ALSO BY CATHERINE LACEY

Nobody Is Ever Missing

The Answers

Certain American States

Pew

BIOGRAPHY OF X

BIOGRAPHY OF X

A Novel

CATHERINE LACEY

FARRAR, STRAUS AND GIROUX

NEW YORK

Farrar, Straus and Giroux
120 Broadway, New York 10271

Illustration credits can be found on pages 393–394.

Library of Congress Cataloging-in-Publication Data
Names: Lacey, Catherine, 1985– author.
Title: Biography of X : a novel / Catherine Lacey.
Description: First edition. | New York : Farrar, Straus and Giroux, 2023. |
   Includes bibliographical references.
Identifiers: LCCN 2022053340 | ISBN 9780374606176 (hardcover)
Subjects: LCGFT: Novels.
Classification: LCC PS3612.A335 B56 2023 | DDC 813/.6—dc23/eng/20221108
LC record available at https://lccn.loc.gov/2022053340

Designed by Gretchen Achilles

Our books may be purchased in bulk for promotional, educational, or business use.
Please contact your local bookseller or the Macmillan Corporate and
Premium Sales Department at 1-800-221-7945, extension 5442,
or by email at MacmillanSpecialMarkets@macmillan.com.

www.fsgbooks.com
www.twitter.com/fsgbooks • www.facebook.com/fsgbooks

1   3   5   7   9   10   8   6   4   2

This work was partially supported by a grant from
the Illinois Arts Council Agency.

AUTHOR'S NOTE

———————

This is a work of fiction. Names, characters, businesses, organizations, places, events, and incidents either are the products of the author's imagination or are used fictitiously.

The endnotes of this book contain attributions not mentioned in the text.

BIOGRAPHY OF X

_____

C. M. LUCCA

FARRAR, STRAUS AND GIROUX

NEW YORK

Farrar, Straus and Giroux
19 Union Square West, New York 10003

1   3   5   7   9   10   8   6   4   2

CONTENTS

BIOGRAPHY OF X

The first winter she was dead it seemed every day for months on end was damp and bright—it had always just rained, but I could never remember the rain—and I took the train down to the city a few days a week, searching (it seemed) for a building I might enter and fall from, a task about which I could never quite determine my own sincerity, as it seemed to me the seriousness of anyone looking for such a thing could not be understood until a body needed to be scraped from the sidewalk. With all the recent attacks, of course, security had tightened everywhere, and you had to have permission or an invitation to enter any building, and I never had such things, as I was no one in particular, uncalled for. One and a half people kill themselves in the city each day, and I looked for them—the one person or the half person—but I never saw the one and I never saw the half, no matter how much I looked and waited, patiently, so patiently, and after some time I wondered if I could not find them because I was one of them, either the one or the half.

One evening, still alive at Penn Station to catch an upstate train, I asked a serious-looking man if he had the time. He had the time, he said, but not the place, as he'd been exiled from Istanbul years earlier but never had the nerve to change his watch, and looking into this stranger's face I saw my own eyes staring back at me, as I, too, could not un-locate myself from the site of my banishment. We parted immediately, but I have never forgotten him.

It wasn't a will to live that kept me alive then, but rather a curiosity about who else might come forward with a story about my wife. Who else might call to tell me something almost unfathomable? And might I— despite how much I had deified and worshipped X and believed her to be pure genius—might I now accept the truth of her terrible, raw anger and boundless cruelty? It was the ongoing death of a story, dozens of second deaths, the death of all those delicate stories I lived in with her.

Or maybe what kept me alive was all the secretarial work I had to do, as I'd become X's secretary by necessity—she kept firing the others. I sometimes found a strange energy to shuffle through her mail in the middle of the night—signing contracts I barely understood, reviewing the amendments made "in the event of the artist's death," filing away royalty statements in the manner that X had instructed, and shredding the aggravating amount of interview requests addressed to me, the widow. The Brennan Foundation had invited me to come receive the Lifetime Achievement Award on X's behalf, not knowing that she'd planned to boycott the ceremony in resentment for how long it had taken them to recognize her. There was also an appeal from a museum that had been eagerly anticipating X's contractual obligation to make one of her rare public appearances at the opening of her retrospective that spring; by overnighted letter, they asked whether I, as a representative of whatever was left of her, might fly over to London in her stead? I sent back my regrets—*I am currently unable to explain how unable I am to undertake such a task.*

Tom called, despite a thirty-year silence between us. He'd learned of my wife's death in the papers and wanted to tell me that he had been thinking about me lately, about our strained and ugly childhood as siblings. His own wife, he said (it was news to me that he'd married), had been given another few months to live, maybe less. His daughter (also news to me) was fourteen now, and there was a part of him that wished she were younger, that believed she might be less damaged by grief if she were protected by the abstraction of early childhood. *What an awful thing*, he said, *to wish my daughter could have known her mother for fewer years.*

But I did not find this so awful. Grief has a warring logic; it always wants something impossible, something worse and something better.

When Tom was fourteen and I was seven we lived in a clapboard house on a dead-end with our mother and assorted others, and that summer as we were eating spaghetti in the kitchen Tom stopped moving, and sat there with his mouth open and the noodles unraveling from his poised fork as he stared into nothing, everything gone from his eyes, and he kept staring, unblinking and frozen as our mother shouted, *Tom! Stop it! Tom!* His eyes kept draining, nothing and nothing, then even less than nothing as Mother shouted for him to stop, to stop this horrible prank, until she finally slapped him hard in the face, which still did not bring him back but freed his fork from his hand and sent it into my lap. That night, slowly, he did start to come back, and later a neurologist was excited to diagnose him with a rare kind of epilepsy, which was treated with a huge pink pill, daily, and for months after my wife died I'd often find myself in some abject, frozen state—sitting naked in a hallway or leaning against a doorframe or standing in the garage, staring at the truck, unsure of how long I'd been there—and I wished someone could have brought me such a pill, something to prevent me from pouring out of myself, at odds with everything.

Tom and I were living in different griefs now—his imminent, mine entrenched—but I wondered if the treatment might still be the same, and I asked him if there was any kind of pill for this, some pill like that pill they used to give him all those years ago, but Tom felt sure there wasn't, or if there was he didn't know about it, and anyway, it probably wouldn't work.

REGARDING MR. SMITH

After two years of ignoring his letters, I took a meeting with Theodore Smith, at X's request, to put an end to his nonsense.

"I can't believe it's really you," he said, "I can't believe it. X's wife—incredible."*

Though it was 1992, I was unaccustomed to such fawning, as she and I avoided the places where such people lingered. The sole purpose of this meeting, which I recorded for legal purposes, was to inform Mr. Smith that X would not cooperate with his supposed biography; she would not authorize it, would give no interviews, and would allow no access to her archives. As my wife's messenger, I encouraged Mr. Smith to abandon the project immediately, for he would suffer greatly trying to write a book that was ultimately impossible.

"If you truly want to write a biography," I told him, "you must first select a subject who is willing to comply, advisably a ghost."

Mr. Smith sat there blinking as I explained, in slow detail, our total disapproval of this endeavor. The estate would not license any reproductions of any of X's work, nor would he be allowed to use any of the portraits of X to which we held the copyright. We would not give permission for him to quote her lyrics, essays, scripts, or books, and of course X had

---

* Theodore Smith, conversation with the author, June 18, 1992, Café Vesper, New York.

no time to answer any of his questions, as she had no interest in his interest, nor any respect for anyone who intended to exploit her work in
this way.

"It is her explicit wish not to be captured in a biography, not now and
not after she's gone," I reminded him, my tone absolutely cordial, or at
least judicial. "She asks that you respect this wish."

But Mr. Smith refused to believe that X would choose to be forgotten,
to which I explained that X had no such intention and already had plans
for what would happen to her archives in the event of her death; all I
knew of those plans at the time was that access would require forfeiture
of the right to biographical research.

"Her life will not become a historical object," I explained, as X had
explained again and again to me. "Only her work will remain."

"But she's a public figure," Mr. Smith said, smiling in a sad, absent
way. (How odd to remember the face of someone I hate, when so much
else is lost to the mess of memory.) He slipped a page in a plastic sleeve
from his briefcase. I glanced down—it was unmistakably her handwriting, dated March 2, 1990, and addressed to *My Darling*, and though I
should have been that darling, given the year, I had a way of overlooking
certain details back then.

"I have several others," he said. "The dealers always call me when they
come across one, though they're rare, of course, and quite expensive."

"A forgery," I said. "Someone has ripped you off."

"It's been authenticated. They've all been authenticated," he said.

I thought I knew what he was doing—dangling false artifacts to en-
trap me and compel my cooperation—but I would not budge. The letters
must have been (or so I wanted to believe) all fakes, and even if X *had*
written such a letter to someone else, which she most likely had not, she
would've never associated with anyone treacherous enough to sell her out.
This pathetic boy—no biographer, not even a writer—was simply one of
X's deranged fans. I don't know why she attracted so many mad people,
but she did, all the time: stalkers, obsessives, people who fainted at the
sight of her. A skilled plagiarist had merely recognized a good opportunity and taken it, as people besotted with such delusion hold their wallets
loosely.

"You must understand that my wife is extremely busy," I said as I stood to leave. "She has decades of work ahead of her and no time for your little project. I must insist you move on."

"She won't always be alive, you know."

I did not believe myself to be such a fool, but I was, of course, that most mundane fool who feels that though everyone on earth, without exception, will die, the woman she loves simply cannot, will never.

"Whether she wants there to be a biography or not," Mr. Smith went on, "there *will* be one, likely several, after she's gone."

I told Mr. Smith, again, to cease all attempts to contact us, that we would file a restraining order if necessary, that I did not want to ever see or hear from him again; I was certain that would be the end of it.

Four years later, on November 11, 1996, X died.

I'd always thought of myself a rational person, but the moment she was gone I ceased to be whoever I thought I was. For weeks all I could do was commit myself to completely and methodically reading every word of the daily newspaper, which was filled with articles about the Reunification of the Northern and Southern Territories, a story so vast that I felt then (and still feel now) that we might never reach the end of it. I gave my full focus to reports of the recently dismantled ST bureaucracies, the widespread distrust of the new electricity grids in the South, and all the sensational stories from inside the bordered territory—details of the mass suicides, beheadings, regular bombings—and even though my personal loss was nothing in comparison to the decades of tyrannical theocracy, I still identified intensely with this long and brutal story, as I, too, had been ripped apart and was having trouble coming back together.

Reading the paper gave a shape to my boneless days: each morning I walked the length of the gravel driveway, retrieved the paper, walked back, and read it section by section in search of something I'd never find—sense, reasons, life itself. Immersed in the news, I felt I was still in the world, still alive, while I remained somewhat protected from the resounding silence she'd left behind.

In early December of that year, I read something in the arts section that I could not, at first, comprehend. Theodore Smith had sold his biography of my wife to a publisher for an obscene advance.* It was scheduled to be published in September of the coming year. For a few days I succeeded in putting it all out of mind. I thought, No—no, it is simply not possible, it will fail, they'll realize the letters are frauds, that it is a work of obsession, not of fact, and when I, executor of X's estate, deny them all the photo and excerpt rights, that will be the end of it. How could there be a biography without any primary sources?

As it happened, the editor who'd purchased the book was someone with whom I shared a close friend. She called me that winter—*a courtesy*, she said, as she was under no obligation to gain my approval. She insisted the research was impeccable. *Scrupulous but respectful*, she said, whatever that means. She assured me that Mr. Smith truly revered and understood X as an artist, as a woman, and that he had so many wonderful insights about her work, but of course, some would find the book a little controversial, wouldn't they?

Your wife never shied away from controversy, the editor said.

Is that so?

The editor suggested I come to her office to meet with Mr. Smith while there was still time to correct the text, that I might want to dispel some rumors he'd been unable to detangle, and though I'd been sure I'd never see Mr. Smith again, by the time I'd hung up I'd agreed to the meeting.

Two days later I was sitting in a conference room with Mr. Smith, his editor, and two or three lawyers. The cinder block of a manuscript sat on the table, practically radiant with inanity. I asked for a few moments with our author, and once alone, I asked him how he'd done it.

Oh, just, you know, day by day, he said, the false modesty so pungent it could have tranquilized a horse.

But what could you have had to say about her? What could you have possibly known?

He insisted he still had plenty to go on without the archive, as she'd given thousands of interviews since the 1970s, that she rarely repeated

---

* Elinor Snow, "Recent Publishing News," *The New York Times*, December 2, 1996.

herself, and of course there were the ex-wives, ex-lovers, the collaborators, others. They all had plenty to tell him, and lots of original letters to share. It had all gone quite well, he said, except for his interactions with me, of course, and the fact that he'd never been able to speak with X herself—a miscarriage he still regretted. But I did not care what he wanted from me and only wanted to know who had given him interviews. He listed a few inconsequential names—hangers-on and self-important acquaintances— then, surprisingly, Oleg Hall.

Mr. Smith must have known about the enmity I'd long been locked in with Oleg. The only comfort in X's death was that I'd never have to see him again, her closest friend though I could never understand why. I'd disliked everything about Oleg, but I thought the very least I could expect of him was that he'd protect X's privacy.

You must have been so glad she died, I accused Mr. Smith. *And so suddenly! A nice dramatic end. I'm sure you were thrilled to hear the news.*

Mr. Smith squirmed in his chair as I berated him, calling him (apparently) *a groveling fraud, a useless little leech with no talent,* an insult he later quoted in his book, and though I don't remember saying those words, I do approve of the characterization.* However, I am sure I did not, as Mr. Smith alleged, accuse him of killing my wife. I was indeed grief-wild, but I've never been a conspiracist, and it's clear Mr. Smith lacks the fortitude to accomplish a murder from afar, undetectable by autopsy.

I'm trying my best to include you, he pleaded.

I do not wish to be included.

Then why did you come here?

I could have said that I was attempting to wake up from this nightmare, that I came to somehow stop his book from existing, to ensure it was never published, to spit in his face, but I didn't say anything. Why did I go anywhere? I had no idea anymore, now that she was gone, where to go or how to live or why I did anything. I started to slip out, leaving the manuscript behind, ignoring the clamor around me, refusing the editor's assurance that X would be remembered "*so fondly*"—I could give a

---

* Theodore Smith, *A Woman Without a History* (New York: Brace & Sons, 1997), 3.

shit for anyone's fondness—but when she made the suggestion that the biography would likely inflate the market value of X's work, I do recall telling her to fuck off as soon as possible and never contact me again. It was my fault, I'll admit, for hoping any of those people could be reasoned away from profit.

The night after my first meeting with Mr. Smith in 1992, as I was falling asleep beside X, she sat up, turned on the lamp, and asked, *What did the warning mean?*

X was a nocturnal woman, but also a diurnal one—in fact, it seemed she never grew tired, or jet-lagged, not even weary on a warm afternoon—while I've always just been a regular person, tired at certain intervals.

What warning?

We warned Mr. Smith to cease his research, she said, *but what did we warn him with? What was the threat?*

Of course I hadn't threatened him in any specific way. She was neither surprised nor content with this answer and suggested we could send someone to his apartment to intimidate him, or to mess it up while he was out. I laughed, but she continued—we might as well get right to it and have someone break his legs, or maybe just one leg or, better yet, a hand. Did I notice whether he was left- or right-handed? I felt then, as I often felt, that I was a mobster's wife, better off looking the other way.

Well, it's something to think about, she concluded, *if he tries to contact us again.*

From the very start, I knew that X possessed an uncommon brutality, something she used in both defense and vengeance. She was only a little taller than me, but her physical power was so outsize that over the years I'd seen her level several men much larger than she was, sometimes for justifiable reasons but also in misplaced rage. The longer we were together, the more I understood that I, too, was at risk of being the object of her anger, that there was always the possibility, however remote, that she might turn against me, if not physically, then emotionally or intellectually, that she could destroy me totally should the whim ever arrive.

I fear I am the sort of person who needs to feel some measure of fear in order to love someone. My first love had been—privately, embarrassingly—God itself, something that made me, something that could destroy me; every mortal relation that came after, until her, had always fallen short of the total metaphysical satisfaction I'd felt in prayer.

But I never needed to fear X's strength. Other things, yes, but never her strength.

Months after that disastrous afternoon in that office, I received an advance copy of Smith's book accompanied by a terse note explaining that the "scene" I'd made had been included in the newly added prologue. I left the book on the floor of the garage beside the trash bin until one morning—something must have been extremely wrong with me—I went to the garage and, instead of the daily paper, brought in that book and did not stop reading until I reached the last page.

Though I had failed to prevent this book from coming into existence, Mr. Smith's horrific prose and lightless perspective seemed to be the more atrocious error. His writing is—both aesthetically and in substance—page by page, line by line, without interruption, worthless. The only thing impressive about it was that he managed to take a subject flush with intrigue and grind it down into something so boring, so absolutely pedantic and without glamour, that I often laughed aloud, alone, so sure it would fail, that the book's primary weakness was not the estate's lack of cooperation, but that it simply wasn't any good.

I slept easily that night, certain I'd reached the end of this entire charade.

I am not bitter that Theodore Smith's *A Woman Without a History* was met with such acclaim—let him drown in his spurious success—but I am surprised that such a dull book has captured the attention of so many. I am not even appalled by his depiction of me—unflattering to be sure, but I have no interest in the flattery of a fool. What bothers me about it is that his lies have been held up as the definitive account of X's life, that his work speaks the final word about her groundbreaking, multihyphenate career and its impact, that every reader and critic seems to believe that Mr. Smith successfully navigated the labyrinth of secrets X kept around herself, and that he illuminated some true core of her life. This is far from the case.

It is no secret that my wife layered fictions within her life as a kind of performance or, at times, a shield. Mr. Smith described this as "a pathological problem" and called her "a compulsive liar, crippled by self-doubt, a woman doomed to fortify herself with falsehoods."* Though it is true that not even I always knew where the line was between the facts of her life and the stories she constructed around herself, my wife was no liar. Anyone who was ever fortunate enough to be a part of X's life had to accept this hazard—she lived in a play without intermission in which she'd cast herself in every role.

That was the first reason X refused to authorize a biography: it would necessarily be false, and this work of falsehood could only serve to enrich whatever writer was shallow enough to capitalize on her infamy. And yes, I realize I am that writer now, but over the course of this work, my reasons and aims for it have shifted as the story around X shifted; Mr. Smith wished to warm his cold hands on her heat, while I have been scorched by it.

X believed that making fiction was sacred—she said this to me many times, and mentioned it in her letters and journals and essays repeatedly—and she wanted to live in that sanctity, not to be fooled by the flimsiness of perceived reality, which was nothing more than a story that had fooled most of the world. She chose, instead, to live a life in which nothing was fixed, nothing was a given—that her name might change from day to day, moment to moment, and the same was true for her beliefs, her memories, her manner of dress, her manner of speech, what she knew, what she wanted. All of it was always being called into question. All of it was costume and none of it was solid. Not even her past was a settled matter, and though anything else around her might fluctuate, that unsettled core—her history—was to remain unsettled.†

---

* Smith, *A Woman Without a History*, 92, 209.

† X, "List of Self-Attributes," April 10, 1981, box 15, item 2, The X Archive, Jafa Museum Special Archives Annex, New York. (This collection is cited hereafter as TXA.)

"A biography," she wrote in a letter to her first wife, "would be an insult to the way I have chosen to live. It's not that I am a private person; I am not a person at all."*

I've since discovered another, more specific reason that X did not want anyone to fact-check her past prior to 1972, the year it seemed she had materialized out of nothing, without a past, without a beginning. Of Mr. Smith's many egregious errors, his misidentification of her parents and birthplace is perhaps the most fundamental, though it is true that X made uncovering that fact nearly impossible, as she obfuscated every detail, planted false narratives, and never came clean.

In fact, until I set about doing my own research, even I did not know where she'd been born. She once told me she had no memory of her life before she was eighteen, and another time she said she could not legally reveal the identity of her parents, but occasionally she claimed that they were dead, tragically dead, or that they'd kicked her out, or that she hated them so much she couldn't remember their names. She sometimes said she was born in Kentucky or Montana or in some wilderness, raised by various animals, or that she'd been born illegitimately—an ambassador and his maid, teacher and pupil, nun and priest, some doomed union. There was one allusion to an orphanage, or a childhood on the run, or no childhood at all. "It depends on how you look at it," she said in one interview. "It only seems to be a simple question—*Where are you from?* It can never be sufficiently answered."†

There were rumors she'd been rescued from a sex-trafficking ring somewhere in the West, or had escaped the Southern Territory, or that she was a spy from the Soviet Union, but I had long assumed that the truth was more likely quite simple and sad. She seemed to me to have the face of someone who had been given up by her mother and had spent the rest of her life refusing that initial refusal, as if her own mother should have been able to recognize the enormous capacities that burned inside that soft infant, and now the whole world would be punished for it.

After she became better known, fans and strangers alike claimed to be

---

* X to Marion Parker, undated carbon copy, item 134a, TXA.

† Penny Saltz, "23 Minutes with X," *The Underworld Magazine*, June 1982.

her long-lost parents or siblings, calling up reporters and insisting they were her true mother or brother or husband, finally willing to tell the story of their daughter, their sister, their wife. When contacted to verify or dispel these new stories, X said they were true, all of it was true—that she'd been born a thousand times, that she was the child, the sister, the anything of anyone who said she was such. It confused people until it amused them, amused them until it bored them. The interest in her past would subside for some years before returning again, always unfinished.

When I read the chapter in Mr. Smith's book about X having been born in Kentucky to Harold and Lenore Eagle, I knew this to be one of her objectively false stories: Harold and Lenore were actors whom X had hired many years earlier. Though it was just one of the many details Mr. Smith got wrong, the birthplace error bothered me more than any other.

I never intended to write a corrective biography—if that is what this book is. All I wanted at first was to find out where my wife had been born, and I imagined I might publish my findings as an essay, an article, or perhaps a lawsuit, something to quickly discredit Mr. Smith. I did not know that by beginning this research I had doomed myself in a thousand ways, that once the box had been opened, it would refuse to be shut.

Perhaps it doesn't make sense to marry someone when you don't know some of the most basic things about them, but how can I explain that those details did not seem relevant to how I felt about her, the sort of buzzing sensation I had in her presence, as if I'd just been plugged in? Early on, I sometimes asked about her past, but I soon accepted she would be both the center of my life and its central mystery, excused from standard expectations. Love had done that, maybe—love or something more dangerous—but now that Mr. Smith's false narrative was out there and I was in our cabin alone, I had nothing to do but avenge him and his lies, to avenge reality itself, to avenge everything.

The title of this book—as titles so often are—is a lie. This is not a biography, but rather a wrong turn taken and followed, the document of a woman learning what she should have let lie in ignorance. Perhaps that's what all books are, the end of someone's trouble, someone putting their trouble into a pleasing order so that someone else will look at it.

Early on, certain people kindly and less kindly advised me to give up my research or, if I could not give it up, at least avoid trying to make sense of it. I certainly shouldn't attempt to publish it in any form, they said. Some believed that I was jealous of Mr. Smith's success or that I was being a self-destructive fool. X's gallerist told me I was delusional, that X's biography had already been published and I should accept it and move on. Others thought I was not in my right mind, that I was grieving inappropriately, that I should be patient, let another year or two pass, that I should back away from grief as if evading a large animal—go slowly, be patient, make no sudden movements. On one occasion I did put the manuscript aside, briefly believing it to be hopeless. That afternoon I set out for a long hike in the woods, but as the hours passed I felt increasingly hurried, as if I were running late to meet someone, only I didn't know whom.

And obviously X would have vehemently objected to this work, and still I am waiting for her to find a way to argue with me about it from the other side. If she ever does, I know I will lose that argument, no matter who was wrong or right. I can imagine her disapproving of this endeavor just as I can imagine her disapproving of anything, pacing in the kitchen and telling me all the ways in which I (or someone, or something) was wrong. No two ways around it: No. Absolutely wrong.

A passage from her journal, 1983:

*There is no such thing as privacy. There is no experience or quality or thought or pain that has not been felt by all the billions of living and dead.**

But even if I had quoted her own words in my defense, she would have continued making her case against this book, blistering me with accusa-

---

* X, journal entry, June 9, 1983, box 4, notebook 46, TXA.

tions. *A derangement of nostalgia, an indulgence, a wallowing.* Every time I shuddered at the news of a friend's death, she insisted I never mourn the dead, as *they know what they're doing,* but I remain unconvinced.

Some days it seems she is only away in the next room, and when I go to that room she has fled to another room, and when I reach that one she is in yet another. So often I am sure I hear her voice on the other side of a wall or door, but she never stops moving—lecturing, arguing, laughing, making and remaking her case, always—insistent, scouring, spiraling, clear. Even now, with all these years gone and all these stories stacked up irrevocably against her, I keep hearing her footsteps come steadily down the stairs, and I swear some afternoons I can hear her taking off her boots at the back door and padding up the hallway after an afternoon hike. In anger, in longing, in both, despite myself, I strain to hear those steps.

LETTERS

From the first moment we met in April 1989, there was an unnamable sentiment between us, one that arrived so quickly there was no moment to question it. It wasn't just love, nor was it lust or obsession. It was something both visceral and beyond viscera, and as much as I have tried, the only way I can find to accurately describe this feeling is to first explain something that occurred in the marriage I ended to be with her. Those interested only in X and not in the life of her widow (a reasonable position) may find it appealing to skip ahead to the next chapter. Please forgive this interlude. I needed to put this story somewhere, and there was no better place than here.

Early on a Saturday morning in 1984, not yet a day after I'd met Henry Surner—the sculptor, the man who would later become my husband—I woke up struck with the certainty that I would marry Henry and have children with him. I'd never before hoped for such things, and what's more, I knew almost nothing of this man. We'd met the night before, at the birthday party of a colleague. I had not planned to go, but I'd just finished an article about a small massacre in a Manhattan apartment and felt too unsettled to be alone.* The party was at a bar nearby the office, and immediately upon arriving I stepped on Henry's toe and apologized; neither of us spoke to anyone else for the rest of the evening.

I was a nervous young woman, and without the armor of conducting an interview for work I had trouble with conversation, but all of that was gone, somehow, when I spoke to Henry. He told me he was a sculptor and taught art classes in a private school, and later I wondered if I found it easy to speak to him because he was so accustomed to speaking to children, in safe and neutered tones. We left the party to go for a walk—it felt natural for us to hold hands—and when he kissed me good night, gripping me by the shoulders, I felt that I was a towel with which he was drying himself, a prone and useful thing.

When I woke the next morning with that odd certitude of our future, I knew I couldn't tell him without sounding completely mad—yet I knew I was not mad. A bright and grim sense of calm took over. I was so sure that Henry was my life now that I began writing a letter to "Henry of the Future," the only person I felt could accept my prescience. I wrote of how clearly I could see the decades: the birth of our children, their youths, the years going on, the grandchildren, our aging, our deaths, the finality of it all. It frightened me, but it also felt unavoidable, and though I'd always been a slow writer—always editing myself in doubtful circles— that morning I typed a dozen pages with the urgency of an approaching deadline.

Henry and I had plans to meet that afternoon in a park where we sat side by side under a tree to watch people as they passed by, and I was glad not to have to look at him because I feared I would faint, though I had never been that sort of woman, a fainting woman. In past relationships I'd been accused of being cold, of being distant, of never loving anyone as well as they had loved me. I'd never known what to make of those accusations, had never been able to discern my own coldness or distance, but as I sat there talking with Henry, his mere presence pressing me so firmly and warmly into the present, it became clear to me that this was it, this

* C. M. Lucca, "Chelsea Gunman Kills Five, Injures Two," *The City Paper*, August 30, 1984.

was love, and all those past partners had been right—I had never loved them. I must have believed love was something that arrived in your life and told you what to do with it.

Each morning that week I wrote a letter to that future Henry, and for the next two years I wrote more letters recording dozens of days and dates, inconsequential afternoons we spent together, trying to keep track of all the details that would otherwise pass unremembered. I kept all the letters in a file labeled FOR HENRY IN 1986. As it happened, Henry and I married in March of 1986, and shortly before the wedding I told him about the letters. I thought he would be moved, but he only seemed confused.

What letters? Why wouldn't you have given them to me back then?

I was afraid, I said.

Afraid of what?

I had no answer to this.

What was there to be afraid of? he asked again. *Didn't I fall in love, too?*

And I didn't like this question, this "*Didn't I?*" (Hadn't he?)

I retrieved that file of letters, and assuming he'd want to read them immediately, I asked him to wait until he was alone, saying that it would be too much for me to watch it happen, but he just smiled and put them on the coffee table, there amid the old magazines.

I could not sleep that night. I hadn't reread any of the letters, an unedited spew of nearly 150 pages. Some of them had footnotes, and demented marginalia, grand statements of devotion. I wanted him to read them immediately, to tell me I was right, that he'd had the same feelings, too, that our reality was the same one, or perhaps I wanted him to read those letters and tell me I'd been mistaken, that we had both been mistaken, that we should call off the wedding since I was not the woman he thought I was and he was not Henry in 1986.

The letters sat on the coffee table for a few more days, and after they vanished I told myself his silence must have been his approval. After the wedding we went on a road trip through California, and late one night while we were feeling optimistic about ourselves, I asked him what he'd thought of the letters, but he didn't remember any letters, and I had to explain to him what I meant, to which he admitted he hadn't finished them. It was just too much. It was too long.

How many of them did you read? I asked.

He couldn't remember. Three or four pages.

There are reasons that people vacation in a place renowned for its cliffs when they're feeling very clear and glad—when they're enjoying immense success in love or money and not at all at risk of stepping over a precipice—because in that moment I felt I should leave the cabin and lurch into a ravine and leave it at that. I had been wrong about us.

Instead I locked myself in the bathroom, turned on the faucets, and stared into the mirror until I could forget who I was and return to bed beside this ambivalent man I had married, a man who could simply not be bothered. He was already asleep. That night I concluded that the problem with throwing myself over a cliff was that I didn't want to kill myself—or rather, I couldn't kill myself, as I was already dead. We never spoke of it again.

Almost immediately upon meeting X a few years later, I realized that she had been the subject of those letters, that she knew every word of them without having ever seen them. I realize this is nonsense, in a way, that I hadn't even known of the *existence* of X when I'd written them, but it is also true that what I had begun feeling had changed me into a person who would not make sense to herself until X introduced me to who I was. I'd somehow known her before I knew her, or perhaps writing toward the future had created an absence in me that only she, for whatever reason, could fill.

X would certainly scold my sentimentality here, but I can think of no other way to explain how I had the wherewithal to abruptly end my marriage in 1989, just weeks after meeting her. There was simply no alternative—or it seemed that way to me then: I had to abandon that safe inertia in order for my life to become recognizable as my life.

———

An irony: Henry had been the one to first introduce me to X's work. He'd read one of her novels, *The Reason I'm Lost*, after hearing it described as one of the most important books of the twentieth century.* He'd given it to me and insisted I read it, so sure I would love it that I was surprised when I did. Henry only read books that had been unequivocally praised, books wearing gold stickers; since he didn't read often, he only wanted to read "the best." *After all*, he explained, *I'm an artist. I spend my whole day making art. How am I supposed to come home and unwind with someone else's art?* Most evenings he watched sports on television.

I learned how to block out the sound of a cheering crowd and his occasional howls as I read. Henry was such a remote, dispassionate person that I enjoyed seeing him experience an extreme emotion, even if the feats of strangers were the only thing that seemed to rouse such feelings from him. The fact that I wrote all day and came home to read, he said, proved that being a journalist wasn't taxing in the same way that being an artist was. I never disagreed with him. I did not understand what Henry did in his studio or why. At home, we spent our time together engrossed in opposite things, and this had seemed like one of the things a person had to do in marriage—accept differences, block out certain noises, be alone. There may be nothing inherently wrong with living a life like that, and perhaps I could have safely remained married and had his children and gone along with the original plan. It's not as if I would have died from it. Not immediately.

Other than the issue of the letters, our conflicts were few. Henry was amiable and pleasant, and had been spared most of the neuroses common in other artists. He was best known for a series of bronze statuettes of young boys, an homage to Degas's dancers, but according to his artist statement their subject was "*toxic masculinity*," a topic that had become popular after men had, millennia too late, become aware of its existence. When we were first dating, his work had begun to sell at higher prices, and Richard Serra had just taken him under his wing. Henry regarded Serra as a god walking the streets of New York City, and this mentorship

* Clyde Hill, *The Reason I'm Lost* (New York: New Directions, 1973).

was often held up as an indication that Henry was destined for unequivocal prosperity.

We did have one recurrent issue, however; fidelity was always beyond our reach. Six months after we met, I'd been sent out of town on assignment with a photographer, and one night something had simply happened. When I got back from the trip I told Henry about the indiscretion, expecting to finally see his anger, but he didn't seem angry, just surprised. *Wow*, he kept saying. *Wow*. Really? I begged his forgiveness, but he just kept shaking his head and saying, *Wow*. After a few chilly days he seemed to forget about the whole thing, though I later realized he had simply metabolized my betrayal into blanket permission for his own infidelities. His confessions, too, were alarmingly easy to handle. I forgave him. I said I understood. Several more missteps and reconciliations occurred and reoccurred in the years after, and the worst that ever happened was that we'd spend one night feeling bitter, but by morning it all seemed forgotten, long behind us.

Perhaps I never admired him in the way he wanted to be admired, and perhaps he never seemed to pay close enough attention to me, was always missing crucial details. And these failures—my failure to celebrate him and his failure to comprehend me—led us to wander, to look for comprehension and celebration elsewhere. We did not know how to belong to each other. But there's no point in trying to write an autopsy of a marriage, as either side would be insulated with falsehood.

1989

It was April 27, 1989, when everything changed.

X's gallery was throwing a lavish opening for her new series, *The Amnesia Triptychs*. Henry and I had been put on the guest list as Richard Serra's plus two.

I didn't like Richard Serra. I didn't like him at all. He always—without hesitation or caveat—introduced me as "Henry Surner's wife" and found endless occasions to pat my lower back. When I told Henry about this he seemed flattered, thrilled even, that his hero was apparently "*so fond*" of me, and he assured me Richard was merely being friendly. None of this, Henry said, would bother me if I knew him a little better, and anyway Richard's support was too valuable to question. I was thirty-two that year, but I still lacked the confidence to assert myself or clearly describe my complaints. Like many other women at that age and time, I harbored a swelling anger that I did not know how to express, as if a new organ had grown inside me but had not yet begun to function.

The gallery was crowded when we arrived, and no one could see the paintings, though of course that wasn't the point. I was pressed between my husband and Serra when X appeared before us, just like that, this woman who would soon destroy my life as it had been.

All I knew about X then was that she'd held some strange notoriety in the music industry, and that I'd read one of the novels that she'd published under a pseudonym. I was confused about who she was and why she seemed to matter so much to certain people, and how she managed to have a single letter as her entire name. I'd never seen any photographs of her, so I don't know what I was expecting, but in the gallery that night she was radiant—not so much with beauty, as no one would have called her conventionally beautiful—but with life itself. That seems simplistic—it is simplistic—but how could you see in someone's face anything meaningful about her life? With X, you could; her ferocity was evident in her body. And photographs did it little justice, could never convey the feeling she sent into a room, her hunger, her velocity.

I rarely agreed with the way that other people described my wife, except for the quote from Lynne Tillman that was included in one of the obituaries.* She'd said X was "voracious for people . . . one of the great devourers of all time. But her method of devouring was to entice. If you had a room full of twenty people and X came in, there was an energy uplift. It got everybody off their boring number. Here was this glamorous freak."

The night I met her, X wore a baggy black suit and bright white brogues. Her hair was cut short and slicked back. Serra introduced me to her as Henry Surner's wife. She took my hand and looked briefly at me. Years lay between us.

I hear the paintings are genius, Serra said. *If only I could see them through the crowd!*

What does it matter, Richard, she asked, *when art itself is so worthless?*

He claimed to always look forward to her shows. X smirked, and I felt I could hear her say, *That's because you want to be seen here.* But she didn't say that, or at least did not say it aloud, and though I do not believe in extrasensory perception, I did hear her voice in my head, as if she had broken in like a burglar. I wasn't sure how to feel about another person's voice in my head. I thought only I was in my head. I thought I preferred it that way.

What X did say to Serra and Henry was that she did not attend contemporary art shows and she advised the two of them, if they cared

* Amos Spiegel, "Contentious Polymath, X, Dead at 46," *The New York Times*, March 17, 1996, C1.

to protect their minds, to do the same. Bad art is a contaminant to be avoided, she said, but Henry changed the subject by asking X how she knew Serra.

As I remember it, X said, *I looked up one day while I was getting fucked and there was Richard, fucking me. Of course we didn't call it "getting fucked" when it was Richard. We used to call it "getting beaten up." Isn't that right, Richie?*

She left us then, and Richard said something crude once she was out of earshot and Henry laughed and looked at me, waiting on my laughter, but I did not laugh, and later, as we were leaving the gallery I reached into my skirt pocket and found a slip of paper with an address on West Twenty-Fourth Street. *Tomorrow, 3 p.m.* I knew the note was from her, that she'd pick-pocketed me in reverse. I looked up, expecting to catch her watching me, but she wasn't there. Wasn't there or I didn't catch her.

Henry, Richard, and I went out for dinner after the opening, and I asked about X's work and reputation.

Maybe she's a genius or maybe she's just a menace, Serra said.

Prolific but not to be taken seriously, Henry said. Then he asked Serra with an embarrassing eagerness if it was true, if he had slept with her. *I didn't know she went for men*, he said.

As far as I can tell, she goes for pretty much everybody, or used to anyway, Serra said. He explained she'd been using "disguises" when he met her, different identities—he must have fucked one of them and didn't know it was her.

They both laughed, and Henry asked if he believed the Southern Territory rumors.

Absolutely not! Richard shouted. *She's just some art cunt, not a goddamn Houdini. The fact is she's a* dabbler—*books, films, music producing, painting— it's too much! A dilettante when it comes down to it.*

They kept on talking but I stopped listening and thought seriously about the phrase *"art cunt."* Serra meant it as an insult, I knew, but the things he believed to be serious were often of private amusement to me. The rest of the night he and Henry spoke of reviews and critics and other artists—rising and falling reputations, rumors, the worth of any given work, who was in bed with whom.

Henry had been taking me to art shows since we'd first met, and I invariably hated the work that he thought was the most genius, and anything I admired he did not seem to understand. I suspected that his opinions had more to do with what other people thought than Henry's own feelings. He repeated lines from reviews as if they were proven truths, and I tried not to hate him for this. After I'd complained about how boring and soulless one show had been, Henry defended it by telling me that Hamish Henklin said these sculptures were all about the subjective point of view of the object. I asked him what that even meant.

Well, it's the point of view of an object, the object's subjective point of view, he said.

Immediately, I blurted out that I loved him, because I wasn't sure, in that moment, if I did.

This is all to say I approached my meeting with X with a fair amount of cynicism about successful artists, about what they did and why they did it. She must have known I was a journalist, I thought, and perhaps she was planning some kind of stunt—that or she recognized me as someone meek, someone she could manipulate, and I had to admit to myself, though fearfully, that I would allow myself to be manipulated by someone like her.

When I arrived at the address she'd given I found nothing but an empty lot. I checked the note again—I was in the right place. I waited a few minutes; then, as I turned to leave, I noticed a rope ladder swaying from the abandoned elevated track that ran above Tenth Avenue. One bare arm waved at the top, then slid out of sight, and even now, all these years later, I do not understand how I had the nerve to climb that ladder. It was the first time since childhood that I discovered I was capable of more than I'd previously believed, an expanding sense of possibility that defined my years with her—a stark contrast to the smallness I felt in Henry's home. Once I reached the top of the tracks she helped me over the edge—her hands on my arms and back. I stood and looked out over an impossible sight—a long, narrow meadow running through the city, overgrown with vines and tall grass.

I thought we could take a walk, she said.

We headed north. I cannot remember what we spoke about, only that it felt as if we were resuming a conversation we'd been having for years. What do people ever talk about at times like this, the first meeting of years and years of meetings? It seems at such times that we are the least in a hurry to explain ourselves, intuitively knowing there is time to get to all of it, that there is plenty of time. And when I learned, reading page after page from a chest of letters, that a late-afternoon walk on those derelict tracks was a move she'd made on many others before and after me, I still believed, at least at first, that our particular afternoon walk must have been the most crucial one, the real one from which all the other walks deviated. I would like to believe that I'm less of a fool now, that in the course of this research I've come to a better understanding of my overlapping significance and insignificance in her life. But I know now a person always exceeds and resists the limits of a story about them, and no matter how widely we set the boundaries, their subjectivity spills over, drips at the edges, then rushes out completely. People are, it seems, too compli- cated to sit still inside a narrative, but that hasn't stopped anyone from trying, desperately trying, to compact a life into pages.

At one point on that first walk I told her that I'd heard about her work, and that I found it all quite suspicious.

There's nothing to suspect about me, she said. *I don't hide anything.*

I said I wasn't so sure of that.

And you shouldn't be. You shouldn't be sure of anything.

Richard Serra called you an art cunt.

I'll have it printed on a calling card, she said, skipping upward to click her heels.

It was only when the sun began to set that I realized how much time had passed, us talking about nothing in particular while trespassing on restricted property for hours. In the golden light—that which usually transforms one into a more beautiful version of oneself—I noticed something newly sinister and menacing in X's eyes, something almost abhorrent; then it was gone. I felt a sudden need to get away from her and told her I had to be going, so we climbed off the elevated tracks by using a fire escape on a neighboring building, and as the rusted steel swayed and shook in my hands I began to cry, afraid that the whole structure would rip from the brick and fall to the street, crushing me and this woman beneath it. What would Henry have thought of his wife dying like a cat burglar? By the time I reached the ground again, I feared it had all been a mistake, that a cop was going to catch us, that I'd be arrested, or ticketed, perhaps have to stand trial. But no one seemed to care that we'd just climbed down from the tracks. Two old men were playing backgammon nearby. A pair of women were relaxing on a stoop, enjoying cigarettes. They waved at X; she waved back.

Are you crying? X asked.

I searched for a taxi.

Why are you crying? she asked.

I'm not crying, I said as I smiled, stupefied, a grown woman indeed crying and denying it.

A taxi appeared, but as I opened the door I momentarily had no idea where to go. I looked back at X, her frame both willowy and imposing, a hard invitation in her face. Then the taxi driver shouted—*Get in or get on with it*—so I got in.

When I got out of the taxi minutes later, I realized I'd mistakenly given my old address, on East Second and Bowery, an efficiency studio with wonderful light and terrible everything else. I looked up at the windows where I'd lived in such happy squalor, and cried. How completely idiotic I was being. It makes no sense to grieve years. Be reasonable. Go home.

As I walked north toward our building, I lingered at each of my private graves on Second Avenue—the bench where I'd had the relationship-ending fight with a girlfriend several years ago, the bar where I'd read *The House of Mirth* for the first time, the café where I'd once met my estranged father for a painful coffee, and the Italian restaurant where Henry and I had soberly discussed the decision of marriage. I'd always been someone over whom the past had a powerful hold, easily importuned by nostalgia, but that evening each of these locations seemed to have lost their power. I walked right into the café where I'd had that coffee with my father, though for years I'd crossed the street to avoid passing it. I ordered a glass of wine as if I belonged there, had belonged there all along.

There was a newspaper on the bar, and in it I found a lukewarm review of X's latest exhibition.* The review mentioned that two out-of-print books from her "persona period" were being reissued that summer: 37, which she had first published under the pseudonym Cassandra Edwards, and "the tetralogy of novellas by Cindy O." It was only then I remembered that I'd read one of the Cindy O novellas while I'd been in journalism school—Old Families. The paperback had been passed among a few of us. We'd all loved it, but I couldn't remember why.

Though I'd been unsettled by my afternoon with X, I did not yet believe I was in love with her. I only felt that I had been changed—though being changed by a person is far more dangerous than simply loving them. It would have been much easier to dismiss my feelings if I had thought I was merely falling for her. In our five-year marriage, Henry and I had each seen a handful of affairs down to the sobering bottom of the well, and I believed I understood the power of such escapism. But this was not that. Sitting at the bar, I took notes I didn't read again until recently: "Could it be that the best thing that could ever happen to a person could also be the worst?" I then wrote, with a fervor that warped my handwriting, as many lines as I could remember X saying during our walk: "To be rebellious and to distrust rebellion is the plight of the tragic artist . . . Nature has no origin . . . Corrupted by the cruelty in beauty, is art a luxury or necessity?" A page later I remembered more: "This cowardice, unknowingness in the face of my own feelings is why I betray those I love, verbally, when I refused to express my feelings for them . . . The world is cluttered with dead institutions."

It was well after dark when I returned home. Henry was waiting to hurry us to a dinner reservation I'd forgotten. He didn't ask where I'd been, as

* Hamish Henklin, "Paintings One Won't Soon Forget, for Better or Worse," *The Village Voice*, April 28, 1989, 15.

he never asked such questions, nor did I, an avoidance we had justified as an advanced level of marital independence. All through dinner I couldn't stop smiling, though I also felt an ambient distress, and as we walked home I heard myself blurt it—*I think I'm leaving*.

He did not believe me—why would he when I hardly believed myself?—and instead directed the discussion toward the ongoing riddle of our starting a family, and when to do so, and the duty he felt to have children, and my repeated failure to cross the boundary between theoretical and actual pregnancy. I kept making appointments to have my IUD removed, then canceling them or forgetting to go.

You're just depressed, Henry said. *I know you.*

But he didn't know me anymore, as the trouble with knowing people is how the target keeps moving.

I repeated that I was leaving, but he scoffed, almost laughed. *Not just like that you're not*, he said, and we walked in silence for several blocks and I wondered whether there was any ideal criteria for this, whether there was a correct way to end a marriage on nothing more than an amorphous sense of another life just out of reach, a life that might kill me, it seemed, if I didn't live it. Once inside our apartment again, he asked me to at least keep living with him for another month, to accompany him to his cousin's wedding, to give him a chance to make the case for our life together, and I agreed to it, hoping that it would make sense, that the simpler course—staying together, staying the same—would come to seem to be the correct course.

During those last weeks in his home I had vivid dreams in which X appeared repeatedly. I'd never put much stock in my dreams, but suddenly only dreaming seemed real, and days were just time to endure between nights. Often I was chasing her through a city or a forest, or trying to find her in a crowd. Other times she and I were accomplices in some sort of performance or stunt. Or we were swimming in a sea, just swimming, for miles. Foolish to think too much about dreams, I know, but perhaps even more foolish to ignore them completely.

Each morning I arrived at work there was a letter from her on my desk. As I read through the letters now, they seem innocuous, even dull—love letters tend to expire—but at the time it was rapturous to read them.

I began arriving earlier and earlier to the office, hoping to catch her delivering one, though I never did. She never explained how she got those letters to my desk. I had no means to reply to her—no return address, no phone number. I suppose I could have left a message for her at the gallery, but I never had the nerve to do so.

It began to feel possible she could be around any corner, at any moment, and she often was. She appeared on a park bench where I was spending my lunch hour. She emerged from crowds to slip a note into my pocket, then vanished just as quickly. She rushed past the diner where I was having a coffee, locked eyes with me through the window, and was gone by the time I ran outside. A more reasonable person, perhaps, would find it troubling to be followed in this way—to be, quite frankly, stalked—but I had ceded all control of my life to this feeling of a storm approaching and the glad certainty it would demolish everything I knew.

One night, as a break from the turgidity in that apartment, I went out for a walk, and after seeing a little flake of cigarette ash fall in front of my face, I looked up to find X sitting on a tree branch. She climbed down and walked with me for a while. We did not speak of our feelings for each other. We walked in silence or spoke about the nonsense of the world, or about how beautiful we found some pile of trash we came upon in the street. Our walk ended around three in the morning when she dived into a cab that sped away. I went home and looked at Henry's sleeping face, slack on the pillow. He was such a handsome man. I sat up for a long time, just looking at him.

The next day the letter from X on my desk was brief—the address of her loft, no other instruction. I went home, packed my few things into two suitcases, and called Henry to tell him I was going to make him dinner that night, to be home by six. He sounded victorious, as if this dinner were my entire life. He told me he'd come home early, though it was quite late when he arrived. I had no appetite, I said, another detail he failed to notice. Once he was done eating, I said I'd made a plan for my life, a way to proceed. There was no more time. I was leaving right away.

He did not understand and neither did I, and now I cannot comprehend how I had the nerve to leave him when I had so recently thought of Henry as the only permanent part of my life. On my way out the door, I delivered a few panicked and false justifications about how broken and doomed we were, but people will say the most heinous things when they're trying to justify their own failures and madness.

My office phone rang constantly that week—either it was Henry telling me to come home, or it was one of our friends or his mother advising me to be reasonable, saying that I didn't know what I was doing; that I must have been in pain, real pain, to self-destruct this way; that perhaps I needed to speak with a psychologist; that perhaps I needed to be medicated. I had already accepted the possibility that I had lost my mind, that it was possible I was wrong about X, that perhaps I had simply left the fantasy of a stable marriage for the fantasy of a total transformation of the persona, yet I had never felt so unafraid and clear in my life—the clarity was physical, a vibration in my skin, my feet, my clavicle. Nothing had yet occurred, but in that nothing, everything had occurred.

X was not exactly a person to me yet, but a possibility, a different way of life. I deified her then and for a long time after, believed her to be an oracle, almost inhuman. Now it is so clear to me that love is the opposite of deification, that it erodes persona down to its mortal root. She was always human, difficult as it was for me to admit that; I made so much trouble for myself by refusing to see it.

MONTANA

When she died, all I knew about X's distant past was that she'd arrived in New York in 1972. She never told me her birthdate or birthplace, and she never adequately explained why these things were kept secret. X often repeated a line from RuPaul (one of the few artists she openly admired), "You're born naked and the rest is drag," but she pushed the thought further—that even the body is drag, all our names are drag, and memory was the most profound drag of all. Early in our marriage I thought the day would come when she'd explain everything about her past, but she insisted that all that mattered was the present, and though I couldn't refute this notion, living in it constantly was unnerving.

A diary entry, 1981:

The circumstance of someone's birth should have no bearing on their life, and any insistence on the importance of those accidental facts is violence, ignorance. A person can be understood only through the life they choose, the people they choose, the things they do, and not the things that are done to them.*

---

* X, diary entry, July 30, 1981, box 3, notebook 7b, TXA.

"Maybe the closest friends and the friends of those friends know something about her life," a journalist for *Artforum* wrote in 1994, "where she came from, where she was born, how old she is, how she lives. But she never talks about that, 'since it's very personal.'"[*] The only thing she did disclose about her early life in that profile was that she was born with rigorous and exacting taste, despite her jejune surroundings. When asked if she read anything trivial as a child, she said she had read *Moby-Dick*.

X, of course, was not her given name, and neither was Dorothy Eagle—the name on the ID she used when she first arrived in New York—and neither were the several other names she used at different times, for different purposes, from 1972 to 1981—Deena Stray, Clydelle, Bee Converse, Clyde Hill, Martina Riggio, Yarrow Hall, Věra, Cindy O, Cassandra Edwards, and others. Though she was occasionally accused of being deceptive, deception was never her intent; a single name simply failed to contain her.

Nathalie Léger once described X's names in an essay: "Who knows if it was in order better to conceal her self or to expose her self, if it was in order to escape her self or to understand her self; five names, according to some, though I only know of three. With a name nothing is ever clear, on the contrary, everything becomes more opaque."[†] Léger was one of the few past acquaintances I contacted who seemed to have a wholly uncomplicated relationship with X.

"To me it seemed like a reasonable solution to a person, being a self," Léger told me over the phone. "You have to get through—how to put it?—shame, essentially, yes that's it—the shame and boredom of talking about yourself." She later added, "Shifting between so many names, between selves—it must have relieved some of that shame."[‡]

Yet isn't it natural to want to know where your wife was born, to see photographs of her as a baby, a child, to know something of her earliest world? Early on, I obsessed over these omissions in the most mundane

---

[*] Julie Thompson, "Solving for X," *Artforum* 33, no. 1 (September 1994): 45–46.

[†] Nathalie Léger, "The Right Mess," *Dorothy Magazine* 25, January 1995: 42.

[‡] Nathalie Léger, telephone conversation with the author, March 4, 2001, tape 3.40–41, CML audio collection, TXA.

moments—staring at her over the dinner table, or watching her sneer at a magazine while we waited for a plane, or waking in the middle of the night to find her side of the bed empty.

Perhaps this was why the widespread acceptance of Mr. Smith's erroneous biography enraged me so. I had to discredit the book by discovering X's true birthplace, and yet that discovery bled into other discoveries—I cursed myself. Is anyone ever sufficiently admonished by admonitory tales, or are such myths simply maps of inevitabilities?

Many who knew X personally believed "Dorothy Eagle" to be her legal, given name. It made sense, almost. X held a state-issued ID for Dorothy Eagle. The photograph didn't look much like her, but she told me she was wearing wax prosthetics and stage makeup that day, that she didn't want her real face photographed back then. Dorothy's story was that she'd been born to a poor family in Lexington, Kentucky, that she ran away from home as a teenager after discovering her father had murdered someone. She ended up in Montana, where she worked at a deer processing plant for some time before hitchhiking to New York with a hundred dollars to her name.

I began my research in Missoula, Montana, to first determine how she'd been given this form of identification and why. The phone book listed four deer processing plants in the area; I had no luck at the first two—they'd both opened in the early 1980s, years after X would have left. No one at the third plant would talk to me. The fourth one appeared to be closed until I found a young man drinking from a thermos at the side of the building. I asked him—though he seemed too young—if he'd ever heard anything about a woman working there in the late sixties.

Not the sort of place most women like to work, not with all the guts and everything, he said. The neck of his T-shirt was stretched out, and two flecks of blood were dried onto his collarbone. His father, he explained, had worked here long ago. He was retired now and lived down the street a ways, a brown house with a red door.

Dennis B. Kimball wouldn't tell me what the "B" stood for, but he offered me a can of soda and sat with me on his stoop, allowing me to record our conversation.* I told him his son had sent me over, that I was trying to find information about a woman he may have worked with processing deer in the late sixties.

He nodded for a while, a slow squint coming across his face. "Dorothy," he said. "Wasn't that her name? You don't often come across a woman that comfortable with carcasses." He nodded, picked at his fingernails. "What do you want to know?"

"Anything," I said, though I wanted to ask him if she ever told him where she was from, or where she lived, and did he remember what she looked like, what her voice sounded like, and was she as oddly enthralling back then as she was later, was everyone in love with her, and did he remember any of her stories, and had he ever stood close enough to her to smell her skin and was it a grassy smell, and did she tell anyone she was leaving town or where she was going or did she just vanish. I was still romanced by grief, and stupidly hopeful that reconstructing her life might resurrect her, but I hid in the costume of an objective, detached reporter.

On the tape I hear myself saying, "Anything could be helpful. Anything at all."

"Tell you the truth, I didn't know her so much as this other fella did, Dave, David Moser. He was the one who brought her in, got her the job. Dave works at the courthouse last I heard, couldn't tell you what. Spends a lot of time at the pool hall, as I understand, down there—down in some place near the . . . I forget . . . [unintelligible]."

I pressed him on Dave and X, but he remembered very little.

"I was married at the time, so I tried not to [muffled], and it's nothing but trouble for me, is what I mean. Some of the other guys, they might surely have known her better than I did. Something cheerful about Dorothy—I recall that much. Everyone had a nickname then, but she didn't want nobody to call her Dottie—she made that pretty clear if I remember—but you oughta talk to Dave. He'd know where she's gone to—"

"She's dead," I interrupted.

---

* Dennis B. Kimball, interview with the author, October 11, 1997, Missoula, MT, tape 7.51–53, CML audio collection, TXA.

Mr. Kimball nodded. He was old enough not to be surprised by the news of a peer's death, just reminded. "Sorry to hear that. She must have been a bit younger than me . . ."

He wrote down Dave's full name, circled the courthouse on my map.

"They had some kind of arrangement, Dave and her. I don't know exactly what, but that was what people said—there was something worked out between them. I couldn't say exactly what, and I don't know. It, well, it wouldn't be right of me to speculate, that's all. Not in female company."

Such an old-fashioned attitude about women is still somewhat common in the Western Territory, as its people were so isolated from the Northern Territory after the 1945 Disunion. I found this meek sexism more amusing than insulting, so I reminded Dennis that he could speak freely with me, that I was a journalist, a professional, but he remained quiet. He mustn't censor himself, I insisted, as it was important that I gather as much information as possible about Dorothy. But his Western tendency toward neutrality remained.

"Wouldn't be proper," he said. "You ask Dave now. That's what you ought to do. Talk to Dave."

Image: Missoula, Montana, courthouse, 1969

———

The woman at the courthouse seemed to find it strange I was looking for Dave Moser. I told her I was trying to get some information on a woman who lived in town some years ago and I thought she might have known Dave.

Oh, I'd bet she did know him, she said. *I'd bet she sure did.*

Though I pushed, she declined to divulge what she meant, and when a male coworker entered the room, her tone became formal.

Yes, ma'am, Mr. Moser has been retired about a year now, but I believe you may be able to find him at Hawthorne's over on Main. Seems that's where he's occupying himself.

She drew a little map on the back of a form that explained how to contest a parking ticket.

Dave Moser was right where the clerk said he'd be, and when I approached him and spoke his name, he didn't startle.

In the flesh, he said, not glancing up from the pool table.

I was wondering, I asked, *if you knew a woman named Dorothy Eagle?*

He narrowly missed a shot, stood upright, and looked at me.

Might have, he said, bowing toward the table again, sinking the five into a side pocket.

This was October 1997, more than a year since X had died. Dave Moser looked a rough decade older than X had been, and I had to stifle the loathing I sometimes felt when meeting anyone who'd lived longer than she had. Dave and I sat in a creaking wooden booth, and when I told him that she—that Dorothy, that X—was dead, he cleared his throat several times, grunted, then coughed heavily.

You're a reporter? he eventually asked, wiping at his eyes.

I said I was and asked if I could record our conversation.

Rather you didn't, he said. *Least not until I get a sense of things.*

He was quiet for a long time, and I felt a heaviness between us as I asked if I should leave him alone.

He shook his head. *I always knew I'd have to answer to what I did.*

I asked Dave where he'd met her.

Here, he said. *Ain't nothing has happened to me in this life didn't happen to me in this pool hall. Every woman I knew, every friend, enemy, paychecks lost or doubled . . .*

Then, as if it could be so simple to know, I asked him if he knew where she'd come from.

See, that's a complication, he said. *I made a promise to her.* He frowned with his lips clenched, like a child refusing medicine. *Lady, I gotta get some air,* he said.

So I followed him out a back door. He stood in the alley, lighting a cigarette and squinting at one of the mountains that stood guard around the town.

Damn, he said, then, louder, *Damn! I should've never lived this long.*

He'd never imagined having to hear she was dead, and though I knew his grief was real, my own loomed larger. I asked why he didn't want to be recorded.

For one thing, he wasn't going to betray her in case she was still alive, and for another thing he'd done this favor for her, taken a risk that could still get him in an awful lot of trouble if anyone found out.

It was the right thing to do, he said, *though illegal. But, you see, people don't know much about right and wrong. They think they do, but they don't.*

Later that afternoon Dave allowed me to record him on the stipulation that I would not publish his confession until after his death. Though it now seems foolish to have made such a promise to a source, I agreed. He died in 2002.

Dave Moser had come up with that name—Dorothy Eagle. He'd forged her birth certificate and driver's license shortly after he met X in the summer of 1968. She'd beaten him in pool, he told me, that's how they first met. It was late and he'd been on a winning streak and had moved from beer to whiskey when she challenged him.[*]

[*] David Moser, interview with the author, October 11, 1997, Missoula, MT, tape 7.54–58, CML audio collection, TXA. All quotes from David Moser in the following paragraphs are from this interview.

MONTANA DRIVER'S LICENSE

PRINT OF TYPE
FULL NAME ___ **Dorothy**   **Eagle** ___
                   FIRST   MIDDLE   LAST

ST & NO. ___ **4481 Livingston Ave.** ___

CITY &
STATE ___ **Missoula, MT 59801** ___

DATE OF BIRTH

SEX	EYES	WT.	RACE	HAIR	MO.	DATE	YEAR
F	Gry	120	W	Brn	01	01	1950

THIS
LICENSE   LEAVE THIS SPACE BLANK
EXPIRES   6/8 1975   170608

RESTRICTIONS ___

FOLD HERE TO FIT WALLET

OCCUPATION ___ **Domestic** ___

USUAL
SIGNATURE   *Dorothy Eagle* ___

The person named hereon is hereby licensed to operate a motor vehicle
as an OPERATOR only unless otherwise authorized, and when validated
by Postage Meter No. 132679 cancellation stamp on reverse side.

Alf R. Stephenson
SUPERVISOR, MONTANA HIGHWAY PATROL

"She won every cent I had on me," Dave said. The rest of the summer she was there every night. "The girl with no name—or rather, if she had one, she wasn't telling it. Scrawny kid, wasn't hardly nineteen from the looks of her, and she wouldn't tell nobody what her name was . . . Had a dozen names, depending on who asked—Saralynn or Kendra or Halle—no end to new names."

Eventually Dave realized she was living in a broken-down car parked around the corner from Hawthorne's.

"I would have just as soon stayed out of it, but she ended up digging me out of a real pit of trouble one night, and there wasn't no way I could turn my back on her after that."

Dave had a somewhat inaccurate reputation as a man with money to spare instead of what he really was—a middle-class courthouse clerk with something of a gambling problem. Most of Hawthorne's other patrons worked at factories or in construction, so Dave's office job, his reputation for being a lush, and his uneven pool skills made him an easy target for scams and favors. For decades, Dave was known as "City," a nickname he always hated but was unable to escape.

One night the summer that X arrived in Missoula, two men appeared at the pool hall looking for City, one of them claiming to be the brother of a girl City had gotten pregnant. Dave, by his own admission, knew it was possible that he could have "gotten someone or another pregnant" in those months, but he felt sure these guys were lying. They claimed to need two thousand dollars for an abortion and "incidentals."

"I made a lot more than my share of mistakes in those days," he explained, "and I thought it was just a matter of how I could love people too much, fell in love like it was nothing, but now I know that's just something people tell themselves to justify it . . . to justify the trouble I made for myself and others. But I didn't have two thousand dollars! I didn't have two thousand anything, not with the sort of wife I had and the kids."

Noticing the confrontation, X stepped in to challenge one of the men to pool. *City's not going anywhere*, she told them. *Just wait for him to get drunk enough, and he'll give you whatever you need.* After she'd beaten each of the men easily, Dave said, he saw her whisper something to one of them, and then they both left. She said she knew who they worked for.

"Some guy running a scheme out of Bozeman," Dave said. "And that was that. They never came back."

He never knew exactly how she'd done it, but the gesture put him in her debt, so Dave convinced his wife to let X move in to the spare bedroom in their garage. It was then he came up with the name—Dorothy Eagle.

"My wife was a real serious Christian," Dave explained, "and couldn't resist helping out a charity case like ol' Dorothy." By winter, however, he'd fallen in love with her; the two began an affair that lasted until she left Missoula in the autumn of 1970.

Keeping pace with Dave, I drank two beers as I listened, trying to convince him and myself that I was simply a biographer—gathering evidence, gathering facts—though I was shaking and had to go to the bathroom several times just to breathe alone.

X's real name, Dave said, was Caroline Luanna Walker Vine. She was born in Byhalia, Mississippi, in 1945.

That was the year the wall went up around the Southern Territory, the year of the Great Disunion—a strange balance to the fact that she'd died in 1996, just weeks before the wall was torn down, as if her very existence were tethered to that dangerous, doomed boundary.

X had told Dave about her birthplace and escape a few months into their affair, and he'd immediately understood how dire her secret was. All these years he'd kept it, never told anyone; he could hardly believe he was telling me now.

"Who would have trusted me anyway?" he asked, drunk enough for his sadness to look like a kind of joy. "A girl like that escaping the territory. I never even knew the whole story of how she got out, never asked. She felt guilty about whatever it was—I could see that."

In the months after Dorothy left Montana, she sent him letters on hotel stationery from all over the country, and though over the years the letters came less frequently, they always came. A letter a year, or every two years. He wrote back to all of them until 1991—the year his wife died—and when he stopped replying, the letters stopped coming.

"It was almost like . . . whatever I felt about Dorothy depended on my wife being there. Like my wife was a lamp that had always been on—and

in that light I could see certain things, and now that it's gone I can't see anything. That's what it felt like, still does, like I'm sitting in a living room with no lights on, just sitting."

Dave was grinning to stop himself from tears, so I assisted his avoidance by asking if he'd ever seen any of X's art, read any of her books.

"I was never one for reading, and I never bothered trying to figure out what art was, why people did it. But I felt proud of her all the same, knowing she was out there, making her way, living. That I had some kind of piece in that. In Dorothy."

Just before I left, Dave asked me, "Did you know her? Did you ever meet her just once?"

And I don't know if I surprised myself when I said, *No, never, not really*.

Image: Photograph by David Moser

INTERVIEW, 1983*

ROBERT STORR, INTERVIEWER: There's a letter in *The Reason I'm Lost* that reads: "This is the poetically licensed story of a woman who finds it difficult to reconcile certain external facts with her image of her own perfection. It's also the story of a woman who cannot reconcile these facts with her image of her own deformity." So you have, again, the split personality. It is almost the archetype of the narcissistic dream of perfection.

X: Yeah, it's called ambivalence, Jake.

STORR: How consciously did you structure this according to psychological or psychoanalytical models, or how much of this was organically coming out of your own experience?

X: It came out of my own development.

STORR: Your own development?

X: Yeah.

STORR: What do you mean by development?

X: Are you familiar with photography, the process of photography? *Storr hesitates and half laughs as he squints at her.*

X: You put the photo paper in the developer and what happens?

STORR: What I was asking—

X: What happens, Jerry?

STORR: The photograph develops.

X: Good boy, Frank, good boy. The photo develops. And this is what life is, little Waldo Emerson, little Charlie, darling. You put people in situations and their personality develops. Their little freaky heads. *X lights a cigarette. A long silence.*

STORR: I—well, I had one more—

X: Come on, Billy, just go with it, Billy Boy, ask me another smart question of yours. Have a look at your notes, find some genius in there!

---

* "X interview with Robert Storr," New York University Arts & Humanities Festival, 1983, transcript, item 499.2, TXA.

STORR: Not much is known, um, about where you were born or when.

X: Is that all you got?

STORR: Though there are theories, and many believe you were born in Italy, or that your father may be—

X: And back to your question about personalities—I'm going to take it seriously this time, your serious question—this is what happens with people, they don't stay the same unless they're dead, unless they're born dead, certainly you've seen them in New York City, haven't you? The dead people in all their skyscrapers, banking, eating lobster tails?

STORR: It's also been rumored you were born in the Southern Territory.

X: It's been rumored that Tuesday is in disguise as Thursday. It's been rumored that Shakespeare was a ball of twine that gained consciousness and grew a beard. It's been rumored Emma Goldman was the greatest tap dancer of all time and kept it a secret, and of course it's long been rumored that I've got a wad of cherry licorice between my legs, and everyone knows licorice is outlawed in the Southern Territory so it should be obvious what's true and what's fantasy, shouldn't it?

STORR: Do you have anything to say to—

X: Name anyone who's made it out of that place alive. Can you? You can't. You can't and you won't, and neither will I.

A long, tense moment. X speaks again softly into the microphone.

X: Jonnycakes, my darling little Jonnycakes, be a good boy. Don't show up at this fancy place for all these fancy people just to insult those people who are living through the very real, very bloody, very authoritarian war we all know is happening on the other side of that wall. Don't stoop to that level, little Jonnyboy, little Babycake Jonnyboy? Huh? Can you play nice? Can you?

STORR: My sincerest apologies. Let's move on.

X: That's the spirit!

THE SOUTHERN TERRITORY

T he theory that X had escaped from the Southern Territory quietly persisted over the years, though it lacked evidence and seemed impossible. With rare exceptions, such stories ended in deportation, imprisonment, or death. A 1958 tripartite treaty among the Northern, Southern, and Western Territories had declared harboring or aiding a Southern escapee to be a federal crime; if David Moser had been caught making that driver's license and birth certificate for X, he could have been put in jail for a minimum of thirty years.* The perception that escape from the ST was impossible protected the secret X most wanted to keep.

Though I expect most readers will be well aware of the Great Disunion of 1945, in recent years—and especially after the dissolution of the Southern Territory's fascist theocracy—many Northern and Southern politicians have attempted to revise our country's history, to simplify or sanitize it. And though the historical record so often belongs to the victors, the 1945 secession of the Southern Territory earned victory for no one. Strife in the North continued. Buildings were burned on both sides of the division. Political and religious leaders of all kinds were assassinated both by the territorial governments and by that looser form of govern-

---

* The 1958 treaty, as described in Senate Bill 113c, defined "harboring or aiding any citizen from the Southern Territory who has illegally escaped their homeland" as a felony.

ment known as a mob. Many of the newly "free" people of the Southern Territory are still too fearful of retribution to speak of their lives under the ST government. Worse, many Northerners still believe that Southerners brought suffering upon themselves and deserved their oppression.

For the sake of contextualizing the world into which X was born, I will attempt to briefly outline the history of the Great Disunion and the nature of the Southern Territory's theocratic rule from 1945 until 1996. Granted, America's radical bifurcation, and the nascent Reunification (if we achieve it), is a large topic. These notes are simply here for any future readers who might be unfamiliar with this complicated conflict.

Image: Satellite photograph of the Northern, Western, and Southern Territories, 1993

On Thanksgiving Day 1945, twenty-two million America citizens woke up to news that they were no longer living in America—a wall had been erected between much of the Deep South and the rest of the country by an insurgent theocratic government that now controlled the newly anointed Southern Territory. The state governments of Mississippi, Alabama, Georgia, the Carolinas, Tennessee, Florida, as well as parts of Virginia, West Virginia, Arkansas, and Louisiana, had been cooperating in secret for nearly a decade to enact the mass exodus. Kentucky's self-exclusion was a response to the teetotaling Southern Territory leaders' insistence that it dismantle its whiskey industry.* By mid-1946, when it was clear that what remained of America's Western and Northern states could not come to a consensus regarding diplomacy, a peaceful unguarded border was established between the Northern and Western Territories; the North took an aggressive stance in its relations with the South, while the West was more laissez-faire.

Though the Disunion seemed sudden from the outside, the so-called Christian Coup and its wall had been in the works for years. The most rural portions of the massive structure had been built long before the wall's official completion in late 1945; recently declassified documents show that prisoners had been forced to assemble modular sections of the wall as early as 1942; day laborers, police officers, and volunteer militias built the rest.† What may have seemed like a coup from the outside was actually a slow mutation of a conservative democratic state into a country overtaken by an invasive delirium—the fear of God—and ruled by whoever could most convincingly claim to know *His Divine Laws*.‡

In the years preceding the Great Disunion, while the U.S. military and

---

* For more information, see Chris Offut, *My Father, the Distiller* (Lexington, KY: Haldeman Press, 1998).

† Cora Currier, "Declassified FBI Files Reveal Intricacies of 1945 ST Coup," *The New York Times*, January 7, 1998, A1.

‡ *His Divine Laws* (1945) was the title of the 478-page document listing 1,364 laws that ST leaders used as a replacement for the individual legal codes of the southern states prior to the Disunion. Another 5,449 laws were added to the document during the ST leaders' reign.

the federal government had been engrossed in World War II, the Southern Territory's future leaders had—through a steady propaganda campaign of radio shows, newspaper reports, posters, pamphlets, and youth outreach programs—convinced a majority of Southerners that every state in the North was being secretly controlled by the Communist Party; an invasion of the South, they said, was imminent. Those who weren't convinced of a Communist invasion were unsteadied enough by the widespread misinformation to feel there was no longer any objective truth, a belief that numbed any part of the population that might have objected to the forced theocracy.

But years before the rampant propaganda, political discontent and xenophobia had been on the rise. By the mid-1930s, a majority of Southerners lived in abject poverty, and the influx of immigrants and refugees that was shaping Northern cities led many to believe that their situation would only become worse if the rise of socialist policies swept the country.* Emma Goldman, in particular, became a lightning rod for Southern hatred. In the two decades before the wall was erected, Goldman—the Russian-born anarchist turned socialist governor of Illinois, then chief of staff to Franklin Delano Roosevelt—had become an unexpectedly influential figure in American politics. In her time as governor, she was credited with hastening the changing perception of workers' unions and popularizing what has been called Socialist Capitalism through her innovative legislation and galvanizing public speeches. As FDR's chief of staff and closest adviser, Goldman was responsible for the most controversial policies attached to the New Deal—the plan to phase in same-sex marriage rights, a near abolition of the prison system, and a series of bills that led to the Twenty-Second Amendment, on immigrant rights. Southern newspapers dubbed this "Goldman's Devil Trinity."†

By the time she was assassinated in 1945 (infamously followed by FDR's somewhat sudden death just three days later), Goldman had radically reshaped American politics. The Socialist Party (renamed the Goldman Party in 1946) had gained so much power through the 1930s and '40s

---

* Saidu Tejan-Thomas, "The Dismantle," Northern Public Radio, July 8–15, 1997.

† Renata Adler, *Nowhere to Go: A Month Undercover in the Southern Territory* (New York: Farrar, Straus and Giroux, 1978).

that the previously dominant Democratic and Republican Parties were pushed to the margins for the rest of the twentieth century. This sudden reshaping of the mainstream political agenda left many Southerners feeling that the federal government was oblivious to their needs and culture.

Part of the New Deal of 1933 included the creation of the Tennessee Valley Authority, an effort to develop Southern waterways into sources of hydroelectric power and to modernize their irrigation systems; many Southerners objected to these infrastructure improvements on the assumption that their existence condoned the social policies to which they objected. One TVA project on the Tombigbee River, which flows through northeastern Mississippi and into northwestern Alabama, was destroyed with several amateur bombs in 1937, an act of protest of Goldman's "heathenism." The bombing resulted in severe flooding of nearby towns, but the governors of Mississippi and Alabama accused Goldman *herself* of setting off the bombs.* It was not a difficult story to sell—she was already

WOMAN OR WITCH?

---

* "Report of the 1937 Bombing of TVA Waterway Project on the Tombigbee River," January 13, 1983, National FST Archive, University of Virginia, Ida B. Wells Library.

viewed as a tormentor of children, a traitor to her sex, and an enemy of all Christians. A group of factory owners, fearing that Goldman's pro-worker agenda might trickle southward, had been paying for a series of radio and print advertisements vilifying her.

Talks of secession were increasingly common during those years, but when Southern politicians raised the issue in Washington, others openly mocked the idea, which only served to further stir unrest. Among their constituents, support of secession by any means necessary grew rapidly. At Southern public schools, children were taught the Lord's Prayer instead of the Pledge of Allegiance. Sermons turned political. Political rallies became religious rallies. Many people lost their jobs or were disowned by their families for not supporting the "South First" ideology; thousands fled to the West to escape political persecution. Propaganda posters declaring WE WANT QUIET AND ORDER! hung in every town square, and many people wore buttons bearing the same message.

On that autumn day in 1945, the quiet orderliness began. Phone lines were snipped. Radio stations were shut down—some by violence and executions, others by willing consent. Local newspaper production ceased. Electricity and running water were rationed in the small number of homes that had any to begin with. Sunday church attendance became mandatory. Libraries were purged of unlawful texts. Schoolhouses were abandoned—all education took place in churches now. Armed guards stood at attention at the few places where it was possible to cross the border; snipers were stationed along the rest of the wall. No one was allowed in or out, and those who dared to defy these orders were shot dead.

The writer Susan Howe has aptly described the Great Disunion as a time when "the original American conflict between idealism and extremism was being acted out again."* The Southerners believed Northerners to be naïvely and dangerously radical, while the Northerners viewed the Southerners as diseased by religious extremism and willful ignorance. But even now, nearly a decade after the dissolution of the ST, some citizens

* Susan Howe, *Our Southern Territory: The Poetry of Rebellion* (New York: Jackson & Howard, 1982).

are nostalgic for their previously despotic leadership, despite the high cost. It was, at least, an orderly and quiet time, a time when Southerners knew exactly what they would and wouldn't see in public, when everyone knew exactly how to behave. There was a rigid dress code, laws about speech, and a universally followed daily schedule that dictated work, chores, prayers, meals, and sleep. Girls were not allowed to ride bicycles or drive cars; men and women were prohibited from speaking to one another in public; the only sanctioned radio station played nothing but the Lord's Prayer and hymns on repeat.

Perhaps most crucially, the theocracy found a way for its populace to police itself: by the late 1980s, a majority of Southern citizens were either directly or indirectly involved with the Guardians of Morality, a network of citizen-informants much like those who worked with the Stasi in East Germany. The GMs rooted out and reported anyone suspected of sinful or unpatriotic behavior—those who engaged in vanity, sloth, or covetousness; those who practiced "aesthetic pastimes" such as embroidery; those who were perceived as gluttons or homosexuals; those who read unregulated books; those who doubted the government; those who complained about the health-care system; those who practiced any form of birth control or had sex for pleasure or missed a church service for any reason.*

One of the more staggering statistics for Northerners to understand about the Southern Territory is that up to 45 percent of the total population was imprisoned at some point in their life. While Emma Goldman's dream of total prison abolition was not fully realized, the Northern and Western Territories came closer than many ever imagined. The ST, in contrast, used detention at the hands of the government more widely and wildly than any other nation in modern history—despite the fact that such practices were repeatedly proved to be ineffective at controlling crime. Some ST citizens never left captivity, though many were "rehabilitated" as devout patriots. Systemic racism was clearly evidenced in the ST's judicial system, as Black citizens were imprisoned at rates far above those of the white population. (In this regard, however, the Northern

---

* FBI, *Report on Guardians of Morality in the Southern Territory*, 1969 (amended in 1970, 1974, 1982, 1988, and 1991; declassified in 1996).

Territory saw similar rates, as does the reunified country today.) Further-more, prisoners in the South included children as young as nine. Even more shocking, roughly a third of all prisoners were "auto-admitted"—that is, they turned themselves in without being charged.

As we can see now from both the ST's official records as well as pri-mary materials such as diaries and letters going back to the Disunion's beginning, the degree to which ST citizens trusted in the righteousness and infallibility of their government was extraordinary. It seems this widespread nationalism was created and fostered almost exclusively by the fear of God and the force of the Church. By 1952, nearly every cit-izen in the territory was convinced (or at least claimed to believe) that the Second Coming of Christ would happen in their lifetimes. Devotion to the ST was not merely a matter of politics or societal acceptance, but instead was a choice between everlasting life and eternal damnation. For many Northerners, this kind of religious belief is difficult to understand, as the Anti-Religion Movement of the 1940s and '50s has been so fully integrated into our culture. Aside from scholars and historians, few in the North have any firsthand experience with religion of any kind, nor do they know anything of the coercive force such faith can have in a community, the acts of violence carried out in the name of God, the wild and seductive power of a belief in the divine, or the boundless joy and fear that can be experienced when heaven and hell are believed to be inevitabilities.

The very few uprisings in the ST were quickly and violently stymied. Participants were portrayed by the state-controlled media as lost souls or Satan worshippers. All were executed. After all, what else could com-pel someone to rebel against God or turn their back on a community in which all their needs were met? "Jobs, housing, childcare, medical services, funeral benefits—both the Northern and Southern Territories delivered state-guaranteed basics. And both were rewarded—at least for a time—with support from large majorities of their populations," Marc Fisher, a leading historian of the Disunited Era, and professor of theoc-racy and comparative politics at Harvard, told me in a letter. "The popular consensus broke down when the ST government's inability and unwill-ingness to provide the standard of living anywhere near that of the North was revealed to be the result of deliberate policy, a corrupt wizardry manipulated by the old men behind the curtain."*

Now the stories are well-known—how in its final years, a strong current of paranoia overtook the South in the larger cities first, then across the rural majority. Much of the territory experienced extreme famine and drought. Many people believed God to be speaking to them, though it was later determined that bacteria in the water supply had caused widespread hallucinations. Hundreds of children vanished. There were rumors about prison revolts, enemies at the gate, a coming war. The belief in the suffering and depravity of the Northern Territory broke down. Prisoners escaped. Several factories exploded. Jesus was repeatedly sighted, hitchhiking, pumping gas, loitering. Cotton fields caught fire. Grain silos caved in. Farmers' weather diaries detailed constant tornadoes, fish hail, and blood rain. The belief that Judgment Day was imminent was a comfort to some and a nightmare to others. Then, in November 1996, following an incident of mass hysteria on Halloween that inspired 2,488 leading theocrats to take their own lives under divine orders to do so, the North successfully invaded the South, the wall was demolished, and the Reunification began.

As I write this, barely a decade has passed since that day in 1996; I do not belong to the era of writers who will be able to make any sense of this particularly turbulent chapter of American history; one cannot make a bed while still tangled in its sheets. By that logic, however, I will never understand X, either, will never be able to get far enough away from her to see who she was or to comprehend the facts and contradictions of her life. Yet there are things one cannot help but do, or try to do, no matter how doomed they may be.

* Marc Fisher to author, April 3, 1998, folder 7, item 3, CML papers, TXA.

CAROLINE

———

X was born to Angela Mae Walker (née Irving) and Leon M. Walker in Byhalia, Mississippi, on April 9, 1945. Her given name was Caroline Luanna Walker.

Though I visited the Former Southern Territory in 1999, three years after Reunification had begun, passports and travel visas were still required—ostensibly to protect the South from being invaded too quickly by Northern developers, but also to prevent journalists from swarming and sending out a bevy of bad press. Bureaucrats and police from the North and South had a tenuous, patchwork alliance in the newly "liberated" territory, but the FST Border Regulation Bureau still controlled which journalists were given entry.

Braver writers refused to abide by the remaining shreds of such a notoriously inhumane government, but I had no such courage. As a younger reporter I'd once gone undercover in a cult, but X's death had aged me quickly; I no longer had such youthful nerve. In January of 1999, after waiting nearly a year for my research visa to be approved—I found myself in a small car with Nancy George, a woman of sixty-eight who'd just begun working for the FST's Travel Mentor Program. The car—a bright blue sedan—would have looked unremarkable anywhere else in the world, but Nancy, whose eyes were both youthfully expressive and hardened at once, commented several times on how *future-like* it felt. This was one of the first new cars imported into the South in half a century.

During my trip Nancy drove me everywhere, steering clear of restricted areas and ensuring I never left my hotel unescorted. When she met me at the newly constructed Memphis Airport she gave me a manila envelope containing a notebook, a pen, the FST-approved tape recorder, and a disposable camera. I was not permitted to bring my own notebooks or recording devices on the trip, and I had to sign an agreement allowing all my work to be reviewed before my departure. Though almost all of my written notes were left intact (my handwriting is generally illegible to others), the tapes were occasionally censored and only half my photographs survived processing.

Despite these limitations, I felt that the Travel Mentor Agency was the only viable route I could take to successfully reach those whom X had known in the Southern Territory. Even if I had found contact information for any of her family members, most FST citizens did not have phone lines and the understaffed postal system holds a millions-long queue of letters. Every one of my meetings in Byhalia in 1999 was arranged by the agency.

A week before my arrival, the agency sent me a photocopy of a letter from Angela and Leon Walker, X's biological parents. (While I was in the ST, I called X by her given name—Caroline, or Carrie Lu for short—though I found it unsettling.)

"We would be glad to welcome you in our home to discuss our beloved daughter, Carrie Lu, rest her soul," Angela wrote in the letter. "May the

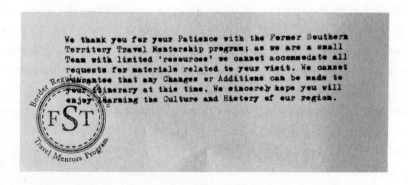

We thank you for your Patience with the Former Southern Territory Travel Mentorship program; as we are a small Team with limited 'resources' we cannot accommodate all requests for materials related to your visit. We cannot guarantee that any Changes or Additions can be made to your Itinerary at this time. We sincerely hope you will enjoy Learning the Culture and History of our region.

FST

Border Regulations · Travel Mentors Program

Lord bless your travels."* The letter was accompanied by an itinerary—a list of names and dates, though I didn't know who any of the people were until I met them.

One of the Articles of Reunification required the FST to permit a certain quota of journalists and researchers inside the borders. The fact that I'd spent my short career mostly as a crime reporter worked in my favor by suggesting I was concerned with justice as an abstract—though I was not, and have never been. I titled my proposed article "The Human Cost of Rebellion" to give the impression that I might be an ST apologist, or at least anti-rebellion. My fallacious statement of plans explained I was focused on young rebels from the sixties in an attempt to discern whether undiagnosed mental illness underlay uprisings of that era. I was beginning my research with Caroline Walker, I lied, after I'd discovered her name in a few heavily redacted pages from an FBI report about a failed insurgency in Byhalia the late 1960s. This, at least, was somewhat true. I still did not know how X had escaped the South, but based on the limited information my request under the Freedom of Information Act had uncovered, it seemed her involvement in this rebellion would have been relevant. Of course, FST officials did not know, or did not let on that they knew, that Caroline Walker had become X or that I had been married to her, that I was her widow.

Renata Adler's undercover reporting from the Southern Territory in the 1970s found that in the rare cases that a Southerner successfully crossed the border or was killed while attempting to do so, the government often told the surviving family members a false story. These falsifications were typically a variation on a theme: their lost son or daughter had been killed by Northerners while working as a secret Southern operative. "The more cultivated elements of theocratic fascism," Adler wrote, "have evolved their own schizophrenic logic—a seamless garment of nonviolence in the one hand and a blood-soaked rag hidden in the other."†

I did not know what story the Walkers had been told about their daughter's disappearance, but I assumed that they would have learned the

---

* Angela Walker to author, January 13, 1999, folder 15, item 5, CML supplement, TXA.

† Renata Adler, "The Invisible Insurrection," *The Yorker*, July 16, 1976.

truth by now. The expansion of the Freedom of Information Act into the FST had mandated that Southerners be given access to any files that had been kept on them, their deceased family members, and their "vanished" family members. Nearly every citizen had a file: memos about their behavior in public, detailed records of their confessions at church, surveillance footage, covert photographs, and reports from their bosses, spouses, friends, children—anyone they knew who had been a GM. Anytime a Southern citizen was arrested, he or she was usually given the chance to trade information—even unfounded rumors—for leniency in punishment.

The Walkers, however, either did not read the files on Caroline, had been given bad information, or had simply refused to believe what had become of their daughter.

The Walkers' home was the first stop on our itinerary the day I arrived in Mississippi.

The two-story clapboard, surrounded on all sides by a white-painted brick wall, was located on an oak-lined street teeming—as much of the FST is—with stray cats. (Neutering animals is still illegal there.) Four large dogwoods and a pair of live oaks crowded the front yard. As I stood at their door, travel-jumbled and nervous, I braced to see X's eyes stuck in someone else's skull, or her cheekbones set into a stranger's face, but when Angela Walker opened the front door, I was relieved to find an unfamiliar old woman. She looked nothing like my wife.

Mrs. Walker wore an old pink housecoat and had her gray hair up in curlers; my visit was more a chore, it seemed, than an event. When I thanked her for taking this meeting, she brushed it away and insisted that Nancy and I call her Angela. "Makes me feel old when people call me Mrs. Walker!" she said, and though she was old—nearly eighty, it seemed—there was a stubborn sense of youth in how quickly she moved around the room, setting out a plate of shortbread and pouring cups of coffee. Nancy and I had not yet sat down when Angela frantically began talking.

"Well, let's just start at the beginning, shall we? Carrie Lu was a terrible baby. Just terrible! She cried if we tried to hold her, but she sang to herself when she was alone . . . That was the first peculiar thing about that girl . . . Just obstinate. She came out obstinate from the get-go. And lonely, I think. She was a very lonely child."*

They rarely took photographs of the girl, but Angela showed me the few she had.

"She was not a pretty baby—I loved her all the same, not that you really get a choice—but I did not fool myself about her beauty. She grew into that face, in a way, but all that dark hair just made her look pale, unhealthy. And that underbite! She looked an awful lot like a bulldog when she smiled, not that she smiled much. I'm still glad we had it fixed when we did, though Leon sure did make a fuss about the surgery, costly as it was."

Angela looked down at one of the photographs for a long while, then turned it to me. It was Angela as a young woman, holding baby Caroline by the armpits and looking confused. Though I'd wanted to see these photographs so desperately and for so long, I feigned—with much effort—a detached examination of them. Though Angela had permitted the agency to make photocopies of other photographs, she did not allow any of her daughter as an infant to be included, as they embarrassed her. "Imagine all that trouble of being pregnant only to have a baby this ugly handed to you. Even the midwife cried," she said.

"Even though the house was full of other children—her brothers and sisters and all the neighborhood children were in and out of this living room all day, just playing and carrying on—Caroline was always sitting off on her own, in the girls' bedroom most the time. Reading or drawing, I always thought, but one day I was walking past the door and I heard her in there talking to herself, which made me nervous . . . You see, I had this sister named Clara. One year older than me. And she was peculiar even as a child, but once she was grown up, she got all kinds of terrible *ideas*, and they had to put her away . . . And you just never know what sorts of things run in family lines, now, do you? You never know until it's too late."

* Angela Walker and Leon Walker, interview with the author, January 22, 1999, tape 11.2–3, CML audio collection, TXA. All quotes from Angela Walker and Leon Walker in the following paragraphs are from this interview.

Angela was distracted for a moment, as if listening for some distant trouble in the house—a whining furnace, a squirrel chewing into the attic. Then she took her empty coffee cup to the kitchen and shouted back toward us. "So I said to her, 'If you don't take care, you're going to be like your aunt Clara. She was peculiar.' And Caroline said, 'What happened to her?' 'She was shut away,' I said. 'She had to be.' Then Caroline said, 'If anyone ever shuts me away, even a little, I shall die.' I said, 'You say that. You're just talking.' 'Oh no,' she said, 'I am not just talking. I shall die.'"

She stood still before me, holding the coffee pot, smiling unhappily.

"She said it just like that! 'I shall die.' She couldn't have been eight years old. 'I shall die.' Imagine hearing a little girl say something like that. Of course it's funny, because she's so young, so you don't take her seriously, but it's also troubling, it's concerning . . . 'I shall die.' . . . Of course I told her what any good parent would tell her, which is that she should pray about her troubles instead of doing all this talking out loud, making all this noise for no reason."

She poured more coffee into our cups, filling each to the brim.

"You know, it really is nice to remember about her with someone. I hadn't really given her much thought since the accident. Then all these years go by, and what do you have left?"

Angela stared at the floor for a moment, then looked up with an odd brightness.

"It's just that it was much easier to deal with everything when we were independent—the territory, I mean. We all had something in common. We were in it all together, which is so much more than we can say for us now—how divided it is. It used to be that everyone believed in the same values, and we all worked to uphold them. We all believed. Everyone believed the very same things."

Without an explanation, Angela left the room, but kept talking all the way down a hall.

"We understood each other, can you imagine that? Nobody up north knows that kind of understanding. They don't even know a thing about it . . ."

She returned with a shoebox, from which she took a blue notebook.

"And this here . . . this was a real comfort to me after Carrie Lu was gone. I gave it to her and told her she could write her prayers to God. It was something my pastor had recommended to me, you know, because of all her talking to herself. And she took right to it, and filled up several of these notebooks over the years, but this one was my favorite to read—it's from the time before she got mixed up in all that trouble, back when she was really doing right, really living in the light of God. It's still a comfort, and not much is a comfort, you know. She had her troubles, sure, everyone does, but she was trying to do right . . . At least she knew how to ask forgiveness. At least we taught her that."

Angela held one of the journals open to a page covered in bulbous cursive.

"What I am asking for is really very ridiculous. Oh Lord, I am saying, at present I am a cheese, make me a mystic, immediately . . . But why should He do that for an ingrate slothful & dirty creature like me?"*

"A cheese," Angela said. "Now, what on earth did she mean by that?"

She allowed me to photograph the notebook page, but seemed to change her mind as the flash went off.

"One photo is quite enough I think," she said, taking the open journal from the table and shoving it back into the shoebox.

Nancy, as if to save Angela from this shame, shouted something about some documents she'd left in the car. She ran outside, came back a minute later with a folder, and spread several forms on a table—statements for each of us to sign affirming we had met of our own volition and that we were not collecting or supplying information about this meeting to any unnamed parties. I had to sign several such documents each day, forms that confirmed Nancy had driven me here or there, that nothing I collected in my research could be legally used against any citizen of the FST for any reason.

"Where's the other source?" Nancy asked.

"The other source?"

"Says right here that Leon Walker was confirmed to be a source in the appointment."

---

* X, photograph of an undated journal entry, folder 7, item 2, CML photo and research collection, TXA.

"Oh," Angela said. "Well, he's just out in the garage—he's not one for talking, so we figured I'd take care of it."

"But we need to have him sign—says right here."

Angela closed her eyes the same way a child will when they want the world to be different. Then she opened them, went down a hallway, opened a door, and called out her husband's name. After a few moments they both appeared in the room. Leon Walker had a narrow and secretive look—a face like a folded note.

"It's the reporter," Angela said, her voice much flatter now. "From up north."

"Pleased to meet you," Leon said, not seeming pleased and not offering his hand.

"She's the one researching about Carrie Lu," Angela said. "The mayor's office sent that letter about it."

"I remember," Leon said.

"Do you really need to talk to him?" she asked, as if Leon were not standing there with us.

Before I could answer, Nancy insisted he stay, telling him that the papers stipulated his participation.

"I do have some thoughts on the matter," Leon said, his voice grave and clear.

"All right, well, I'll fix you a cup of coffee," Angela said. "Everybody's having a cup of coffee, so you should have one, too, if you want it—do you want one, Leon? Do you want a cup of coffee like everyone else is having?"

"That'd be nice," he said, "wouldn't it?"

Leon's presence accelerated Angela's already accelerated behavior. She emptied the shoebox into her lap—Carrie Lu's report cards, school portraits, letters home from camp, drawings of the Crucifixion, Christmas ornaments made of colored paper and tinsel.

"It doesn't bother me looking through all this now," Angela said as she hunched over the artifacts as if to protect them. "It used to bother me, but I made my peace with it. We gave her a nice life, and the Lord took her back when she was needed."

"Is that so?" Leon asked.

"It is so, it is. Now, here, look at this one," she said as she handed me a photograph.

Like all the others, it looked much older than it was, as most of the photo processing equipment in the South was frozen in time—pre-1945, before the Disunion.

"We took Carrie Lu to see this cannon one time, and she just loved that big ol' gun. Talked about it for weeks after, don't you remember? She just loved it. Had to have her photograph taken with it."

"It's interesting, ain't it?" Leon said, almost to no one. "A cannon. Why a cannon?"

"Says it's a gun," Angela said, pointing to a sign in the photo: KEEP OFF THIS GUN.

"Too big to be a gun," Leon said.

"Too stupid to read a sign," Angela muttered.

Image: X as a child

We were all quiet for a moment as we looked at the photograph, their bickering lingering in the air. Then I carefully asked if they might give a basic timeline of Caroline's life.

Leon began, "Caroline was a normal baby except for the hair and teeth. Then she got a plague of warts when she was three, and we had to take her out of preschool until it was over. Then she wasn't much trouble, I reckon. Kept to herself. Minded. Did right. All until she was about fourteen, I'd say."

Angela tried to interrupt, but Leon disregarded her.

"Then she had a rebellious streak, you see, which we didn't know how to deal with. I think the only problem was that she had too much time on her hands. Then of course she went and got herself pregnant by Paul Vine when she was fifteen, though Paul had the good sense to marry her before it got too far along."

I have it on tape—this first moment I learned of my wife's actual first marriage, and her pregnancy, but I don't recall how I felt. Perhaps I was too overwhelmed already to be overwhelmed again; perhaps I just blocked it all out, had to do so in order to continue.

"I'd say motherhood straightened her up for a time, or at least it seemed to," Leon continued. "She was so good with Zebulon when he was a baby, and it was the first time I'd seen her happy in a long time—a long, long time, maybe ever. They lived with us since there wasn't any room at the Vines' house, all the older boys there with their wives and all. So Paul and I fixed up the shed out back into a little room for them, seeing as there wasn't much in here, with our older sons both married and having children. And as far as I ever knew, Carrie Lu and Paul got along, and none of us—not even Paul—knew what foolishness Carrie Lu had gotten into with that group, so when the accident happened that was the first we heard of it—the first I really heard about her being wrapped up with any kind of . . . dissidents."

Leon looked to Angela for a long moment. She was sitting with her arms crossed, looking out the window.

"It really made our life tough with the Guardians after that," he went on. "They were reading all our mail and wanting to see this and that, searching the house for books, and asking all these prying questions. And of course there's poor little Zeb at the center of it, no mother anymore, which was the *real tragedy* of the whole situation—"

"I think that's a bit too much to say, don't you?" Angela interrupted. "Don't you think that's a bit too much to say?"

"No, Angela, I surely do not think that is too much to say. The boy was seven years old, and he needed a mother, and that, to me, is the real tragedy—"

"Our daughter went and got herself blown up and you're saying that Zebulon having only four grandparents and a father and a whole host of aunts and uncles—you're saying that was the real tragedy? That's what you're saying?"

"You don't have to put it so ugly. The boy lost his mother."

"Well, it is ugly, Leon. That's the ugly truth of it. She got blown up to bits and that's what happened."

There was a long silence before Leon said, so softly I had to strain to hear it, "You don't have to say it like that."

I didn't say anything, though I wanted to ask what Angela was refer-ring to when she said Caroline had been "blown up." My confusion must have been apparent.

"Well, isn't that why you're here?" Angela asked. "About all that trou-ble at the rifle factory? It's just about the only thing she ever did in her life."

"She gave us Zebulon," Leon said.

"And left us to pick up the bill for the rest of his life. What a thought-ful gift that was! Why, I should have sent her a thousand thank-you cards for it, shouldn't I?"

"Could we start with her earliest signs of rebellion?" I asked, my voice suddenly assured and firm. "Maybe you could elaborate about this rebel-lious streak in her teens?"

LEON: Well, all of a sudden she started questioning why we had to go to church.

ANGELA: That's not how it started.

LEON: That's how I remember it. She came to my den and asked if she could skip church the next day and I said, "No, ma'am, you may not." Then of course I had to whip her for asking and even still she had the nerve to ask why she had to go to church and of course you don't tell children about your reasons—

ANGELA: Because you never even knew yourself—

LEON: Because children have to learn to do right without knowing the reasons! That's why. But Carrie Lu, well, she wanted to know and kept asking—I said, "It's the law." Then she wants to know why it's the law, and on my word, I tell you, that's really when the devil really got hold of her and wouldn't quit.

ANGELA: It was not a matter of the devil.

LEON: You can excuse it however you want, Angela, but I know the devil when I see it. It wasn't *her*. Nothing was wrong with *her*—

ANGELA: It was not a matter of the devil—you write that down in your notebook. It was a matter of something with Carrie Lu. Eventually she *chose* selfishness, indulgence, and stopped being our child—

LEON: When the devil got hold of her.

ANGELA: You are making us sound ignorant in front of this lady reporter.

LEON: There's nothing ignorant about knowing what you believe. Nothing ignorant about right and wrong, about good and evil. That's just the way the world turns. Ask anybody—it's the same everywhere, same story.

ANGELA: She studied the Bible very seriously at a young age. She read a passage in the Old Testament about not eating pork—which was something, I don't know—something logistical that doesn't apply anymore, but after Carrie Lu read this she came home and wouldn't eat pork anymore. I had to leave it out of her portion of everything and she wouldn't touch the Easter ham, none of the funeral hams neither, even though it had been her favorite all her life—she loved Easter ham—but she was trying to do right—

LEON: Angela Mae Walker, you do have some kind of selective memory. Caroline quit eating ham because they made her dissect a fetal pig at that animal husbandry class and she just couldn't get that smell of the formaldehyde out of her nose. She didn't read it in her

Bible. Who knows if she ever read her Bible—she didn't seem to know much about it—

ANGELA: She most certainly did read the Bible. I sat up with her many nights talking about it. I was concerned about her not eating ham, so we went through Leviticus together, and I pointed out there were a lot of things in there we didn't do anymore and some, of course, that we did—Ten Commandments, and all that—but it wasn't her job to figure the Bible.

LEON: And you see, that's what troubled her. Who was setting the laws and why did we have to follow them just because someone said so. Weren't they human, wasn't everybody human? You see, that was the real heart of the problem—she had a terrible stubbornness, never really grew up, never wanted to mind anybody else. And you can see how dangerous that is. Went and got herself killed because she couldn't stand anyone telling her what to do.

ANGELA: Well, there you have it. The gospel according to Leon, amen.

"But what," I asked again, "did she do during her teenage rebellion?"

Unsurprisingly, Carrie Lu's offenses could only be considered rebellious in the Former Southern Territory. She once wore pants in public; she tried to hug her father; she tried to leave church early; she did not close her eyes during prayer. This occurred in the years before the state lowered the imprisonment age from fifteen to ten, or Carrie Lu would have likely been taken in, but her behavior caused the Walker household to be put on a watch list. They were visited three times a week by a GM who ensured their home was in perfect order, and they were required to arrive at church two hours before the service to sit in silent prayer. Carrie Lu's behavior did seem to calm down for a time, until she came to her mother to confess her period was late.

ANGELA: And there was no sense in being angry, so I wasn't angry, wasn't angry at all, and I just asked her what any mother would ask, which is whether *God* had told her to go lay with Paul Vine or whether the devil had, and she said it was God that had told her, so that was that. Zebulon was a gift to us, and you can't question a gift from God. You just can't. No matter if it comes earlier than you'd like. God has His own time. So I took Carrie Lu and Paul both to the church that very afternoon, and by suppertime Pastor Elliot had given them his blessing to get married that Sunday.

LEON: I was a little turned around by the whole thing.

ANGELA: Wasn't nothing to be turned around about. Lots of girls got married at that age. Bethany White got married at fourteen and is still happily married to this day with seven children and four grandchildren already . . . And anyway, Caroline always needed to be *occupied*. And Paul Vine couldn't have been a better husband for Caroline. He hadn't once missed a church service in his whole life, not even when he fell off his bike and broke his arm, you remember? He sat through the whole service with a swole arm. He couldn't have been but ten years old. So reliable. So focused. It's a shame she had to go and ruin his life. I guarantee he would have been the most respected man in the community if she hadn't gone and messed him up like she did.

LEON: What I wondered was why he chose *her*. That was the real mystery of it.

ANGELA: The most important thing is that Zebulon was a gift from God. He was the most beautiful baby. It was a wonderful time for Carrie. She was so happy in those days. She just glowed and glowed—see, here I have a picture of her. See how pretty she was? Zebulon was a real big child for his age—he looks like he's two here, but I would guess he was hardly more than a year. He practically ate us out of house and home. Nothing better than a big strapping child, now, is there?

She looks too young to have already carried a child—even younger than the sixteen or seventeen that she is in the picture. Maybe X already knew how to fold herself into other selves to survive, or maybe there was, as her parents believed, simply something wrong with her from the

(opposite page) Image: X and her son, Zebulon Vine

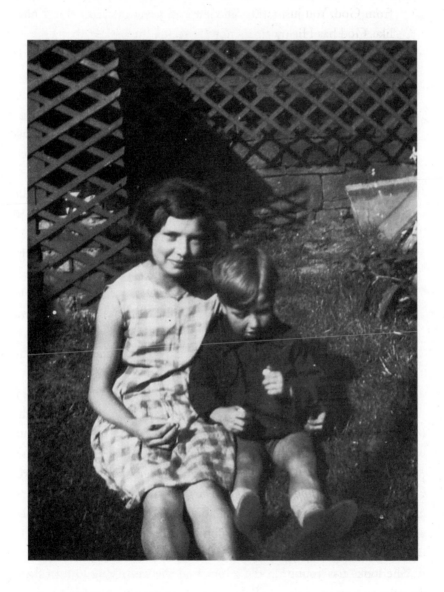

start, something cruel and destructive. She'd had a son and left him. I'd never thought of X as a mother, and she had never mentioned it. I have stared at this image many times now. It seems impossible that I'll ever understand it.

> LEON: At some point she must have just turned on us.
>
> ANGELA: Oh it's not as simple as just that.
>
> LEON: She was a good mother for a time, but I think once she lost sight of what Zebulon needed, once she started focusing on herself too much—
>
> ANGELA: Oh, you would say that. It's not in a person's nature to just be one thing, you know. No one ever faulted you for being more than a father, did they?
>
> LEON: It works different for mothers. I'm not alone in thinking that.
>
> ANGELA: Because that's what men think, men who don't know anything but how to ruin the world—so how about you just stick to the topic at hand, Leon? This lady didn't come all the way down here to get your opinions.
>
> LEON: The problem was, Carrie Lu started going to the library all the time. That's where she met up with the others.

For the next hour the Walkers argued over details about their daughter's involvement in a small insurgency group that had something to do with a library. I knew from the FBI report that X had been involved in a plot to blow up a gun factory (all ST citizens were given state-issued rifles), but I hadn't yet been able to find any documents about the outcome of those plans. Leon believed that Billy Vine—Paul Vine's older brother, who led the group—recruited Caroline because he jealously wanted to ruin his brother's marriage. Angela believed that Carrie Lu was trying to run a covert mission within the group, that she was trying to turn them back to the Lord and simply failed to do so in time to save her own life.

"I may just be a woman, but I'm no fool—let's be clear on that," Angela said. "I loved my daughter while she was my daughter, but when she stopped existing, that was that. I'm a pragmatic person, *a pragmatic woman*, Leon—imagine that! Because I'm not one of these women who thinks her children are always her children, forever. At some point they become other people, and with Carrie Lu that moment came all at once."

Nancy stood suddenly, said our appointment was complete, and thanked the Walkers for their time. As I followed her outside I felt utterly dazed. I was a widow who'd known nothing of my wife's past, while her parents had known nothing of their daughter's future, and we'd sat there in that room for hours, none of us admitting or even knowing who we really were to each other, people who had—in one way or another—loved the same person.

The FST never responded to my requests for additional information about the Revelation Rifle Affair of 1968, but in 2001 I met Jill Charlet, a historian specializing in insurgencies within the Southern Territory who was writing a book on the subject.* Through her own channels she had obtained the handwritten police reports from that night, as well as a series of memos between ST officials coordinating the lie they would tell the surviving families. Charlet had also been able to secure access to a still classified FBI dossier on this and several other incidents. The following is an excerpt from her book, which she has graciously allowed me to print here:

> Around 1:45 a.m. on January 1, 1968, two black vans parked outside the Revelation Rifle factory located at 99 Brine Street in the northeastern corner of Byhalia.
>
> Cathlyn Wilkerson, twenty-five, the factory owner's daughter and mother of four children, and Kathy Boudin, twenty-six, stood guard as two young men unloaded boxes from the back of the van. Those men were Ted Gold, twenty-seven, an employee of Byhalia Automotive, and Billy Vine, a twenty-nine-year-old woodworker and the mastermind of this nascent, unnamed group of dissidents.

---

* Jill Charlet, *The Objectors: Insurgent Activities Within the Former Southern Territory* (New York: Knopf, 2002).

Billy Vine had sent Terry Robbins, a twenty-one-year-old engineering student, and Diana Oughton, twenty-eight, into the factory's basement to begin assembling one of the bombs for that night's plot. After the first van was unloaded, Caroline Walker Vine, a twenty-three-year-old mother of one boy and sister-in-law to Billy, drove the emptied van to the other side of the factory, where she was instructed to keep watch. Should anyone appear, her alibi was that she and her husband got lost trying to find the First Baptist Church and her van had broken down—the imaginary husband had walked back to town to find a mechanic. The lie was supposed to be a momentary distraction before she killed any such witnesses with the pistol hidden beneath her dress.

Around 1:57 a.m., Robbins and Oughton were fastening some doorbell wire from a cheap dime-store alarm clock through a small battery to a blasting cap set in a bundle of dynamite. Near them were boxes of more alarm clocks and batteries, additional wire, perhaps a hundred other sticks of dynamite, a number of already constructed pipe bombs and "antipersonnel" explosives studded with roofing nails, and several more blasting caps. Just before two o'clock, one of the wires from the bomb they were assembling was attached in the wrong place, completing the electrical circuit.

The explosion rocked the entire area, shattered windows up to the sixth floor in the office building across the street, blasted a curtain from the front window onto a railing forty feet away, and punched a two-story hole, twenty feet in diameter, through the wall of the building next door. Within moments two more blasts erupted and the gas mains in the cellar caught fire. The interior of the factory exploded into a cloud of dusty debris, leaving only the back and front walls temporarily intact. Flames then roared up through the opening and leaped out the blasted windows, and an enormous cloud of smoke billowed into the night.

Though the local authorities reported that all seven young people involved in this plot were killed, it is now evident that Kathy Boudin, Ted Gold, and Caroline Vine all disappeared that night and managed to assume new identities in the Northern and Western Territories.

A member of the Southern Border Guard, Derick Patrick, a close friend of Billy Vine's and covert sympathizer, allowed Boudin, Gold, and Caroline Vine to escape through checkpoint H-56 on the northwestern portion of the wall, intentionally firing above the car as they sped past. This information was known to the Southern Territory authorities only after Patrick admitted to the crime in his 1982 suicide note.

When authorities arrived on the scene shortly after the explosion, Mrs. Wilkerson and Billy Vine were found semiconscious, dazed, and nearly dead on the sidewalk in front of the factory, covered with dust and glass cuts. Flames licked up the front wall of the factory, and a part of it collapsed just as Billy Vine and Mrs. Wilkerson were shot.

Inside the demolished factory, two other people lay dead. Terry Robbins's body, recovered late that night, was crushed and mangled under the century-old beams, a victim of what the coroner called "asphyxia from compression." In the basement the torso of Mrs. Oughton was found four days later, without head or hands, riddled with roofing nails, every bone in it broken, and it was not until seven more days that she was identified, through a print taken from the severed tip of a finger found nearby.

The bodies of the rest of the criminals, the authorities reported at the time, were so thoroughly blown apart that there was not even enough of them left for a formal identification or burial. The young people involved in this plot were not idle troublemakers or crazed criminals, but members of a group of dedicated revolutionaries who represented one of the last strains of opposition within the Southern Territory. The Revelation Rifle Affair quickly became an admonitory tale for anyone who spoke up against their government. Thus, starkly, amid ruins and lies, did any remaining insurgency within the Southern Territory come to end for nearly a decade.

The Walkers believed that their daughter had died that night, and it is possible they'll live the rest of their lives without learning the truth, and they most likely wouldn't recognize the impassioned, ruthless version of their daughter that lived on. Carrie Lu was dead to the Walkers then; she is dead to them still. "Revolutions do not follow precedents nor furnish them," she wrote to Ted Gold years later. "I do not want pity. I transfer to others the hate in my humiliated heart."*

Night had fallen by the time Nancy and I left the Walkers' home. The sky was moonless and blasted full of stars, and as I looked at them, exhausted into naïveté, I felt almost fearful of the vastness above me. I'd read about the Southern Territory's infamous night sky, a darkness that Northerners, accustomed to our bright megalopolis, could not comprehend until standing beneath it. Supplying electricity to the many dark acres of the South was a large task that remained, years after the wall had fallen, mostly undone.

As Nancy escorted me into the lobby of the Byhalia Regency, my assigned hotel, I realized I'd hardly said a word to her all day. On the drive she'd explained that the hotel, like all hotels in the Southern Territory, is owned by Northern investors and run by a staff of Southerners who'd undergone a thorough vetting process. After the wall had fallen, the hospitality jobs that sprang up a year later were coveted, but applicants had to prove they had no allegiance to the prior theocracy, a position that most people had difficulty proving after living for decades under a government that required total devotion. As a result, most hotel workers were in their early twenties and had openly resisted the theocracy during their late teens; many had been released from political prisons when the wall came down in 1996.

I'd assumed that the vast majority of those released from the ST's prisons had accepted asylum in the North, and though it's true an exodus occurred in 1996, nearly a third of those who left returned to the South by the end of 1997, a repatriation rate that would later exceed 50 percent. That trend contradicted the North's belief that we had been "welcomed as liberators," and as a result the statistic went underreported, with the exception of Durga Chew-Bose's excellent and extensive article, which was published shortly after my visit to the FST.*

Jeremiah Green, the desk attendant that night at the Byhalia Regency, was an example of such a "prisoner returning to his cell." He spent much of his teens incarcerated—first for petty offenses, like failing to recite certain Bible passages from memory or being late to church, but those punishments only turned him further from the ST. By the time he was sixteen, Jeremiah doubted the divine authority of the state, though he also believed that God was speaking to him—two experiences that he was legally obligated to report to his pastor. Instead, Jeremiah told his best friend, Thomas Haley, and found that Thomas, too, had been hearing the voice of God. (It has been estimated that between 60 and 75 percent of Southerners claim to have heard the voice of God at least once in their lives.) Thomas believed God was telling him to learn carpentry and to marry a certain girl to whom he'd never spoken, while Jeremiah's transmissions were more incendiary—that the Southern Territory government was controlled by the devil, that money had corrupted the church, that every politician and preacher was a heretic.

The day after Jeremiah had confessed this to Thomas, four armed men representing the Guardians of Morality entered his home and pulled Jeremiah from his bed. For years he believed Thomas had reported him, but after his release from prison, Jeremiah discovered it was his own mother who had alerted the GMs. She'd sewn a recording device into the interior of his backpack. Upon learning this in 1996, Jeremiah readily accepted a resettlement package in the North, but after a few months in Chicago he felt unmoored. He'd spent his whole life hating everything the Southern Territory stood for, yet now that he'd escaped it, he longed for the familiarity of home. He even attended a secularized "church" that was a part of the Religious Studies Department at the University of Chicago, but this

* Durga Chew-Bose, "Returning to the Cell," *The Yorker*, May 7, 1999, 19–27.

only alienated him further. Why did anyone bother with church without the threat of damnation?*

After a few months, Jeremiah took a train southward, renounced his refugee status at the border, and showed up on his mother's porch. Since Reunification, she had been jobless and living on the pale zucchinis from her garden and the emergency meal replacements that were occasionally air-dropped in. When Jeremiah realized he was eligible for a job at the new hotel that would soon open in Byhalia, he felt like it had all been a part of a plan, a way to save his mother. For $4.15 an hour, he works twelve-hour shifts six days a week.

He told me all this as I stood there at the front desk. He seemed accustomed to reciting his story to curious Northerners. There were only a few other guests staying at the Regency and was little else for him to do to pass the time.

"I was angry," he said, "and I'm still angry, but you can't really be angry with a place unless you love it. You have to love it to wish it could be better, to wish it could be different. If I didn't love Byhalia, I would have been able to forget about it, to stay in the North, to give up."

As I listened to him, I tried to imagine what X would have thought of Jeremiah—whether she would have said he wanted something impossible, that his return to the ST was an act of self-destruction, of fear, of foolishness—but I struggled to hear her voice that night. It may be true that you have to love a place to be angry with it, to want something better for it—and X, too, must have loved the South for a time, loved it in her own harsh way as she tried to blow up that gun factory. How closely our lives drift past other lives; how narrowly we become ourselves and not some adjacent other, someone both near at hand and much too far away.

Nancy was an hour early to pick me up the next morning; when I looked out the window she was sitting on the hood of the car, drinking a paper

* Jeremiah Green, interview with the author, January 22, 1999, tape 12.1–3, CML audio collection, TXA. All quotes from Jeremiah Green in the following paragraphs are from this interview.

cup of coffee. Looking at her with the winnowing lens of distance, I could see an aloof confidence in her movements, one I'd previously seen almost exclusively in men. Her face was placid and alabaster, as if even her skin, like everything else in the Southern Territory, had been untouched by the passing years. She was wearing pants, a garment newly legal to her, but one she seemed to wear with an old ease. The majority of the women I saw on this trip still wore the long dresses that had been required by the state before 1996; it's often difficult to change the most mundane details of our lives. I watched as Nancy downed the end of her coffee, crumpled the cup, and tossed it like an athlete into a trash can fifteen feet away. It sailed in perfectly, one clean arc.

Two meetings were on the itinerary for my second day in the FST, starting with Bree Morton. All I knew about this woman was that she'd been childhood friends with Carrie Lu and that she'd been given a different name at birth—Mary Magdalene Morton—but had participated in a 1997 program that allowed certain FST citizens to legally rename themselves. Bree was born in 1947, just after a law had passed requiring all Southern Territory children to be given biblical names. The traditional, ordinary names were popular at first, but eventually children were christened as Psalm, Leviticus, and Galilee, and later the names got stranger—Resurrection, Crucifix, TheBlood.

"They said you could come downtown and get yourself a new name, so that is just what I did," Bree explained with easy cheer. "I never felt quite suited for that name, Mary Magdalene, though I know some people had stranger ones than I did."*

Bree Morton was fifty-two when I interviewed her, but her age seemed stunted by her clothing—a long-sleeved pink dress that fell past her knees and thick white stockings despite the warm weather. She'd never married and still lived in her childhood home with her two broth-

* Bree Morton, interview with the author, January 23, 1999, tape 11.6–7, CML audio collection, TXA. All quotes from Bree Morton in the following paragraphs are from this interview.

ers. When Nancy and I arrived the house was silent in a glassy, fragile way. We sat in a room facing a part of the front yard where dozens of wooden crosses were stuck in the ground.

"A few months back, I wanted to move them somewhere less apparent," Bree said as we stared out at the dramatic assemblage, "but my brothers wanted to keep them, so we did. They wanted the house to stay the same after Mother and Father left."

Bree was alert and eager all through our interview, as if I might give her a grade at the end. She'd already retrieved everything she had pertaining to Carrie Lu—a few photographs and several notes the two had passed each other at school. "She'd throw mine in the trash, but I'd pick them out and keep them." They'd been close the summer Bree was ten and Caroline was twelve.

"I thought she was the most glamorous person I'd ever known—I don't know any other way to put it. Funny to think anyone could look at a twelve-year-old and think that, but it's true. I never really understood why she took an interest in me that summer. For the longest time I thought it had to do with the bike accident, that it might have made her a little funny, or made her feel sorry for me."

Bree told the story—and medical records later confirmed—that X had to get six stitches on the top of her head and another twelve on a gash along her arm during the summer of 1957. "Parents report the child fell off a bike," the doctor's notes said, "Injuries sustained unusual for such an accident, but father insists child fell off bike on Stark Street this afternoon." In a letter she wrote to Bree Morton that September, Carrie Lu reported on having her stitches removed:

> Today Momma took me to the doctor & he took off the
> bandages. He held a mirror over my head. The scar is so ugly
> I can hardly bear to look at it. When I first saw it I said, "Oh
> no, is that my flesh?"*

"When I was a kid," Bree said, "I wondered if those stitches in her head had given her some kind of blessing, because she could do the queerest things—like, she would go crouch on the ground somewhere for not two minutes and she'd come back with a handful of four-leaf clovers. And she could write backward just as quick as she could write forward—even in cursive and everything—just as fast as if she were writing it the right way. You had to hold it up to a mirror to read it. She came over once and started playing my piano and she was playing and playing and my mother came in and asked her who she took lessons from and Carrie Lu said she didn't take lessons. So Mother said, 'Don't lie, Carrie Lu,' since lying was sinning, but she said she wasn't lying, that she hadn't taken lessons, she just woke up one day and knew how to play. I couldn't have her over to our house after that. She had no shame—that's what my mother said."

In the middle of the interview, one of Bree's brothers came into the room to say he wanted a sandwich. Bree went to the kitchen to prepare it, and when she returned she resumed her story as if no time had passed.

---

* Caroline Walker to Bree Morton, photograph of undated note, folder 8, item 29, CML research supplement, TXA.

"So Carrie Lu couldn't come over anymore, but I still got to see her at school, but of course I remembered what Mother had said—about Carrie Lu not having shame. I thought, gosh, well, maybe I need to help her get shameful, don't I? There were a lot of stonings then, and I sure didn't want her to be stoned."

I later learned that Bree was referring to a period in early 1957, when the ST deemed it lawful for a stoning to be undertaken by the public as long as twenty men could agree a crime had occurred. In February of that year, the Guardians of Morality had uncovered a plot of domestic terror—two hundred revolutionaries were planning to bomb dozens of government buildings on Easter Sunday, a discovery called the Prevention of the Easter Massacre.* The ST released a list of suspects and gave its citizens blanket permission to stone them to death.

"Papa told me all the time that the devil had his eyes on Carrie Lu, and he said she'd looked back at the devil when he'd looked at her. I thought about that a lot. How did he know it? And how did Carrie Lu know she was being looked at? How could anyone know for sure the devil was looking at you?"

There is a long silence on the tape at this point.

"People had a lot of ideas about Carrie Lu after what she and the others tried to do," Bree continued, "but I never saw the devil in her, no matter how hard I looked, even when—gosh, this was so long ago, but I remember it so clear—even when she told me she'd seen a dead girl, another Mary Magdalene (there were a lot of us), and, well, Carrie Lu wasn't supposed to see her, she said, but she had snuck around and followed her daddy out to the field where they buried people after a stoning. So I asked Carrie Lu if she knew what Mary Magdalene did and she said, 'She was unrepentant, but they didn't say what for.'" Bree paused for a moment. "Unrepentant. I always had a hard time knowing if I'd ever been repentant *enough* when I prayed, so that just about frightened me half to death. But nothing frightened Carrie Lu. Nothing. She was so unafraid, which was, you know, unusual on a girl."

* Michael Spies, "The Uprising That Wasn't," *Mother Jones*, June 21, 1998.

Bree's testimony was broken by the entrance of her second brother, who stood at the room's threshold to ask Bree to pour him a glass of milk. A grown man unable to pour himself a glass of milk, I thought. This is the sort of person an authoritarian theocracy produces. The brother stared at me as Bree left the room.

"You're from up north," he said.

"Yes," I said. On the recording I can hear a tremble in my voice that I cannot recall feeling in the moment.

"And you like it up there? You think it's a good place?"

I was never exactly proud to be from the Northern Territory, had never been optimistic in that way, so I didn't know what to tell him. Just as the policies of the South were believed divine, but instead were cruel, those of the North were often fair in theory but chaotic in practice. Political power still seemed to be a necessarily corrupting force. The North never became the socialist utopia so many had imagined, and instead had been locked in an ideological debate for decades, a snake chewing and regurgitating its tail, endlessly. A crash came from the kitchen and Bree called out—"I'm all right!"

Her brother shrugged. "Stupid idiot picked a name that ain't even a name."

Bree seemed scattered when she returned from the kitchen, but when I asked if we needed to cut the interview short she insisted she was fine and began to enthusiastically recount Carrie Lu's wedding.

"I was so glad for her. I thought, Well, now that should settle her down, shouldn't it? I knew her life would be much easier, so much happier, if she just calmed down. And Paul Vine was a real nice boy. Everyone thought so. As a wedding present, I made an apron for Carrie Lu in sewing class, and it took me a whole two weeks to do it. I'd never made such a nice apron."

Bree didn't see Caroline or Paul much after the wedding aside from exchanging glances at the grocery store or smiles across the sanctuary during church. Their age gap widened when Caroline became a wife, and they had little to do with each other anymore, Bree explained. Then her expression collapsed inward. She began to cry and cover her face.

"Never could forgive myself after the rifle factory," she said.

She sobbed for a long time before I asked her *why* couldn't she forgive herself for something she'd had no part in.

"I could have witnessed better to her. I knew she needed to submit herself to the will of God. She wasn't submitting herself—I could tell she wasn't. And isn't letting the same as doing? Even all this time later I still think it is. She was fighting every minute, like she'd confused the Lord for the devil. I hoped a lot for her, but hoping ain't doing, either. Her death is on my heart forever—I know it is. Even my pastor agrees. It's the reason I can't marry, can't have children—"

"But she lived," I said, a reflex.

"She died," Bree said, shaking her head. "She got blown up."

"That's just what they told you."

Nancy looked at me sternly, clearing her throat.

"Is she still alive?" Bree asked.

I had not become accustomed enough to X being gone to speak of it naturally, and I can hear my hesitance on the tape before I said, "No—I'm sorry, no. I misspoke."

Nancy told Bree it was time we left, and she began to cry again and say incomprehensible things, perhaps prayers, in a low voice. I told her not to worry. She cried more. I told her I didn't think she did anything wrong, and for a moment that seemed to calm her, or maybe she was just shocked. It seems no one had ever said such a thing to Bree Morton.

Just before leaving, I saw her brothers standing in the backyard beside a fenced pen full of dogs—Rottweilers, it seemed. The brothers were throwing dead cats or rodents into the cage, laughing as the animals scrambled and sparred for the meat. One of the brothers noticed me watching and held a hand up as a wave or a warning.

Once we were in the car again, Nancy explained she'd once gone to the same church as the Mortons. They'd been a very close family, but Nancy had heard from friends that Bree and her brothers had been trying to *avoid* Reunification, something common in this part of the FST. But the Mortons, Nancy assured me, weren't *representative of the whole territory.*

According to Nancy (or whatever script she'd memorized in her travel mentorship training), the suicides had cleared out the most extreme. A kind of halo of suicides had followed, people who felt left out, I guess. Then there were the people like Bree and her brothers.

They don't know how to change, Nancy said, with an unusual nervousness. *They don't want to. It's human, of course, to want to keep things familiar. Don't you think it's human?*

I agreed with her.

And what you told Bree at the end . . . You know, you really can't go around telling people that. Whatever you might know or think you know, it doesn't help anything now. It can only upset people.

I apologized, but Nancy brushed it away. Now I can see how foolish it was to trust her as much as I did, to assume that she wasn't reporting back to the FST about my behavior. I asked what she knew about the Revelation Rifle Affair.

I don't know anything about it, she said.

We drove awhile in silence after that. Then she pulled over beside a disheveled wooden shed and told me it was time for lunch, that we were going to have something called catfish.

As we approached the shed, I realized it was newly built but had been designed to appear old and broken-down. The interior was decorated with nets full of plastic fish and vintage fishing rods. Feather lures dangled from the ceiling. The chalkboard menus were supposed to look as if someone had jotted down the offerings that morning, but they'd been carefully painted. I told Nancy it looked like a movie set, and she told me I must have an eye for such things because that's exactly what it was. Some Hollywood people, she said, had filmed there last winter, just after the border opened up. Apparently, they needed a restaurant scene and none of the ones they could find were exactly right, so they built this one and left it to the people who owned the land.

Every table was full, but I heard as many Northern accents as Southern ones. I overheard conversations about land development and legislation. Was this just the place where the agency sent all the out-of-towners? Nancy admitted that it was, that there were only so many places they were allowed to take us.

The catfish was fine—I think. I didn't know what it was supposed to be like.

As we were leaving, a woman called out to us—*The Lord be with you! And also with you,* Nancy repeated.

Now you say your part, the woman said, cheerful and expectant. *Say it.* I stood there confused.

Say your part, she repeated, smiling.

And also with you, I said, unsure of what, exactly, I was wishing upon her or what was being wished upon me.

The afternoon's meeting was with a man named Gregory Charleston. The only notes beside his name on the itinerary read: *Formerly incarcerated. Recordings subject to bureau approval.* It turned out that Gregory spoke slowly enough to allow me to record nearly his every word in writing.

Gregory was living in a repurposed motel—housing for recently released prisoners that was meant to be temporary but had become semi-permanent for the 150 men who lived there.

"I knew what I was doing was wrong," he said as he idly looked around at the battered office furniture he'd salvaged from a nearby junkyard—file cabinets, desk chairs, and a large drafting table.* A calendar hung in the corner displaying the wrong month, the wrong year. A state-issued cot was turned on its side in the corner. He slept on his back on the floor—prison habit.

"But do you still think it was wrong," I asked, "now that everything's changed?"

"I was right about what I thought, but I was wrong about what I could do about it," he said, a line he'd clearly been repeating to himself for years, rehearsing what he'd tell all the journalists who came to ask him about what led to his thirty-six-year imprisonment and recent release.

Several journalists had already interviewed Gregory by the time we met. The profile by Mike Spies had been the first major exposure his story

---

* Gregory Charleston, interview with the author, January 23, 1999, tape 12.1–5, CML audio collection, TXA. All quotes from Gregory Charleston in the following paragraphs are from this interview.

had up north, and the halo effect of his influence was the subject of Avery Trufelman's oral history of the ST's major rebellions.* The filmmaker Alex Prager, one of the first Northerners allowed into the FST on the Unified Works Project, had made a startling, nearly silent documentary entirely focused on Gregory.†

Accustomed to attention, he spoke in a steady monologue for the first hour of my visit, needing no questions from me. He told me about his involvement in the banned-books trade, how he hid thousands of illegal titles about world history, philosophy, and nonreligious fiction by fashioning fake covers for them, then filing them in special parts of the Byhalia Public Library. Slowly and selectively, Gregory chose a handful of young readers he felt could understand the contraband ideas in those books. Over a decade, he assembled a cohort of young rebels, some of whom eventually took actions that led to Gregory's discovery and arrest in 1960. His original sentence stipulated ten years of nearly solitary confinement, followed by ten years of religious rehabilitation in a medium-security prison, but his release date kept getting pushed back for months, then years, without explanation. He committed himself to exercise and meditation regimens. He wrote hundreds of poems and essays without pen or paper—memorizing them and reciting them to himself daily.

When I met him, Gregory was sixty-seven years old. The wall had been built when he was fourteen; he was a part of the generation that could remember life before the Great Disunion, a group of men who were imprisoned in such high numbers that the Southern Territory's birthrate dramatically dropped in the mid-1950s. Notably, this trend led to the establishment of birth-houses, hospitals where hundreds of teenage girls were kept to be impregnated by older men, most of them officials and pastors in the government. X's childhood journals mention these birth-houses and describe girls who'd been sent there, older sisters who had just returned. These revelations change how we might interpret much of her performance and film work from the late 1970s—such as her controver-

* Avery Trufelman, "The Charleston Project," Northern Public Radio Audio Library, 1998.
† Alex Prager, dir., *The Lonely Librarian*, Unified Works Project film, 1999.

sial installation *The Pain Room*. Gregory's project, to make sure that the younger generations in the ST did not come to understand such heinous rituals as commonplace, was as valiant as it was doomed.

In the years since Gregory had been released from prison by Northern forces, he began collecting and organizing propaganda posters and paraphernalia of the world he had known before he was detained. His archive, likely the most extensive and comprehensive in existence, has become an invaluable research tool for scholars of the Disunited Era. Since 2002, the Charleston Archive has been housed at the Library of Congress in Douglas-Washington, DC.

Every object in Gregory's collection was its own lesson in the ST's national mythology and means of control. One poster depicted a pantheon of Southern governors as loving fathers, angelic beings. The cover of the Guardians of Morality handbook had a striking illustration of a church as a courtroom—Christ as judge, those same governors as the jury. Gregory calmly gave context for each object, as if he were a boy and this were simply his stamp collection, not the detritus of his captors. I asked several questions I didn't need to know about before I managed to ask about X, about the first time he met Caroline Walker.

"Carrie Lu," he said, his voice now smaller and more somber, as if delivering a eulogy. He then proceeded:

It was July of 1958. She was thirteen, so she wasn't in school anymore. Her mother sent her to the library to do some research about how they could get their tomato plants to yield better . . . At first I wasn't sure about Caroline. She had this intensity, and I couldn't tell if it was the intensity of faith or anger—they look the same sometimes. She asked for a certain title—she wanted to read *Why Plants Grow* by Bernice Shannon. Of course, there is no such book; it was a sort of code, the title and cover I used to hide *The Collected Essays and Speeches of Emma Goldman*. For Carrie Lu to have known about that title, one of the older kids would have had to tell her about it, so I asked her why she wanted to read *Why Plants Grow*, and she said Paul Vine had told her about it.

Paul was one of the first boys I'd started giving certain books to. An enormously bright child, he was one of the few who never got arrested, though he eventually gave up on resisting, not that it matters now.

But—that Goldman collection had all the classics, as I remember—that famous first speech she gave as governor, her best philosophical essays, her writings on the Marriage Equality Act . . . It even had some of those early speeches when she was still an anarchist—of course, Goldman frustrated everyone, eventually. She seemed like a radical to conservatives, but the rest of us knew she'd had to make many compromises to get as far as she did. I still admired her greatly. Nothing could change that, I don't think. My father took me to see her give a speech in Chicago when I was eleven. We took the train up—it was the only trip I ever took outside the South before the wall. It was the early forties, that period when Goldman was getting old but was still quite active. There was this feeling then, with the war and everything, that fascism might come to America. Goldman herself feared that the South would secede, and unfortunately she could see the future quite clearly. She said as much in the speech that night in Chicago, and my father started to cry. Afterward she came down into the audience and shook the hands of all the children. When it was my turn I told her I was from Byhalia, Mississippi, and she became very solemn. I suppose not many Southerners were traveling north to attend her talks—and there she was, one of the greatest American orators and politicians of the twentieth century, a woman who always had something to say. She just stared at me, so quiet, then asked if I would promise to serve the working class and the poor in my state, and I said I would. It was a very sudden and solemn moment in the middle of this festivity. There were balloons everywhere. And cotton candy. For some reason I remember the cotton candy.

When she was assassinated and the wall went up—well, I was still quite young, only fourteen, but I immediately felt old. Men were celebrating in the streets, really glad she was dead, and I couldn't believe it, I still can't. Something had ended. I didn't know how to . . .

Well—what was I saying? Ah, the Goldman essays, the first book Carrie Lu first asked for. You see, it was a very important book to me. My father had a copy of it before they came and took all the unapproved books away. We hid it with some others in our chicken coop.

Gregory fell quiet. He and Nancy shared a quick glance, perhaps feeling too close and too far away from each other at the same time, as they had each survived the same despotic rule but lived very different lives within it. Soon he returned to the subject of Caroline—

"She came to me in tears because she read that Goldman had been shot the same day that she'd been born—April 9, 1945. She said, 'Mr. Charleston, I feel so happy and so sad at the same time.' She even had Goldman's mugshot, which she'd clipped out of a newspaper and kept in a locket."

This explained the locket I'd found in an old cigar box among other seemingly random objects—a thimble, a skull bead, a single playing card.

"So Caroline was immediately a part of the fold, as it was," Gregory continued. "Maybe there were six or seven of them who knew about the so-called *illegal* collection. I was starting to get a few new books through the underground channels, and I thought the ST might really change if enough people knew what it really was, though I can't help but wonder . . . Well—if I'd been more strict with how we handled things, maybe I could have avoided the raid."

After Gregory told me the story of his arrest and his farce of a trial, his face went slack for a long moment, that brief corpse face that comes when living is too difficult.

"I was right about what I thought, but I was wrong about what I could do about it," he said for the fourth or fifth time that day. "I've had a very long time to think about this. And perhaps it's wrong to say, but I'm not one of these people who thinks its valiant to die for your beliefs. Maybe I thought so at first, but when I heard about Revelation Rifle, I knew it was my fault. They had all been my students . . . and it made me wonder if the truth isn't always what people need. It can be just as dangerous as lies— no, much more dangerous than lies. Maybe it would have been better if I'd found a way to live in the territory without needing to rebel—then none of those children would have died. I can forgive myself for a lot of things, but not for that . . . never for that. It was the only thing that made me feel I deserved to be locked up forever."

I forced myself not to speak—not to tell him that a few had survived. I didn't know how or if he'd ever find out about them.

We stared at the stained motel carpet for a while, and he didn't look at me when he asked, "That's what you're writing about, ain't it? The accident at the factory?"

I told him, no, I wasn't writing about the accident.

"Then she got out, didn't she?"

"Who?"

"Caroline," he said.

I smiled out of nerves, then pretended to be confused as I asked him an innocuous question about some other book in his illegal library.

Soon Nancy told us our time was up, that we had to be going now, and he looked at me again—"She's still alive, isn't she?"

"No," I said. I wasn't lying. "She isn't." I thanked him for his time and left.

Nancy didn't speak as she drove me to the hotel. The sky had taken on a kind of tornado gloom, but no tornadoes came. It rained all through the night, and I slept as if I were some other person on some other planet, not a widow, not myself. I dreamt X was driving a truck through fields of fire and I was sitting beside her. "I think about you every single day," I said, but she didn't hear me. I woke up in the middle of the night feeling so certain—with near insanity, really—that the world would have ended by now if she and I had never met. It was a mad clarity, the kind that passes overhead like a brief cloud on a bright day, a short repose before the truth returns—of course the world would have gone on, and so easily. I don't have dreams like that anymore.

When I met Paul Vine I did not believe myself to be nervous. I felt sure that X, that Carrie Lu, had been forced to marry him, that it was not something as special as a marriage of young love or blind enthusiasm, but even if it had been, the stain of old love would have faded long ago. He was living an hour's drive from Byhalia in the Greenwood Men's Facility. I didn't understand what this facility really was. A prison? No. Nancy said it wasn't a prison. A hospital, an asylum?

It's a facility for men who can't handle their liquor, she explained.

A hospital, then.

Not really. It's run by the state. It's not mandatory that he live there, but at the same time it sort of is mandatory. It's hard to explain. You'll see. Or you won't.

The Greenwood Men's Facility was a large gray building behind an iron gate. After a half hour with security we were allowed in, but when Nancy and I found Paul Vine in the garden watching the chickens roam around him, it seemed he'd forgotten we were coming.

"Are you Paul Vine?" Nancy asked.

"Most of the time," he said.*

* Paul Vine, interview with the author, January 24, 1999, tape 11.14–16, CML audio collection, TXA. All quotes from Paul Vine in the following paragraphs are from this interview.

I introduced myself.

He said, "You've come to get the real story, the real story from the real jackwagon himself, is that it?"

I immediately resented his charm, his Labrador ease, but there was also something alien and nervy about him. More than anyone else I spoke to, he seemed the least touched by the Reunification, and his clothing—a linen shirt that had been worn and patched many times at the elbows and twill pants held up by suspenders—stood out as if it were a costume. I asked if he would speak with me about Caroline Walker.

"Might as well," he said with a grim smile. "I'd like to set some records straight."

We conducted the interview in a small greenhouse, and as I was setting up the recorder, Mr. Vine—I had resolved to refer to him formally—ripped some sprigs from a mint plant and began chewing on the leaves.

Image: Paul Vine, approximately 1990

"Gotta get your kicks somewhere in this place," he said. "I used to chew tobacco, but they don't allow it. You only get one cigarette after meals, but you have to eat the whole meal first, and that plainly don't suit me. I don't prefer to live like that."

He chewed his mint and offered me some. I declined.

"Habits," he said.

"When did you first meet Caroline?"

"Oh, we were kids. Church. A girl like that—you don't meet her, not really . . . There hadn't been a moment of my life I didn't love Caroline. Even after all the trouble she caused—and how does that make sense? Lot of fellas think all women are dangerous, but I don't agree. It's not the women themselves, it's the compulsion that gets between certain people—it's the compulsion that's dangerous. Women themselves, they're not dangerous. Not a minute of their lives are they dangerous, not really. But the compulsions that sometimes take hold of two people—that's what you have to look out for. That's what makes it trouble."

He stopped for a long moment, spit out his mint, and then leaned over my recorder and spoke loudly into it.

"Love is breakable, it can go away. But compulsions! They don't go nowhere. Once you get one, that's it. It's you and your compulsion till death do you part. And you see, once she was gone, the compulsion had to go somewhere. That's the nature of the compulsion, you see? I hadn't had a drop of liquor in my whole life until that night. A month later there wasn't a moonshiner in the county I didn't know. I tried to take care of Zeb, and of course I love that boy with everything I got, but the compulsion! It was easy for me to hate my brother for getting Carrie Lu mixed up in that trouble, but I still had that compulsion about her, you see, and it had to go somewhere. I loved her is what I'm saying, and I can't help it. I can't help it any better than I could shoot it. So there you go. That's what I've got to say."

It was immediately apparent that Mr. Vine was nothing like anyone else I'd met in the Southern Territory—reserved, passionless people who were exactly the sort X pitied and had no interest in knowing. The un-usual demeanor of this man, her first husband, the father of her child, gave me pause. I had only been prepared to speak to a source, some innocuous person in whom X held no real interest or love. But, despite myself, I recognized something in Mr. Vine—an agitation, an erratic pulse, a certain power—some quality that had never failed to magnetize my wife to a person.

"Could you tell me about the beginning?" I asked.

"The beginning?" Mr. Vine said, then jumped onto his bench and began to quote from Genesis in a mock-dramatic tone, throwing his arms around. "In the beginning God created the heaven and the earth. And the earth was without form! And void! And darkness was upon the face of the deep!" He kept on for quite some time until he stopped, abruptly. "You think I'm crazy, don't you? You're looking at me like I'm crazy."

"I don't think you're crazy," I said.

"Well, how can you be so sure, huh?"

Mr. Vine sat back down, smiled to himself, and began to tell the story.

"Well, the first thing you have to know is how dark a night could be. No one had electricity back then—we only got candles for Christmas, and there were laws about fires or lanterns, so for most of the winter the whole town was in bed by seven, eight. Even now that some people have electricity, at least part of the time, hardly anybody keeps their lights on after dark. You get into a habit, you know, you get into your ways." He paused, then smiled. "But the dark has advantages of its own. Especially if you are a teenager dating somebody you can't be seen with."

He was fifteen and Carrie Lu was fourteen when they started to meet covertly in the cover of night.

"Her house was set off from the street by a white wall, just above eye level," Mr. Vine recalled, "and I found a spot behind that wall where nobody would notice me as the sun went down. I'd wait hours for her, maybe two or three. It didn't matter. When she came outside she'd peer into the darkness, not seeing me at first, but she knew I was there. At first we walked in silence, and we kept an arm's distance from each other until we were sure we wouldn't be spotted, and once we were a ways out of the neighborhood, out in the fields, we could hold hands and talk. It was a full year of that—not even one kiss. Just holding hands and talking."

They walked through the night, scattering pine needles in their wake. This is not the sort of thing that shows up in satellite photographs. When we analyze the Southern Territory from afar, we don't stop to think that in the middle of this black hole—in this bleak, dark country where millions were imprisoned, tortured, killed—there were also children walking in the dark, hand in hand, intensely in love. They spoke of their families, their classmates, the church, Bible passages, the books they'd read in Gregory Charleston's library, and whether it was okay to read those books, and whether the feelings they had for each other were godly or ungodly.

"Because it was either one or the other," Mr. Vine said. "All good or all evil. We were so sure of that—I don't know how or why. Why couldn't it have been a little good, a little bad? Most things, you come to realize later, are some of both, but at that age, I didn't see it that way. But when it comes to Carrie Lu . . . I could keep telling you pointless things, or I could just go ahead and tell you the long and short of it."

Mr. Vine crossed one leg over the other, leaned toward my tape recorder, and said, "We were in love a while, then she tried to kill me."

There is a short pause on the tape, after which I hear myself saying, as if imitating someone else, "I see."

"Tied me to the bed and stabbed me in the leg so she could go get herself demolished with my brother and those fools. A lot of good it did anyone."

He crossed his arms and leaned back, studying my face—I thought—for evidence that he'd impressed me as I averted my eyes and waited for him to continue.

"It was a normal night . . . We'd put Zeb down and gotten into bed and gone to sleep—the whole lot of it, a regular night—but then I woke up and saw her getting dressed, and all she said was I better not to try to stop her. And I said, 'Stop you from doing what?' And she said it would make sense later, so I started to get up, but she went and clocked me upside the head with an elbow. It was a real shock—there was never any violence in our house on either side—and by the time I had my wits about me, she'd tied up both my hands and one leg to the bedposts, and I'll be damned if I couldn't get loose! And as I was kicking my one free leg, and trying to stay quiet so I don't wake up Zebulon, out of nowhere

Carrie Lu stuffed a shirt in my mouth, stabbed me in my free leg, and tied up that last ankle. Then she was just *gone*. We had a little house behind her parents' house, a shed we'd fixed up so nice, and she loved that little house, took such good care of it—then just like that she was just gone and I'm there bleeding, can't nobody hear me, and I'm thinking the devil himself is carrying my wife off and it'll be hours before anyone finds me, by which point it'll be too late. She wasn't even twenty-three years old yet and hadn't ever been nothing but lovely to me, and then she was just . . . whatever she was."

In the diaries I later obtained, Caroline's hesitance about her husband is more evident than it was to him. "I marry Paul with full consciousness + fear of my will toward self-destructiveness," she wrote on the morning of her wedding. "It seems the Lord intends for me to marry him, but perhaps he also intends for me to implode."* The page before this entry, she had copied out a passage from Marguerite Yourcenar's *A History of Certain Women*, one of the books that Gregory Charleston had covertly included in his library—disguised as a copy of St. Augustine's *Confessions*:

I smiling wife do promise these things. Newly identified, do I smother my childhood and my father's name, as my mother smothered her own? Is my cordial smile artificial? The light mock light? . . . Cordelia refused to be falsely cordial to her father. Whose smile? Is the smile Society's Giant pleasure at its Vesuvian power to force me into Custom's lair, or sunshine to warm my cordial acquiescence? There are no cords in cordiality.†

Mr. Vine had made the common mistake of seeing an absence of conflict as the presence of devotion. In a later notebook, not even two years after they'd married, X observed, "In marriage, every desire becomes a decision." And later, it's worse—"Whoever invented marriage was an ingenious tormentor. It is an institution committed to the dulling of feel-

* X, undated journal entry, box 1960, items 3–8, TXA.

† Marguerite Yourcenar, *A History of Certain Women* (New York: Pantheon, 1943), 115.

ings. The whole point of marriage is repetition. The best it aims for is the creation of strong, mutual dependencies."*

While she was cleaning his house and raising his child and cooking his meals, she felt acutely aware that the banner she labored under, the banner of family, was waved and held and belonged only to him. She'd had more control of her life when she'd been a child—when she had been the one who told him when to come to her, where to stand, how long to wait. They decided together where to walk, and what they spoke about, and how long they stayed out. When they married, her body and time became his. But it is unsurprising that Mr. Vine was shocked by his wife's departure—he'd never contended with her presence deeply enough to imagine that her presence might be contingent upon anything.

"I sometimes wondered if it wasn't . . . Well, I wonder if the real problem, the reason she got wrapped up in Billy's extremism, was just a problem of us not having more children," he said. "Because once she had Zebulon, she . . . Well, isn't it natural that having a child changes a person? And maybe she was the sort of woman who needed to be changed a few times over to be satisfied with life. I couldn't understand why God didn't give us more children. I still can't understand it, though I don't waste my time blaming God about it now, not anymore."

Gregory Charleston had mentioned that all his acolytes read a book on reproductive health since birth control of any kind was forbidden, so it was likely X knew how to avoid another pregnancy. I was only unsure of how she'd allowed herself to ever become pregnant in the first place— whether it was an error of passion, a miscalculation of days, or a choice. I was unable to locate any diary entries or anything else she wrote on this issue. Her papers rarely mention the existence of her son.

"Are you married?" Mr. Vine suddenly asked.

"Yes," I said, immediately realizing it was no longer true.

"Do you ever get the feeling when you look at your husband that you don't know him at all? Not one little bit?"

I sensed Nancy listening with him for my answer. I'd been advised by

---

* X, journal entry, September 29, 1963, box 19, item 2, TXA.

a number of journalists that the very concept of homosexuality baffles and horrifies most Southerners, so I didn't correct him on the word "husband." I shook my head and said I wasn't sure I understood.

"I was a little better with it in my second marriage," Mr. Vine went on, "after I realized that just being married to someone, even having a child together, doesn't mean as much as it seems. There's no special power in marriage. I was just at the periphery, living with clues, trying to collect more clues . . . But maybe I don't know anything about marriage, since of course my second wife left me on account of the drinking and the church here won't give you a third chance. And, you know—I don't think they should. Maybe I was never the marrying kind, and there was never any hope for me. I forget too much, forget what's been said to me or what I've said."

At this he took out his wallet and handed me a scrap of paper that he'd kept for many years, the farewell note from Carrie Lu the night she vanished.

"I've been carrying this around all this time and I still don't know what she's talking about. I don't know what she said to me 'that night,' and I don't know what she means by the 'distant call' and I don't know why she thought being married would 'silence' anything. Silence what? All I can come up with is that there would be these occasional moments, say, when she had some serious look on her face, staring out a window or stirring something at the stove—this expression she'd make only when she didn't think anyone was looking—and I didn't know that woman. I may have known some of the other ones she'd be in a day, but I didn't know that one. And why would I? I was frightened of that one . . . But I never thought she'd *leave*. Nobody ever left anybody—it was as good as impossible. It does me no good to think about . . . *Still*, I keep going over and over it, thinking that maybe if I'd been some other kind of husband to her, she would have never been at the factory that night."

Mr. Vine sat in silence for a long time after that and I knew that he, too, had been ruined by losing her. But it was not a comfort to sit with someone whose pain mirrored mine. I don't know what it was. He shook his head—

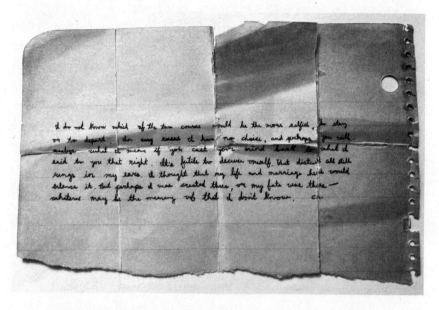

I do not know which of the two courses would be the more selfish, to stay or to depart. In any event I have no choice, and perhaps you will realize what I mean if you cast your mind back to what I said to you that night. It's futile to deceive oneself. That distant call still rings in my ears. I thought that my life and marriage here would silence it. But perhaps I was created there, or my fate was there—whatever may be the meaning of that I don't know. C.M.

"What I said earlier—well, I say it all the time, but it's not really true—she didn't try to kill me. She did stab me, though. Real quick one in the leg, not too deep. I know she wouldn't have gone through the trouble of really doing me in."

(One night shortly after I'd first met X, she told me that when she thought back to people in her life who had abandoned her, it seemed to her they were dead, and when she thought of the people she had abandoned, she sometimes felt she had killed them. I told her this seemed to indicate that she rated her own company rather highly—that to be denied her presence was death itself. She laughed. Maybe so, she said. We were so newly in love, spending one of those endless days in bed, delirious over ourselves. But who would ever abandon you? I asked. Impossible! I had just left my husband to be with X, and my father had left my mother when I was a child, so I thought I knew a thing or two about abandonment. Of course I didn't. Not really. Not then. Let's not speak of such things, she said, and this became our agreement. New lovers are always digging their graves and lying down, smiling, scooping the dirt in with their clean hands. We rarely spoke about those who had abandoned us or those we had abandoned. They were all dead to us now.)

"They say the women here were happier before they got set free," Mr. Vine said. "Did you ever hear that? Read about it?"

He was referring to a recent study on the mental health of Southern Territory women post-theocracy conducted by several sociologists and psychologists.* Though the women here were now free to behave however they pleased—to pursue work, to travel, to terminate a pregnancy, to deny their husbands sex without retribution—a majority of them reported feeling stultified and discontent, burdened by choice.

Even stranger, the fall of the Southern Territory correlated with a massive increase in diagnosed cases, almost exclusively among women, of migraines, vertigo, digestive disorders, tremors, skin allergies, insomnia, and other ailments. (This trend was evident before any changes were made to the FST's prohibitively expensive and ineffective health-care system—

---

* Sara Richardson et al., "A Comprehensive Study of Psychological Abnormalities Among Southern Women After 1996," *The Journal of Socio-Political Health* 38, no. 439 (December 1998): 112–39.

that is, an increase in medical attention after private health insurance had been abolished was not the instigating factor in the trend.) For instance, in one county in Alabama in the autumn of 1996, more than two dozen women and one man were suddenly struck with atonic seizures—characterized by a sudden loss of muscle tone, causing a person's body to collapse to the ground, paralyzed, for anywhere from fifteen seconds to three minutes. In Tupelo, Mississippi, not far from Byhalia, seventy-two women were diagnosed with severe cases of res-ignation syndrome, a rare psychological disorder in which a person re-fuses to eat, speak, or even move. Housewives were simply retreating to bed and staying there until they were carried out to the hospital or the morgue.*

Such stress-induced disorders in the FST mirrored similar discoveries about women freed from communist regimes in Europe around the same time, though for nearly opposite reasons. Equality of the sexes, theo-retically, was an integral part of post–World War II communism in the Eastern bloc. Women there were educated alongside men and comprised an important part of the workforce. There were state-mandated maternal leave policies and free child care, and though this did not create a society void of discrimination, their lives were stable, predictable. While women in the Southern Territory were subordinate to men in every way, what they lacked in equality was made up for by the fervency of their faith and the religious structures around them. Just as it was in the Eastern bloc, the opportunity costs for giving birth in the South were low, but motherhood was also a woman's sole opportunity. Of course both the ST and the Eastern bloc rigidly controlled the media—there was no access to information about life beyond their circumstances. Both behind the iron curtain and within the ST's walls, the burden of possibility was wholly un-known. It was not equality that bred women's contentment, but limits—as an ignorant happiness can thrive in the most dreadful conditions.

Knowing all this, I listened to Mr. Vine go on about how the ST was a better place for women than anyone realized, how his wife (my wife)

---

* Rachel Aviv, *Resignation Syndrome in the Former Southern Territory* (New York: Routledge, 2001), 87.

had simply mistaken the simplicity of her life as a form of oppression. This is one of the darker, less contested realities of authoritarian
governments—that the human animal is a meek thing, easily manipulated. No one wants to admit that they, too, might live quite happily in
a simulation, in a simulacrum of life. No one wants to believe that they
are, at heart, more interested in comfort than in truth.

"It was Gregory Charleston's fault, you know," he said, facing away
from me. "Are you going to talk to him?"

I knew to avoid an answer, but Mr. Vine didn't wait for it.

"They shouldn't have let him out. There's blood on his hands."

I thanked him for his time and said I had to be going, then thanked
him again, though on the tape I sound more professional than I felt. Just
before I left, he asked me why I'd chosen her, Carrie Lu, of all the people
I could have studied. The tape recorder was no longer running, and I cannot remember exactly how I explained myself, only that I was lying and
hoping not to be caught in my lie, and when he asked if I'd ever known
her, personally, I felt my skin prickle and chill. I insisted, flustered, that
I hadn't known her, as it was impossible—I'd been a child in the North
when she died in the South. This lie came out more easily than I would
have expected.

Oh, she died here, did she? he asked.

Nancy's eyes were on me. I shook my head.

Of course, Mr. Vine said. Then, with a smile—more sinister, less
charming—he leaned too close to me and said it was a shame I never
met Carrie Lu because she had this real special way about her. It wasn't
that she was particularly beautiful, though she was all right, and it
wasn't that she pretended to be happy all the time the way other women
were, but it was this other thing. *It was like a black hole or something, a
gravity feeling,* he said. *You're supposed to get clear on certain matters as you
get old, but I never did feel clear about anything with her. I don't understand.
I just don't understand it.*

How close I felt to him, close against my will. Despite every trouble
she caused me, and despite all the falsehoods I was left to untangle, and
despite the rage I sometimes feel these days toward her, I wanted then
and still want now to be singular in X's life. Was that all this was? An

attempt to prove myself to be irreplaceable, the victor, the most crucial and true love in her life? I didn't know that trying to prove this fantasy would so certainly undo it.

As Nancy and I exited through the metal detectors and patdowns at the Greenwood Men's Facility, one of the armed guards smiled and said, "God bless," and I felt his sincerity, despite his weapons. It was a reminder of the enormous paradoxes in a religious worldview that holds as much dazed and romantic hope as it does fatalism—the possibility of heaven for some, and the certainty of hell for others. One of the most difficult and least explored aspects of Reunification, it seems to me, is within the Northern imagination. How can we see through the men who pulled levers within a sinister hyper-capitalist theocratic government and into the vivid humanity of those who had—through their all-encompassing trust in the power of God, the church, and authority—neutered their own needs and desires at the feet of the divine? It's not that the people of the ST who were oppressed for their gender, poverty, or race were duped—as so many in the North seem intent on believing—but rather that their ability to love a concept as large and appealing as God was used against them again and again.

According to extensive research conducted by the journalist Imara Jones, the vast majority of Black Southerners (after some uprisings in the 1950s) came to tacitly accept that the intensely racist structure of their society, the tailwind of slavery, was simply "God's plan."* All the while, as governors and preachers bloated themselves on power and wealth, the intense faith shared by individual citizens often created networks of unfathomable charity and harmony just beyond the reach of authority.

In the first decade of the ST's formation, new legislation swung between extremes. After it was abolished in 1945, the death penalty was restored, and public execution by hanging or lapidation had become

* Imara Jones, "Every Day I Pray for What I Have," *The Atlantic Coast*, July 19, 2000.

commonplace by the late 1950s. The expansive homeless shelters set up in buildings over which the ST had initially declared eminent domain—newspaper printing facilities, theaters, dance halls, and so on—functioned smoothly for nearly a decade, as did the public cafeterias that fed both unhoused and low-income families. Small vegetable farms, orchards, and textile factories sprang up, creating self-sustaining economies where there had previously been dire poverty. By the later 1950s, however, the state enforced strict control over the shelter system, using anti-miscegenation laws to re-segregate these communities. By 1960, the shelters functioned more like concentration camps for groups of people deemed unfit for proper society.

Many other liberal policies—initially justified on certain religious grounds and later terminated on different religious grounds—rose and fell in the early years of the ST. Perhaps the most notable was the 1949 Referendum on Reparations, which passed by a narrow margin after years of debate. The bill mandated that weekly checks be sent to all adult citizens of the ST who could prove they had a relative who had been previously enslaved. What constituted proof varied from county to county, but by the mid-1950s, at the program's peak, at least 82 percent of the Black population in the ST had been enrolled. By 1961, however, when a few Black Southerners began to reach a standard of living that rivaled that of their white counterparts, the payments ceased without explanation.

In more rural parts of the South—isolated pockets that escaped the ST's campaigns of propaganda and public stonings—grassroots organizations blended the values of the New Testament with anarchistic ideas. These self-sufficient, radically generous communities built their own roads and waterways, shared resources equally, and naturally began to flourish.* As with the shelter systems, their success led ultimately to their demise: the central government came in to dismantle any community aid programs deemed to be in contradiction to the ST's Protestant work

* The most well-developed of these anarcho-Christian communities could be found in Panola County, Yazoo City, and Clarksdale, Mississippi, as well as Valdosta, Georgia, and Lookout Mountain, Tennessee.

ethic. A radically benevolent society struggled to be born, but the idealists were ever beaten back by the dictators.

On the drive away from Greenwood, I began to see the imprint that this place had left on my wife and I could almost hear, again, that dark tone her laughter took when the rumors of her Southern birth came up. X had always held me to extreme standards of love and devotion; she believed two true lovers should be able to read each other's minds, that my every third thought should be of my wife, that I should need the company of no one else, and if at any moment I seemed to stray from this vision of what our love was or should be, a childish look would fall over her face, that of a scorned girl, smarting in what she saw as my neglect. A violent history and a romantic belief in a divine, all-encompassing love sit closely together in the place she was raised. And she—a woman born the same year as the wall, perpetually discomfited, restless, at war with herself—she could have been from nowhere else.

But what good is this after-death clarity? Must this be the way that people see one another—can we get a clear image only once we're too far away to touch?

The empty afternoon on my penultimate day in the ST had been filled, Nancy told me; the office had unexpectedly heard back from Zebulon Vine, Carrie Lu's son.

X had kept so many secrets about herself that the secret of her child, I wanted to believe, was merely one of them. Nothing significant. Childbirth is ordinary, a basic biological event. It needn't define my wife, nor any other woman. Yet I had to admit that the fact of her son unsettled me. This child, this man, a whole other human who'd begun inside her body; when I thought of him I felt grief in reverse. I was forty-one years old, yet I had never felt more strangely naïve.

Though X seemed to hold an intricate and freely espoused opinion about everything, I couldn't remember having ever spoken to her about having children, and though there was one night early in our relationship that I told her that I was not interested in parenthood, she'd only replied, *It's a question of existence or nonexistence, which means it's not a question.* I didn't really know what she meant by that, and I didn't ask her to explain, afraid she would be frustrated with me for not immediately gathering her meaning. The matter was settled.

Between the interview with Mr. Vine and this last-minute meeting with Zebulon, Nancy dropped me off for an hour's rest at the hotel, and it was then that I began to feel quite ill. I felt sure that this young man would see through me, that he would recognize me as a thief, an impostor, a part of the world that had taken his mother away. I scolded myself for such magical thinking, swerving from fear to shame to fear as I tried to talk myself into believing that I knew what I was doing.

When Nancy and I arrived at the Walkers' house that afternoon, where the interview was scheduled to occur, Angela answered the door dressed in a bright green dress, her hair sprayed up into a gray cloud. She wore tawny lipstick, a new luxury, I knew, a product only recently available in the FST. She offered us coffee and a basket of warm cornbread.

I always make it when Zebby comes for a visit.

You spoil that boy, Leon said.

How nice to have company again. Isn't it nice?

We waited for a nearly an hour for Zebulon to arrive. Leon and Angela picked at each other like old cats. She called him senile; he said he knew she wanted to poison him, that the thought must have crossed her mind.

What an interesting idea, she said, her gaze settling on the floor. *What a very clever idea.*

Mercifully, the doorbell rang.

Zebulon was thirty-seven and had eyes just like hers—goddamn it— and the same nose. But he had another sort of mouth, jaw, hands—Mr. Vine's, maybe, though I'd already forgotten his face. The son wore plain blue slacks and a gray shirt with a stain on it, and he ate three pieces of cornbread in quick succession as I asked a series of pointless, timid questions, to which he gave blunt replies.*

---

* Zebulon Vine, interview with the author, January 24, 1999, tape 11.20–23, CML audio collection, TXA. All quotes from Zebulon Vine in the following paragraphs are from this interview.

"I don't remember."

"It's just been a long time."

"It's hard for me to remember."

Then, as if he were growing tired of being himself, he suddenly slipped into a different voice, formal and jaunty, as he said, "I simply don't recall," and winked at me.

For a moment I saw one of X's faces emerge in his, startling me. Zebulon looked over my head as he spoke and held long pauses in the middle of his sentences, just as she had. Though he still hadn't said anything of any use, I was overwhelmed again and excused myself to the bathroom to try to relax. When I returned, Mrs. Walker asked me if everything was all right—"I hear Northerners have sensitive stomachs," she said, piercing. "I wonder why that is."

As I was unable to push the interview in any meaningful direction, Mrs. Walker sometimes interrupted to brag about Zebulon's days as a high school quarterback, about his volunteering, about his skills as a carpenter—a profession that seemed to simultaneously please and displease her. "All my other grandsons ended up in more intellectual fields—two lawyers, one pastor, and two doctors—so it is so nice to have someone in the family who is handy, isn't it?"

Eventually, Leon burst through her monologue. "The topic is Carrie Lu, not Zeb!" he shouted. "This lady isn't here to know anything about Zebulon."

"Don't be so rude," Angela said.

"I'll tell you one thing about Carrie Lu," Leon said. "The fact is . . . she just wasn't one of us. She wasn't really a Walker—"

"What on earth has gotten into you?" Angela shouted, appalled. "Of course she was a Walker! She was our daughter, and she belonged here as much as any of us. You'll have to strike that from the record, dear . . . Leon is clearly going batty in his old age. It's *really* so tragic."

We all sat quietly for a moment. Then I asked Leon what he meant, but Angela berated me before he could reply—

"I don't know what you're insinuating, Miss Reporter, but I do believe you owe me an apology. I just can't imagine coming down here, being invited into our home for the second time, and then being so ugly to us."

"It's been such a long time, and Carrie Lu's gone now," Leon said to his wife. "I don't know why you can't just come out and admit it."

Angela shouted at him, but Leon picked up the recorder and spoke directly into it—

"You get old, you stop caring about some things—they don't have sway over you like they did once. It just don't bother me about her. I don't have to answer to what she did. I don't have to explain it. She had nothing to do with me. Her wickedness was *her* wickedness."

Angela ripped the recorder from his hands, held it tightly for a moment, and at last handed it to me. The stop button had been pressed in the scuffle. Nancy brightly chimed in that we best be going, and as Zebulon signed one of her papers, I looked once more at him before I left, not saying goodbye to anyone, and went out to wait beside the car.

That night in the hotel, the phone rang. I expected it to be Nancy confirming the time she'd take me to the airport the next morning, but it was Jeremiah from the front desk asking me if I was expecting any visitors. I told him I was not, and, sounding like a child trying on a formality many sizes too large, he said two gentlemen were there to see me. I heard some muffled speech in the background, and after the sound faded Jeremiah told me the men had left. They had asked for me by name? He said they had, then apologized in confusion.

A few minutes later the phone rang again—it was Nancy asking if I was okay and not waiting for a reply before she told me not to go to the lobby until she called for me tomorrow morning. I was not to see any visitors and not to take any calls for the remainder of my trip, and anyone who might try to contact me outside the proper FST channels was breaking the law.

I told her I understood. I recalled that a journalist had been badly beaten in a hotel parking lot in South Carolina last year. He hadn't died, which meant the incident went largely unreported, but the battered man lingered long evenings at Café Loup with his crutches and eye patch, telling and retelling the story as a warning. His assailants fled before they could be identified, but they were suspected to be part of a group of re-secessionists called the American Freedom Kampaign, a domestic terror group that was gaining significant power in the FST at the time.

Just to be on the safe side, Nancy told me, I should probably stay away from my windows and keep the lights in my room off. I said I would. We said good night. I did not sleep.

When Nancy drove me to the airport in Memphis the next morning, I didn't know I'd never return to the Southern Territory. I was already planning to request another travel visa to interview X's many siblings, other friends, former in-laws—but each application I placed for a subsequent visa was denied. My attempts to contact Nancy through the Travel Mentor Agency were unsuccessful, and every letter I wrote to the Walkers or to Bree Morton was returned to me, marked as undeliverable. In January of 2002 I flew to Memphis without a visa, as certain travel restrictions had been lifted, but after a two-hour interrogation by the Reunification Police Alliance, I was sent back to New York. It was for my own good, they said; my name was Code Red on the Do Not Admit list, though it would be another year before I learned why.

Bree Morton's brothers were both involved in the AFK. Cain Morton had been elected chairman in 1999, and Joseph Morton was chief judicial officer. Around the same time I'd visited the FST, the journalist Rachel Kaadzi Ghansah had undertaken a groundbreaking investigation of the AFK.* In a telephone interview with Cain Morton, he explained his group's plans to reclaim the Southern Territory and reestablish their independence.

"Hitler and Gandhi are the decisive models for me," Cain said. "I am a normal man. I am nice. I am friendly. I am a totally normal man with two feet on the ground and in spite of that, I am considered both a hero and an enemy of my government. I am forty-nine and I am sitting

* Rachel Kaadzi Ghansah, "A Year Inside the AFK," *The New York Times*, June 23, 2000, A1.

here talking to *The New York Times*. Of course, I am an extremist. I am a dictator. But this is no democracy. This is an authoritarian society. In time, it will come to me."

In the course of her investigation, Ghansah covertly attended the annual Revelation Rifle Bar-be-cue, a public celebration of the deaths of the seven men and women believed to have died there during the botched 1968 terrorist attack. The ritual of throwing seven scarecrows into a bonfire had been suspended that year, 2000, as the AFK had just discovered declassified documents stating that Ted Gold, Kathy Boudin, and Carrie Lu Vine had escaped the ST that night. Four scarecrows were burned instead, and Cain Morton gave a speech vowing to bring justice to the other three.

Ghansah also found that the Mortons' sister, Bree, had gone missing in late 1999. Though Cain and Joseph had filed a police report, they'd written her name as Mary Magdalene Morton; according to Ghansah's sources, the recency of her name change sent Bree's case into a kind of bureaucratic eddy. No formal investigation of her disappearance was ever undertaken, but several anonymous sources confirmed that Bree had been stoned to death by a mob of men, led by her brothers, for allowing a Northern journalist into their home. I was, it seems, that journalist.

"Everyone in town knows the truth," a source told Ghansah, "only nobody wants to hear themselves say it. Nobody needs to know . . . Reckon we all belong to the Church of Nobody Needs to Know."

Bree Morton's body was assumed to have been fed to the dogs.

Of my many missteps—nearly every step taken seems to have been mistaken—none was quite as costly as my avoidance of a clue X had planted for me, years before her death.

Behind our cabin, affixed to a fence post at the gate to the garden, there was a metal box embedded in the wood. X had installed it there during our first summer away from the city. The front of the box was engraved with the phrase IN THE EVENT OF—the preposition stranded without a complement—and X never told me what the box was for, nor did I bother to ask, as I felt, innately, that it would rouse one of those withering, disappointed stares that came when I asked a question to which she felt I should know the answer.

As I was regaining basic capabilities in the months after X's death, I thought of the metal box several times, aware that we had now reached and passed the "event" in question, yet I could do nothing more than regard it from a distance, never stepping too close to it, all the while knowing that a sturdier, more reasonable person would have immediately wrenched it from its place and opened it, as it clearly instructed me to do.

A few weeks after my visit to the FST, feeling reckless but lacking anything to wreck, I took a crowbar from the garage and dislodged the box from its wooden post. It came out more easily than I expected, but I found the box had no lid or latch or lock—no obvious way to get it open. It was a gloomy, overcast afternoon punctuated by erratic wind gusts as I stood over the box, bludgeoning it, until one of the welded edges burst and I was able to pull out a tightly wound scroll. When I unrolled it I found X's neat handwriting filling the long and borderless page, and though my eyes had adjusted over the years to read her meticulous long-hand, here it was so small I could decipher it only under a magnifying glass. The document, clouded with legalese and clauses crowded with clauses, laboriously decreed that the only people who would be allowed unfettered access to X's archive and permission to use it in any way they pleased, were the founding members of BASEL/ART, that is, the Black Americans for Southern Equality and Liberation through Art, Resistance, and Terror.

This was not entirely surprising to me. X had frequently cited the group as the only thing that made her hopeful about the future of art in the Northern Territory, an opinion she'd made explicit in her most controversial and bridge-burning essay, "The Remarkable Laziness of the Northern Territory Artist," a screed often cited as evidence of her genius as a critic or her cruelty as a person:

> Few notions are more mentally toxic and aesthetically boring than
> the idea that "art" is the result of an artist's "self-expression," yet I

am galled to discover that the exploration of these supposed selves
is the primary activity of so much contemporary *stuff* being currently produced by individuals in the Northern Territory whom
we permit to call themselves *artists*. Have we no pride, no decency,
no original thoughts? Have we no hope as a society, as a nation,
as a group of *Homo* fucking *sapiens*? Ah, but perhaps I am being
too harsh. Am I being too harsh? Indeed, self-expression could
be the worthy pursuit of anyone in possession of a self worth expressing. As it stands, the self-expressers seem to be expressing a
carbon-copied army of beings allegedly calling themselves *people*.*

X then went on to name names, to make an example of thirty-nine
of her peers and their most celebrated works, which she deemed "full
of unredeemable pettiness, violent anti-intellectualism, and fatuous no-
tions of insight." Her primary thesis was that "art is an expression of
the society from which it emerges, not the artist in themselves," and
her primary complaint was that the relative comfort and political apa-
thy of the Northern Territory had produced at least three generations of
"money-driven fluff machines . . . that insult the very notion of art as a
matter of existential survival."

After calling out the artists she defined as the worst offenders, X spent
many long paragraphs praising the work of the artists she classified as
"legitimate," most of whom were not American, including an unnamed
movement of radical feminist sculptors who came out of Iran in the mid-
1980s, two midcentury French Vietnamese performance cooperatives,
and several painters from Italy, Japan, and China. (Being creator, critic,
and crank naturally made X's own artwork a target for sharp criticism
after this manifesto was published. However, with a few drastic exceptions, criticism of her visual art did not seem to penetrate X.)

The only American artists who received her unequivocal praise were
Adrian Piper, Nancy Spero, and several members of BASEL/ART. Piper,
it should be noted, published a sort of rebuttal to X's essay, stating that

---

* X, "The Remarkable Laziness of the Northern Territory Artist," *Harper's Magazine*, March 18,
1987, 21–26.

though she did not disagree that the majority of Northern artists were lazy and attention seeking, X had succumbed to "the myth that the critic may impersonally efface herself and her subjectivity in order more accurately to deliver objectively valid pronouncements about the criticized object."* In her private diaries X admitted that Piper had been right, but in letters she complained that Piper's essay had missed her point completely.

At the center of the writers and artists who founded BASEL/ART was Arthur Jafa, one of the very few Northerners who openly identified as a Southern Territory refugee, having been granted asylum in the late 1960s on a complex set of legal technicalities. Though he was pursued by the AFK for decades during which he refused to cease appearing in public for lectures, presentations, and performances, Jafa was both a genius of disguise and an intrepid escapologist whose methods and feats may not be understood in his lifetime. X had always spoken of Jafa in such admiring tones that I once surrendered my pride to ask if she'd been in love with him. *Oh no*, she said, *he's quite out of my league*, a notion I never heard her use regarding anyone else.

Of all of his work, the most well-known was his 1980 installation, *Love Is The Message, The Message Is Death*, in which Jafa went undercover into the Southern Territory, and covertly replaced every Bible in ten Mississippi Delta churches with decoy Bibles in which the statement "Love Is The Message, The Message Is Death" was printed at intervals into the text.† Upon discovery, each of these churches burned the errant Bibles in a public ceremony, events that Jafa, still embedded and disguised, photographed: religious extremists burning what appears to be their own text.

When the documentation of this performance was exhibited at Quarry (which was also X's gallery), it was one of the rare moments that a work of art became the topic of national media attention. BASEL/ART, the somewhat marginal group that had financially aided the work,

* Adrian Piper, "Toward a Politically Self-Aware Art Criticism," *The Newer York Times*, March 30, 1987, C22.

† Arthur Jafa, *Love Is The Message, The Message Is Death*, art installation, Mississippi Delta, 1980.

suddenly received a huge influx of attention and support. Within two years the group was multinational; it has since been credited with exerting a significant effect—through various outreach programs and attention-commanding public artworks—on global politics through the 1980s and '90s, without which many historians agree that the Southern Territory's wall could have easily stood solid well into the twenty-first century. (Again, it should be noted, I am far from an expert in the complexities of the legacy of BASEL/ART, and none of this should be seen as comprehensive. Those looking for further reading on this subject would do well to begin with the 1998 anthology *Black Futures*, edited by two of the group's cofounders, Jenna Wortham and Kimberly Drew, which provides both a detailed history of the organization and dozens of essays and contributions from other members suggesting possible futures for the Northern and Southern territories in light of Reunification.)*

At the bottom of X's densely worded scroll, there was a signature of a witness, Chioke Nassor, and a phone number to call regarding "how to entrust the archive to BASEL/ART, and other pertinent details." I immediately called and, upon hearing Mr. Nassor's voice—sonorous and low and casual, with moments of lilting brightness—I felt sure he must have been more than a mere witness or an administrative contact, that he had the sort of voice that X would have been drawn into. When I told him who I was, he immediately knew why I was calling. He spoke with such ease and intimacy about my late wife that I found myself trying to prove that, of the two of us, I had been the one to know her better, and in this state of threatened competition I told him—my tone embarrassingly overeager—that I had just returned from the Former Southern Territory, where, "you might be alarmed to learn, X was in fact *born*."

"Byhalia was it?" he asked. "Caroline Luanna Walker—ha! What a name! She went through hell, didn't she?"

For a moment I silently tallied all the months I'd spent in search of the information that this man, this stranger, had just revealed so plainly,

---

* Kimberly Drew and Jenna Wortham, eds., *Black Futures* (New York: Lennard-Knopf, 1998).

realizing that some man in Brooklyn had been casually keeping X's secret all along. I stammered for a moment, and Mr. Nassor explained that X—who was using the name Deena Stray when he met her—had lived or had seemed to live in his building in Fort Greene. One Halloween in the 1970s they'd somehow come to take large doses of psilocybin and listen to Pink Floyd's *Dark Side of the Moon*, during which she had confessed her whole life story and swore him to secrecy. But why, I asked him, hadn't he felt compelled to correct the mistake in Mr. Smith's biography?

"Someone like that isn't quite worth the trouble, are they?"

I wanted to agree, but given that I was still caked in the dust I'd kicked up while going through all that trouble, I could not.

"She told me about you once," he said, "when she was still chasing you around, trying to get you to leave your husband . . . She came by with some beers past midnight and climbed in my window on the second floor—I never knew *how* she did that—and anyway, she woke me up, said we had to talk, said she'd been changed by someone, that she'd never really been changed by someone before."

It seemed to be all I had ever wanted to know—how I might have changed her, what effect I'd had upon her. She had always seemed to me too powerful a mind and heart to ever fully breach, least of all by someone as fearful and flimsy as myself. I asked him if he could remember what effect I'd had on her, but he was vague.

"But I'll never forget that night," he said. "She was saying something about how wrong it was that you were across the river, sleeping in a bed with someone who could never understand you. She kept saying it was an 'icy way of life,' that you were trapped, that she knew you were living with answers to questions you hadn't yet thought to ask yourself yet—"

"How would she have known any of that for sure?" I asked, interrupting his dreamy remembrance of her, a woman he never truly had to endure, to suffer beside, a woman who'd simply crawled into his bedroom window from time to time, and I felt so horribly far from that young woman who'd believed in everything that X had convinced me to believe—destined love, doomed love, real love at all.

"Oh, she knew things. Who knows how she knew them, but she did . . . She asked me this question that night—she said, Is it possible that the best thing to happen in your life could also be the worst? Something like that."

"No," I said. "She didn't say that. I said that. That was what *I* thought."

Mr. Nassor, who must have realized by then the depth of my derangement, apologized and changed the subject back to the details of the archive.

I'd become someone, I know now, who also wasn't quite worth the trouble.

TED GOLD

———

It was easier to find Ted Gold than I'd anticipated. A few weeks after his involvement in the Revelation Rifle Affair and his escape from the ST with the others, Ted had taken the above-board route as a political refugee; he turned himself over to the FBI in Chicago, seeking asylum in the North in exchange for any intelligence he could offer on the Southern Territory. Ted was granted citizenship after several months of questioning in a secret prison, where he vowed allegiance to his new country to gain protection from his former one. Against everyone's advice, Ted insisted on keeping his name—it was the only thing that was his, he explained—though the FBI gave him a new alibi for his past, and by August 1969, he was regarded as one of the bureau's foremost experts on the Southern Territory.

It was only when I met him, in the autumn of 2002, six years after the wall had fallen, that Ted Gold began talk to anyone (aside from the government) about his life in the South. He'd been retired for several years, but when the AFK put a bounty on his head in 2000, the FBI provided him with a security detail. After a series of background checks and a rigorous physical inspection, I was permitted into his Chicago apartment for an interview. I found Ted sitting at his kitchen table with several manila folders laid out before him. As I introduced myself, he told me he already knew who I was, that he had been following

X's career since before she was X. He'd even been keeping a file on me since 1989.*

"Habit," he said, holding it up and shrugging. "She took all the awful things in life and transformed them, didn't she?"

But I only wanted to know about the part of her past for which I had no records or documents.

Ted eagerly recounted the days after the Revelation Rifle Affair, when he, Carrie Lu, and Kathy Boudin had stayed in Kentucky at a safe house. Billy Vine had arranged for this through an underground channel connecting the rebels in the Southern Territory to sympathizers in the West and North, and though Billy's letters had indicated seven defectors, no one seemed surprised when only three showed up—a natural cost of this work. For a week they slept under blankets on a wooden floor, no one daring to put away the four empty pillows beside them.

---

* Ted Gold, interview with the author, October 21, 2002, tape 65.1–7, CML audio collection, TXA. All quotes from Ted Gold in the following paragraphs are from this interview.

Image: Ted Gold

"I remember feeling," Ted explained, "that I needed to be some kind of compass for the other two, Kathy and Carrie Lu. I know it's silly, but I thought I had a certain responsibility as the only man in the group—but I wasn't a leader like Billy was, and I couldn't come to any firm place about what we should do next, whether we give up and disband or change course or go back to keep fighting . . . For days we talked a little about it. One minute we were all sure we had to continue working to liberate the South, and the next we'd feel the opposite. Some days I wonder how we ever figured it out, how any of us ever got out of Kentucky."

Just before this interview, after hiring a locksmith to break into a safe X had kept in our basement, I'd found a collection of manuscript pages

Image: Kathy Boudin and X

titled "Everything I Can Remember About Everyone I Knew,"* which seems to be an incomplete and fictionalized memoir. In it, X wrote:

> The memory of poor T in the woods, weeping like a child. Didn't he know that some of us might get killed? How quickly he became useless, pliant, erratic. I've never felt more like someone's mother. When I told K about T in the woods, she said, "Well, it's over, you know, men don't protect you anymore." I said, "Not that they were ever so good at it," and she laughed. It's a wonder he ever made it out of that place.

Ted had a few photographs of X that he'd taken when she and Kathy had both made their minds up that they were going to shed their past lives for new ones—new names, new histories, new haircuts and costumes, new gestures, new voices.

"They were both at work for a month solid," he remembered, "almost like girls playing dress-up or something, but of course it was something else . . . You know, I can't say I ever understood a woman in my life. I was taught that girls were something else entirely, that they were something more earthy, more natural than men—I can't seem to unlearn it, even if I know it's not exactly true. And that month that Kathy and Carrie Lu were making up new lives for themselves . . . Well, I tried a couple times, but I couldn't do it—I couldn't get away from being who I was. But they did just fine, tried out personalities like trying on clothes. And I thought, Well, they're going to survive and I'm not. That's why I went to the FBI so quickly—I had no hope."

Ted showed me a variety of artifacts from his personal files—the map of the route they drove from Mississippi to Kentucky, the plan that Billy Vine had written up for the bombing, and the grainy xeroxes of newspaper clippings about the explosion, including his own obituary, which had run in *The Byhalia Daily*.

"'Mr. Gold, Lord save his soul, was killed in an explosion of his own

---

* X, "Everything I Can Remember About Everyone I Knew," undated manuscript, folder 39b, item 1, TXA.

devising at the Revelation Rifle Factory early on New Year's Day,'" he said, reciting it with a smile.

But when I asked Ted about other memories of my wife, he didn't recall anything about her that I didn't already know. When I asked him if he ever saw X after leaving Kentucky, his expression scattered.

"I can't say," he said. Ted was in his sixties, but his face—especially his eyes—still held the dizziness of childhood.

"You can't say?"

"I can't explain, and I can't explain why I can't explain."

Not yet an hour into our interview, it was beginning to seem a waste to have come all the way to Chicago to talk to him. There was something grating about him, and I felt I could no longer abide his company. As I stood to leave, he silently took an accordion file from a side table and handed it to me.

"She was so determined to leave it all behind," he said, "but she also didn't have the nerve to really throw it away."

Just before X left Kentucky, she'd given Ted the one notebook she'd brought with her from the Southern Territory. Leaving it in the South would have been dangerous, but she didn't want to carry it as she traveled into the West.

"She was hoping, I think, that someone in the future would want to know why she'd believed what she believed, why she'd done what she'd done," he told me.

It's a common hope of the young—for later acclaim to redeem the insignificance of earlier years—though most twenty-three-year-olds haven't just carried out an act of terrorism against a despotic government. I opened the file to find a tattered notebook, a supposedly precious primary source, but I was unmoved. I had been conducting this research for years and was now annoyed by how many journals and letters I kept finding squirreled away, almost as if X had laid this scavenger hunt as a kind of revenge for anyone who undertook it.

"Oh, and before you go, there's actually one more thing," Ted said as he darted to another room.

It was then I realized I hated Ted Gold in the same irrational way that I hated the people who would approach X with an apology and a supplication—how intensely they loved some painting or song she'd made, or a book she'd written or a performance or a photograph, whatever, but I knew they were simply fawning over her fame. If a person respected her work as much as those strangers claimed to, they would not have the nerve to come over and intervene in her life with their trivialities, diverting her attention upon themselves. As the years passed, I even feared that all this vacuous admiration might warp X, that her ego might saturate like gauze filling with blood, at which point she might abandon me for one of those young admirers, leave me just as abruptly as I had left my husband—a balanced retribution, a fate foretold. I knew it was foolish, but I felt it all the same, lost sleep to it, threw fits over it.

There was, however, one occasion when this scene inverted. X and I had gone to see a late showing of *The 39 Steps*, then for a midnight dinner somewhere in the Village, a low-lit bistro that felt like a diner, a place where real life happened—a couple forever making out in one corner and someone sobbing in another. A woman slightly younger than I slid up to our table, apologized to X, and turned to me and asked if I was C. M. Lucca. Regretfully, as the main reason I'd used initials in my byline was to be more invisible, I confessed that I was. The young woman told me that an article I'd published some years prior—a long feature about a series of unsolved homicides that I connected back to a cult leader—had changed her life. (Though that article was and still is the strongest piece of reporting I ever did, the passing years transformed my prior pride into embarrassment, as I feared the piece had been a fluke and I was not a real journalist and thus I had not earned any of the laurels that work had laid upon me.) The woman who had interrupted our dinner said she was also a journalist, but she'd felt painfully directionless in the years after school and feared she might tread water for decades, comply with whatever her editors wanted from her, and die without having ever followed a story on her own initiative. Immediately after she'd read the article I'd written, she quit her job at a luxury magazine, went freelance, poured all her time and savings into investigating a child abuse scandal at an orphanage, wrote and published a piece that instigated a federal investigation and several arrests, and just that night she'd found out she won a Northern Magazine Award. She was out celebrating. *And it all started*, she told me, *with what you did—you changed my whole life, and I'm so sorry to interrupt, but I had to thank you for it.* I do not remember what I said; I just remember the hot feeling in my face, and the realization that I had been wrong about the nature of such an interaction. As that woman stood above me, she was not suppliant so much as she was powerful; her adoration had a way of leading my blood around in my body like an obedient dog, and I even found myself thinking she was radiantly beautiful, that she had such a powerful beauty she must have lacked the aggrieved heart that beats in the chest of any decent writer—yet of course it should be obvious why I found her so stunning. She had not thrown herself at my feet with these compliments, but rather picked me up by the neck, put me in her control, and after she left us, X smiled in conspiracy, stirring her soup. So now I knew.

When Ted Gold came back sheepishly holding a second shoebox—this one with some letters she'd sent him over the years—I still wasn't sure why he reminded me so much of those fans, but as I read over everything that night in the hotel, I understood. Knowing what he knew about X and withholding it from me in this way had given him a certain power.

Prior to reading the journal and letters from Ted, I'd always assumed that X's artworks and subsequent fame had been incidental, a side effect of her life. "I entered the art field by accident," she once explained to a reporter, "when a coincidence of geographical, personal, and legal matters resulted in indefinite vacations which, through a mixture of boredom, curiosity, and vanity, led to my present profession."*

Even if I had been slightly skeptical of the accidental nature of her career as an artist, now I could no longer hold on to that vision of who she had been, as these papers from Gold demonstrated that she had, from the start, staunchly believed her vision and resolve and intelligence to be powerfully superior, destined for respect. Many of the letters she sent Ted in the 1970s are addressed to her "*biographer*," though she'd told me many times that she was intensely opposed to her biography being written. But this younger version of my wife was not just seeking fame, but renown—her goal was to be revered by people who'd not yet been born.

"Carrie Lu gave me one piece of advice the last time I heard from

* X, interview with Francis Alÿs, *Art-20*, PBS, October 14, 1988.

her," Ted told me as I was leaving. "She said, 'Beware of anything that you hear yourself saying too often.' I still think of it, sometimes more than once a day. I suppose it's become one of the things I hear myself often saying . . . I've got that sort of problem, I suppose. Repeating myself, getting stuck. Chicago, for instance. I thought I'd live somewhere else since I'm free now, free to go anywhere, but I can't seem to leave. I travel, sure, for the State Department, but even with all the security, I never feel safe out there. I only feel safe here."

The year after I met Ted, the American Freedom Kampaign finally met their promise to assassinate him, the sole survivor of the Revelation Rifle Affair. While Ted was changing planes at Schiphol in March of 2003, a young woman disguised as a flight attendant threw a vial of the nerve agent known as VX into Ted's eyes, then smothered his face with a handkerchief laced with the same poison. Ted convulsed on the ground as she fled, the scene so unusual that no one could tell, at first, what had happened. Security footage shows the woman immediately blending into a crowd of flight attendants, the assassin anonymized as if in a school of fish. Twelve minutes later, Ted Gold was dead, killed in the most gruesome manner for having been so audacious, long ago, to have believed in a better world.

Much of the diary X had kept in her last year in the Southern Territory was written in a cipher, the key to which had been copied out on a notecard she added after her escape. "Husband is charming, cheerful," she wrote. "He knows how to leave well enough alone. That's what I must learn from him. How to leave well enough alone." A few days later she wrote out a memorized passage from one of Emma Goldman's essays so that she wouldn't forget it, but a day or two later she crossed it all out. Then she rewrote it the following week, again followed by the advice of her husband: "Paul says we must not speak of such things anymore. He can put the past behind him—how vacant his face becomes at church. Must learn to use masks the way he does, the only way to survive time." But the entries become grim and foreboding as she continues: "It may be, if the time comes, that all this will be gone: house, child, husband, church. Or will I fall asleep in this grave?"*

As teenagers, both X and Paul had read through much of the secret library, but after those books were confiscated, it seems they did not speak of them for years. In one of the last entries before she left, X asked Paul if he ever thought about Gregory Charleston—did he think it was right of the ST to put him in prison and, if so, did that mean that they, too, should be put away? Paul did not respond, so she asked if he thought the ST government was corrupt, or if he ever thought of life on the other side of the wall—then he grabbed her, covered her mouth, and told her never to say such things, that he didn't want to hear it.

"Paul says we have to choose our battles, by which he means to choose no battles," she wrote after the incident, later adding, "Isn't this the fate of women? Even in the Bible, even there—we are asked to be alone, to go faithfully into solitude, to ease into misunderstanding, to inhabit it, to make it warm and beautiful."

Though she is careful never to explicitly mention, not even in the code, her involvement in the planning of the bombing, her mind melts toward escape:

> *What if I could be taken to wherever Gregory Charleston went? Would it be worse than here or better or the same? Cannot stand another day in this kitchen . . . Billy says there are times in a life when all the stories break down, and how we chose to react then says everything about who we are.*

As the date for the attack at Revelation Rifle comes closer, her entries stiffen and become fragmentary, and it seems her disquiet became apparent to others:

> *Mother said I seem nervous lately. Am I praying enough? Yes, plenty. Praying for you, mother, even you. Oh how nice—bless you, she said.*

---

* X, diary entries, September–November 1968, box 3, items 18 and 19, Ted Gold archive, TXA. The quotes from X in the paragraphs that follow are also from these diary entries.

But I know praying is where the trouble begins, not ends . . . Argument
with Paul. He asks: Who are you being right now? He didn't care for
my tone of voice, or the way I moved, or what I said to him. Didn't
recognize it. Let him not recognize it. Little good it will do him to try
to recognize me, to wonder who I am. Little good.

The last entry before her escape is the briefest—"Life's metaphors
becoming increasingly unsubtle. Oh, enough with it. Enough with the
metaphors"—though she doesn't say what those unsubtle metaphors
were. The diary goes unused for a month; then some notes are jotted
sideways across the last pages—phone numbers, addresses, and lists of
which I could never make any sense, a mix of memories, tasks, anxieties.

It seems she did not write anything in Kentucky, except for a hectic,
page-long letter to Kathy and Ted on the night she fled the safe house
without warning. The letter is an onslaught of apology, of self-pity, of
an inward-facing debasement common to those swept up in revolution
or religion. Knowing X would have hated my quoting it here, I won't
include it.

A few weeks after she left, X sent letters back to the safe house for
Kathy and Ted. She wrote of the personas she created while hitchhiking—Marley, Angel, Joan, Luella—each with her own backstory, man-
nerisms, accents. Most of the time she did farm work in trade for a place
to sleep, but occasionally she found ways (she doesn't say how) to earn a
little money. She asks how the garden is faring or whether Kathy is still
there or if their neighbor's lost dog has been found—but each letter came
without a return address. Months later, when she called the house in
Kentucky, she got Ted Gold's new address in Chicago.

For a time, her letters to Ted took an explicit turn—not toward him
but about herself. "I want it more than both ways—I want it all ways. I
only want a dick because boys look at me more than girls do and it seems
a shame to go around empty-handed."* She writes of lovers, but never
love. She writes of fucking so frankly, it seems she'd shrugged off her up-
bringing in the ST like an old coat. If these letters are to be trusted, she

---

* X to Ted Gold, May 2, 1969, box 4, item 6, Ted Gold archive, TXA.

seems to have spent an incredible amount of time pursuing sex, having sex, planning new pursuits of sex. In one twenty-four-hour period she had a trio of threesomes with five different people. Why? A compulsion, a fit, a need to outweigh all the dying with warm bodies, maybe. Living in the shadow of her friends' deaths, she catapulted herself from bed to bed.

"A waitress told me I looked 18 so I have just been telling people I'm 18, a five-year lie. It's useful for getting around," she wrote on a postcard. "You have to seem young to get away with this kind of vulnerability, standing on a road's shoulder, showing the pale underside of your arm. You must seem totally harmless, but still liable to knife somebody."

X was using the name Angel Thornbird at the time; Angel told anyone who asked that she was fleeing an abusive family in Kentucky. She wore a red wig and worked mostly as a motel maid, though for at least a month she found a more lucrative job as a clerk at the Elkhorn Ranch. From there she sent more frequent letters, sitting at that desk all day with little else to do. In the longest letter—fourteen pages of stationery fatly folded into an envelope—X writes with a diaristic privacy.

She describes and re-describes the day her father beat her with a tree branch for asking why they had to go to church so often. She obsesses over Paul, wondering what he might be doing now, whether he remarried, whether he was secretly happy that she left: "I knew I was really too much for him, all along, far too much for him—though too much of what, I still do not know." Again and again she writes out every detail she can remember about the night she left her husband: "I want to find a way to describe his face, that last face I saw him make—it was his real face, the only time I saw it." But she is never satisfied with her descriptions of Paul. "I never knew him," she concludes. "I married someone I never managed to know." In the margin, she immediately berates herself for her fixation on him, upset that she's still carrying that marital poison, still obsessed by what the church told her was her worth. She does not write a word of Zebulon.

The letters to Ted Gold also contained—on the backs of Elkhorn Ranch envelopes—drafts of the songs that she would, years later, record with David Bowie, Susan Lorde Shaw, Connie Converse, and others.

During her short time as a music producer, X had a reputation for

being chaotic and destructive—she would sometimes take a hammer to taped demos, or lie flat on the floor of the studio mid-recording, refusing to get up. She once burned a whole notebook that belonged to Tom Waits while they were in the middle of an artistic dispute. Another time she halted a session with Susan Lorde Shaw and would not begin it again until she'd made her famous squash casserole. Infamously, she also destroyed several notebooks and demos belonging to Shaw, who was a critical darling and commercial success, which made X the enemy of many. Fans were confused when Shaw chose a photograph taken by X as an album cover for *Locations*.

But X was also known to be suddenly possessed by highly productive streaks, to write songs in single bursts—lyrics, chords, everything. One of the many inaccuracies in Theodore Smith's book crept in because he was fooled by the myth that X would often lean over a piano and spontaneously create a perfect new song. In fact, many of the lyrics to those inspired hits can be found in papers that go back to the late sixties, when

Image: Susan Lorde Shaw

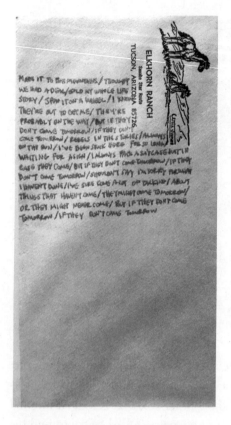

she was a total unknown. She'd likely had them memorized for years until they found a use.

The best-known song from that time was "If They Don't Come Tomorrow," popularized by David Bowie's 1976 recording. In Bowie's performance, it seems to be sung by an artist contending with his own ambition, both anticipating and craving acclaim, an audience, while worrying it may never materialize. But seen in this context—knowing it was written by a woman exiled from her home, rightfully paranoid that she might be hunted down and killed—the lyrics take on a new meaning.

A few months after I had moved in with X in 1989, she found me crying in the empty bathtub, suddenly emotional over how I would likely never see Henry again, worried that by leaving him I had made him dead; I had wanted to be with X, and being with her meant leaving him, and leaving him had meant each of us dying in the world we had lived in together. I had committed a bloodless murder-suicide, and I wept over it, though even my own sorrow seemed pitiful to me, and when I'd exhausted myself of tears, X calmly told me that regret was an emotion that could only bend someone backward, that it had no use except as a self-poison.

"When it is necessary," she said, "I will put anything or anyone out of mind."

Immediately, I could see the back of her head as she walked away from me, unbothered, into some other life, an image that frightened the regret from me.

This is all to say that it was difficult for me to recognize the anxious young woman in Ted Gold's papers as the same woman I knew. She seemed more like someone X could have known a long time ago, a troubled and rootless person, a person she couldn't help but kill. How else can I explain her own obsession over the way she left Paul? She wrote to Ted:

Keep thinking of Paul, the slit I left in his leg, hole the shape of an eye, and if I'm capable of that, what else could I be capable of?—he could have died, I came at him with a knife and he could be dead, he could be dead right now—if not from the wound itself then from blood loss and if not from blood loss then from infection if not from infection then from other complications, and there are always complications— and though, maybe, it is unlikely that Paul is dead, it is possible that he is dead, dead because of what I did—in haste or of necessity I am not sure—so I can and must logically conclude that the by the virtue of the existence of the possibility that Paul is dead, I am, in my heart, a killer.*

Ted kept copies of all the letters he sent to X, and many of the originals were returned to him, undeliverable. He often pleaded with her to come to Chicago, saying that she needed some measure of institutional protection. Ted had been using his position in the FBI to try to find his comrades. Every week, he reviewed hundreds of mug shots and photographs of unidentified corpses that police departments in the Western Territory shared with the FBI. In 1969, Kathy Boudin appeared in one of those photos taken by the San Francisco Police. Her body had been found in a flophouse in the Haight; she died from an apparent overdose.

X was living in Missoula by the time she received news of Kathy's death. In a lewd and confusing letter she wrote back, X connected Kathy's dying to her own promiscuity:

A kind of cicada season . . . Kathy dying high & my fucking. An invisible thread between us, she always said that. I said it, too. Dying is a remarkable thing, the only remarkable thing—but there's nothing

* X to Ted Gold, undated letter circa summer 1970, box 4, item 10, Ted Gold archive, TXA.

remarkable about fucking. That's what's so nice about it. Nothing to say. Nothing to it. When you're done you take a shower. I once thought I could fuck myself into some kind of knowledge. How stupid! I used to think that anything removed from my life could be somehow returned to me. God must have told me that.

Aside from mapping X's travels through the Western Territory during this itinerant and previously uncharted period of her life, the letters in the Ted Gold archive provided little insight, or if there were insights, they were insights I did not want to see. There was one line, however, isolated on a page from 1969, that stood out:

The price of having an identity is the inability to transform it.

At one point during her hitchhiking, X passed through Chicago for a few warm days. She recalled in a later journal how she approached Ted's apartment building once, considering but ultimately deciding not to enter. After 1972, X sent fewer than one letter a year to Ted. Most of these later letters were simple and short, and revealed very little. In 1984, however, in what seems to be her last letter to him, she writes entirely in second person—"You have had an abnormal childhood," the letter repeats several times. "You will have to live your childhood over again."

CONNIE

Often X made the argument that our supposedly liberal society was illogically puritanical about age differences in romantic partners, that "some" fourteen-year-olds were more mature and capable than adults well over twice their age. I agreed this was a possibility, but it seemed sagacious teens were in shorter supply than lecherous adults, and lust itself has a transfiguring effect, a way of taking action and justifying it later. I'd once had a professor who'd pursued me while I was his student, and though I was technically and legally mature enough to consent, the imbalance of power seemed to me a warning. To this, X groaned: Didn't I know that personal experience blurred the truth? And furthermore, she said, the professor obviously hadn't been appealing enough to me, so it wasn't an adequate example. I did not bring up the fact I'd been quite attracted to him, as I never mentioned any attractions I'd had in the past; I even found it difficult, in her presence, to remember them clearly, so completely my sense of desire and sexuality seemed to rest in her hands. We never reached a conclusion to this disagreement; we simply concluded and re-concluded that there was no use bickering over abstractions, though abstractions continued to be the sole subject of our bickering.

X often spoke of the truth as if it were a stable, glowing object—something just within her grasp—but she argued for the opposite as well, that reality itself was a shifting illusion, never to be known. I believed her on both accounts. I believed nearly everything she ever said.

But the memory of our abstract bickering came to me as I tried to understand X's long-ago relationship with Connie Converse—whether they were a couple or an intense pair of friends, or whether such a distinction even mattered. Connie was twenty-one years older than X, roughly twice her age when they met, but each of them needed the other—intensely at times—and each of them behaved irrationally about the other in ways that suggest theirs was not a wholly platonic bond.

In November of 1971, after her affair with David Moser was uncovered and she was fired from her job at the deer processing plant, X began traveling vaguely eastward for a few weeks, forging a path of accidents, brief rides between small towns, soup kitchens, gas stations, and women's crisis centers. "Another crisis center," she noted in a journal. "It's beginning to seem I may be having one."*

In her backpack X carried a little cash, a notebook, two photographs, two changes of underwear, a pair of clean socks, a camera, and several newspaper clippings. She had a folding knife tucked into her bra. If anyone asked, she would have said her name was Dorothy Eagle, that she was twenty-one, that she'd been born in Kentucky. If anyone offered her anything, she took it—rides, food, a place to stay, money.

X had no home, no family, no connections—and yet she moved with a propulsive forward force, sure of her fate. She had forgotten her origins and thought only of the future, all her allegiance placed in the years to come.

Her aimless months of hitchhiking away from Montana landed her in Ann Arbor, Michigan, where, on Thanksgiving Day 1971, she met Connie Converse at a soup kitchen where X was eating and Connie was serving. For years, Connie had been living in a deepening depression; volunteering—the only human contact she had aside from her secretarial job—was her primary salve. Connie's younger brother, Phil, told me she

* X, journal entry, November 14, 1971, box 1971, item 15, TXA.

had become preoccupied with the Southern Territory at this time, and the more she read about the famines and prisons and oppression down there, the more pointless life seemed, and the more pointless life seemed, the more she wanted to know about the world's cruelties.

As is often the case with betrayed love, Connie and X remembered their first meeting differently. In writing, each casts the other as the nexus of their entanglement, remembers herself as the clueless bystander caught up in the other's plans. In Connie's unpublished memoir, she wrote that "a young woman named Dorothy Eagle" approached her in tears, saying she'd been turned away at the women's shelter and needed a place to sleep for a few nights.*

"She caught me off guard," Connie wrote, "and I could hardly believe myself when I said she could stay with me. I don't know why that seemed like the right thing, as it makes no sense looking back at it . . . Then some months passed and she was still there—I suppose I forgot she was supposed to be looking for a place. Forgot or just didn't mind."

X's diaries—though perhaps they are not to be trusted—tell a different story:

> *This lady picked me up in a soup kitchen and has put me up in her place for now. Her line was that she was a writer, too, as she'd seen me with my notebook. I can't imagine how desperate a person has to be to approach a stranger to say that—I'm a writer, too. But I was tired of crisis centers and park benches. Been here a week or something, and every night she starts getting panicky after the sun goes down, like she isn't sure what to do with me, like something has to be done. I'd say it's probably doomed.†*

Connie had been living in Ann Arbor since 1960 after a fifteen-year stint in New York. When she dropped out of college in March of 1945, she'd been certain of her talents as a musician and a writer. Her drive

---

* Connie Converse, memoir, undated pages, folder 5, CML papers, TXA.

† X, diary entry, December 1, 1971, box 1971, item 15, TXA.

toward a career as an artist was derailed by the Goldman assassination in April of that year, then extinguished when the Great Disunion occurred that autumn. Like many others in their twenties, Connie threw herself into protest and activism nearly full-time—marching, writing letters, volunteering, or reading the horrific news between her temp jobs. When the pace of the movement to liberate the Southern Territory slowed in 1946, returning to her pursuit of folk music and fiction seemed absurd. In a letter to her brother from May of that year, she sums up her problem: "Is life in the small things, in songs or stories, or is it in the large things, in the country, its laws, in the liberty and safety of others? I feel it cannot be in both. I cannot be in both. I am so weary, Phil, I can hardly sleep but I can hardly get out of bed."*

As the years went on she tried to remain in both worlds. She wrote her dour ballads, and occasionally a political essay, while still attending and helping to organize rallies and sit-ins and letter-writing campaigns. Both pursuits were rife with rejection. Demanding liberation of the ST was increasingly Sisyphean, but Connie's attempts to get a manager for her music career were just as hopeless, and she was losing stamina for open mic nights. Activism became her tool for avoiding her creative ambition, and her music seemed like a time-wasting escape from the urgent reality of her activism. This stalemate continued into the 1950s, punctuated by occasional moments of success—a good show, a new song—and in 1954 she was invited to perform on *The Morning Show* with Walter Cronkite. None of it was ever quite enough.

The same year as her *Morning Show* performance, Gene Deitch invited Connie to perform at his salon, a regular event he held and recorded in his Greenwich Village apartment. Connie arrived in a long shapeless dress, leading someone to quip that she'd "just come in from milking the cows," to which she retorted, "I'll milk *you*," then took up her guitar and began to play.† She impressed the crowd that night, though they still found her strange and old-fashioned. The problem, perhaps, was that

---

* Connie Converse to Phil Converse (photocopy), April 8, 1946, folder 4, item 2, CML research collection, TXA.

† Connie Converse, recorded by Gene Deitch, 1954.

Connie had all the qualities a male folk musician was allowed to have in the 1950s and none of what was expected of a female singer. She was bewildering when she should have been seductive, rugged when she should have been glamorous. Her songs were about steely women when they should have been about powerful men. Her voice had a stilted, pedantic quality—the sort of irregularity celebrated in Bob Dylan—instead of the nostalgic, mellifluous tone of a woman. A booking agent told her she needed to buy some lipstick and high heels before he could get her gigs. Shades of equality could be seen elsewhere in the Northern Territory, but stages and spotlights still demanded a beautiful docility. At the time, few noticed or cared about correcting the prejudices in an industry seen as ultimately frivolous.

Connie met similar hurdles with her writing. A prominent editor once rejected one of her short stories on the grounds that it was "too morose." Her essays were often accused of being vitriolic, irrationally negative, or obsessed with trivialities. Now that Emma Goldman's policies had delivered paid maternity leave, federally mandated equal pay, and subsidies for housework, what did women have to complain about? In 1960, Connie gave up and moved to Ann Arbor, got a job as a secretary, and mostly gave up her creative work. X's arrival in 1971 diverted Connie from her plans to drive her Volkswagen off a cliff she'd chosen in Canada.

When X and Connie met, each had reached a sort of impasse that seemed to winnow their focus on each other. While Connie had been discouraged enough to believe the impasse was the sole destination of her life, X was young enough to believe she could hurtle herself over it. "I only know that I have to create a powerful monster, since I am such a weak one," X wrote in the journal she kept while living with Connie. "I have to create a monster apart from me, someone who knows much more than I know, who has a world view, and does not get such simple words wrong."*

Early in December 1971, Phil Converse stopped by to check on his sister, and wrote a letter to his mother about what he found:

> There's this young woman, a Dorothea [*sic*] Eagle, living
> with Connie for now. Must be half her age. I think it's a little
> strange to just take in a woman we don't know (homeless?),
> but it does seem the company has done Connie some good.
> She has to set her mind on something or else she gets all
> flustered. She's cooking in earnest—there was even a big cake
> under a dome, like a holiday.†

When Connie admitted she'd once been a musician, X asked her new friend to sing for her. Connie refused. X kept asking; Connie kept refusing. It was only after X found two tape reels in a closet labeled MUSICKS VOLUME I and MUSICKS VOLUME II—Connie's home demos and the

* X, journal entry, December 28, 1971, box 1971, item 1, TXA.

† Phil Converse to Betty Converse, December 10, 1971, folder 4, item 6, CML photo and research collection, TXA.

recording of the Deitch salon—that X first heard her talent. Arriving home from work that evening, Connie was chilled to hear those old recordings again, a past self sneaking into the present.

This sort of gesture—to force someone into feeling what they wanted to avoid—was something X did all her life to anyone she felt she had the right to change. It seems that the more she loved someone, the more pain she wanted to dredge up, the more demanding she became, no matter the cost, no matter the damage. In her notebooks, Connie recalled that odd morning that her friend Dorothy found a new strategy to force Connie to become (or recall) the sort of person X wanted her to be:

> It was a kind of drag, I guess. She layered all these clothes on, kind of stooped a little, wore this wig and dark sunglasses. She came out of her room looking like that and we sat there, eating breakfast. I remember saying, "Well, good morning, and what's your name?" And she said, "Bee Converse." And I asked if that meant she was my sister and she said, maybe. My brother, my wife, my husband? Cousin? She kept saying "Maybe" or "Who knows?" And later she went to the piano and started playing "The Ash Grove" and other songs. I sang with her on some of them, something I hadn't done in years. I didn't know she played piano. But that was just how we went about things—not having to explain ourselves.*

Connie's brother, Phil, stopped by unannounced one evening that winter and introduced himself to Bee, not realizing she was Dorothy. Having fooled someone without even trying, X had the confidence to go out in public as this new persona. One night in March 1972, Bee joined Connie and a few of her co-workers at a pub. With their two-decade age difference less apparent beneath the costume, they were pegged as a couple right away.

Eileen Ellman, who worked with Connie at *The Journal of Conflict Resolution*, remembered, "It was so clear how happy they were, would've

---

* Connie Converse, undated memoir notes, folder 5, CML papers, TXA.

been silly to point it out. But nobody had ever seen *Connie Converse* with a *date*. It would be like seeing a cat wearing shoes . . . Then to hear that they had the same last name—where they married already? Or cousins? They tried to shrug it off—just old friends—but nobody was buying it. You could tell from the way Connie looked at her. *Some*thing was going on."*

In X's archive, I could find only one note from Connie, an inscription in a Thomas Bernhard novel: "We are a pair of solitary travelers slogging through the country of our lives."

When X told Connie she was planning to move to New York that spring, Connie discouraged her, insisting that New York was a cesspool of hacks and frauds who just want fame at any cost. "Anyone will stab you in the back to get ahead," she said, "and no one wants anything to do with you unless you're ahead of them in the game, and even then what they most want is to defeat you, take your place . . . That's all it is, a place full of people eating. Just people eating everything right up."

But Connie's objections were no use. At the end of March, X hitch-hiked away as suddenly and easily as she'd arrived. Connie stayed in bed, barely ate, lost her job, stopped bathing. Her brother came by to check on her, but she wouldn't speak to him. A month later, she found several letters in the hill of mail piled up at the front door:

Dear Connie,
    Please get in your car and drive to New York City. My address is 23 Grove Street.

    Your Friend,
    Bee Converse

Dear Connie,
    It would do you some good to get out of Ann Arbor. My

---

* Eileen Ellman, telephone interview with author, September 9, 2000, tape 18.1–2, CML audio collection, TXA.

address is 23 Grove Street in New York City. Bring your
guitar.

> Your friend,
> Bee Converse

Dear Connie,
>   See my other letters. I am not kidding around here.
>   23 Grove. New York, NY. That's *Manhattan*.

> Your friend,
> Bee Converse*

X also sent a letter signed by *"Dorothy"*—three pages of yellow stationery in bulbous cursive. "I cannot imagine what might be keeping you in
Ann Arbor when there is so much life and opportunity for you here. It
is certainly not the same city that you left in 1961. You won't recognize
it. You may not recognize yourself, either. Bee complains of your absence
all the time," she wrote. "People do cling to consciousness, and under the
most dreadful circumstances. It shows you that it is all we have, doesn't
it? Waking up, the first and the last privilege, waking up once more."†
She must have known, whether explicitly or implicitly, how close Connie
always was to suicide.

That night Connie got out the shoebox where she'd hidden the few
things that X had left behind—a lighter, a barrette, several bobby pins,
and a clipped-out article from a magazine, a profile of a man who'd been
orphaned when his unmarried mother murdered his wealthy father. The
story, Connie remembered, had been headline news when she'd first
moved to New York—a crime of passion, gossip fodder—but she wasn't

* "Bee Converse" [X] to Connie Converse, undated, ~ late April 1972, folder 15, items 9–19, CML
photo and research collection, TXA.

† "Dorothy" [X] to Connie Converse, April 1, 1972, folder 15, items 9–19, CML photo and research
collection, TXA.

sure what interest X would have had for it. The next morning, Connie pocketed the article and the lighter, clipped the barrette into her hair, left a note for her brother saying she was going to find a new life for herself, and drove to New York City. Phil would not see his sister again until he was called in to identify her body, nine years later, in 1981.

As I tried to make sense of X's relationship with Connie, and as I failed to uncover the truth of it, I sometimes recalled—though I wished I could forget it—that old fight of ours about romance over age gaps, and X's claim that my personal experience had warped my ability to see this issue clearly. With them, however, expectations were inverted—Connie was the one helplessly in X's thrall, despite her being twenty years older, and I wonder now if X had always been a thousand years older than anyone, that everyone she ever loved was always a child to her, always something to be molded, to control. Or perhaps it's all much simpler than that: we cannot see the full and terrible truth of anyone with whom we closely live. Everything blurs when held too near.

OLEG HALL

T here is only one line in X's notebook from the day she met Oleg Hall, her crucial patron and (at times) close friend:

April 16, 1972
*What myths am I trading in?** *

X had less than sixty dollars left in her purse. For two weeks she'd been renting a bed at a women's shelter in the garment district. She'd lost

---

much weight, and her attempts to find a job had failed. The nuns who ran the shelter were beginning to court her—what other options did she have? Despite this poverty, X first met Oleg—allegedly while she was being stood up by someone else—at a champagne and caviar bar called Brenda's, a place frequented by wealthy diplomats and real estate moguls.

Given the specific variety of fame Oleg had at this time, Brenda's was one of the few places he could go without being hassled by strangers, reporters, or women who overlooked his exuberant homosexuality and tried to set up this wealthy "bachelor" with their daughters or nieces. Oleg took a late lunch at Brenda's a few times a week: caviar and blinis, oysters Rockefeller, and a few grapefruit sodas. His preferred seat at the bar was perpetually reserved, and he'd sometimes stay all afternoon, leafing through magazines as the waiters changed the tables from the day setting to night. This was not the sort of place a broke, connectionless young woman would have stumbled into by accident, but X already knew surviving New York meant ensuring that her appearance belied her situation. She hand-washed and ironed her clothing every other night at the women's shelter, and budgeted salon visits above food. She spent several afternoons studying the women shopping at Saks, teaching herself to mimic their gestures, the bored way they laid a gaze upon whatever they wanted.

"I'm waiting on someone," X told the bartender, once, then again when he offered her the menu a second time. Oleg watched as X delicately removed her gloves and folded them into her patent leather handbag, a little out of date and cheap, he thought, but somehow stylish in this woman's hands. Some time passed. X's date, if he ever existed, continued not to show.

"I couldn't help but pity her," Oleg explained on the first of my disastrous interviews with him. "I was feeling a little lonely myself, I suppose—I'd just called off an affair with a married man. I was doing that sort of thing back then, and—I don't know—I suppose seeing this young woman waiting on someone who clearly wasn't coming . . . Well, I felt sorry for her. I recognized her."*

Oleg claims not to remember who spoke to whom first. If he does remember, he was careful not to remember it in my presence. The nature of their friendship's beginning is one of many aspects of Oleg Hall's role in X's life that has long confused me, especially since Oleg almost immediately began financially supporting her, and lavishly so. Love—and I hesitate to use that word, though I am left with few alternatives—rarely moves with that sort of velocity without involving sex, deception, or dependency. Yet in what seems to have been a matter of twenty minutes their lives were deeply and unquestioningly intertwined; the situation was never romantic, nor did they seem to lie to each other or themselves about the nature of their friendship, and unless we understand Oleg Hall to be paying for this young woman's company, there was nothing directly remunerative about the arrangement, either. After Oleg bought her lunch at Brenda's, they left for a walk in the park, a trip to the Met, dinner at one of the clubs to which Oleg belonged, and, finally, cocktails at a jazz bar.

"By midnight she'd told me things she'd never told anyone, things she'd never tell anyone ever again, not even you," Oleg said.

I refused, then, to believe he could have known anything about my wife that I did not know. His insistence on calling her Dorothy leads me to believe he may not have known that name was simply an alias, but perhaps he was just attached to it for no reason other than it was the name he first associated with her.

"It was immediately clear to both of us—Dorothy was my entire family, and I was her entire family. We were each other's whole, entire family all in one person."

This has long been his line on the matter.

"She's my only real family," he told a reporter in 1985.† "She's the

---

* Oleg Hall, interview with the author, December 10, 1999, tape 9.1–2, CML audio collection, TXA. All quotes from Oleg Hall in the following paragraphs are from this interview.

† Oleg Hall, quoted in Lucy Sante, "Lost Ones," *Vogue*, April 1985, 89.

sister I never had, the mother I don't have anymore," he told another in 1988.*

That first night, when Oleg realized X had been living at a women's shelter, he refused to allow her to stay another night there—"You mustn't trust the nuns!" he said.† He packed up her things, paid off her balance, and checked her into the Waldorf Astoria, a choice that was as macabre as it was opulent, given Oleg's personal history with that particular hotel.

For much of the mid-1960s, Oleg could hardly set foot out of his apartment without being hounded by tabloid photographers, though his star—if that is what you want to call it—has since faded significantly. Even in 1989, when X tried to explain Oleg's past to me, it seemed too large and strange to be believed—that his mother shot his father and herself in a suite at the Waldorf Astoria, orphaning Oleg but leaving him as the heir to his father's estate.

"All I remember of my mother is that she wanted the very best for me," Oleg told the director Ross McElwee in McElwee's 1991 documen-

tary about X.‡ "She got a weekly allowance from Father, but she'd spend it all on me and leave nothing for herself . . . It was almost as if my existence made her feel as if she no longer existed. Children can tell things, can't they? About their parents? Anyway, it's part of the reason Dorothy and I always got along so well, I think. Something about that . . ."

Off-camera, McElwee asks, "Something about what?"

Oleg immediately replies, "Existence. Something about existence."

* Oleg Hall, quoted in Joshua Rivkin, "The Erasing Woman," *Vanity Fair*, February 1988, 45–47.

† X, journal entry, box 1972, folder 8, item 44, TXA.

‡ Oleg Hall quoted in *Portrait of an X*, dir. Ross McElwee, A22, 1994.

Image: Nina Kolodnaya, mother of Oleg Hall

After the murder-suicide, Oleg was left in the care of his aunt Eloise, who'd known nothing of her nephew and parented him with open hostility and violence, thinking of him as the child of her brother's murderess rather than as her own blood. On his eighteenth birthday Oleg had his aunt evicted from his home, as it was now legally his, and when his butler informed him a decade later that poor Aunt Eloise had suffered a heart attack in a dressing room at Macy's and was pronounced dead on the scene, Oleg immediately replied, *Don't be silly. She didn't have a heart.*

By the mid-1960s the tragedy of the murder-suicide was far enough in the past to give a mysterious sheen to Oleg's wealth and good looks. A 1967 article in *The New York Times* society page reported that Edie Sedgwick was seen sitting in Oleg's lap at a nightclub, stroking his face and mussing his hair, and later the same evening Truman Capote chased him though the crowd, trying to pinch his ass.* Elizabeth Taylor often threatened to marry him if he wasn't careful. Robert Frank, enamored with the angles in Oleg's face, photographed him several times, alone and in clusters of beat poets. The notorious were drawn to him the way the notorious so often are—magnetized by his living drama, his constant audacity. Oleg alternately courted and detested his status as a tragic celebrity. "Like all famous people Oleg Hall constantly attracts new people," Susan Sontag once wrote in a letter to X, "and he doesn't have to cultivate old friendships, resolve disputes, soothe ruffled feathers. He can just move on."† It is true that Oleg repeatedly lured people in with one hand and quickly pushed them away with the other—Sontag was one such victim—but X, a chiral sibling, held his loyalty.

Oleg has lived alone on Park Avenue since his parents died, though every time I have witnessed him there he always seems like an uneasy visitor. The sitting room where we conducted our few interviews was still decorated with his father's formal 1940s furniture and oil portraits of relative strangers. He's never renovated, redecorated, or even rearranged any of

* Rachel Syme, "Gossip Dispatches from the Diamond Set," *The New York Times*, June 28, 1967, D4.

† Susan Sontag to X, May 14, 1981, box 1981, item 56, TXA.

the furniture; everything is pristine and ghostly, an unpopular museum's most forgotten wing.

I asked Oleg for an interview several times before he granted it. He was either out of town or not in the mood or too busy. Each time I called I could clearly see the scene: the butler carrying the rotary phone on a silver platter to Oleg, who is languishing through another empty day of his life, tossed across the chaise longue, smoking, flipping through a magazine as he explains there is simply no time in his schedule. The first few times I called, he taunted me with the existence of Theodore Smith's book, which had been filled with verbatim and self-aggrandizing quotes from Oleg, then hung up without warning, but a few weeks later I drew Oleg out for a while as I ran the tape recorder.

"There are simply so many things you'll never know about her," he said. "It's such a pity, really. If it weren't so amusing to watch you exhaust yourself, then it would almost be a tragedy, wouldn't it? You've just been mistaken about her for so long."

"She married me," I said.

"Yes," he said, "I did notice that."

After a long silence I asked, "What is it that you have always had against me, Oleg? What is so wrong with me?"

"There's nothing wrong with you, dear, but can't you see there's nothing so right with you, either?"*

It was typical Oleg, a glamorous sadist, yet there was nothing he could do or say to harm me then. I'd been to the Southern Territory earlier that year, and I was now feverish with the kind of focus and obsession that seems to come early in a project as large as a book—a feeling not unlike new love, though a motionless, silent sort of love, so inward and tightly wound that from the outside it must look like paralysis. My implacability in the face of his insult seemed to compel Oleg to agree to an interview at his penthouse that evening.

After I arrived and set up the recorder for our first face-to-face meet-

---

* Oleg Hall, telephone interview with the author, December 10, 1999, tape 8.3, CML audio collection, TXA.

ing, he sipped a glass of his evening sherry, then a second glass, before he reclined on the couch as if I were his analyst. At last he launched into a long monologue, only some of which was useful.*

"I never felt like I *belonged* anywhere—a lot of people say that, sure, but you can't imagine how true it was for me—how true it still is. I've only stayed in Daddy's penthouse all these years because I didn't have anywhere else to go. I had—I've always had a hard time with relationships . . . romantic ones, you know. They haven't come naturally to me. I don't like anyone to stick around too long, but with Dorothy it all made sense from the very beginning. You can't understand how much I loved her, how pure that love really was."

Within days of their first meeting at Brenda's, Oleg had purchased an apartment for X on Grove Street and set her up with her own bank account. He brought her to all the social events he'd been avoiding—receptions and dinner parties and galas—and introduced his new friend as if she were the guest of honor everywhere they went. Their photograph regularly appeared in the society pages throughout 1972 and '73, always captioned *Oleg Hall and Guest*, as Dorothy Eagle would always be a nobody from nowhere when she stood beside Oleg. She grips his arm in all those early photographs, her smile wide but unsure.

Among the few pictures X kept from that time is one of Oleg and herself: a blurry shot from the summer of 1972, taken by the poet Frank O'Hara. She'd gone out to Fire Island with Oleg and a few of his acquaintances to celebrate the anniversary of O'Hara's 1966 brush with death—when he was hit by a jeep and nearly died at the hospital. Oleg looks exceptionally young with a rare clean shave, and X is wearing a long blond wig, trying on a new personality around new friends. On the back of the photograph X had written *Two beautiful little children with nothing to hide.*

With each other they'd found the possibility of reliving the youths they'd been denied, a redemption, and that feeling must have come with some raw power, the restoration of the bliss of having not yet lived, of

* Oleg Hall, interview with the author, December 10, 1999, tape 9.1–2, CML audio collection, TXA.

being unburdened by memory. It had been an aspect, too, of what I'd felt when I met her—an expanding sense of the future and of what could be known or felt in this life. Still, listening to Oleg recount his earliest memories with her during the first interview, I was surprised to find myself actually moved by the confessions of a man so committed to being cruel to me.

I'd first met Oleg in late 1989, several months after I'd been living with X. He'd broken several dates that he and X had set for him to meet me—*The new girlfriend*, X sometimes said, winking. I didn't like that word, *new*, as it placed me in a passing parade of new girlfriends and old girlfriends, past girlfriends and future girlfriends. Oleg canceled our initial plans on the grounds that he'd fallen ill; then he was ill again, then he had to go abroad suddenly for a funeral, then he'd stayed in Paris for a long vacation to recover from the funeral, then he accidentally double-booked us against some unmovable engagement, then he simply admitted he didn't feel like it, didn't feel like meeting his best friend's new *girl*.

It's just that you're always introducing me to these people who supposedly mean so much to you, I remember him explaining to her over the phone, speaking loudly enough that I could hear him, *but they inevitably disappoint you, don't they? You might as well admit that you're just like me . . . We're not made for conventional relationships. We're just not.*

X had been holding the receiver away from her ear, rolling her eyes and smiling at me while telling him that she could see where he was coming from but that people change sometimes, don't they? (How intensely I committed this moment to memory, so full of hope I was that this and this alone was the life for me, a life with her. I was old enough to know I'd been wrong about many things of which I'd once been certain, but still young enough to see possibility and perfection in new certainties.)

People don't change, Oleg said over the phone that day, his voice full of resignation. *They try to change, they act like they change, but they don't. They never do.*

X was looking straight at me as Oleg's voice boomed over the phone. She leaned in to kiss me for a moment, a kiss I thought was meant to

(opposite) Image: Oleg Hall and "Dorothy Eagle" (X)

invisibly spite him and everything he was saying, and then she replied to him, her mouth still close to mine, that he, of all people, must have known that she was nothing like other people, that maybe normal people don't change, but if anyone could really change, she could, strange as she was.

Which is why it's insane for you to try to commit to anyone, he said.

X bent double in silent laughter, her hand over her mouth as I stood there, trying to seem unbothered. Eventually Oleg conceded, and a new date was set for a week later at his penthouse. When we arrived his butler led us to the drawing room on the east side of the building, and we waited in the dim afternoon light for nearly an hour before he came in, embracing X for long enough to make a point, muttering secrets into her ear.

Then he scrutinized me—the trouble—before beginning his inquisition.

Where was I from, and what did I do, and what were my ambitions, and how did I meet *Dorothy*, and did I really think I could keep up with her, and did I realize what a special person she was, and could I truly say that I could handle the life that she was apparently offering to me? A life with this woman, this intense and remarkable person?

She is, he said, *and I mean this quite seriously—she is a dangerous person, an incredibly dangerous person—do you understand that? Do you understand what I mean by that?*

I answered this and the rest of Oleg's questions with the calm certainty of the insane or the newly enamored, and when his inquisition was over, he asked to be left alone with X for a moment so that they could *discuss something personal*. I pressed my ear to the other side of the door and listened to Oleg cry and hyperventilate before X came out and led us quickly to the elevator. He was afraid of being abandoned, X explained. It was something they were "working" on.

Over the years I found my wife's friendship with Oleg to be as intense and inscrutable as any marriage. They could converse across a room in a silent code, mimic each other's handwriting, perfectly imitate the other's voice, and I often observed X pick up the phone to call Oleg, only to find he had called her, an occurrence so common that they no longer called it uncanny. Of course they thought of each other simultaneously. Of course they did.

In his 1988 *Vanity Fair* profile of Oleg, the writer Joshua Rivkin explained their bond as a "complex arrangement of love and domesticity."* Before I arrived in 1989, X and Oleg had spent nearly all their free time together—cooking meals, playing hours-long backgammon tournaments, singing, reading side by side, sometimes even reading the same book at once, taking turns turning the pages, always on the same sentence. I always suspected that Oleg Hall's money had been what had truly drawn them together, as X's first years in New York would have been financially impossible without a patron. However, it is true that when X came into wealth of her own, she was quite generous with Oleg, but it was a cheap generosity, ultimately—as the wealthy can throw money around without much care or meaning.

When Connie Converse arrived in New York City in May of 1972, she was the first to witness the intensity of this new pair. Connie sat in her VW Beetle across from 23 Grove Street and for a moment considered driving back to Ann Arbor, forgetting all about it, but then her friend appeared, beaming in the afternoon's golden light. Oleg was there, too, his annoyance apparent when Connie unloaded two suitcases from her car. "He looked at me like I was carrying a couple of severed legs," she later wrote.†

When I asked Oleg about Connie's arrival and tenure in the Grove Street apartment, he gave me a scattered, dismissive look.

"I don't recall it," he said.

What about the year that Connie lived with Dorothy?

"Who?" he asked.

"Connie Converse," I reminded him, "the folk singer from Ann Arbor?"

---

* Joshua Rivkin, "The Erasing Woman," *Vanity Fair*, February 1988, 45–47.

† Connie Converse, undated memoir pages, folder 5, item 5, CML papers, TXA.

"Oh, well, I simply don't remember anything about her. She was just so old! And she wore the most dreadful clothes and had no manners. Anyway, I was never interested in country music, and it just seemed like she wanted everyone to know how much she suffered. Of course, we're *all* depressed—what made her depression so special? Why couldn't she just hide it like everyone else?"

When I pressed him further, Oleg yawned. "She was a lunatic, not important," he said.

What about the songs, the albums she wrote with X? What did he remember of that?

"Dorothy was a very talented person, as you know, and there were a lot of hangers-on. It was nothing more than that."

In a letter I obtained from one of Oleg's scorned former friends, it is obvious he felt jealous of Connie. He refers to her as "that elderly woman" and says he is annoyed when X declines invitations to parties because she's in the middle of working through a song with her. "And why on earth does Dorothy insist on wearing that hideous wig when that woman is around? It's so obvious she's manipulated herself into Dorothy's life."*

Like an animal marking his territory, Oleg made his ownership of the Grove Street apartment more obvious, trying to push Connie out by leaving her no room to live in. He hired a contractor to remodel the living room and kitchen, but Connie simply took to sleeping in the bathtub until it was complete. Then Oleg had a baby grand piano lifted by crane through the third-story window; he had it placed atop Connie's pallet on the floor, but she then made her home beneath the piano, even tacking up curtains for privacy.

All through Oleg's campaign to win back X's undivided attention, Connie and X kept writing dozens of songs, recording them in the bedroom in the middle of the night. All that year Oleg tried to schedule and control X's every hour. When she mentioned wanting to learn Italian, Oleg hired her a tutor four days a week. There were almost always evening engagements—if not a party, then a play, a dinner, a film Oleg wanted to see, a double feature.

* Oleg Hall to Sean H. Vanderslice, December 1, 1972, courtesy of Vanderslice.

"Oleg Hall was an astonishing number. I mean, the *things* he would say! The expressions he would invent. One of them was: 'You have a flair for the obvious.' *He* certainly didn't," a longtime friend of his, Mark Doten, told me in an interview. "Or at least not after Dorothy showed up. Before her, I always thought Oleg was something of a boor, so serious . . . But the new Oleg once showed up at a party wearing a bright red wig, and Dorothy had this fake mustache, and the two of them hunched together laughing the whole time . . . For a while I never saw one of them without the other—out at things of course, but also shopping, walking . . . practically everywhere. Oleg's one of those people who can't stand to feel alone—has to have someone at his side whenever possible."*

Connie's presence apparently threatened to upend that arrangement.

In the autumn of 1972 something happened between Connie and X, though neither clearly recorded the details. In her letters and notebooks from that year, X calls it "The Incident," while Connie wrote of it recurrently and hazily in her memoirs, referring to it as "that night," or "that strange night," or "the night when everything changed." But neither woman explains, in writing, what exactly changed or how, and though this was clearly a turning point in how they felt about each other, their habits remained largely the same. Most of their time together was spent playing guitar and piano or writing songs; Oleg intruded as often as he could, taking X away and leaving Connie to write her ballads alone.

The less time Connie spent with X, the more melancholic and powerful her lyrics became. She wrote and recorded nearly fifty songs without X that year, though none of the tapes were released until after her death. Some reference a lover slipping between disguises, songs of unrequited love in heterosexual costume; even though gay love stories were easily mainstream by the 1970s, Connie was still bruised and constrained by the homophobia of her youth. In the song "Trouble," she describes her months sleeping beneath the baby grand:

* Mark Doten, interview with the author, February 12, 2000, tape 19.1–2, CML audio collection, TXA.

I sleep without a home
a piano blocks the sky.
Trouble goes out, trouble comes in
and she won't tell me why

The song's speaker lives in the periphery of someone referred to only as "trouble," though she's unsuited for anything else:

Go out and stay away
but if you say we're through,
where will I find another soul
to tell my trouble to?*

One day in late October of 1972, Oleg went to Grove Street in search of "Dorothy," only to find Connie alone in the apartment, drinking a glass of beer for lunch. Neither knew where their friend was, as each had been told that she was spending the day with the other. Uneasily and in silence, they waited all afternoon. Late that night, X arrived home, though dressed in a way that neither Connie nor Oleg had seen before. She'd cut her hair short and wore dark lipstick and smeared black eyeliner. Her shirt was sleeveless, her jeans ripped. She wore clunky combat boots and stank of ammonia.

"She looked at us both like she had no idea who we were, and of course we must have been looking at her the same way," Oleg recalled. "She took this awful clump of wet cash out of her pockets and went over and drank water straight from the tap. I was . . . I was absolutely scandalized."

Horrified, Oleg asked what had happened to her hair. She shrugged and was quiet for a while before she told them she'd gotten a job pouring drinks at a place called Big Bar; she'd told the manager her name was Clydelle and claimed to have been a bartender at the Rainbo Club in

---

* Connie Converse, "Trouble," from the album *The Complete Connie Converse* (vinyl), Pulse-Kinsella Records, 1980.

Chicago. This false résumé and her attitude were sufficient to get her two shifts a week.

When I asked Oleg if X's sudden adoption of alternate identities and costumes came as a surprise, he nearly shouted—"Not at all, not for a moment," though this contradicts X's own diaries, how he cried about her hair, even though he knew she'd lately been wearing a wig when she went out as Dorothy. From the very first of our interviews, Oleg claimed to have known about X's plan to live in New York as several people.*

"Of course it all made sense to me from the very start," he went on, "as there was hardly a separation in our minds from one another. Every idea she's ever had, every word she wrote, everything she did had something of me in it—I was her catalyst."

Since my wife's death, Oleg has repeatedly and publicly insisted that he was the most important person in her life and that if I didn't pity him so much perhaps I would feel insulted. I do not dispute that Oleg Hall was one of X's first great enablers, as he was always ready to put up the money she needed for a project or make introductions on her behalf or give her total privacy if that was what she required. In some ways Oleg was X's first wife—the first to try to give her anything she needed—and first wives have certain a right, however facile, to gaze with a wizened rue at the girls who come after. As he wrote once in a letter to an ex-boyfriend, Oleg thought it was sad how X's girlfriends and wives so often "possessed the touching temerity to harbor ambitions of their own," adding, "Eventually X tires of anyone, as she must; then these girls all join the grim sorority. They go mad with startling frequency."†

I was X's wife when he wrote that letter; he couldn't have known that instead of going mad, I, her last wife, would go quite sane in the end, as I've never felt more starkly clear than I do now, as I write this, all my research behind me, unhindered, uncontrolled, nearly invisible in the world. Unfortunately for Oleg, I also discovered the truth of what actually brought X into his life in the first place.

---

* Oleg Hall, interview with the author, December 10, 1999.

† Oleg Hall to Juan Soramizu, June 6, 1990, courtesy of Soramizu.

———

Though my wife went to great lengths to maintain the illusion that she and Oleg met in seraphic happenstance, a life like hers—one so continually constructed and arranged—contains few accidents. I always felt that Oleg's financial support was simply too necessary to X's survival in New York to have been coincidental, a suspicion I managed to confirm.

In 1967, *Time* magazine ran a three-page profile of Oleg Hall during which the journalist accompanied Oleg through an aimless afternoon in Manhattan, caviar at an unnamed East Side bar, an afternoon of shopping, then a long dinner at one of his clubs.* X found a copy of this issue of *Time* at some point prior to her arrival in New York; she clipped out the article and kept it before leaving it, according to one of Connie's letters, in Ann Arbor.

X had also summarized the article's details in a notebook she never bothered to expunge, listing the places where she might meet Oleg, coming up with plans about how to charm him. The day before their fortuitous meeting at Brenda's, X put in an application to be a coat-check clerk at a club in which Oleg was a member, as well as in the men's department at Bergdorf Goodman. Oleg, in all his "touching temerity," was never aware he was being hunted.

Connie broached the subject of how X and Oleg met at least one time on record, during one of her and X's bedroom recording sessions in late 1972.† The first part of the tape is clouded with static, but the conclusion is clear enough—

CONNIE: . . . about Oleg?
x: Well, you mean after I saw that article about him?
CONNIE: Yes.
x: It did have something to do with it.
Connie strums a few chords.

---

* Hermione Hoby, "A Man Very About Town," *Time*, May 13, 1967, 55–59.

† Connie Converse, audio recording, December 15, 1972, box 1975, item 2–9, Grove Street sessions tapes, TXA.

CONNIE: How about "Two Tall Mountains"?

x: All right.

Connie begins to play, then stops.

CONNIE: So—you planned it? You went somewhere you might find him?

x: As much as you can plan these things.

CONNIE: Right.

x: And you can't plan whether someone will . . . get along with you all right.

CONNIE: I suppose not.

x: You ready?

They begin playing.

At the end one of our later interviews in 2003, feeling weary of Oleg's repeated insistence that the primary commodity exchanged between "Dorothy" and himself was love, I snapped and told him he'd been fooled, that X had known all about his inheritance and had searched him out in premeditation.* I could have backed this up with proof—her notes about the article, the recording with Connie—but it seems to have confirmed a fear he'd held all along. Oleg's face flared in anger, all his cool calm gone, as he told me to get out of his house. I did, glad as I went. I now see it was foolish to alienate an important source like this. A real biographer would have had more tact.

Who loved her more? Who knew her better? There can only be one widow, I told myself as I took the elevator down. The rest are exes.

---

* Oleg Hall, interview with the author, July 4, 2003, tape 9.18–22, CML audio collection, TXA.

DOWNTOWN

A journal entry from the summer of 1972—

And now there is the nightmare, the one and only nightmare, of living. Of the importance of living. And of the importance of succeeding to live. Or simply of succeeding. In other words of becoming something. Something more or less than what one is. *

Big Bar, the East Village dive where X (using the name Clydelle) began working in late 1972, was chosen not at random, but rather as a portal into an alternate world. Prior to this, X had spent her time in the city at Oleg Hall's side, and though her months of passing as a socialite had been a feat, she'd had the advantage of expert guidance. Her proximity to Oleg hid her ignorance of table etiquette, of haute couture, of how to behave on a yacht. She knew that entering the downtown scene—a supposedly lawless world that was in fact rigidly policed for authenticity—would be much more challenging.

X successfully convinced the manager of Big Bar that she was qualified for the job, and indeed it seems she blended in well enough, by spending a few weekends observing and taking extensive notes on how dive bars

* X, journal entry, July 3, 1972, box 1972, folder 8, item 3, TXA.

worked—how to operate the tap, the cash register, the ice maker, the dishwasher. She took notes on how and when to intervene in fights, when and how to deny service to someone too drunk or hostile for more, and perhaps most crucially, how to pick someone up at the end of the night.

Working at Big Bar was X's way to be both invisible and omnipresent within the world she planned to infiltrate. She eavesdropped on gossip, took note of rivalries and factions; each night the machinery of the scene became clearer. A few of the regulars from that time who remembered "Clydelle" all confirmed that she never spoke about herself, not even when asked. Even the young women who lingered around until closing time to take her home rarely got more than a few words.

"I thought she was some kind of urban legend until I went there my-self," a woman named Rebecca Novack told me. "But word got around that the chick with the shaved head would take a girl home at the end of her shift and screw you like a lightbulb—that quick! She wouldn't say hardly anything, wouldn't even ask your name, and she'd be gone before you realized it. It sounds kind of, I don't know, rude? But it was more like . . . well, kind of a community service. Yeah, she was doing a real service for the community."*

It was late in 2002 when I met Rebecca and several other women who'd slept with X at this time. Other people's memories of my wife had clouded my own by then, which perhaps had been the point all along—not to see her more clearly, but to understand I never knew her in full. I'd been given Rebecca's phone number by the man who managed Big Bar while X had worked there; we met on a cold bench in Riverside Park. She'd become a psychologist in the years since, and she looked at me with the synchronous answering and questioning gaze so intrinsic to thera-pists. She specialized in post-wall trauma and mentioned that several of her patients were lesbians, newly liberated from the FST.

"It's horrifying to learn about what they were going through while we were all up here, just fucking around, living as we pleased."

---

* Rebecca Novack, interview with the author, September 4, 2002, tape 23.1–3, CML audio collec-tion, TXA. All quotes from Rebecca Novack in the following paragraphs are from this interview.

My eyes filled immediately, though I tried to conceal this. Of course this woman had no idea that X had been born in the ST, carried a child when she was still a child, and risked her life to flee. It had been six years since the wall had fallen, but chaos and horror still dominated the papers—new atrocities uncovered, new threats or actual violence enacted by the AFK—and all through that public grief I'd been locked in my private one. When Rebecca looked at me that afternoon, I knew she'd seen the simplest image: a widow wobbling toward tears. Her training took over. She placed a hand on my wrist and whispered, "Is everything okay?"

There are some times in grief when being witnessed is the only thing you need, and there are others, months and years in my case, when nothing suits but invisibility. I controlled myself, thanked Rebecca for her time, and cut the interview short.

Tim Holt, a book editor X befriended that year, was the only Big Bar regular who didn't quite belong. He arrived each Friday at five to attend to his customary three martinis as he read through a stack of book submissions. The bar was nearly empty at that time—quiet enough to read for an hour, then busy enough to distract him from all those desperate pages. Holt noticed the cheap paperbacks X kept in her back pocket and started bringing her books from New Directions, his employer, gifts she countered with shaking larger drinks, the runoff served in a tumbler on the side. I spoke to Holt by phone, as he'd retired and moved to the Western Territory.*

"Whatever I gave her on Friday she would have read by the next week," he said. "I remember her loving Kay Boyle and Borges, though even then she always had some kind of sideways thing to say, never the obvious comment . . . I was just about burned out at the time, but I started looking forward to Fridays, to our little talks."

One week Holt arrived in a dark mood; it had been months since he'd acquired anything new, and what he'd published that year had done badly.

---

*Tim Holt, telephone interview with the author, February 2, 2002, tape 22.3–5, CML audio collection, TXA. All quotes from Tim Holt in the following paragraphs are from this interview.

The industry itself was the problem, he said, the most common complaint of those who comprise it. He bemoaned the idiocy of mass market books, all the dull submissions, and the riddle of how what sells is rarely good and what's good rarely sells.

"Then Clydelle leaned over the bar and said, 'Why don't you just write one yourself? Write one that's good *and* sells.' Ha! I would've assumed she was kidding, but she wasn't one for jokes. It was like getting advice from an alien—Just *write* a book. As if books just waited around in someone's head, waiting to be let out. Anyway, I knew better—writers are a miserable lot. Literature isn't written by the content. Why would I suffer to write when reading is so much more pleasurable?"

Holt went on to explain the hypothesis he had about writing, that trying to translate ideas and feelings into story and language is unnatural, perhaps even poisonous. "Our thoughts don't sit easily in words," he said, and I recognized this as the reason X had often given for why she didn't write books anymore. But in 1972, X still seemed to believe that writing a good book should be a simple matter, that if Holt knew how to recognize good writing, he should be able to produce it.

"I told her it wasn't typical for editors to publish themselves," Holt said.

You can use a pseudonym, she told him.

And I suppose that solves the trouble of actually writing the damn thing.

It's actually quite easy.

Well, if it's so easy, I'd appreciate if you'd come up with one.

All right.

And I'd like it by Friday if you don't mind.

Holt was so sure this would just become a running joke between them—the novel Clydelle would never write—something to ask about each Friday, the impossible thing.

Two days later, X arrived at Oleg's penthouse with a typewriter and a ream of paper. She took over one of the guest bedrooms, asked the cook to leave a pot of coffee at seven, four plums at noon, dinner at six, and two snifters of brandy at eight. She needed four days, she told Oleg; she was writing a book, the whole thing all at once, and she wanted to be left alone.

"She did everything she ever set out to do," Oleg told me the following year. "She was immensely powerful, determined. I wasn't surprised at all when she walked out of the room with a full manuscript. Not surprised in the slightest."*

It was Thursday afternoon, a full day ahead of her Friday deadline, when X arrived at the New Directions office, announced herself as Clydelle, asked to see Tim Holt, and laid the manuscript for *The Reason I'm Lost* down on his desk.

"She'd taken me seriously!" he told me. "I could hardly believe it. Of course, I sort of dreaded it, too. What were the chances it was going to be any good? Would it even be readable? I'd likely have to find a new bar . . . But then—what in the hell? It was actually *good*. Naturally, I thought she must have been working on it for some time, had only finished it now. But she insisted it had really taken her just four days . . . Even months after it had been published I was worried we might find out it had been plagiarized, but even the manuscript itself looked like was typed straight through—you can see the way the ink ribbon ran out slowly over the course of a few pages before it got replaced. She wasn't even jumping around or editing as she went or anything . . . But I'll be damned. It still doesn't add up."

New Directions published *The Reason I'm Lost* that fall, November 1973. Clyde Hill, a pseudonym's pseudonym, was credited as the debut author, and the alias deepened the mystery surrounding the book, a novel that emulsified fact and fiction so completely it was often misfiled under biography. New Directions sent the royalty checks to Dorothy Eagle— her little sister, Clydelle claimed—in order to further protect her anonymity. (This was, however, merely a matter of logistics. Dorothy Eagle was the name on X's only official ID, and the name on her bank account.) The back flap of *The Reason I'm Lost* features a grainy, out-of-focus photograph of someone (X, perhaps, with Clydelle's buzzcut) who is osten-

---

* Oleg Hall, interview with the author, July 4, 2003, tape 9.18–22, CML audio collection, TXA. All quotes from Oleg Hall in the following paragraphs are from this interview.

sibly Clyde Hill. The biographical note is just as perplexing—*Clyde Hill promises not to write another book. He knows a little about boats and owns a hatchet. Letters of complaint may be sent to New Directions.*

Holt brought fan mail and hate mail in twine-bound batches to X each Friday, but the ritual eventually gained notice; a theory began that the stoic bartender with the shaved head was *Clyde Hill*, gossip that spread so quickly that Big Bar, which was actually quite small, became unbearably crowded at all hours—readers with their copies of *The Reason I'm Lost*, looking for a signature. X played dumb, said nothing, poured drinks, but her behavior just fanned the flames. After two weekends of this spectacle, she quit; the job had now outlasted its original purpose. For a full year, a sign was posted in the window at Big Bar—WE DON'T KNOW SHIT ABOUT CLYDE HILL SO DON'T BOTHER ASKING.

New Directions forwarded the letters to Dorothy Eagle's apartment from then on, and for years X wrote occasional responses, each of them signed by "*Clyde.*" One of the correspondences that arose was with the writer Denis Johnson, author of *Jesus's Son*, though he'd not yet published a book at the time. His first letter to Clyde Hill arrived in 1977:

> Dear Clyde Hill,
>
> I hesitated to write to you, as I was holding out hope that you'd break your promise and publish a second, third, fourth book—then, I told myself, I'd write in relief. Instead I keep rereading this book, year after year, sometimes more than once a month. Maybe you don't need to write another— maybe you don't have to. In fact, just yesterday I opened a musty copy of *The Reason I'm Lost* and read about Gabe Smith and Danny Osgood . . .
>
> I turned first to a five-page passage late in the book—an argument between Osgood and his girlfriend Maureen, the first bit of dialogue I'd ever scrutinized for its ups and downs, the turns and turns-about, the strategies of the combatants . . .
>
> I looked back at the novel's opening paragraph, and by midnight I'd read the whole thing again and found myself just as moved as I'd been the first time—the first dozen times—every time. *The Reason I'm Lost* wasn't just an exercise in exemplary prose. Ultimately this book, and my envy of it, were about a life fraught with glamour and ugliness and every kind of love—thwarted love, and crazy love, and victorious love—above all, the love between these two friends.*

Johnson wrote for another two pages about the novel and his struggle to write something as "perverse and hypnotic" as *The Reason I'm Lost*. "But I'll do it, somehow. I have to now because your book has done me some damage . . . I don't recognize myself anymore—and all I want to know, sir, is who are you and where did you come from? It may be too much to ask, but I'm asking it. Can't help but ask."

---

* Denis Johnson to "Clyde Hill" (X), April 5, 1977, folder 12, item 7, CML photo and research collection, TXA.

X wasn't writing many Clyde Hill letters at the time Johnson's letter arrived, but she was moved enough by his prose that a regular correspondence began. Her first reply was uncharacteristically optimistic, an outburst of almost unlimited encouragement for young Johnson's future as a writer:

> Whatever happens to you,
> you put it onto a page, work it
> into a shape, cast it in a light.
> It's not much different, really,
> from recording the movement
> of clouds across the sky and
> calling it a film—although it
> has to be admitted that the
> clouds can descend, take you up, carry you to all kinds of
> places, some of them terrible, and you don't get back to where
> you came from for years and years. I have no doubt you'll
> do this many times, that your work will mean so much to
> so many. As for myself, I did it once and now I am thinking
> of other things, not books, not anymore . . . But it's nice to
> think you have a skill, you can produce an effect. Or that you
> once had a skill that once produced an effect.

The seven-page letter, the first of many Johnson received, ends abruptly—"I once entertained some children with a ghost story, and one of them fainted."

For the next year and a half the two exchanged letters regularly. Johnson wrote about his addiction, his jobs, his travels. Clyde Hill wrote back praising his style and his talent, encouraging him to write about whatever

Image: Clyde Hill, author photograph

pained him the most, whatever seemed too horrible to say, to start there, move quickly, and never look back. X's final letters contain many ominous non sequiturs; it seems she was unable to keep her real life from bleeding through the guise of Clyde Hill. In the middle of a long approbation on Dostoevsky, she wrote, "Connie is likely dead and how I miss her" before resuming the prior train of thought.*

Johnson permitted me one brief visit to his cabin in the Western Territory so that I might see the letters he'd kept preserved in plastic sleeves and binders. He seemed distracted and uninterested in speaking with me, but he left me alone with the pages, which I read, searching for something I did not find. The final letter came not from "Clyde Hill," but from "Dorothy Eagle." This, the shortest letter of all, was the only one I asked to photograph rather than simply take notes on.

Much has been made of the fact that X spent the majority of the 1970s using a dozen pseudonyms, slipping into and out of certain corners of New York, faking expertise, using accents, claiming various fictional histories. Though I've recounted portions of that era in this work, those interested in every alleged detail of this time in X's life may consult Theodore Smith's tedious reconstruction—her tenure at the Times Square sex show, her time spent in drag as a man, her short-lived punk band, the crashing of the Warhol parties, her various social stunts, and on and on. Merve Emre's review of Mr. Smith's book—the only legitimate review in my opinion—pointed out the basic fallacy in his point of view. "Smith portrays X's life as an unwinnable battle between her public self and her private self; to this end, he traffics in the crudest of oppositions: appearance versus character, mind versus body, intellectualism versus eroticism, persona versus private self," Emre writes. "Anyone who has paid any attention at all to X's work or interviews can see it plainly—she recognized no such borders and lived a fully boundless life."†

---

* "Clyde Hill" (X) to Denis Johnson, undated, folder 12, item 12, CML photo and research collection, TXA.

† Merve Emre, "Consider the Source," *The New Yorker*, October 8, 1997, 47.

Dear Denis

Thank you for your letter. I don't know what else to say. Clyde died unconscious, and this morning very early we went to the crematorium.

A sunny day, a *cold* sun, and a lot of flowers but it made no sense to me.

I feel that I've been walking a tight rope for a long, long time and have finally fallen off. I can't believe that I am so alone, and there there [*sic*] is no Clyde.

I've dreamt several times that I was going to have a baby—then I woke with relief.

Finally I dreamt that I was looking at the baby in a cradle—such a puny weak thing.

I don't dream about it anymore.

Dorothy Eagle

It's so *cold*.

X's repulsion at the idea of a writer attempting to summarize those years was the primary reason she refused to authorize a biography. "I have earned the right to call myself anything I like," she often repeated in interviews. "No one but I have paid for that privilege."* She assumed—and, as it turns out, was correct in her assumption—that a biographer would make the mistake of treating the minutiae of those years in particular as meaningful.

Furthermore, X explicitly stated, in her seminal 1982 work, *The Human Subject*, that the exhibition itself was the only accurate portrayal of that time. Mr. Smith's painstaking attempt to catalog what was left out of the exhibition betrays his misunderstanding of X's meaning. Though Mr. Smith certainly would have read X's "Disclosure," which appeared at the start of *The Human Subject*'s catalog, he clearly did not comprehend it.

For his sake and for yours, I am reprinting it here:

DISCLOSURE

My name is X and my name has always been X, and though X was not the name I was given at birth, I always understood, before I understood anything else, that I was X, that I had no other name, that all other names put upon me were lies. The year and location of my birth no longer pertain—few know that story, some think they know it, and most do not know it and need not know it. From 1971 until 1981—a youthful decade—I suspended the use of myself; that is, I was not here, I was not the actor within my body, but rather an audience for the scenes my body performed, a reader of the fictions my body lived. If this sounds ludicrous, that's because it is ludicrous; it is ludicrous in the exact same way that your life is ludicrous—you who have convinced yourself, just as nearly all people do, of the intractable limits of your life, you who have, in all likelihood, mushed yourself into the most miserly allotment of what a life can be, you who have taken yourself captive and called

* Robert Storr, "Another Interview with X," *BOMB* 13 (Fall 1985): 77–79.

it living. You are not your name, you are not what you have done, you are not what people see, you are not what you see or what you have seen. On some level you must know this already or have suspected it all along—but what, if anything, can be done about it? How do you escape the confinement of being a person who allows the past to control you when the past itself is nonexistent? You may believe, as it is convenient for you to believe, that there is no escaping that confinement, and you may be right. But for a period of years I, in my necessarily limited way, escaped.

Still, you may insist, such an escape is not possible. Indeed, it is not possible; however, attempting the impossible is always possible, always imperative. My attempt lasted ten years, and though it served me then, it no longer serves me now.

I am, in one sense of the word, myself again. I have admitted to this.

I am asking you now to understand that those years, a period I will refer to as *The Human Subject*, are not to be understood to be years of my life but years that I exempted from my life. I was a part of my audience, just as those who spoke to, touched, listened to, or otherwise interacted with "me" were also a part of the audience.

Is there anything more tragic than seeing an empty theater before the performance begins? The stage is so clearly a lie when naked, but when the actors, the performers, the dancers suspend their disbelief, then we, the audience, will pick up the bill. Rarely do we all get deluded together.

But I wanted that—a total, ongoing delusion, a work of art that overtook a life so completely that no seams could be seen, not even by the self who sat suspended inside the body as that body became the stage, the actors, the ticket, the script itself. I leased my body to a theater beyond my direction. The director was the world itself, the possibilities that world presented. Rehearsals occurred simultaneous to the thing itself. For this reason I am requesting that anyone who has played an unwitting part in *The Human Subject* to understand the boundary set around those years. The play has concluded. Go home.

Here, in the detritus memorializing *The Human Subject*, you will find various documents and props of the characters who comprised *The Human Subject*. Some characters wrote books of varying quality, some made films, paintings, music. Some of them made nothing but trouble. Most of them, in fact, spent most of their time trying to find something to do. Any memory a person may claim to have about additional events that purportedly took place within *The Human Subject* is lying. What I reveal here, in images and text and film and artifact, is the full extent of *The Human Subject*. There is nothing more.

There was no con, there was no crime. There was only fiction. The names, the activities, the voices, the histories—all of it a fiction. Are you following? Those people were not people. The self escaped the body. The body went around with me in it, but I was not there. I abstained from myself, just as you, too, may on occasion abstain from yourself. What a relief, what a relief it was.*

It is true that many events involving characters from *The Human Subject* were left out of the exhibition, but it is not true, as Mr. Smith suggests, that this was an attempt to "erase history." It's a juvenile idea—erasing history. There is no erasing history, just as there is no photographing history, no escaping, no holding, and no direct reconstitution. The exhibition catalog for *The Human Subject* consists almost entirely of primary sources—letters to and from those involved, diary entries, photographs, the books written, the articles, the interviews, the films. What Mr. Smith attempts to add to that archive of a ten-year performance are the warped memories of those who were not crucial enough to *The Human Subject* to have been included in its final form.

Though much of Mr. Smith's book reeks of self-regard, the tediously paced section on this period of X's life is by far most foolish—as if he has mixed up a palette of pastels and given himself permission to brighten a Rembrandt. He even attempts to diagnose X as a sex addict and manic-depressive suffering from extended delusions of grandeur; it should have

---

* X, "Disclosure," in *The Human Subject* (New York: Taschen, 1984), ii–x.

been clear to him that X was able to complete this ten-year performance not through detachment from reality, but in a vivid grappling with its limits.

Moreover, much of Mr. Smith's "reporting" can be immediately disproved by contents of X's archive, to which I, admittedly, denied him access. And though I later discovered that X intended for her archive to be eventually made available to the artists and writers involved with BASEL/ART, to be used for any purposes they saw fit, any others who accessed her papers would be prohibited from writing about their contents.

This may lead the careful reader to wonder: What, precisely, do I think I am doing? Though I did once respect X's wish not to attempt to explain or summarize her life after death, I have discovered an unforgivable trespass against myself and my privacy on X's part, and will no longer be respecting her wish to remain unsummarized. But for as much ire as I may have for my late wife, Mr. Smith remains our common enemy, a facile, silly man who foolishly wanted to interview famous people about things that simply did not matter—for instance, what do we even make of the fact that David Byrne told Mr. Smith that X was "a woman incapable of returning friendship,"* when the woman he believed he was referring to was not a person but a character? And who cares that Patti Smith did not feel that she could *trust* "Deena Stray,"† when trust and authenticity were never goals of the work?

In what may have been the most outlandish error, Mr. Smith accuses X of trying to *pass* as these different people. There is abundant evidence to contradict this claim, but I will give one example.

Simultaneous to the months X worked at Fun City, the Times Square sex show where she first met the writer Kathy Acker, she also regularly attended poetry readings in the East Village; there she introduced herself as "Pamela Reno," wore prairie dresses buttoned up to the neck, and read her sexless sonnets in a whisper. When Kathy Acker recognized "Pamela" as her coworker "Deena," albeit wearing a wig and a drastically altered

* Theodore Smith, *A Woman Without a History* (New York: Brace & Sons, 1997), 111.

† Theodore Smith, *A Woman Without a History* (New York: Brace & Sons, 1997), 89.

personality, X didn't deny it; she simply tilted Kathy backward and kissed her deeply on the mouth.

"At readings when people ask what I'm working on, I never say writing or art," she wrote in a journal page later used in the exhibit. "Instead I tell them I'm doing a sex show! And they say wonderful, great."*

Mr. Smith, instead, writes of X's time at Fun City as if it were some kind of scandal, despite the fact that it is intricately documented in *The Human Subject*. X felt no shame or regret over her time there, a place where everyone had a fake name, where everyone well understood the human desire for self-mythology and how all desire costumes itself in one way or another. To this end, X and Kathy took pleasure in devising their own scenes.

* X, journal entry, August 2, 1973, box 1973, item 18, TXA.

Image: "Deena Stray" (X)

"In one of their routines," Chris Kraus writes in Acker's biography, "Acker played a patient confessing her sexual Santa Claus fantasies to her aroused psychoanalyst [played by X]. They worked Acker's shaved head into the act: she's become Joan of Arc, she's completely delusional."* After Kathy quit ("I'm sick of fucking and not knowing who I am," she explained), X's performances became even more bizarre and much less popular. In one she entered the stage as an elderly woman—a gray wig, cane, and gaudy muumuu. Then through a series of rip-away costume changes she aged in reverse—a stately older woman, an exhausted mother, a new mother, a bride, a teen, a preteen, a girl—until she was writhing on the ground as an infant, naked and seemingly orgasming. Indeed, X explored odd corners of the psyche in this work, but shame was never her concern.

* Chris Kraus, *After Kathy Acker* (Cambridge, MA: Semiotext(e), 2002), 177.

CONNIE, AGAIN

A t first I had rules for researching X's life and I followed them.
The first rule was that I would read only the part of the
archive that X had left "in order," nothing else. The second rule
was that once I discovered her birthplace, I had to stop. The third rule was
that if I was unable to follow the second rule, then I could only research
the years before the work on *The Human Subject* began in 1971. The fourth
was that I was to write only one essay dispelling Theodore Smith's many
errors, and that was it. I have broken every rule I ever set for myself. And
now I am busy, so busy, day and night, ruining my life.

One night, thinking nothing of it, I brought out all the disordered materials X had kept in milk and wine crates in the attic; soon enough the
"orderly" portion of her archive had become so mingled with the rest that
I no longer knew which items belonged where.

"Putting everything in order" was a task X sometimes brought up
in a grave mood, on the darker edge of dusk, often after enduring some
perceived affront to her work—after being passed over for an award, or
feeling snubbed by an invitation lost or never sent, or after reading a
bad or even a tepid review she might later claim to have never seen. No

one's opinion mattered to her, yet everyone's opinion mattered to her. She desperately wanted recognition, yet she was also unable to respect any laurels given—she'd been misunderstood; viewed in bad faith; defaced by a critic's ignorance, errors, or lazy standards. Her only retaliation would be an impeccable archive, the one thing she could totally control—*It's time I put everything in order, isn't it?* She always stated it as a question, but she was never asking a question, as she never asked anyone, not even herself, what to do.

It is unsurprising that I was first interested—to the exclusion of nearly everything else in those papers—in the letters to and from the old lovers, significant and less so, the charcoal portraits, the photographs, and the diary entries detailing every fluctuation of those courtships. I pored over them so carefully that I couldn't even glance at the mirror as I brushed my teeth those nights, so gross the trespass. I justified my behavior by believing that a woman is the most interesting version of herself when she's enraptured, but that's not true. Romance is a closed circuit. Nothing makes a person less comprehensible to others than being in love.

Satisfied and unsatisfied, I moved on to the things pertinent to her work and its impact—manuscript pages, notebooks, blueprints, the ephemera from the Bowie years, set photographs from *The Coma Game*. X claimed to despise the awe surrounding her more popular works—a frequent complaint: *Produce a few songs with a pop star and you'll never hear the end of it*—yet the irony is that if anyone had ever known of her Southern Territory origins, her proximity to celebrity would have ceased to matter.

Acclaimed for the *wrong things*—her constant and unsolvable complaint.

At the opening for her 1994 retrospective at the Museum of Modern Art, she was so irritated by the congratulations—*You are attending my funeral. Why would you congratulate me for that?*—that she made us leave early. Her lack of gratitude embarrassed me. So many people at the museum had worked long hours on the installation and reception, which were both elegant and respectful, but I knew better than to mention it. *Imbeciles, all of them,* I muttered in agreement as a cab carried us away.

I often wondered how her past girlfriends and wives had dealt with this recurrent mood of hers, if any of them had developed a viable strategy for calming her down or redirecting her focus. In my most desperate moments I imagined looking one of them up, maybe even calling her first wife to ask for advice on this matter, but of course I never did. Once this research was under way, I found it difficult to even arrange for any of the interviews with anyone she'd been involved with, fearful that traces of X might still be apparent in their bodies—the way they smoked, certain turns of phrase, a gesture, a piece of jewelry, a scar.

The person I most wanted to speak with—Connie Converse—had been dead for some time; all she'd left behind were her plangent songs that tell me so little and her unfinished memoirs that reveal little more. It seems that she and X were always straining toward and away from each other in uncertainty—never sure if the other was the cure for her pain or the cause of it.

On December 30, 1973, X returned to 23 Grove Street after a long shift at Fun City to find every gift she'd ever given Connie piled on the coffee table—several books, records, a scarf, an unused daybook, a figurine of a donkey, a chunk of pink crystal, a pocketknife. Connie's keys to the apartment were in the kitchen, in a glass of water. She'd left no note.

I found several of X's ripped-out journal pages from this time in a shoebox duct-taped shut. At first she wonders if Connie's sudden departure is a ploy, that she'd come back soon, but after a few weeks the entries become more frantic. She starts calling all the hospitals and morgues in the area. She takes a string of consecutive shifts at Fun City, where her routines become increasingly absurd, with animal costumes and pies to the face. Her journals veer deeper into nonsense—conversations with herself, odes to Connie, screeds of self-evisceration. Oleg Hall remembered X being "in a foul mood for a while that year,"* though he didn't attribute it to Connie's departure, an event he must have welcomed. X's diaries are maddening conversations with herself, or rather with "Bee":

---

* Oleg Hall, interview with the author, July 4, 2003, tape 9.18–22, CML audio collection, TXA.

I said to Bee—All pain enrages. Why am I not in contact with my anger? What do I feel? And Bee said—Depression. But that means I am "depressing" another emotion. Despair, then. But despair is a conclusion drawn from a history of pain (it's happening again). And there's no conclusion. I conclude nothing.

So I said—Everyone who has had a bad childhood is angry. I must have felt angry at first (early). Then I "did" something with it. Turned it into—what? (rebellion) Self-hatred > Fear (of my own anger, of the retaliation of others). Despair. To be logical about pain, then to dissociate.

Bee said: "I can't think of anything more warping to one's personality than liking one's parents." But they have nothing to do with it.

Then Bee says I talk about depression like someone who has never been psychoanalyzed. I told her of course I haven't been psychoanalyzed, but that she hasn't been psychoanalyzed either.

Bee: Yeah, but I don't talk like it.*

By October of 1974, almost a year after Connie left, X's depression had transformed into anger: "Could I write to C in several weeks: *I'm outraged, I'm hurt, I'm angry. I won't let you do this to me.?*" she wrote in her diary, adding, "But there's nowhere to send the letter!"†

A letter from Connie arrived a few days later; she explained her new life with uncharacteristic ease and good humor: "This is the loveliest place you can imagine—everything about it: OK and just as I'd hoped (except the name: Morningside Heights, who are they kidding—however I am getting used to that). Also several (many) years of steady drinking hasn't made me calm about cockroaches I notice . . . Never mind everything else is fine."‡

The day after this letter arrived, as X was still drafting her reply, the phone rang. It was—speaking as if no time had passed—Connie. She was

---

* X, diary entry, January 8, 1974, box 45, items 7–8, TXA.

† X, diary entry, October 9, 1974, box 45, item 16, TXA.

‡ Connie Converse to X, October 18, 1974, folder 35, item 9, TXA.

going to a concert that night with some friends and there was an extra ticket. X took down the address of the venue. The scribbling seems to indicate an unsteady hand.

It is possible that the two never spoke of Connie's year of absence; if they did speak of it, that conversation goes unmentioned in her papers. Connie, however, frankly describes her departure from 23 Grove in her incomplete memoir. Feeling ignored by Bee, she impulsively moved into a week-to-week studio uptown—pest-infested, but affordable. She had a job at a launderette on West Sixty-Fifth Street, but when she came into work in early March of 1974 with pink eye, her boss sent her to a nearby clinic.

I'd been considering offing myself, Connie quipped during the exam, *but I plan to keep using both my eyes until then.*

The doctor sent her down the hall to a psychiatrist who diagnosed Connie as manic-depressive and put her on lithium.

Perhaps if I'd thought twice I wouldn't have taken those pills, she wrote, *but it wasn't a very thinking time.*

On lithium, Connie no longer despised the downtown music scene; she started going to concerts again, and to some auditions with booking agents, now unfazed by the rejection. That autumn an agent booked her for an opening gig when one of his clients was abruptly sent to rehab. The main act that night was Tom Waits, on his first tour of the East Coast from his home in the Western Territory.

Waits was immediately charmed by Connie, describing her to a friend as "a sort of minotaur . . . part librarian, part truck driver. She sings like a grandmother telling a dirty joke."* New York was the last stop on Waits's tour, and he'd planned to stay awhile. He invited Connie to come out to a few concerts that week, and though it had been nearly ten months since they'd spoken, Connie called X as casually as anyone calling anyone— would she like to come along?

A full dramatization of those events is unnecessary—so of course Mr.

---

* D. S. Paris, "Interview with Tom Waits on Acid in a New York Loft," *Rolling Stone*, August 28, 1979.

Smith's book drones on about it for dozens of pages—but this was the fortuitous night that Waits first met X, or rather "Bee Converse."* In a burst of optimism, Connie told Waits that Bee was "a music producer," though the only production she'd ever really done was press a button on a tape deck in a closet lined with blankets.

Over the next few weeks, Waits practiced piano at Grove Street so often that X gave him a key. In a diary, X wrote that she knew she could respect him because unlike so many other musicians, he understood that "the importance of succeeding in life is a noose. It's nothing but a noose."† The admiration was mutual; Waits soon invited her to Electric Lady Studios, where he'd been gifted some time that winter. ("She was like a broken toy that works better than before it was broken,"‡ Waits told Mr. Smith.) Of course, no one at Electric Lady had ever heard of any "Bee Converse," but there was no need to ask for her qualifications or which records she'd worked on. Arriving with Waits was credential enough.

One of the many mysteries about X that I was unable to solve was how she learned to use a sound board or any other equipment prior to that day at Electric Lady. It is true that in the years we lived together X never needed to consult an instruction manual, and seemed to know innately how to operate any machine—the VCR, the security system, the dishwasher. After buying an old truck, she spent a half hour speed-reading an auto mechanics textbook, and from then on she took care of all the truck's maintenance. The few times I ever complimented or even commented upon the speed with which X could absorb a new skill, she insisted—not out of humility, but in frustration—that there was *nothing* to it. Other people, it seemed to her, were simply too indolent to teach themselves anything, and though it seemed this accusation included me—as I never repaired the car or installed heavy machinery or even attempted to operate our clock radio—I chose not to press her on this point.

It is possible that X's unorthodox approach to music production was simply an invention of necessity, something to distract from the fact that

* Theodore Smith, *A Woman Without a History* (New York: Brace & Sons, 1997), 203–57.

† X, diary entry, November 20, 1974, box 45, item 9, TXA.

‡ Theodore Smith, *A Woman Without a History* (New York: Brace & Sons, 1997), 19.

she was still learning how use the equipment. She asked Waits to sing a certain line of a song over and over, giving him mercurial notes after each attempt—*This time you're an old shrub* or *Make it sound like a slice of pie*—as she hunched over the controls.

"When she likes something, she goes crazy—she'll knock over your keyboards and mics because she's so affected by it. But as soon as she hears a sound that she doesn't like, she completely shuts down—it's impossible for her to listen to bad music," Waits told *Rolling Stone* in 1979. "She's a remarkable collaborator, a butch goddess and a trapeze artist, all of that. She can fix the truck. Expert on the African violet and all that . . . That's who you wanna go in the woods with, right?"*

At the time of the Waits session, four years after Jimi Hendrix's death, many at Electric Lady felt Hendrix's emanation hanging around. Several were convinced that Hendrix's ghost was responsible for blessings and curses, but no one was sure if Bee was the former or the latter. Word spread quickly about this odd new talent, but when anyone attempted to book her, she was nowhere to be found. Though the studio manager at Electric Lady, Eddie Kramer, had a phone number for Bee Converse, there was usually no answer, and when there was an answer it was someone named Dorothy Eagle, who called herself "Bee's manager" and always declined the work, explaining that Bee was too busy, didn't want to work with that person or band, or simply wasn't in the mood.

"Rumor and hearsay are far more effective tools for advancing a nascent reputation than plastering one's unwanted name all over the place," X wrote in a journal years later.†

By the spring of 1975—only a few months after their reconciliation—Connie again ceased all contact with X, stopped visiting the Grove Street apartment, stopped calling, stopped answering the phone. Her memoirs don't explain why, but they do give a direct account of the night it happened: "It occurred to me, all at once that evening of the snowstorm,

---

* Michelle Dean, "What Happened to Bee Converse?," *Rolling Stone*, April 10, 1979.

† X, journal entry, April 22, 1979, box 1979, journal 12B, TXA.

when she didn't hold open a door for someone behind her at the Jeweled Thief, that I did not like Bee Converse at all, not even a little. I did not like her moods, her unyielding selfishness. I never saw her again."*

After a few weeks of not hearing from Connie, X went uptown to her apartment—sure that something must be wrong with her telephone or the mail. She buzzed number 5. No answer. She held down the buzzer. Still nothing, so she shouted up at Connie's window, then, as someone was coming out of the building, she caught the door and bounded up the stairs to bang on Connie's door until the super found her and kicked her out.

X's journals from this time worry over the lack of continuity in her life. It seemed the people she'd loved the most were either dead or dead to her. (Tellingly, she makes no mention of Oleg Hall.) She kept losing track of the people she loved, and losing track of herself along with them. She no longer thought of herself as a unified person, but rather as several people, all of them disappointing and inert. She turned to alcohol, opiates, and uppers. She picked up women at bars or let herself be picked up by men—a different name, history, and voice each time—but that, too, bored her. For pages upon pages, she seems to regress into a heartbroken teenager, all of her entries chaotic and self-scrutinizing:

> I'm writing now because I just shot a little cocaine (it seems like 90% of the times I write in here I'm high or else it's a girl). But the new development I've been going through lately amounts to this (is it good or bad that it takes so much longer to write than think—it's bad?)—amounts to this: the incredibly excruciating self doubts I get to that point that I find absolutely every manifestation of my "self"—from the way I dress to the way I walk, sing, write, etc., profoundly embarrassing to the point that I want to completely withdraw. The feeling is intensified by every drug I know—grass, speed, coke, psychedelics (though with psychedelics it may only happen for very short periods—I can hardly remember it being many weeks since I've really used any)—except heroin, which completely destroys the possibility of experiencing feeling.†

* Connie Converse, memoir, undated pages, folder 5, CML papers, TXA.

† X, journal entry, June 3, 1975, box 445, item 82, TXA.

I can hardly recognize my wife in these and other passages, as I had never seen her rendered so molten and desperate. During our marriage I often worried that if I ever left her, she would have weathered it just fine, that perhaps I had never changed or challenged her well enough to be intractable. This is not to say she did not love me—only that we loved each other at different rates, with different needs. I made X's life a little easier, and we had a way of softening each other, but I do not fool myself—I was not irreplaceable. It seems that Connie was.

EUROPE

I n November 1975, X apparently survived an attempted kidnapping.
According to her diaries, she was walking down an alleyway
around Forty-Fourth Street when a man tried to throw her into the
back of a van. After a struggle she escaped and sprinted the twenty blocks
to Oleg's building.

"They know where I am," she told him as he cleaned and dressed her
wounds.

"She was horribly worried, all bruised and bleeding," Oleg remembered. "But the worst was her paranoia—it was so unlike her. She kept
asking me, 'How did they do it? How did they find me?' And of course I
knew it was just a random attack. No one was *after* her."*

I never explained to Oleg that since X had escaped the Southern Territory, she had good reason to believe that agents from the ST may have
been following her. If I had, perhaps he would have claimed to know
about that already, though this anecdote reveals his ignorance.

She stayed at Oleg's house for several weeks after the incident, then
hired a private investigator to follow her around the city in search of
anyone else who might be tailing her, and though the PI found no tail,
her nerves were not calmed. She began taking all the producing gigs she'd

---

* Oleg Hall, interview with the author, June 18, 2003, tape 9.19, CML audio collection, TXA.

been turning down and spent as much time in public as she could, intent on never being alone. At a poetry reading one night she ran into Kathy Acker and, according to a letter Kathy wrote around this time, wouldn't leave her alone for weeks. "That chick from Fun City has latched on. Something wrong, something altogether truly fucked."*

In January of 1976, David Bowie invited X to West Berlin to work on a new album. X had previously insisted she had no interest in working in pop, nor did she care for the collaborative environment Bowie described—as two other producers, Tony Visconti and Brianna Eno, were already working in Berlin with him—but leaving the country held strong appeal. Connie was still not returning X's phone calls or letters, and her nerves were wrecked from fearing that an ST agent might spring up at any moment.

Shortly after X, as Bee Converse, arrived in Berlin that March, Bowie played the demos they'd completed so far. According to her journals, she listened in silence, "feeling obdurate and pissed."† With each song, Bowie appeared to grow more anxious. Once he was done he asked her what she thought of the tracks.

After a long exhale she replied, "I would have never agreed to work with you if I'd known what a happy person you are."

But what did she think of the songs? he asked.

"If you can't hear what's wrong with them," she said. "I can't help you."‡

She told Eno that night she wasn't cut out for this kind of work, that she knew about folk and rock and jazz, but pop music was simply too confident, that it was "the sound of only thinking one thought at a time." Eno was the one who convinced X to stay, though for the first few days she only watched as everyone worked, sometimes sitting silent for hours before yelling something incongruent or banging out a sequence on the piano like an angry child. Visconti was especially wary of the supposed brilliance of Bee Converse, but Bowie was charmed by her antipathy.

* Kathy Acker, diary entry, December 1975, box 4, folder 14, MSS. 434, Fales Archive, New York University.

† X, journal entry, undated 1976, box 446, item 2, TXA.

‡ Box 50, item 11, Bowie collection, TXA.

Eventually, her outbursts began getting worked into the songs. As Bowie was recording vocals on "Breaking Glass," X shouted, *You're such a weird person. But you got problems. I'll never love you.* Bowie added these lines immediately to the song, incongruent as they are.

Of the many rumors about Bee Converse and how she worked, the most impressive was that she wrote songs out of thin air, that when she was struck with a song she only needed to sit at the piano and it would arrive in full. In truth, X had a backlog of songs she'd been writing and memorizing for years, some of them appearing in her journals as far back as the late sixties. "Be My Wife" was the only song she contributed to *Low*, the first album from Bowie's Berlin era. The lyrics are suited for a Connie Converse song—lonely and aimless—but the melody is pure pop. It was also nearly a perfect inverse of a track she wrote for Tom Waits a few months prior, "Better Off Without a Wife." Bowie occasionally said "Be My Wife" was his favorite song on the album, but unlike most of his other singles, it never entered the U.K. or U.S. charts.

Over the summer in Berlin, Bee tended to vanish for weeks at a time, and though her irregularity was an annoyance, each time she returned from wherever it was she went, she'd present a full, new song to them, then manage its recording so quickly that no one could complain she wasn't pulling her weight. One of the better-known songs from that era was "If They Don't Come Tomorrow," later shortened to "Tomorrow."

X first wrote those lyrics in one of the darkest parts of her past—as she was hitchhiking through the Western Territory—but Eno's minimalist synths and Bowie's voice transformed the song into something sparkling and eternally present. In an interview with Max Porter in 1988, Bowie described the experience:

PORTER: You actually worked on and recorded the song "Tomorrow" with Bee Converse. Bee worked with you on that.

DAVID BOWIE: She did. It came out of a conversation that we had about appearances and personas . . . about being ashamed of something you want.

PORTER: Was that exciting for you to work with Converse?

BOWIE: Oh hell! She was one of the major influences on my musical life. I just thought she was the very best of what can be done with rock and roll. And I felt much akin with her. She would rifle the avant-garde and look for ideas that were so on the outside, on the periphery of what was considered mainstream. Then she would apply them in a practical manner to something that was considered populist and make it work . . .

PORTER: Were you surprised that Bee Converse was all an act?

BOWIE: An act? I wouldn't call it an act.

PORTER: That she was one of X's personas.

BOWIE: It just seemed so perfect within the time, that that really represented what the seventies was all about. There was such a feeling . . . Coming out of the fifties and sixties—there was a real opening up of attitudes in the sixties—and then in the seventies everything became—it was the pluralistic seventies, you know? There were so many sides to a story in the seventies . . . Nothing was right. The idea of absolutes was kind of starting to disappear.*

When *Low* was released in January of 1977, the journalists who assembled for the press junket were surprised to learn that Bee Converse—the reclusive newcomer to the industry—had agreed to give interviews. That Bee Converse had reportedly destroyed several notebooks and demos belonging to the beloved young musician Susan Lorde Shaw alienated several journalists who then refused to cover her projects. The few journalists who tried to get interviews, however, rarely made it far.

Footage from that stark hotel conference room in Berlin shows X (as Bee) in a staunchly uncooperative mood. (She seems also to be high.) When an earnest Australian radio journalist asked her if it been hard to leave behind all the excitement in New York to focus solely on Bowie's work, she rolled her eyes. "They say that I have no hits and that I'm difficult to work with," she said. "And they say that like it's a bad thing." The journalist pressed further, as if trying to sell her on her own niche appeal, and the way she seemed to emerge, fully formed, from nowhere:

* Max Porter, "Interview with David Bowie," *Pop Today*, BBC2, December 3, 1988.

BEE: It's a lie. There were five of me going out just like the Drifters in the old days.

INTERVIEWER: You think there are?

BEE: I know there are. Two of them are up here. We've been mutating. Genetic damage.

INTERVIEWER: Do you like producing?

BEE: No.

INTERVIEWER: Why do you do it?

BEE: Because I don't like it.

INTERVIEWER: You like doing things you don't like?

BEE: Yeah. That's a paradox, isn't it?

INTERVIEWER: It sure is.

BEE: I know.

INTERVIEWER: You're just a bundle of paradoxes.

BEE: Well, when I'm faced with paradox I become paradoxical.*

A few weeks after this 1977 interview, X left Berlin for the last time, leaving behind nothing but lyrics and a demo of what became one of Bowie's best-known singles, "Heroes." Though that song has always been understood as an anthem against the Berlin Wall, seen in the light of X's escape and exile from the South, it tells a different, though parallel story—an oblique retelling of the Revelation Rifle Affair. X was fascinated by the Berlin Wall, which could be seen from Hansa Tonstudio, where the entire Berlin Trilogy was recorded. Eno remembers watching her stand in the street, just staring at it, not saying anything, not moving for what seemed like hours.

A decade later, in 1987, David Bowie's performance of "Heroes" at the Platz der Republic Festival was so powerful—the stage was built against the wall itself and a large crowd of East Germans gathered on the other side to listen—that West Berlin government officials later credited Bowie with increasing the pressure to dismantle the divide. Whenever X was asked about this or any of the other songs she wrote for Bowie, she usu-

---

* Patrick Y. Cottrell, "Interview with Bee Converse," Melbourne Music International, January 5, 1977.

ally pretended she'd done no such thing, or that she'd never heard of him, or that she'd never liked pop music anyway.

X had been in Europe for at least a month when Connie Converse appeared at Oleg Hall's building, looking for her friend.

"Oh it was truly pathetic—she had this dreadful pink woolen suit, which must have been her tragic idea of elegance. And fake pearls and white gloves and lipstick that was never straight. You could have just cried looking at her if it wasn't so funny. The doorman called up and said he had a 'Mrs. Converse' there in the lobby and I thought, Oh dear, here we go. Well—I wasn't letting her up of course, so I suggested we take a walk toward the river—a good thing we didn't get there or she probably would have jumped in! . . . Of course she wanted to know where Dorothy was. So I said, 'If Dorothy didn't tell you where she was going, my dear, don't you think there might be a reason for that?' And immediately Connie was crying like a little girl, sitting on a street curb just . . . abject! Like her world was over."*

Oleg felt Connie was being maudlin and childish, but the world only exists insofar as it exists between people. Without those worlds there is no world, and whatever else Connie may have known or not known, she felt certain (and was correct) that her life with Bee, with X, was over. They would never see each other again.

---

* Oleg Hall, interview with the author, July 4, 2003, tape 9.18–22, CML audio collection, TXA.

GIOIA

———

The first weekend of January 1992, X and I flew to Rome—she was accepting an award from an arts organization that has since dissolved—and I suggested we extend the trip by taking the train up to Milan, maybe over to Venice or Florence. I'd never been to Italy before, and three days in Rome did not seem to be an adequate introduction, but X insisted it was out of the question, especially Milan, a horrid city, nothing there of any note. *Terrible food, terrible people.* As I wasn't feeling up to the task of paying for her anger, I didn't press her to explain why she felt this way. All through our marriage I tended to respect the walls she built, without warning, around certain things. By the time of that trip, four years or so into our life together, I had gathered that X had studied and spoken Italian in her twenties, but I didn't know why she'd chosen that language in particular, or whether she was fluent. There were several photographs in *The Human Subject* exhibition that were simply dated *Italy, 1976,* and from this I'd inferred that she must have traveled to Italy while she'd been working in Berlin, but whenever I tried to nudge her toward the topic, she left out all the specifics. Yes, she spent time in Italy. No, she would not tell me why.

In the years before X died, when we mostly lived upstate in the cabin and kept to ourselves, she and I sometimes made a forty-minute drive to an Italian grocery store because they carried a specific, imported brand of canned tomatoes and handmade pastas. Every time we went there I noticed the same old man sitting on a wooden bench in the parking lot, smoking a pipe as he watched people enter and exit the store. Occasionally, someone tried to speak to him, but he always replied in Italian, shrugging, smiling. Once, as I was putting our groceries in the truck, I looked up to see X sitting beside the old man, casually talking to him. His face had softened into shock—and he may have been crying, though I was too far away to tell—and as X walked away from him he called out to her, his voice pained and operatic. She waved at him once, slid into the driver's seat, and pulled away. I stared at her as we drove home, hoping to receive (but not expecting, never expecting) a word of explanation. She gave none.

In the disorganized part of X's archives, I found a thin yellow notebook full of her handwriting in Italian—odd notes, names, dates, and a few addresses in Milan.* With it was a stack of about two hundred typed pages, some kind of dialogue between two people identified only as "M.R." and "C.L.," and a photograph of a woman I thought might be X in disguise.

I immediately booked a flight and at the airport the next day I bought an English-Italian dictionary, to try to make crude translations from the notebook—most of it details about places she'd been, people she'd met. When I tried to translate anything from the dialogue, however, I struggled to make any sense; few of those words had been deemed useful for the common traveler.

It was a beautiful spring day when I checked into the hotel, dazed by the travel but determined to get to work. I felt the deranged clarity and single-mindedness that jet lag will sometimes bring about, a feeling I'd come to know quite well while traveling with X, as she refused to believe that jet lag was a real thing. *It's the mock suffering performed by those fortunate enough to travel*, she always said, so no matter how exhausted I felt after a flight, I soldiered on.

* X, notebook, box 4.30, item 9, TXA.

Once I theorized aloud that X's circadian rhythms might have been abnormal, that they might have worked differently from those of the average person, but she asked me to explain how, precisely, circadian rhythms "worked" in this supposedly "average person." What did I know definitively about such rhythms, and could I cite any reputable studies, and was my understanding of this so-called biological process up-to-date? Of course, I had no such information at hand and had to cede the discussion to her; that is, I had to stop talking.

This happened not infrequently—this realization of how little I actually knew and how much I repeated or relied upon information about things of which I had no direct understanding. Though such probing of someone's ignorance may seem hostile, even controlling, I did not experience it as such. Instead, it had the result of deepening my understanding of everything, of relying less upon shorthand, and though I did eventually read extensively about circadian rhythms, there were not, at that time, enough credible studies on jet lag to convince X of its existence.

However, without X around to object, I can say with anecdotal confidence that I was wildly jet-lagged as I ventured out into Milan that evening alone. I went to the first address listed in the notebook, rang the apartment number indicated, and asked for a name on the page: Carla. The person on the other side of the intercom could not understand my rudimentary Italian, so he came outside, a potbellied man wearing an apron.

Carla, I said. *Is Carla here?*

Carla who? he asked.

I didn't know. There was no last name in the notebook, just CARLA, in large block letters. I shrugged, and he laughed and invited me in to have dinner with his family.

Was I an American, he asked. I said I was, and I think he said my Italian was very bad, and I said yes, that I was sorry for that. Then he seemed to ask a complicated question about the situation back in my home country. It was early May of 2000 when I arrived in Milan, four years since the wall had been dismantled and four years after X's death; every newspaper and magazine had been filled with nothing but news from the FST, our flawed attempts at reunification, and the occasional bombings or shoot-ings carried out by militant re-secessionist groups. Part of the appeal of traveling at that time had been in getting away from that madness, being ignorant of the bad news for at least a week.

Of course, I was unable to say anything complex about this matter— *molto brutto, molto triste*—so I apologized again for my ignorance and declined the potbellied man's offer of dinner, something I now realize was foolish, as it is not often that one lands in a foreign country, arrives at a stranger's door, and is invited in to dine with his family. I held up the yellow notebook as an explanation of why I could not stay. *So much work to do*, I said, as if that would explain anything.

As I was trying to locate the next address in the notebook—walking in circles in search of some tiny street—I became unbearably hungry and walked into the first trattoria I found. It was still early for dinner; only one couple was inside—a man and a woman, both very short and old, dressed in tweed suits that seemed to match, each gracefully eating their spaghetti with fork and spoon. The sight of this pair gave me a feeling I often had when traveling abroad—a feeling that our country had gotten so much wrong, almost everything, all of it, wrong, and perhaps I had, too, that I was entrenched in my wrongness, that I had somehow committed myself to it and no longer knew the way out.

I ordered spaghetti, too, and wine, and I ate with such relief and relish that the waiter watched me as if we were sharing a great and mutual victory. Once I was done he brought me an amaro and a dessert in a small crystal dish, and I ate the dessert, too, then ordered another amaro—it was the best and most bitter one I'd ever had. Then I put down my lire and left. As the waiter opened the door for me, I felt that he could see it in my face—I was chasing a ghost. I went immediately to the hotel, though it was still quite early—eight, perhaps—and fell asleep.

I woke the next day wearing yesterday's clothes. A little light from the window—purple and dim. My watch read four. Four in the morning, yet I was wide awake. I took a shower and took my time taking it, early as it was, but as I was getting dressed and looking out the window, I realized it was late afternoon, that a rainstorm had just ended. Sun splintered through the clouds as the people below closed their umbrellas. A storm had passed and the city was restored. I'd slept for twenty hours.

As I stood there at the window, holding my wet hair in a towel, I felt—as I often do—that X was watching me, disappointed by how pathetically I was living in her absence, so I dressed quickly and tried to assure myself of my purpose. I left the hotel as if I knew exactly where I was going and exactly what I was doing, though I knew neither.

If it ever occurred to me how unlikely it was for a person to hold the same city address for over two decades, this did not hinder my search. The next address in the notebook was for someone name Gioia, and this time I found the building on a short side street that I'd failed to find the previous day. There was only one bell beside the huge wooden door, and a moment after I rang, a woman appeared. I couldn't determine her age— she could have been, like I was at the time, in her forties, but she could have been much younger or much older. I simply couldn't tell.

I told her I was looking for someone named Gioia, and when she told me she was Gioia I realized how shallowly laid my plans had been. I held up the notebook and said, *This belonged to my wife.* She smiled as if she understood, then invited me in.

Upon entering the building, I realized it wasn't divided into apartments as I had imagined, but was one whole mansion, something passed down in a family, I assumed, over generations. The ceilings were high, and the walls were made of pale stone with hardwood wainscoting. Gioia explained she'd lived here all her life, first with her parents and siblings, but now alone. (There was a certain wavering in her voice that suggested I should not ask about her absent family.) She showed me to a sitting room. All the furniture seemed to be heirlooms—well kept and meaningful, softened by lifetimes.

Now, Gioia said as we sat across from each other, *what is it that I can do for you?*

I explained, more or less, my situation, my wife, the other biography, and my intention to correct its failures; I had written this explanation out in Italian on a few notecards, but after I had recited it in what I thought was comprehensible Italian, Gioia asked, in a precise British accent, if we might switch to English.

You didn't understand any of that?

I do appreciate your trying, but, no—your pronunciation is a little . . . off.

The prospect of having to repeat myself felt all at once sobering and sad; Gioia must have noticed the change in my expression because she bounced from her seat and went to a sideboard, where she mixed us two drinks, handing me one without asking. She possessed a kind of ageless nonchalance, one I felt was not uncommon among Italian women, as if time itself could not touch her, as if the years may pass if they so choose, but those passing years would have no ill effect upon her. After all, what was time but a series of afternoons, evenings, seasons—something to sprawl over and enjoy, something to possess?

As Gioia twisted a long necklace of small black beads around her fingers, she pressed me with questions, as if she were the one who needed something from me, as if she'd summoned me here. She asked me—with an odd urgency—about my thoughts on traveling, psychology, and sexuality; my greatest fears; the sway of grief. By the time I'd finished the first drink, she was already handing me another. I exhaled, we smiled at each other, and I re-explained, in English this time, that my wife had died several years ago and there had been a biography of her that had gotten important things wrong, and in the course of trying to correct the main errors of that book my journalistic tendencies had taken over (this was the way I sometimes explained it to myself) and now I was intent on understanding the parts of her that I had not known when she was still alive.

Gioia said she was sorry for my loss, then immediately shook her head—she'd always hated that phrase. Weren't the English euphemisms for death the worst of all?

The English language probably thinks it's going to live forever, she said, and for some reason this made both of us laugh for a while, before Gioia took a cigarette from a metal case, lit it, and told me that the whole endeavor sounded quite foolish, looking for explanations for a dead woman, but it was a foolishness for which she had much sympathy.

Tell me, she said, *who was this wife of yours?*

She found my explanation ridiculous—*A woman named X! Only an American would think escaping your own name was possible*—but when I explained that my wife had been born in the Southern Territory, and was initially forced to use and abandon names as a matter of self-protection, Gioia's mood shifted. She apologized, as if her own country's history with fascism had stepped quietly into the room. I told her there was no need to apologize. I had to agree, after all, that a person naming herself X was, to be sure, a little absurd.

Gioia asked if she could see the yellow notebook, that it might help her remember who my wife had been all those years ago. She read through it quietly, saying a few words aloud, sometimes translating them, sometimes leaving them there as they were. Then, all at once, her face burst into recognition.

Martina! Ah! Martina, Martina Riggio. Of course I remember. How could I forget?

I was surprised to hear that name here. X had once operated a small publishing firm in New York under the name Martina Riggio, but I hadn't expected her to have used that name or persona in Italy itself, where passing for Italian would have been riskier.

"Please," I asked Gioia as I started the recorder, "can you start from the first time you met her? When was that, and how?"*

"From Carla," she said, "Carla *Lonzi*," she clarified.

Lonzi, a close friend of Gioia's, had been an art critic in the 1960s until she gave up criticism to focus on activism and running a feminist press and collective in Milan. Feeling that Italy was lagging somewhat behind the rest of Europe with regard to women's rights, and light-years behind America's Northern Territory, Lonzi devoted herself to writing essays and petitioning her government for equal rights.

"You can't imagine how wild Carla was about Martina," Gioia continued, "though she always tried to play it cool. I don't remember where they met—in fact, I think they kept it secret on purpose, their meeting. They liked to make people wonder—just like people wondered whether they were a couple or not—and once it was obvious they were a couple, there was the issue of Martina disappearing all the time, and even though Carla pretended not to care, claiming that she and Martina were so *unconven-*

* Gioia Realto, interview with the author, May 4, 2000. Tape 32.1–3, CML audio collection, TXA. All quotes from Gioia Realto in the following paragraphs are from this interview.

tional, I knew she was upset. Carla could never lie to me—maybe to other people, but not to me."

Gioia's eyes dimmed for a moment, and she lit a second cigarette with the first, then smiled as she confessed that she didn't really care for Martina, had never trusted her, felt she was using Carla, only she couldn't tell exactly how or why.

"I apologize," Gioia said, but I told her not to be sorry, that it was a long time ago, that I didn't know X until much later, and I knew as well as anyone how difficult she sometimes was.

"But I *did* believe her at first," Gioia continued. "We all believed her, even though the story was so crazy . . . Ah! What a story, really, soap

Image:"Martina Riggio" (X)

opera stuff . . . She told us she'd been born in Italy, in a village outside
Milan, but that her uncle had kidnapped her when she was two and taken
her to America, raised her as if she were his daughter and told everyone
that her mother had died in childbirth. She didn't know any of this, she
said, until he confessed on his deathbed—which was one of the details I
didn't find so realistic—he confessed on his deathbed to the whole scam,
that her real name was Martina Riggio, that she was Italian, that he was
her uncle, not her father, that he didn't know if her parents were still alive.
All this from a dying man! Or so Martina said. If you ask me, people in
movies and in books sure do say a lot more on their deathbeds than they
do in real life. In real life, dying isn't the time for confession. Dying is a
full-time thing. But . . . you're saying I was right after all? She wasn't born
here? She wasn't kidnapped?"

Yes, I said, Gioia had been right to be suspicious of Martina—of X.

"Because she was born in the Southern Territory?" Gioia asked.

I told her that was true.

"How awful that must have been," Gioia said. "What gave her away, at
least to me—I mean, Carla never doubted her, never—but what seemed
odd to me was how Martina said the exact same sentences in the exact
same way. She always told her story as if it were memorized, verbatim . . .
And don't you think that there are times—say, on a really wonderful
day—that maybe even the worst memories are fine? Then the opposite,
too, a terrible day—your lover leaves you, you can't zip your pants, your
cat runs away—when even the best things in your life seem a bit ugly,
don't they? . . . So it's natural, isn't it? You tell the story of your life differently as it goes along. Otherwise the boredom would kill us . . . Anyway,
Martina—or whoever she was, X—she told everyone she'd been studying
Italian for years in America and pinching pennies—that's the expression
she used, 'pinching pennies'—it was the first time I'd heard it—she'd been
saving up to come to Italy to find her real family. Instead, she found Carla,
and Carla of course didn't believe in family, in paternity . . . I think it was
the first time I'd met her, your wife, I mean—we were sitting in Carla's
apartment in the kitchen and Carla was telling Martina, 'No, you don't
need those people, they'll only disappoint you, it isn't worth it.' And soon
enough Martina had quit looking, just kept saying 'Carla is my family,

Carla is who I was looking for.' She did this sometimes, Carla did, absorbed people, sucked them in."

Gioia was quiet for a few moments, then said, "Actually, I try not to think of Carla so much anymore. It makes me sad, and I don't like to be sad."

It was a clear confession—not wanting to be sad, as we often fail to hide ourselves in secondary languages.

By then we were a little drunk, and suddenly Gioia leapt from her chair and said she wanted to go out dancing, insisting that I come along, though I'd never been the sort of woman who "went out dancing." "Isn't it too early for dancing?" I asked in protest, but Gioia said she knew a place where people danced at all hours, and she had some friends who were probably there right now, their weekly ritual. She turned off my recorder,

Image: Carla Lonzi

then pulled me out of the chair by both hands. It had been so long since someone had held both my hands at once that it gave me a sort of youthful feeling—and why shouldn't I be a woman who goes out dancing?

She told me to leave my things where they were, that we'd come back for them later, that there was plenty of time to talk later, but now it was time to dance. She led me by the hand as we walked through her house, through a dining room and hallways and a kitchen where a woman in a starched uniform was ironing bedsheets. The woman smiled and called out to Gioia, and Gioia greeted her in Italian with great affection, then announced—*We're going out dancing!*

Beautiful dancing girls, the woman replied, throwing her hands up as if dancing girls were her only god. Gioia's driver took us halfway across the city and waited for us outside the warehouse where she and I plunged into a crush of people, and though I had rarely danced in my life, I found myself quite effortlessly, it seemed, dancing. Gioia tried to shout over the music to introduce me to her friends, and it was only then she realized I'd never told her my name and when I was given a chance to say it, I simply did not, an omission excused by the environment—it was too loud for proper introductions anyway. *She's writing about Carla*, Gioia explained, and they raised their eyes and nodded in understanding.

At one point one of Gioia's friends, a delicate young man with long limbs and serious eyes, tried to ask me a complicated question over the music, half in Italian and half in English, about a recent act of terrorism in New York and how he heard all Americans, in all the territories, owned guns now. Even if I had understood exactly what he was asking, I'm afraid I wouldn't have had anything insightful to say. In the course of the country's reintegration, the fact that the entire population of the Southern Territory owned guns had led to rapid loosening of gun control in the North as millions bought them in fear. Though I'd been appalled by this trend, I, too, had bought a rifle—justifying the purchase by the fact that I lived alone and that X's stalkers still lurked around. But before I could answer this boy's question, his favorite song came on and he twirled out to the dance floor.

The night went on as I imagine nights like this usually go. (I had, perhaps, never been involved in such a night of un-occasioned revelry.)

After some hours a few of us packed into the car that had brought Gioia and me there. Back at her place, she made everyone omelets. Someone asked me what I was writing about Carla, but Gioia answered for me, announcing to the room that I was a feminist historian, that I was writing about all the important European feminists who had been overlooked. *She's correcting the record,* Gioia announced, and everyone raised their eyebrows. A woman named Misha offered to bring some footage she had of Carla's lectures, and Gioia asked her to drop it off the next day, that she'd show it to me then. The crowd of friends thinned down to a handful, and I suddenly felt it was time for me to go as well, and as I gathered my things I pulled out one of the manuscript pages from my satchel and waved it at Gioia.

Any interest in translating two hundred pages this week?

She took the page from my hand and read it, her smile fading as she did. She told me to come back tomorrow, to bring the pages, that she'd do her best to decode them.

It's a strange life, isn't it? she called out as I descended the front steps, and I agreed, though of course there was nothing for us to compare it to.

The sun was coming up. Halfway to the hotel I realized I wasn't wearing shoes.

The next day began predictably late, well into the afternoon. I had to buy a pair of sandals from a store in the hotel and sat in the lobby for a while, drinking black coffee and trying to stir the energy to return to Gioia's place. The past two days made little sense to me. I'd never before been absorbed into a group of friends like that while attempting to interview a source, and now that I looked back to it, it seemed a little suspicious. But then again, what did I have to suspect of Gioia? She'd been nothing but kind to me. Maybe this was just how it was in Milan, that no one here had ever met a stranger and everyone was governed by pleasure and immediacy.

A maid answered Gioia's door this time and led me into the same sitting room as before. My abandoned shoes stood at attention beside a chair. A small film projector and screen had been set up in the other corner of the expansive room.

Gioia came in some time later, offering apologies for having to cut yesterday's interview so short and for having me wait for so long today. It was only then I realized that the light was different from when I'd arrived. At least an hour had passed. I'd been staring out the window.

I wasn't expecting to have to think of her, Gioia said, *I just wasn't prepared.*

Martina?

Carla, she corrected. *She's dead, you know . . . It's been a long time, of course, but I still don't like to think of it. It was just so stupid the way she died. But anyway, you didn't come to hear about that. It has nothing to do with Martina.*

There was a little triumph in her tone—*It has nothing to do with Martina*. She must have believed, just as I had believed (though it is a lie), that being proximate to someone when they died gave your place in their life a greater primacy, rather than what it most often was—a random occurrence. I didn't interrupt. I let her continue as I set up the recorder again.

"Where did we leave off . . . with Martina?"*

"She was absorbed into Carla's life from the start," I prompted.

"Ah, right, right. Well. We all thought of ourselves as revolutionaries, you know, Carla and all our friends—some you met the other night, Nico, Giuliana, Misha . . . So I always felt, well, even if this woman—this *Martina*—even if she was lying about the uncle and everything, that might even be okay, since patriarchy is a fiction, too, or that's how I felt then. If she wanted to make up another story to live in, well, sure. I'm sure Carla felt the same way, you know—everything was an experiment in those days. The only thing we really believed in was there could be no hierarchy, and no respect for hierarchy. Ambition was the worst sin—wanting any dominance over someone else. Nothing could be more ugly . . . But there was always something strange about Carla and Martina—they took each

* Gioia Realto, interview with the author, May 5, 2000, tape 32.4–10, CML audio collection, TXA. All quotes from Gioia Realto in the following paragraphs are from this interview.

other so seriously! Everything was life and death between them, every conversation, every idea . . . Martina moved into Carla's place right from the start—the very first day they met . . . and I thought, well, here is this American woman, she fascinates Carla, Carla wants to know all about how things work between men and women in America, but also . . . everything Martina says enrages Carla! Like what I told you yesterday—the penny-pinching. Well. Martina had no shame about how she'd made that money. A sex show—she'd had sex for audiences, for money. Carla was so angry about this—it worsened the problem of men seeing women as objects . . . Martina had been publicly reinforcing this idea that women *perform* for men. Even worse—the apartment . . . There was some homosexual man, I think, who bought Martina an apartment? Carla thought it was another example of men owning women and stealing their emotions . . . But Martina would say, they weren't stolen—that she got this apartment out of it! It just went on and on like this!

"This was 1976 or '77, I think. And many of us had given up on governmental change and believed that experimentation in social relationships was the only way to practice feminism, raising our children in groups, avoiding men entirely, but eventually that fails, too. A suggestion becomes a precept, becomes a rule, a law. We wanted to free women from dominance, but we couldn't dominate them out of being dominated . . . The agenda eats its own tail."

Gioia went quiet, smiling, then not smiling, and for a moment I could see how her life had accumulated upon her body. Then she regained her glamorous indifference, her light grip on the present. She asked to see the manuscript pages, which she read silently for a moment before explaining these were their dialogues, a practice they had of recording and transcribing themselves. Gioia kept reading, fully absorbed, and in that silence I fixed us a pair of drinks as she had the day before—a bitter liqueur in sparkling water. She drank without looking up.

"I'm sorry," she said. "I should be telling you what's here, but I'm really so bad at translation. I tried for a time to translate Carla's work into English, but I found it all so frustrating. I could never get her voice across, and everything came out sounding flat and . . . I don't know—but I'll try."

She sat up in her chair, almost as if she were readying herself for something physical, a piano concert or a backflip. She took a pen and notebook from her shirt pocket and began taking notes. After several minutes of this she read me a little of what she'd brought into English.

"Men must just be 'abandoned to themselves,' Carla says here. 'Not in anger. Not in hatred. Just abandoned. We're not their counterparts, and they are not ours.' Martina agrees with her, sort of repeats what she said in another way. Then Carla says, 'Men create an attraction through their personality that gives an erotic halo even to their decay. Women realize brutally that the fading of their physical freshness awakens . . . a kind of tolerance . . .' or something . . . 'Men use myth, women don't have the resources to create it. Women who have tried to do so endure so much stress . . . that their lives are cut short.'"

Gioia stared at her notes, then back at the original page, frowning.

"No, that's not it. I'm not getting the right feeling across, I think. Do you mind if I keep reading this for a little while? Maybe it will help me remember."

I told her there was no hurry, and she suggested I watch some of the footage of Carla that Misha had brought over. She showed me how to use the projector, apologizing that there was no sound, that Misha could only find the silent reels.

"I don't know if it will be of any help, really, but maybe it will give you a sense of what Carla was like," Gioia said, before rushing back to the pages, facing away from the screen. The room was just dim enough to allow me to see the projection, a collage of flickering and imperfectly shot scenes of Carla Lonzi giving speeches in small bookstores or in front of crowds in plazas, alternately lifting her right hand in a fist or raising a cigarette to her gently serious face, her long hair parted in the center and pulled into a low ponytail. Though the image often trembled and fell out of focus, I didn't see X in any of the scenes, though Gioia was in most of them, always watching Carla with respectful intensity. After several minutes of these public events and protests, the reel seemed to reach an end, but then footage of a party began. In fact, this party had occurred here, in Gioia's living room, and glancing around, I realized that every piece of furniture and framed painting was exactly as it had been all those years ago.

The camera pans around the room—there's a woman with a feather boa, a man in a long wig, everyone smoking, chiming their glasses together, laughing, kissing—then there is Carla, in black leather pants and a crisp white shirt, and there is X looking different from how I ever knew her—her face softer, eyes wider, her hair cut short and dyed dark. She is almost unrecognizably happy as she clutches Carla's arm. Full champagne coupes rise into the frame, a toast, and Carla turns to the room to say something, raising her glass, too, and nodding to everyone before she leans down to kiss this woman, this softer, undone version of my wife.

The tape ended there like a shove. I turned off the projector and sat still.

After some time, Gioia shouted from her puddle of lamplight in the otherwise dark room. With great agitation, she summarized a part of the manuscript in which Carla accused Martina of having a "patriarchal secretiveness." She thought Martina wasn't being respectful enough of the community around Rivolta Femminile. "Only men and governments ever demanded total transparency," X, as Martina, had said in defense of herself.

"I remember that," Gioia said, shaking her head. "How angry Carla was. Then Martina asked her, 'So which are you, a man or a government?' Ah! Carla was so upset . . . But barely a day later, they announced they were becoming, together, a new person. They were Marla Rigonzi! Marla Rigonzi—someone between them but belonging to neither, belonging to no one—and for a little while this resolved it. They'd sit in Carla's apartment and talk for hours, recording their conversations, later transcribing them, forming it into one monologue, the work of 'Marla Rigonzi.' Some of these pages are from that time . . . It didn't last long."

Gioia asked to keep reading, though I was losing interest in all this intellectual bickering between two women who were both now dead. I reclined on a chaise for a while with my eyes closed, thinking again about that party, about how easy and happy X seemed. Had I ever once seen her in such a mood?

Eventually, Gioia read me more of her translations of a fight Carla and Martina had on Christmas Day, 1976.

"Here Carla tells her—'If one gives priority to the production of art to the detriment of the human relationship, the human relationship inevitably cannot fulfill itself, because the two things are competing against each other . . . When conflicts take place, like between you and me, there are no chances because you give more value to art.' It was always that way for her. Art or love. There was never really room for both."

Gioia looked down at her notes again, perhaps also growing tired of this old argument, but then she found a quote that re-engaged her attention.

"Ah! I remember this so well. Carla said to her, 'You don't have a schedule, you don't have a job, you don't have obligations, but you create a more constraining situation than if you had a job and a boss.' And Martina wouldn't explain herself at all. Martina said—oh, and this part is the saddest of all—Martina says, 'A woman's need for love was created by patriarchy to help men succeed in life. Women give love an independent value, while men give it an instrumental one.' And, oh, she was yelling this part, I remember it, she said, 'You are making the choice to give love an independent value, and you can choose to give love an instrumental value. Then you will be free of this nonsense, this pain you make for yourself. Don't you see? Loving you makes my life more *possible*, but loving you is not my life!'"

Gioia began to cry as she read, then looked up at me as if she'd forgotten why I'd come.

"It was something Carla spoke of often—how it was dangerous to think of life in terms of work and not-work, to define the free time in our life by what it was not . . . not-work. But by the New Year's party that year, they had some kind of truce for a little while anyway. They were so happy that winter. I'd never seen Carla so happy. Right there—they were leaning in that corner."

She pointed to the corner of the room that I'd seen on film, then flipped through a few of the pages in her lap.

"But by January 1977, I think it was, it had broken down again . . . I was there for their last fight, the last time any of us saw Martina. It happened at Carla's place, in the middle of dinner, another stupid fight they had about work, how Carla wanted to go the beach, take a walk with no plan, sing a song, to whistle! And Martina said, 'One cannot make love with someone who whistles.' . . . It's sad. Why did they try to love each other when they hated each other so much?"

Gioia looked up at me as if I might answer her, then looked back to the pages.

"Martina says, 'I came here to learn where I was from,' and Carla interrupts—she says, 'You never will. Do you understand me?' And Martina says, 'For sure.' Then Carla says, 'Okay, now you can go.' *Adesso vai pure* . . . And Martina left without another word. And that was it. Carla was so angry, she painted it on the back of her door because the next time Martina came back, Carla wanted to remember it—*vai pure*."

Gioia took a photograph of the door the last time she was in Carla's apartment. It was breast cancer, Gioia explained, but she wouldn't take the treatments. She hated the hospital, hated everyone there, so she went and saw a healer, and the healer said the cancer had grown out of an unresolved childhood trauma.

"She never spoke to a real doctor again. All her friends became enemies. She made enemies of everyone so that no one could talk to her. At one point—she was delirious, I think, but also very clear—she told me that part of the reason she was sick was because Martina never loved her, that she loved Martina, but Martina didn't love her back, so the love had nowhere to go and it rotted inside her body. She had this elaborate theory about the artist Pietro Consagra, also, a friend of hers whom she almost married when she was very young . . . Carla knew two women who had loved Pietro intensely, one from his childhood and the other in her twenties, and even though Pietro had been friends with those women, he hadn't loved either of them back, not the way they'd loved him. Both women grew these horrible tumors very young, both of them gland tumors, right after they realized he didn't love them. And Carla was so sure it meant something—that loving someone without love in return could cause cancer—that no one could convince her otherwise. She died thinking that."

Gioia's mouth hung open as if she were approaching a word, then she stood sharply.

"What a terrible host I've been, forgive me," she said, and we went to the kitchen, where she decided that she'd make a risotto, no matter the late hour; it was what she wanted to serve me. She stirred quietly as I watched. I'd turned off the recorder. If it weren't for this grand display of hospitality, starting a risotto so long after dark, I would have left. For a while we didn't speak, so I looked around the kitchen at the old, unpolished silver platters, copper pots, the texture of the stone walls.

After we ate, Gioia said that she had to confess something. She spoke without looking at me, as she busied the edge of the table cloth with her left hand.

X had sent several letters to Carla while she was sick, Gioia said, though of course she had no idea of Carla's illness. They'd been out of touch for years by then, but since Gioia was taking care of everything for Carla at that point—feeding her, bathing her, paying her bills—she read the letters and destroyed them without telling Carla, knowing they would only be harmful. Gioia apologized to me for not saving them, as they could have helped my research; she had burned them. They angered her so much—this woman thinking that after she abandoned someone, she could return so casually.

That's a real story, Gioia said. *A real story from a real life. It's never a kidnapping, a deathbed confession. It's always much simpler—letters thrown out. That's a real story.*

I told her I thought she was right to have done this, but she needed no reassurance.

As I was leaving, I thanked her for her time and assured her she'd been helpful, but she told me she knew she hadn't given me the full picture of those pages she had translated. She'd had her own, selfish reasons for reading through them, she admitted, then she said she had a young friend who was a talented translator, a real translator, and that she'd have her come to my hotel tomorrow.

As I was leaving, she paused at the front door to tell me one last thing: she'd known who I was from the start. She'd seen Martina's portrait—no, X's portrait—she'd seen it in a magazine on a trip to New York and since then had tracked down everything she could about her.

I try not to hate anyone, Gioia said, *but I can't seem to stop myself—I still hate her. I know she didn't give Carla cancer, but I don't have any other explanations.*

I hate her a little, too, I said, words that surprised me as they arrived.

Gioia asked if I hated her for dying, but I shook my head. I didn't know why I had said such a thing. At the time I wanted to believe I still loved her, despite everything, and that I missed her terribly, and that the biography was a crucible for my grief, but already it had shifted into something else, something darker, something I knew to be doomed.

———

A day later the translator, Teresa, came to my hotel and took the pages away to begin her work. But she returned the next evening, apologetic and defeated—*I'm sorry*, she said, *but none of it really makes any sense.*

KNIFE FIGHT

Bertha Hurts did not respond to my first letter, and for once I knew it wasn't an old grudge preventing an interview, but the fact that she worked for Brace & Sons, the publisher of Theodore Smith's book; she'd been warned not to speak with me. Once she'd left that job to take another, however, she agreed to a lunch. We met at a Japanese restaurant with high-backed wooden booths, a location I'd chosen purposefully. It was small and busy, but the staff never seemed hurried. Each table was cocooned with wooden panels and thick curtains, lending a lulling sense of privacy. I'd once had lunch there with a magazine editor I wanted to work with, but by the time the check arrived I had divulged so many details about my personal life—stories I rarely told anyone—that I was too embarrassed to ever face him again. In retrospect, I blamed the space itself.

In a notebook X described Bertha as "discreet and guileful . . . in possession of a perspicacity intentionally obscured with feminine costume bordering on the childish: bright jewelry, hair ribbons, pink blush . . . She courts underestimation, she plates and eats it with a dash of salt."* X hired Bertha to run Knife Fight, the small feminist press that she began after returning to New York from Europe in 1977.

---

* X, journal entry, October 23, 1977, box 57, item 2, TXA.

Knife Fight is obviously a mimicry of Carla Lonzi's Rivolta Femminile, but while Carla and the other collective members had tangible issues to revolt against—Italian women were still fighting for rights that women in the Northern Territory had enjoyed for decades—Knife Fight could only fight abstractions. Though women had federally mandated equal pay, free child care, access to birth control, and equal representation in the government and most professions—and even though there was overwhelming nationwide support for the policies that had led to these advancements*—tenacious forms of sexism still existed within the culture, according to many. A majority of the population in the Northern Territory in the 1970s identified as feminist, but the definition of "feminism" kept morphing to suit the needs of whoever claimed it. Scandals of discrimination and harassment sprang up regularly, but the solutions suggested were myriad and contradictory.

"Subliminal cruelty is our enemy," the first press release for Knife Fight read, "and by giving a platform to nonconforming, contentious, or otherwise 'unlikable' women's voices, we will contribute to the erosion of sexist limitations on what is and what is not considered 'female.' Our books will injure you—as they should."†

Sitting across from Bertha in the wooden booth, I watched her eyes widen as she read this old press release, glowing the way a mother's eyes will when looking at photographs of her children. She explained that she'd first met X by responding to her strange classified ad: "Editor wanted. Experience is relative. Pay, competitive. Lack of conventionality a must."

"It sounded like a scam," Bertha remembered, "but I had this terrible editorial assistant job at the time, and I'd finally stopped hoping that it was going to lead to anything. Even if the ad was a scam—at least it was a *different* scam."‡

---

* Northern United Territory, Society Accountability Office, *Attitudes Toward Gender: A Review of Feminist and Anti-feminist Perspectives, 1935–Present* (Douglas-Washington, DC: U.S. Government Printing Office, 1975).

† Knife Fight, press release, box 1977, folder 8, item 2, TXA.

‡ Bertha Hurts, interview with the author, August 8, 2000, tape 40.1–5, CML audio collection, TXA. All quotes from Bertha Hurts in the following paragraphs are from this interview.

Soon after she'd sent in her application, Bertha was called in for an interview, and when she arrived at the Chambers Street address she found
a derelict floor of a warehouse. X answered the bullet-holed door and
introduced herself as Martina Riggio. She'd yet to buy any furniture; the
interview took place as they paced around the large, unheated space.

"She seemed suspicious, of course, but all rich people seem suspicious,
don't they? But at least she was doing something with the money, something I could respect. She told me her grandfather—or maybe it was her
father—back in Italy had earned his fortune in some sinister way, so she
wanted to use her inheritance against everything he stood for. Naturally,
I asked why she wanted to do this in the Northern Territory when Italy
must have needed her help much more. Well, she suggested she would
export the books, and I knew from the way she said it that she meant to
export them into the South. I'd heard of those underground channels of
communication into the ST, and of course this just increased the appeal
of the job immensely—again, I was young and therefore insane. I can't
imagine getting involved in something so dangerous now. How stupid I
was. Stupid and lucky."

Bertha fell quiet for a little while. The waiter set two small bowls of
soup in front of us, and as she wrapped her hands around the ceramic,
she admitted that part of the appeal probably had something to do with
how she was raised. Bertha had been born in New Hampshire to parents deeply involved in the Anti-So movement—Anti-Socialists who
refused the Northern Territory's universal basic income and socialized
health care, often to their personal detriment. Bertha's father in particular, president of his local chapter of Staunch American Atheists, repeatedly protested these social "handouts," arguing the money would be
better spent on a reclamation of the ST and a destruction of their violent
theocracy. Bertha's childhood rebellion had included reading the Bible
until her father burned her copy, as religious books, in his opinion, were
the only ones that merited burning. She'd argued constantly with her
parents, discord that they encouraged as they insisted she never, under
any circumstances, accept authority. When Bertha moved to New York at
eighteen, her parents, like many others in the Anti-So movement, immi-

grated to the Western Territory, then a libertarian haven. It was almost a year before she heard from her father. After an almost deadly encounter with a mountain lion, Bertha's mother suddenly believed Jesus had saved her life. She left her husband, submitted herself to the Southern Territory's strenuous immigration program, and was never heard from again.

"Mom disappeared the same month I started at Knife Fight. I'd been in the city almost a year by then, and I'd finally given up thinking that, somehow, something was going to save me. I could barely pay my bills—even with the UBI checks, like a lot of people—so I was pretty much just living on oatmeal and adrenaline."

Though Bertha had always wanted to work in book publishing, after the Northern Territory's aborted attempt to turn printed matter into a public utility in early 1970s, most publishers were struggling to rebuild. Readers now expected books to come free or very cheap, and the low salaries meant almost everyone in her office had either married into or been born into a wealthy family.

"Most of them tried to hide it," Bertha remembered, "and at the time it seemed like nothing was more shameful than being rich. I even knew a woman who carried her nice purse into the office inside a paper bag and wore a cheap old coat over her expensive clothes."

I found no evidence that X interviewed anyone else for Bertha's position, but it's hard to imagine there was anyone else better suited for it. Bertha was just experienced enough to know what she was doing, but still young enough to take orders.

"As I remember it," Bertha said, "she didn't ask me about my work experience at all—it was just this series of questions that didn't seem to have anything to do with anything. Childhood memories and questions about music—I didn't really know anything about music, but that didn't seem to matter. We just paced around that room, and even though I know now that the accent was fake, I was really charmed by it then. It made everything sound nicer, that up-and-down way she spoke . . . She hired me and I started the same day, I think. We took a cab to the office she'd just rented on Mott Street. Office—I don't know, it was more of a room, really, with some file cabinets and desks and a couple phones—and the next day she came in with Mitchell [Abbott], and told me, 'This is your assistant.' Mitchell was at least six years older than me, and she clearly hadn't told him until just then that he'd be working under someone with less, you know, real experience than he had—well, he was shocked, and I was, too. Then Martina said something like, 'Is there a problem? Does anyone have a problem?' We both said, 'No, of course not.' And how could we have objected? We were paid the same, and in cash, every week. The only difference was that my business card said *Executive Editor* and his said *Assistant to Bertha Hurts*.

"There ended up being so much work to do that we both did pretty much everything, but it was wonderful—one of the few jobs that I genuinely loved. For one thing, Martina never came into the office, and I'm not exaggerating—she *never* came in. But she called almost every day—telling us what to do, usually, but sometimes just calling to say hello—never to Mitchell, just to me. Actually, she was sort of rude to him, bossed him around in ways I found a little, I don't know, a little unfair. If he picked up the phone when Martina called, she wouldn't say anything to him, she'd just clear her throat and he'd hand the phone to me. If she did talk to him, it was just to give him the most menial tasks, but she and I—well, I think we were actually friends? She even called me at home sometimes on the weekend, and I didn't mind it.

"And *yes*, I know that Martina wasn't a real person—though I was late to hear about that exhibition and everything, and quite frankly I didn't get it—but I never met *X*. I only knew Martina. Maybe it's dumb to think my conversations with Martina were real, that she was actually my friend, but, I don't know—she *was* . . . She treated me like I was her equal. It's hard to imagine I would have stayed in this industry if it weren't for her. Sometimes she called me on Sunday mornings because I lived near a church and there were these bells and we'd just sit there, not talking, just listening to the bells together . . .

"Well, isn't this stupid?" Bertha asked, blotting a napkin at her eyes. "Crying over a fake person. I haven't even thought of any of this in years. I suppose she was a wonderful actress, getting this far under someone's skin. Is that what your book is about? How well she could pretend?"

The waiter appeared and took the soup bowls away. I stared at the blank table. It was a strange time in my research. I'd been at work for years, had read through the entirety of the archive and had gone to Montana, Mississippi, Illinois, and Italy, but I'd been avoiding several important interviews, and I hadn't yet looked at any of the papers in X's office, the room where she died. In fact, I had not yet been able to enter that room at all, though I'd tried several times, tried to go inside; right the chair, at least, or, I don't know, do some dusting, or perhaps throw all the furniture from the window and burn it in the yard—but I couldn't. By the time I met with Bertha, I knew I wasn't researching X's life in order to simply dispel the falsehoods in Theodore Smith's book, but I'd yet to fully accept I was compiling research for my own book, something I would have never elected to write if I had known, at the start, what I was actually getting into. Bertha's question—was my book about how well X could pretend—it made me realize what I was doing, what my life had come to, and this realization brought with it a new, encumbering grief.

"I'm not sure," I said.

Bertha nodded, and I saw my emotionless expression reflected back in her face. (*How well she could pretend.*)

"I should tell you about meeting Cassandra Edwards," Bertha said, smiling, gaining a new confidence, and I knew it must have been a story she'd told many times before.

Yes, I said, how wonderful, tell me everything.

During her first year at Knife Fight, Bertha had been able to find only four manuscripts worth publishing in the deluge of submissions—far fewer than the ten books Martina wanted to publish annually. In August of that year, Bertha read a four-hundred-page manuscript titled *37*, sent in by a woman named Cassandra Edwards, whose cover letter had stated she was "an Upper East Side socialite." Bertha often received submissions from self-identified elites, all of them convinced they were the next Edith Wharton, that their high-class tell-alls would be best sellers—but chronicles of the rich were anathema at the time. There had been several large protests against New York City's controversial tax code, which created a kind of financial haven in Manhattan, attracting flocks of wealthy residents in the 1960s and driving up housing costs. By the late

'70s, the wealthy were seen as the city's great embarrassment. But this manuscript—*37*—was something else entirely.

"It was . . . Well, it was the most upsetting book I'd ever read," she said, "More depressing than *The Bell Jar.*"

The novel *37* is a story within a story within a story.* It follows a man named Cass Edward, who writes a novel called *Thirty-Seven*, in which an unnamed woman vows to kill herself once she reaches the age of thirty-seven. The Cass Edward novel is summarized within Cassandra Edwards's novel as mostly being the unnamed narrator's explanations about why she will kill herself at the age of thirty-seven. After the summary of Cass Edward's *Thirty-Seven*, the second half of *37* consists of extended monologues by concerned friends of Cass Edward, each of them arguing against suicide in general and against his suicide in particular, which they fear he intends to carry out after reading a novel they believe to be thinly veiled autobiography. At the end of this book, when Cass reaches his thirty-seventh birthday, he does not kill himself, and just as the book seems to end happily, the final sentence describes how Cass "lived every day of his thirty-seventh year with a serenity approaching bliss, and on the final day of that year, he shot himself square in the face and, over the next several hours in a nearby hospital, suffered a long, torturous death."

"The voice was just so bizarre, so uncanny. I wanted to meet this woman immediately," Bertha explained. "But when I called Martina, she told me she actually *knew* Cassandra Edwards *personally*, that she'd met her a few times, but that she had no idea she was a writer. I insisted Martina read the manuscript immediately; I was so worried another editor would buy it before we had the chance."

What Bertha did not know at the time was that X didn't need to read the manuscript, as she had been the one to write it using a new pseudonym. Since returning from Europe, X had spent a lot of time at parties with Oleg, disguising herself with a raven-black bob and huge sunglasses. While this may have initially been an attempt to throw off the ST agents she feared were still looking for her, at some point the costume became a character of its own.

---

* Cassandra Edwards, *37* (New York: Knife Fight, 1978).

She used a vaguely British accent and introduced herself as Cassandra Edwards. She claimed that she was Oleg Hall's second cousin, that he'd spent many childhood summers with her out on her family's ranch in the Western Territory. She said her father, "Duke Edwards," was a horse breeder and owned a few planes. "He's such a splendidly proud and resourceful man," she once told a reporter for a society magazine. "It gave you a thrill to look at him. Like looking at the American flag. And he's always kept such a low profile, only he could never teach me to do the same! Why, hardly anyone has ever heard of him, even though he's been so successful in business. And that's just how he likes it."*

A few days after Bertha first read *37*, Martina called to say that she'd secured the rights for it and that Cassandra Edwards was going to stop by the Knife Fight office that afternoon to meet her editor.

"I expected her to be strange," Bertha remembered, "but she kept her

---

* Kendra Malone, "A Curious Young Lady Speaks," *The Chronicles*, Spring/Summer 1978.

Image: "Cassandra Edwards" (X)

sunglasses on the whole meeting and said the most ridiculous things. It was more like . . . in fear or something, but after a few minutes I realized—well—that it was *Martina*. Martina in a wig and speaking with a perfect American accent. Mitchell didn't see it—I thought maybe I was being crazy, but I *knew* it was her. The pieces just fit together too easily. But what was I going to do? Accuse my boss of ghostwriting a book by a made-up person so that we had something to publish? Or was she impersonating the *real* Cassandra for some reason?"

This occurred at a time when X began to use new names and costumes more with more audacity and fewer boundaries. Sometimes, with Oleg, she'd attend a party at which most people knew her as Cassandra Edwards, but she would introduce herself as Martina Riggio, *the Italian publisher*. Oleg would pretend it was a joke, that it was just one of the many marvelous jokes she liked to play at such parties. *Such a silly girl, you can't trust a word she says.* Sometimes X would tell people she'd gone to an "Italian finishing school," a detail that struck many as odd; there were English finishing schools and Swiss finishing schools, and some girls had been to finishing schools in the south of France, but an Italian finishing school?

My, isn't that unusual? Oleg recalled an elderly socialite asking X. *My dear, in what region of Italy was this school located?* And when X explained it was in the north, nearly to Austria, the socialite quietly advised her to say she'd gone to school "in the Alps," not "in *Italy*." Another joked that he wasn't aware that the Italians finished anything.*

Despite Cassandra Edwards's antics, Oleg prized her as his ideal *boutonnière*. She was quickly adopted as "The Swan Queen" of Oleg's friends who bonded over debauched nights out. Though I interviewed a few of them, they often spoke at length about things of no consequence. The only story that interested me was about a long drunken afternoon that Cassandra, Oleg, and company spent at the Ritz-Carlton, running up a tab on Cassandra's father's account, to which it seems they were successful in billing for lunch, along with a 100 percent tip. The lunch ended with X stealing several sets of silverware.

---

* Oleg Hall, interview with the author, July 4, 2003, tape 9.18–22, CML audio collection, TXA.

A few of these friends repeated the same dull anecdotes about the group crashing parties at Warhol's factory, but the most commonly told story was how Cassandra scandalized them all by turning down Warren Beatty's advances. The two apparently met at a dinner party, and when he'd asked her to have a drink with him the next night she said she wasn't free, and when he'd asked her to tell him when she was free she told him she was free all the time, free every moment of her life, that she was simply too free to go around with a man like him. This apparently enraged Oleg.

"Warren is not my problem," she wrote to him in a letter.

"But you are his!" Oleg insisted in person the next day.

"Believe me, Warren is not my problem, nor will he be my problem. If he has a problem that I won't let him be my problem, then he's got a problem."*

"Sure, most women would have been flattered by the attention," X wrote in one of Cassandra's notebooks, "and it was flattering, but I knew the game [Beatty] was playing. He told Oleg that I was the only woman that beat him at his own game but I didn't feel like a victor. If I won something, what did I win?"†

When 37 was published, none of X's uptown acquaintances knew anything of it until Geraldine Snow wrote a damning profile of Cassandra Edwards for *The New York Review of Books* in the summer of 1978.‡ Snow made no secret that she hated the book, describing it as "a torrent of tired ideas," and that she found Cassandra to be "the most irritating sort of fraud." Not even Bertha and Mitchell escaped Snow's scorn—when she visited the office of the "dubiously named small press," she met two employees, "the sort of nebbish folk that flow like tepid blood from one publishing venture to the next."

"Nebbish," Bertha recounted during our lunch. "I've been called a lot of things but never that . . . Of course, once Geraldine Snow calls a person anything it becomes a fact, doesn't it?"

* X to Oleg Hall, June 3, 1977, box 1977b, item 2, TXA.

† X, diary entry, June 4, 1977, box 1977c, item 29, TXA.

‡ Geraldine Snow, "I've Been Thinking of Suicide," *The New York Review of Books*, October 14, 1978.

"On second thought," Snow wrote, "perhaps Knife Fight is an apt publisher for Miss Edwards's debut, as they claim their books have come to injure their readers . . . I was so riveted by *37*'s unrelenting badness that I could not put it down, lest I turn my back on it and find the book had risen on its spine to stab me!"

The bad publicity greatly increased sales for *37* and led to invitations from bookstores for readings, of which X accepted only two: one at Three Lives and another at St. Mark's Bookshop. Disguised in Cassandra's dark bob and oversize sunglasses, X met heavily divided audiences on both evenings. Her readers were a mixed lot: serious writing students, the odd punk or two, self-described intellectuals, and considerable numbers of nervous young men, one of whom fainted on each occasion. There were also plenty of gawkers from the publishing world, there only for the controversy, and a handful of agitators, bleating in the back row.

At St. Mark's, in the middle of her reading, someone shouted, *Life is too short for this!*

X replied, *Oh, but what is it long enough for?*

Like every other title Knife Fight published, the book never made a profit. X insisted on the highest-quality production—clothbound hardbacks, embossed lettering, and fine papers. Bertha tried and failed to convince X to print cheaper, lighter editions of their more popular books, but she refused.

"*37* was being stolen from bookstores regularly," Bertha remembered, "so often, in fact, a lot of them wouldn't stock it or had to keep it behind the counter—and, really, who could blame someone for not wanting to pay nearly twice the amount a hardback usually cost? But there was no arguing with Martina. If I brought up something she didn't want to talk about, she would pretend not to understand my English, or else she'd just hang up. After a while I stopped pushing her on anything . . . By the time Martina sent me the manuscript for the Cindy O novellas, I had a lot of questions—for instance, who is this woman and why did she send the manuscripts to you instead of the office and why didn't she let us handle the contracts or payments? But there was no point trying to reason with her . . . I admired the Cindy O tetralogy in some ways, but I knew it would be a commercial dud—of course, money was never a compelling argument to Martina . . . What's really ridiculous to me now is how *obvious* it should have been to me that *Martina* had written those novellas as well. That was the only logical explanation."

The books that comprised *The Tetralogy*, as it later came to be known, four novellas by "Cindy O" (another of X's pseudonyms), were published in April 1980 as separate, French-flapped paperbacks (the sole compromise X made with Bertha) but also as a limited edition hardcover that sold fewer than a hundred copies.* The paperbacks hardly did better, each of them selling nearly a thousand copies before the remainders were pulped in early 1981. Each novella is a story of standard suburban malaise—yawning housewives, depressed children, philandering husbands—and though *The Tetralogy* later grew a cult following when it was reprinted in 1993, its initial arrival passed almost without notice. (Oddly enough, one of the original paperbacks made it into my hands when I was in journalism school.)

* Cindy O, *The Tetralogy* (New York: Knife Fight, 1978).

X somehow sold the Japanese rights to *The Tetralogy*, though no other Knife Fight titles were ever published abroad. As most of Knife Fight's papers were destroyed, it is a mystery how she arranged for this. Almost immediately upon the Japanese translation's publication in November 1980, *The Tetralogy* became a best seller in Japan; Cindy O's few blurry author photographs adorned a raft of fan paraphernalia: dish towels, rubber stamps, T-shirts, and stationery. The fact that she refused to make any public appearances or respond to interview requests fed into her mystique abroad, though her reclusion went unnoticed in the States, as the unpopular author is no more appealing for being unavailable.

The income from the Japanese deal, however, was likely what brought the IRS's attention, in mid-1981, to Knife Fight's tax neglect. Suspecting that the Knife Fight offices were soon to be raided, X destroyed nearly all her papers and stock mere hours before agents showed up. She called both Bertha and Mitchell in the middle of the night—*Don't come back. Don't ask questions. Don't talk to anyone. You don't know anything.*

As Bertha and I left the restaurant, squinting in a bright afternoon,

Image: "Cindy O" (X)

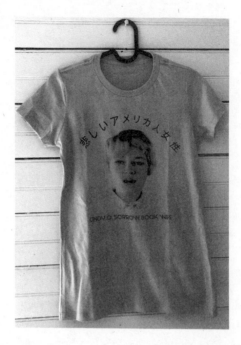

she asked if any of the Knife Fight books ever made it into the Southern Territory. I wasn't sure. Little had survived Knife Fight's sudden demise—just a few books and letters—and it was always difficult to get reliable information from the FST.

"She was born there," I told Bertha, though I hadn't been planning to do so.

She stopped abruptly in the middle of the sidewalk, a hurried pedestrian cursing her as he passed.

"I didn't know that," she said, stunned. "I had no idea."

It was the first time I'd told someone so abruptly. I wasn't yet accustomed to hearing myself say it. Bertha had a dozen questions, but I didn't want to talk anymore. The admission itself had been exhausting, bringing immediate grief. I told her I had to go, lying that I was already late for something, sorry, so sorry, then I was gone.

ZEBULON

In April of 2002 my phone rang—*Well, I'll be damned.*

I knew right away it was Zebulon. He'd barely spoken during that brief, chaotic interview at the Walker household, more than three years prior, but I had listened to the recording of his voice repeatedly, alternately fascinated and repulsed by the existence of X's son, a man closer to my age than I had been to hers. Nancy had given Zebulon my number.

"Wasn't supposed to tell you that," he admitted.

Though he'd been reluctant to talk in person, there now seemed to be no limits to what he'd tell me about his family, his hometown, his irritation with nearly everything in his life. With no way to record him at hand that first day, I am left only with my notes, though Zebulon's drawl was slow enough that I could write down most everything he said.

First, Zebulon said, he wanted to apologize for his grandparents. He'd tried to have the interview happen without them around, but Angela wouldn't allow it and she had enough influence in Byhalia to pay a few visits to the courthouse in order to have "certain knots tied or untied for her." It was an open secret that his mother—Carrie Lu—was not a Walker. One of Zebulon's uncles had told him a long time ago that it was Angela's sister Clara who had given birth to Carrie Lu. Clara had been "carrying on with some men" who worked the farmland behind her house. Not a word was ever spoken about who the father might have been, and after the delivery, she had been forced to give the baby to her sister, Angela, to raise as her own. Clara was sent away, institutionalized, and everyone suspected the same fate might meet Carrie Lu.

"I was told a couple times it was a good thing she got blowed up," Zebulon said. "Better than getting put away somewhere."

Angela had told him the truth when he was seven, but explained he was never to speak of Carrie Lu or Clara ever again. If he even mentioned them, people would think he wasn't adequately ashamed of their sins and would assume there was something wrong with him, too.

"Everybody thinks there's something wrong with me anyway," he said. "Not that anybody will ever tell you, not directly, but you can tell, can't you? From the ways people look at you. You can tell what they see, isn't it so?"

After the wall fell, Zebulon tried to find his biological grandmother, but the asylum where he thought she'd lived had burned down in 1993, and he wasn't able to find any record of her elsewhere. When I asked him why he was telling me all this now, he told me he'd come up with a theory, a philosophy about life.

"I think everybody reaches a point when there's no way forward," he said, "and most people just stop right there. They stop right there and they don't change anything about their lives. Maybe they even start to believe the limits around their life, start to think it's all part of a plan. I must have reached this point some years ago and I didn't do anything—maybe I couldn't do anything—but when the wall came down and everybody else was terrified, I wasn't worried. Wasn't worried at all. Then I realized all those people were scared because they didn't want their lives to change, but I did, and I still do. There's nothing keeping me here—no wife, no kids, nothing—and I never did belong. Maybe I'm like Clara in that way, just different, and if they put men in asylums I'd probably be in one, and when you left that afternoon, well, I felt like I should go wherever you were going."

He paused here for a moment and I could hear him breathing, a sort of intimacy I'd nearly forgotten, as I had not recently come close enough to anyone's mouth to hear air sucked and spent.

"Truth is," he said, "I can't stop thinking about you. My mind just keeps circling back, circling back again."

I waited for him to dispel the implication in this confession, but he did not. Surely he just meant that he wanted to live the sort of life he imagined me to have in the North, to be free, to experience all that hedonism and heathenism he'd been warned against. But there was an unmistakable undercurrent in his voice. I felt a wave of nausea.

"See, I got put on one of those lists. You know about them? And I need a sponsor to move out of here. I can help you if you can help me," he said.

A relief, then—just a matter of logistics. I'd heard of these anti-emigration lists that kept certain people from leaving the FST. I told Zebulon I would help him however I could. He offered to help me with my research in return, saying that he could either send me his mother's journals and letters or at least call me to read them aloud. Since the postal system between North and South was still quite unreliable, I opted for the latter, and for the next two months Zebulon called me every week to read these primary sources aloud.* Most of what was there just confirmed what I already knew about X—that she'd been energetic and idealistic as a girl, that her marriage seemed to have quelled her rebellious impulses for a time.

These calls, however, were unexpectedly emotional, as it sometimes felt like Zebulon spoke in registers or with rhythms that echoed X's voice. I hadn't imagined an absent parent's imprint could find its way into the abandoned child, and at the same time I doubted my own observations, thought I was seeing X because I wanted to see her, wanted to believe she was still somewhere. On occasion I wondered if I should tell Zebulon who I really was—that I had known his mother, had loved her, had married her—but I either justified myself away from this admission or failed to find the courage. Technically, I sometimes thought, I am his stepmother—then: No, technically, I'm nothing and no one.

In return for Zebulon's reading me these materials, I tried to find a way to relieve him of his non-emigration status. I found that he'd been

---

* Zebulon Vine, telephone interviews with the author, April 11, 19, 25, 27, May 5, 15, 23, 30, June 6, 2002. Tapes 80–91, CML audio collection, TXA.

categorized as a "highest risk" FST citizen; he could leave the Southern Territory only if he went into a two-year rehabilitation program run by the Northern Territory's military. There was, I was told, no way around this program, and if Zebulon tried to relocate to the North without first registering, he would risk a long imprisonment. He refused to entertain the rehabilitation program—"The hell I'm ever walking into a goddamn concentration camp. I'm no kind of fool they must take me for."

When he insisted he'd known other Southerners who'd been taken off that list if a Northern citizen sponsored them, I spoke to an immigration lawyer who told me there were different lists, that every citizen in the FST had been assigned a threat level for reasons both concrete and mysterious. Known members of the American Freedom Kampaign, for instance, were not legally permitted into the Northern Territory at all, though of course they disregarded this ordinance and came anyway, blew things up, killed people, tried to make their point.

On one of our last calls I mustered the nerve to ask Zebulon—had he done anything that might have put him on this stricter list? But he claimed he had done nothing, absolutely nothing. Did he belong to any political organizations? He said he'd never been interested in politics. Any leadership positions within a church?

"They'd never trust somebody like me with any of that."

He insisted it didn't make any sense, that they must have had him confused with someone else, and though I did try several paths, I met nothing but dead ends. At first he was indignant, but the longer our calls went on and the more reports I gave him from my sources and methods of inquiry, the less he seemed bothered by his situation.

"It's just nice talking to you," he said one evening with a frankness that worried me again. Later he repeated himself, then asked if I looked forward to these phone calls as much as he did. I said whatever I said, tried to deflect his attention. He resumed reading a note that his mother, my wife, had written to a neighbor with a casserole recipe, some anecdote from church, and a not-funny joke about a squirrel. We both laughed, I supposed, because we still had some amount of intractable love for her, but a few minutes later, as I was lulled into the rhythm these talks with Zebulon often took, I made a grave, unconscious mistake. I started to tell him my own anecdote about X—a story I'd often repeated about an afternoon in France when a seagull had swooped down and stolen my wife's hat right off her head. I laughed for a moment before I realized he'd gone silent.

"She lived?"

Silence lingered, as I had no idea what to say, then he asked, "Where did she go?"

"The West. Then the North."

"But why?"

"I suppose I've been trying to understand that, too," I said, but I hadn't, not really. The violent way she had left the ST had been a surprise at first, but the longer I had reflected on it, the more sense it made. Other things I did not understand about her, but her abandoning that family and that life was not one of them. But I couldn't say this to him, her son, a man frozen in boyhood.

"And you knew her?" he asked.

Again an explanation stopped in my throat, and I couldn't remember what I had said just moments earlier. Had I called her my wife? Had I said the word *love*? Why had I even needed to say anything about her? Why did I find myself returning and returning to memories of this woman who, I knew by then, had betrayed me, had lied to me, had seen me as less than her, something to be controlled, explained, shaped? I began to cry and tried to stifle it. Don't let him know. Don't let on that you loved her.

"You called her . . . your wife? My mother?"

So it was too late. "I did," I said. Then—and if this wasn't on the tape I would not have remembered saying as much—I added, "I survived her."

Another pause on the line, then Zebulon launched into a tirade of violent insults, the words hurled at me from some dark, instinctual place. I sat there with the receiver to my ear, blank-eyed, unable to put it down.

On my trip to the FST I'd been extremely careful, just as I'd been instructed, but I'd been raised in a culture so absent of homophobia that the very concept of it never made sense to me. My only experience of such hatred was secondhand—the stories I'd heard from friends who were twice my age, or those who'd been born in other countries. But the illogical stance of another's sexuality being cause for anger was still an abstraction to me, and it was not until I became the subject of Zebulon's repulsion that I truly felt its warmth. When he slammed down the phone I felt as if I'd been rejected by my own child. I never heard from him again.

Image: Zebulon Vine

GINNY GREEN

I s there any variety of person more odious than a New York gallerist? Cynics, most of them, and cynics of the worst kind—those who may have once been sincere devotees but have since mutated into businesspeople, no longer *seeing* the world but rather blankly gazing at it, the way a calculator would. A shame that those who best know such people are rarely in a position to call them what they are, but I feel neither indebted to nor interested in nor respectful of the so-called art world and its various machinations.

I hate Ginny Green. I've made no secret of this—even Ginny knows—though she immediately metabolizes all disdain, perhaps is even nourished by it. For that I can at least respect her, despite my deep disapproval of Ginny and everything she stands for.

And yet—X loved Ginny. She loved everything about her. She loved being in her company, loved her self-involved monologues, her style, her friends, her loft—loved all of it with such an uncomplicated pleasure that I began to doubt that my wife and I shared any common reality when Ginny was around.

I first met Ginny in 1989, just a few weeks after X and I had gotten together. Tall and sturdy, with a dark black bowl cut, Ginny wore only monochromatic ensembles, including her circular, thick-rimmed glasses, which she must have owned in fifty colors, various tones of white, taupe, and pink, and at least ten shades of blue. She stood like a column at the center of any crowd, holding everything up, forcing everyone to navigate around her. She squinted once at me, immediately forgot my name, and after the tenth time X reminded her of what I, *the new one*, was called, Ginny moaned into her hands and complained that it was such a *complicated* name and suggested that everyone simply call me C. She smiled as she said this, speaking as if I were not present, and from then on that's who I was to Ginny—I was C, if I was anything.

Ginny forgets everyone's name, X explained. I knew this was a lie, as I'd seen her practically sing the names of those whose attention or money she needed—but I excused it. X and Ginny depended on each other to a degree that I knew better than to disturb, though I also knew that X recognized Ginny's cynicism as clearly as I did. My wife and I despised a sizable percentage of the art Ginny displayed and sold at Quarry, though of course X attended every opening Ginny asked her to attend, and would fawn over the artist if Ginny nudged her to do so. X forgave anything Ginny had to do to keep her gallery dominant, a position from which they both benefited.

My wife also began calling me C, and though I'd found the name diminishing when spoken by Ginny, it was another matter on X's tongue. This happened often—behaviors I found repellent elsewhere became pleasurable, even preferable, if X adopted them. After all, she reasoned, I used initials for my byline—why not in the rest of my life? What difference did it really make?

It seemed that names had been given to and taken from me all my life, for reasons beyond my control. My parents had been in disagreement about what to write on my birth certificate, one of them insisting on Charlotte Marie and the other on Cynthia Malone. Until the age of seven I was called both names interchangeably, and when asked as a child what my name was, I gave both in a row: Charlotte Marie Lucca *and* Cynthia Malone Lucca. A few times this resulted in someone calling me Ann after they'd misheard the "and," so for a year at Girl Scouts I was Ann. What's more—my last name is my mother's pure invention, her attempt to get away from her own family, whose last name I have never known, but my father won the first-name argument in the end, and Charlotte Marie was made my legal name, though my mother still called me Cindy and both my brothers called me Malone, Mally, or Loner. Since there were too many Charlottes in my third-grade class, a teacher started calling me Marie and that stuck for a while and I didn't mind. In college I was Charlotte again, by default of roll call, but some people in journalism school called me Lucca—as most of us had adopted the newsroom affectation of calling people by their surnames. When I began publishing I used C. M. Lucca, and though I'd only intended for "C. M." to appear in print, most of my colleagues started calling me C. M. Henry had the bizarre habit of calling me Char, which wasn't a name at all but something you do to a piece of dead flesh, but I accepted this name, too, for no reason other than I had no preferred alternative. X didn't call me anything at first, or if she did I don't remember what she called me—"Henry Surner's wife," perhaps, as a joke—so when Ginny began to call me C and X followed suit, it ultimately felt fine, as it seems I was born under a nameless moon and perhaps that namelessness was what X had been drawn to from the start: I was a house without a foundation.

Before my interview with Ginny, I had not seen her since just after X had died. She'd shown up at the cabin with a quart of soup from one of those high-end delis in town that cater to distinctly incapable rich people. *I'm sorry*, she'd said, almost like a question, standing on the porch in a shimmering midnight-blue suit. I don't remember what, if anything, I said in reply. That quart of soup sat in the freezer for several years, and aside from a few emails from Ginny's secretary about X's work—Ginny silent on the cc line—I'd had no contact with her until, reluctantly, I made an appointment for an interview and, even more reluctantly, went.

When I arrived at the gallery it was Ginny, oddly, who answered the bell, and as I faced her through the glass door, it occurred to me that I'd never seen Ginny *do* anything. There were always people around her—assistants and sycophants—who did things on her behalf as she remained motionless at the center, spewing orders. As we walked through the gallery toward her office, a phone was ringing; the noise carried all over the high-ceilinged space, shrill and lonely. The secretary was out.

She rolled her eyes at the sound of it. "I haven't answered my phone in years," she said. "If I want to talk to someone, I call *them*."*

Though I'd visited the gallery countless times, I'd never been to her office in the back, and it was both a shock and a confirmation to find that her desk was not only empty but also *clear*, a designer box of Lucite. Nearly everything else in the room was either white or transparent—a sculpture of blown glass, clear chairs, clear side tables. There was even a pane of framed plexiglass hanging on the wall, a work by a new artist whose prices were already cresting five figures. The office contained no papers, no books—there wasn't even a computer visible—as if Ginny never did a moment's work, just sat in there, breathing. Maybe this is why fiction about real people so often feels forced—we live in the clunkiest metaphors.

"Everything about X broke the rules of how these things go," Ginny said when I asked her to tell me how they first met. "It was April 1977, and the boy at the front desk came in and said there was someone important in the gallery, but he said he didn't know who it was. Of course, I always had my boys memorize photographs of the major critics and curators, but this was truly hilarious, I thought—how was this *kid* to know, by *sight alone*, whether someone was important? I can't say why I even entertained the notion, but I went out to the gallery and there she was, wearing this loose silk dress that went to the floor, some kind of circular pattern, but it was the way she was looking at the work—with a complete viciousness. I don't know how else to explain it, as if it would be dangerous for her to look at you.

"Was she enjoying the paintings, I asked, and she said, 'Oh, no, not at all.' She didn't even turn to see where the question had come from. I asked if she was a collector, or an artist herself, or . . . ? But she didn't answer, just paced around . . . Eventually, she asked if I was the one to *blame* for these paintings. I told her that I was indeed the gallerist here, and she turned to me for the first time and said, 'I'm so sorry to hear that,' then launched into this explanation about how terrible the work was, how the artist

---

* Ginny Green, interview with the author, December 20, 2002, tape 49.1–8, CML audio collection, TXA. All quotes from Ginny Green in the following paragraphs are from this interview.

had no understanding of color or dimensionality or texture, that he was indulgent, that he had no ideas, that the paintings documented his every missed opportunity. She said—'He didn't put anything in the paintings because he doesn't know how. He doesn't know anything about art, and worse, he doesn't care.' Now, of course I was accustomed to criticism—I even welcomed it on occasion—but no one's opinion ever made me as doubtful as hers. Ah! Then she said this one thing I've thought of many times since—'You have to know what you're leaving out in order for it not to be there. Otherwise, it's not an absence, it's just nothing.' And immediately I had a better understanding of all those void artists back then—there were so many of them. Anyway, I sent the desk boy home early, and eventually this woman said her name was Věra, and I asked her how it was she'd come to her opinions about art. 'Oh, they're not opinions,' she said. Again I asked her if she was an artist herself, a critic, a writer . . . But she just exhaled and went on another diatribe about a different artist on my roster—one of those male artists I'd been pressured to exhibit. Can't remember his name—but his next show was going up the following week . . . He was one of those male artists obsessed with the void. All the male artists were making art about the void, and, you know, it sold quite well. But this one—he'd become frustrated with some of his sculptures—they weren't *void* enough, he said—so he'd burned them and I had agreed to exhibit the ash.

"I knew the ash wasn't exactly *good*, but it seemed clever enough and simple; it would sell. But somehow Věra knew all about that man—she even knew about the ash! Absolutely hated it, she said, then went on and on about how pathetic his work was in general. In five minutes she'd described the entire sweep of art history, from the ancient to the contemporary, and by the end of it I had this knot in my stomach. It was far too late to cancel the show, and collectors were already lining up, but she had seen straight through the whole thing. When she was done she left immediately, as if she was too disgusted to stay another moment. Later I asked the ash guy if he'd ever heard of someone named Věra, but he said he hadn't. A few weeks later she stopped by again, sneering and laughing at the pile of ash, but this time I convinced her to come with me to a bar around the corner—I was still trying to figure out *who* she was, of course, but also I couldn't stand to be in the room with that pile of ash after she'd embarrassed me so much over it.

"I'd never met anyone in New York less willing to talk about herself—still haven't—but after a few glasses of wine that afternoon I finally got some details from her—that she was an artist, but she'd only exhibited abroad, that she didn't respect any New York galleries, and I found myself almost begging her to show me her work—mind you, I'd never begged anyone for anything, and certainly not an *artist*, as they were constantly presenting their own severed heads on a platter at my feet, desperate for my attention, but that was the thing about her—she may have been a con artist, but the con was always honest."

That evening X, known in that moment as "Věra," agreed to accompany Ginny to a few openings, and while X's refusal to show Ginny any of her own work may have seemed like a tactic to string along her interest, in truth X had no work to show. "It was at least a year before she agreed to let me see anything, long after I'd stopped asking," Ginny said.

The first pieces that Věra exhibited with Quarry, in early 1979, were allegedly documentations of performances she'd done in years prior, but in fact X had only produced all this "performance documentation" months after she inserted herself into Ginny's world, a simple fact Ginny Green refuses to accept.

"I understand that Věra was a pseudonym, a made-up person, but the work was simply *the work*. She didn't lie about it—she couldn't have."

When I told her I had proof if she needed proof, Ginny changed the subject.

X's gallery debut, in March 1979, was titled *Provocation*, a name taken from the central piece of the show—*Provocation, 1975*, a series of photographs and documents purporting to chart the purchase and sale of a large rock located somewhere in the Western Territory.* The first sale was from Věra to "Harold Winston Jr." in 1975 for $5. A photograph documented Harold solemnly handing a five-dollar bill to Věra as they stood in front of the rock. A certificate of ownership was displayed beside that photograph, and on it the terms of the rock's ownership were

* Věra, *Provocation, 1975*. Photography, paper, five-dollar bill. Item X550, Quarry Archive, New York.

outlined: "Under no circumstance should the rock be moved," and "The rightful owner of the rock shall have the exclusive right to perceive and be perceived by the rock. No other individual will be able to claim any relationship to the rock unless ownership of the certificate is changed."

According to the rock's "official deed," Winston soon sold it back to Věra for $10. A second photograph inverts the first—Věra hands Mr. Winston a ten-dollar bill. "That was a very exciting day," Věra said in an interview, "because the value of the rock had doubled in a very short time."* Věra then sold the rock a few months later for $25 to a musician she met at a bar. Věra repurchased the rock for $35 a few days later. The next sale came several months later to an anonymous buyer who bought the rock for $250. A few months after that purchase, Věra—according to several letters that documented this alleged performance—pleaded with the anonymous buyer to sell the rock back to her. Eventually, the collector—whose name is blacked out from their correspondence— allowed Věra to purchase the rock for $575. Before the show even opened

---

* Bruce Nauman, "Fat Chance, John Cage: Věra Speaks," *BOMB* (1979): 22–27.

Image: Photograph from *Provocation, 1975*

to the public, the entire set of documentation for *Provocation, 1975* sold for $19,600 to the prominent collector Ayşegül Måks.

Måks also bought a more controversial work, *Continuation d'un chemin de bois pour aller d'un lieu à un autre dans le but d'une quelconque communication* (*Continuation of a wooden path in order to go from one place to another with the aim of making any kind of communication*), another performance documented in seven photographs. *Continuation* depicted someone (possibly X) lying facedown on a sandy beach, their ankles tied to a half-eroded wooden pathway.* Both the title and content were a verbatim copy of a 1970 performance by the artist Gina Pane. When caught, Věra claimed that the obvious plagiarism was simply a coincidence, an audacious lie that might have been more of a scandal if Måks hadn't also owned the photos by Pane; the duplicity had its appeal, as Måks explained: "I'm an art collector, so of course I love nothing more than swindlers, imbeciles, and low-key crime."† However, the one piece in the 1979 Quarry exhibition that was not for sale ended up being the most notorious.

"Everyone points to *An Account of My Abduction* as the reason why I must have known that Věra was an impostor," Ginny said, leaning over her desk. "But it simply wasn't true! I didn't know about any of it—the other personas, her real name, nothing. I thought Věra was Věra, and that was confusing enough, wasn't it? For instance, she first told me she was from a small town in Croatia, but later she said it was Rome, then her mother was French and she'd been born in France but had grown up in rural Denmark—then it was back to Rome, or was it Croatia? If I tried to clarify some detail or another—*Didn't you say Rome last time?*—she'd shout at me—*Try to keep up, Ginny. Try to listen*—so I stopped asking. I got into a lot of trouble with my accountant for writing checks to someone without a last name and no tax forms, but I never knew anything about her overall plan. And, really, other people's opinions bother me hardly at all—you have to have a thick skin to survive, you know—but this idea that I was in on it all along is really quite preposterous and irritating."

---

* Věra, *Continuation* . . . , 1976. Photographic documentation of performance. Item X570, Quarry Archive, New York.

† Calmese Freeman, "Shit-Eating Shit-Talkers: A State of the Contemporary Art World," *The New Inquiry*, April 11, 1984.

She didn't have to convince me. I knew that Ginny knew nothing of X's real plans. And perhaps what most irritated her was not that others believed she was in on X's fictions, but that later, in 1982, Ginny had been a part of X's unwitting audience. But I didn't bring that up, not yet, and soon she suggested we view some of her work.

"There's really nothing other than the work, now, is there?" she asked.

I followed Ginny upstairs to the gallery's archive—a clinically lit room in which every surface was the same dove gray. Ginny spread nine photographs out on a table—*An Account of My Abduction, 1979*. Neither of us spoke for a while, just stared down at the images. A few of them were stills from *The Blue Tape*, the short experimental film that debuted at the Anthology Film Archives in 1979, by an otherwise unknown filmmaker named Yarrow Hall, and the others were the photographs attributed to Věra. Though it is now well-known that both Yarrow and Věra were two of X's personas, this was not known at the time, and Věra's accusation— that she had been abducted by Yarrow Hall and held hostage in her own apartment, tied up, and threatened for hours as Yarrow filmed—was taken quite seriously.*

So much has been written about *The Blue Tape*, but a brief description is necessary. The film is eighty-seven minutes of aimless narrative that cuts between three settings. The first is a static shot of a figure wrapped toe to crown in blue tape, writhing and moaning on the floor, as an off-camera voice makes increasingly graphic threats. The second is silent footage of a woman (who seems to be Connie Converse in the Grove Street apartment) dressed as a pregnant Virgin Mary, smoking cigarettes with someone in a Jesus costume, with the disembodied head of John the Baptist between them. The three of them smile and talk, inaudibly, and Jesus occasionally holds a cigarette to John the Baptist's mouth. The third subject is a collage of surreptitiously taken footage of the artists Vito Acconci and Richard Prince as they strolled around Manhattan. The majority of the scenes of Acconci and Prince are silent, but at one point, while the two are sitting in a café, a long portion of their conversation is recorded by a hidden microphone.

* Yarrow Hall, *The Blue Tape*, 1979. 16 mm film, 87 min, Anthology Film Archives, New York.

At one point Acconci says, "The thing that still interests me about Catholicism is the number of saints. There's no void, no distance between 'person' and 'God.' There are all those saints in between: every misfit, every problem has a patron saint attached. So you're always part of a crowd, and there's no abstraction, everything's tangible." Aside from this one comment, there is little or perhaps no thematic content connecting the three aspects of the film.

The Blue Tape is not inherently interesting (not to me, anyway), but the fact that it documents a stalking of Acconci, one of the very few male artists who found any success at this time, fueled its initial popularity. Acconci's 1969 work *Following Piece*, in which the artist followed and photographed strangers around the city, was widely discussed and generally acclaimed, but it also made him the target of privacy activists who accused Acconci of "social micro-terrorism," and of a few feminists who felt the work was blatantly chauvinist. For the Acconci scenes alone, the film was screened several times at the Anthology Film Archives early in 1979, but after Věra's accusation that *she* was the figure wrapped in blue tape on the floor, that Yarrow Hall had taken Věra hostage in her own home to make that film, the controversy reached a fever pitch. The AFA, citing concerns about performer consent, ceased showing *The Blue Tape*, but the reels went on a small tour of other cinemas and art schools. Later in 1979 it was played at the Museum of Modern Art, until Věra began suggesting that Yarrow Hall may have been a persona of Vito Acconci; amid the scandal, MoMA canceled the remaining screenings.

"*The Blue Tape* played later at Yale where everyone laughed," X said during the only interview in which she acknowledged that she'd made the film herself. "At RISD, they cried . . . It depended on the first responder . . . Everyone followed suit; everyone was on emotional edge."*

After we'd looked at the photographs for *Abduction* for some time,

---

* "Věra" (X), quoted in Beatrice Banks, "I Kidnapped Myself, Ha-Ha: Věra vs. Yarrow," *Bitch Magazine*, May 3, 1983.

Ginny abruptly slid them back into their black folders, and re-stowed them in the drawer.

"Was there anything else you wanted to see?" she asked.

There wasn't, not really, but I wanted to take up as much of Ginny Green's time as I could, so I lied and said I'd like to see the photographs from *Dinner*, a series of guerrilla performances X staged in several five-star Manhattan restaurants in 1980.* She disguised herself as a waiter, rushed up to an unsuspecting diner, and presented him with a silver-domed platter, lifting the lid to reveal a dead rat. The diners each beheld the carcass differently—some shocked, some angry, some calmly dismissing the rodent as not the dish they ordered.

"Ah, of course," Ginny said, her taut voice barely concealing her annoyance.

Dinner had been X's worst-selling series; the wealthy often dislike being the butt of the joke. There were fifteen photographs in the series, three from each of the restaurants she targeted. Ginny arranged them evenly across the viewing table, spacing them precisely, as if it were a proper installation. We looked down at them for a while, quiet, casting our eyes across the three-frame story as it repeated in different settings, with different men, and different expressions of disgust.

At the time of this interview, I'd just read about the 1975 famine in the Southern Territory, which had been covered only by the smaller newspapers, for reasons I do not understand. When the South seceded in 1945, all environmental regulations had been lifted on the biblical grounds of men having "dominion over the earth," but by the mid-1970s three decades of an unbroken hunting season and heedless pollution had nearly eradicated wild game and forage. Drought, crop failure, and a strict trade embargo meant the families who best survived those years had ways of catching the rats, squirrels, and feral cats. But X never responded to the critique that her work seemed to be apolitical for never directly referencing the country's division; nearly every other successful artist in the Northern Territory at the time seemed obliged at some point

---

* Věra, *Dinner*, 1980. Photographic documentation of performance. Item X770, Quarry Archive, New York.

to make work as a statement about the wall, and the fact that X never did so was often cited as evidence of her heartlessness and frivolity.

Standing there with Ginny (who did not know what I knew), I considered how the revelation of X's birthplace changed the meaning of her work. I had never fully understood why my wife's art had earned her as much recognition and money as it had, but seeing it in the light of her escape from the Southern Territory, each piece seemed more interesting, more folded with meaning and complication.

When Ginny asked what else we should view, I knew she wanted me gone, but I felt the impulse to test her—to ask her to bring out the film reels, give me a private screening of *Birth/Sex/Death*, the fifty-minute recording of X whispering pornographic stories to a man dying in a hospital,* or, better yet, *24 Hour Psycho*—Alfred Hitchcock's *Psycho* slowed down to last twenty-four hours. But I hadn't really come to look at X's artwork, and she must have known this. I wanted to know what Ginny remembered of X, who she had been, not what she had done, and I was trying to linger only long enough that she might say something spontaneous about my wife, something I didn't already know.

Stalling, I asked to see the work about Sophie Calle—*Where Are You, Sophie?*—in which X stalked the French artist for three days while Calle was visiting New York. Most of the photos were taken in public, but a few of them were allegedly taken from underneath Calle's hotel bed.† Calle claimed she never knew she was being followed, and refused to speak of it in interviews. "It's her work," Calle sometimes said, "not mine to speak on."‡

Along with the photos and artifacts that comprised the work, Ginny had saved, in a vinyl folder, several printed interviews X gave around this period. At that point in my research, I hadn't seen most of them—since the one thing X rarely kept were articles from the press—but Ginny was visibly proud of them, holding up certain portraits and headlines, making

* Věra, *Birth/Sex/Death*, 1980. Filmed documentation of performance. Item X860, Quarry Archive, New York.

† Věra, *Where Are You, Sophie?*, 1980. Photographic print. Item X990, Quarry Archive, New York.

‡ Nora Delighter, "Calling Sophie Calle," *New York*, June 14, 1982.

xeroxes of her favorites, telling me which parts to make sure to quote. In one piece in *Playboy* from 1981, just months before X retired all her personas, Kendra Malone asked Věra if she had deliberately set out to be provocative with her work:

> I don't think so. For me these are banal situations . . . There is nothing extraordinary or different about these things that happen to many people—having sex, eating meat. I don't have a particular feeling that I want to shock anyone. On the contrary, when I was following Sophie around I was very afraid that it would be a cruel thing to do. That was, until I realized that it was only provocative to other people, not to Sophie herself. In some ways I thought her entire body of work up to that point had been a request for someone to follow her like this. And so I did. I feel sure she enjoyed it. I've never spoken to her, though. I suppose we've said everything to each other that there is to say.*

---

* Kendra Malone, "Interview with an Art Vampire," *Playboy*, October 1981.

Image: Photograph from *Where Are You, Sophie?*

When I told Ginny I had to be going, she said there was something she wanted to give me and I thought I detected the faintest bit of magnanimity in her voice. From a cabinet in the corner of the room she retrieved a small wooden crate containing the sign that had hung on the door in *The Pain Room*.* She seemed to mean this as some kind of gift, or perhaps this was one of the objects that had belonged to X, as I'd long ago neglected to read the emails from Ginny's secretaries about sorting out "last details" that seemed to keep coming. I didn't want to take it with me, but Ginny insisted, then began to explain to me why *The Pain Room* had been so culturally important and how it irritated her that the work had been so misunderstood.

I said nothing. Of course I knew exactly what *The Pain Room*, an installation X staged dozens of times from 1979 through 1980, had been about; in fact, I knew its subject even more deeply than Ginny could have at the time, as its meaning had been transformed by the revelation of X's birthplace and escape.

The Pain Room was designed to be viewed by one person at a time. Viewers had to open the short door, crawl inside the little room, lock themselves in, and sit in a chair to view a six-minute film, a compilation of vile images and scenes—torture, decay, violence, death. If the viewer flinched

or looked away, a brief electric shock was sent through the chair. If four shocks were administered, the film ended and the door popped open—the viewer had failed. If the viewer endured the film to completion, a trapdoor opened beneath the chair and sent them down a slide, delivering them to a hidden party—a circus of half-clothed dancers and actors paid to fawn over anyone who came down the chute, to ply them with whatever

---

* Věra, *The Pain Room*, 1979. Various ephemera from performance art pieces. Item X1100, Quarry Archive, New York.

alcohol or drugs or attention they wanted. Potential viewers had to sign a nondisclosure agreement and waiver just to join the queue, though many who lined up never made it into *The Pain Room* and even fewer made it down the chute. By the end of the run, the secret was out; club kids lined up around the block and nearly rioted when the gallery closed at two in the morning.

Ginny made a fortune touring *The Pain Room* to museums around the North, as X—having moved on to other work—signed over installation rights to Quarry for a percentage. *The Pain Room* was costly to install and run, but the rumors around the mysterious work whipped up attendance like few other things could. After two viewers at the Chicago Center for Contemporary Art had nervous breakdowns, the intrigue around the work gave way to controversy. There were several protests outside Quarry, and articles in art magazines both defended and decried the profits that Ginny and X had made from the work. I asked Ginny if she regretted anything about that time.

"Not at all," she shot back. "All art is about pain and suffering and ugliness—at its heart. Don't you think so?"

I didn't reply. What did I know about art?

"We don't blame gravediggers for death, now, do we?"

"I suppose we don't," I conceded, though I felt that wasn't quite the same thing.

As I was leaving through the gallery—an empty white space between shows—Ginny's secretary returned and smiled at me in a way that made it clear he knew I was "the widow." (Perhaps my photograph appeared on a little xeroxed sheet they all memorized.) The shock of being observed after so many hours dwelling in the past made me realize I'd failed to get what I wanted from Ginny. She hadn't answered my main question: How had X managed to *live* in those last years of the 1970s? In terms of sheer productivity, the timeline was too dense—founding Knife Fight, writing those books, pretending to be no fewer than five people, accompanying Oleg Hall on what seemed like endless socializing, all the work she made and installed at Quarry—she'd even remastered and released *The Complete Connie Converse* in 1981. It simply did not add up to me. How did she have the stamina or even the hours to accomplish all this? Was she falling apart? Taking drugs? Had she had employees of whom I couldn't find records? Just as I was leaving, I asked Ginny some stammered version of this question—How had she done it, how had she gotten through those years?

"She did it because she had to," Ginny said.

It was a reasonable answer, I suppose, but incomplete. I stood still at the door, further frustrating Ginny in my delay. I remembered that day several years earlier when she'd shown up at the cabin, how I'd felt her hands trembling as she handed me that quart of soup. She, too, had lost someone she loved, and I'd failed to recognize this before.

From the way she was looking at me, I thought she was going to give me some kind of unnecessary advice about my grief, but instead she said, "Whatever you write, make sure you leave out what you told me earlier—that nonsense about how she falsified the performances. It's simply not true."

"She left evidence," I said.

But her voice sharpened in reply. "I don't want to hear about it," she shouted. "It is simply not true."

A moment's silence followed; I thought she might apologize for raising her voice; she didn't. But I won't leave it out. It is simply a fact that *Provocation, 1975* was made in 1977. And the plagiarizing of Gina Pane's performance had been made on Fire Island in 1977, too—not on a Mediterranean beach in 1974, as X had told Ginny all those years ago.

"Making such a claim could damage her reputation," Ginny said.

I told her I didn't care. Whatever small amount of kindness Ginny had felt toward me was gone, and it was then I realized why she'd given me the sign from *The Pain Room*—after the protests she'd made a public statement about donating the proceeds from that work to some kind of nonprofit. The work and its detritus had no value. She was simply clearing the storage space.

"You ruin things," Ginny said. "You ruin whatever is good in your life—that's what X always told me about you."

"Oh," I said. "I see."

She could not hurt me. I had no more space, at the time, to hold any new hurts. For a moment it seemed she might apologize, but now I know she was likely waiting for me to tell her that I had discovered X's final, unfinished work (though another year would pass before I learned of it) or perhaps trying to summon the nerve to tell me herself, to hurt me with what she knew.

A few months later, in March 2003, Ted Gold's assassination in the Schiphol airport was all over the news, and just before my interview with Ginny, David Moser had suffered a heart attack in the same Montana pool hall where I'd met him; and when I'd called Gioia in Italy to confirm a few quotes, her son had called me back to say his mother had killed herself that winter, had jumped from a bridge. There were times that year when I was overcome with a drowsiness that I thought could have been death, too. I figured that since all these people who'd been a part of X's life seemed to be falling away in some kind of choreography—well, maybe it was my time. But I didn't die. Not that year, or not exactly.

DISAPPEARING

Y our early pieces had an appearance/disappearance method to them," a critic said to X while interviewing her in 1991 about *The Human Subject*.

"The early work applied stress to the body that then had to adapt, change, open up, because of that stress," X first replied, an automatic phrase—one I'd heard her use often—but then she added, "I wanted to get rid of myself so there could be room for other selves."*

There was an unusually honest and abject quality in her voice, though she wasn't exactly answering the question. The critic soon moved on to the usual topics—her brief and bizarre career in music, the controversial artworks, her various feuds, the perennial debate around her sanity.

"For me, insanity would be like a vacation, or a belief in god; out of desperation, you let yourself fall into it," she said.

But as I sat watching my wife from the audience, I kept thinking of her disappearances. I knew that vanishing was not an abstract concern in X's artwork, but a simple fact of her life.

She and I had been together two years then, and I still lived in a sharp fear. I loved her, but I was frightened of her capabilities, her resolve, her

---

* Naomi Fry, "X & Fry in Conversation," Festival for the Humanities, April 23, 1991, Cami-Tabor Hall, New York University.

inscrutability. Then there was the matter of our agreement—the terms she'd set the moment I moved in with her.

In the spring of 1989, X told me I needed to be prepared for her to vanish at any moment, and for any length of time. She made me promise that I would never report these disappearances, never go looking for her, that I wouldn't tell anyone she was missing, and that I would never ask where she had been when she returned. In thrall, I said yes, yes to all of it. She said it had been a problem in other relationships—that her exes had not loved her enough to trust her completely, but she could tell that I was different. I had a "*ruthlessness*" about life—that was the word she used. I lived ruthlessly, and she had seen it from the start.

It would not be unreasonable to say that X and I, in that moment, did not yet know each other except by instinct. We hadn't yet cohabitated, had endured no hardships, hadn't traveled together, and had only discussed personal matters in the most cursory ways. Despite this, I felt X knew me better than anyone else, and the moment she called me ruthless I believed myself to be so. Prior to that moment, I may have identified as a rather meek person, a fearful person, someone who was terrified of pain, of difficulty and conflict. But here she was—this enormously powerful woman telling me that *I* possessed a rare strain of power. I accepted it completely. I immediately became a new creature, one who could accept—without worry or hesitation—that the most important person in her life would disappear for weeks at a time without explanation or assurance of her return.

At the same time, I still carried around those fearful past selves, and the ghost of Henry's wife still paced in the back of my mind, as did my parents' silent and nameless daughter, as well as the young woman who once desired the most conventional, stable life possible—a nice living room, a face no one would call ugly, a marriage, the approval of others. In that first year or so with X, I was sometimes haunted by their voices and the worries of those past selves, especially when X was gone.

The first time she left it was early autumn. We'd been living together for only a few months, and as we were making spaghetti one night I realized we had no Parmesan, so I went out to the grocery around the corner from our building, feeling triumphant as I slipped in just moments before they closed, but when I returned to the loft X was gone. A pot of water was still boiling on the stove. I tried to reassure myself that she had warned me she would disappear, that I didn't need to be afraid, but I spent most of the night weeping, or silently ashamed that I had just wept, gritting my teeth, and breathing hard before succumbing to sobs again. Three weeks later she came home, and I pressed my face against her neck so she wouldn't see that my eyes had filled at the sight of her in our doorway. I thought I would become better at accepting this fact about X, at not knowing where she had gone or why it had to be a secret or when she would return, but every time she left I raved and wept just as much as the last time, and every time she returned I feigned ease to hide my abjection.

In February 2003 an editor I used to know called to say she'd been contacted by a young reporter who was working on an story about Northern citizens who'd been secretly working for the FBI, and X was one of his subjects. He wanted to speak with me. The editor gave me his number. I called immediately.

I have a credible tip that X may have been used in undercover missions in the Southern Territory, the young reporter said, *and that she may have even been born there. Are you aware of any of this?*

I said I hadn't been aware, but that I wasn't surprised. I asked him who his source was, and he said it was the grandfather of a college friend, a man named Fred Holton, who lived in a retirement home in Maine. Apparently unaware that I, too, was (or had been) a journalist, he told me which home. I wished him luck, hung up, and immediately made plans to visit Maine that week.

At the time I thought the only task left in my research was to gather the nerve to go into X's office and follow up with any loose ends I may have found in there, a task I kept putting off, as I knew it would signal the end of my work and I was unsure of what I would do with myself if I didn't have this hole to hide in. The notion that X had been an FBI agent slid easily into the abundant file of conspiracy theories, yet it also had a strange appeal: an involvement with the FBI would have explained all her disappearances, but if it was true this would have meant X was the kind of hypocrite she had long claimed to detest.

It's hard to imagine someone hating the government as much as X did. She detested Congress, the military, police departments, and the tax administration most of all, but also the postal system, hospitals, public schools, public art, interstates—all of it. She claimed to trust nothing the government touched, convinced of its uniform corruption. She loved hopping federal fences, destroying dollar bills, defacing monuments, shredding flags. Her cynicism was so total that she refused not only to vote but also to discuss the existence of politicians for any reason, accusing the whole system to be as duplicitous and corrupt as organized religion.

Early on, I made the mistake of challenging, however slightly, her monolithic position. Sure, there were problems, even unequivocal failures in our government, but I still found it worthwhile to retain a certain amount of optimism about the Northern Territory, as we were doing a lot better than we had in the past. People used to go into serious debt to afford advanced education, and only the rich received adequate health care, and at one time it was even legal for a CEO to earn a thousand times over their company's entry-level salary. And yes, police were still quick to violence and almost always got away with it, but at least they didn't carry guns anymore! (This was pre-Reunification, before Northern Territory police were armed again.) Didn't it count for something that we'd come so far? But arguments were never an even match between X and me, and when it came to these issues, she'd quickly bury me in statistics and rhetorical headlocks—there was no humanity, she insisted, in any aspect or wing of any federal power, and it was morally indefensible to work for them, respect them, or believe they were anything more than criminals.

The thought of her being an FBI operative alternately amused and horrified me; just imagining it sent me into fits of nervous laughter, and it was then I began to wonder if all this work hadn't—indeed and finally—driven me so mad that I was actually entertaining the veracity of this claim. As I drove to Maine to meet Fred Holton, I recalled those withering looks X gave me when I went to vote, and again I was driven to laughter, the only rational response I had; there was nothing else I could do.

Fred Holton had been living in a retirement home in Maine for the two years since his wife's death, a fact I measured against my seven years of widowhood. When I'd called the home to arrange a visit with him,

Image: Fred Holton, 1985

I'd been assured that Mr. Holton was still quite sharp despite being, at eighty-eight, one of their oldest residents. He loved having visitors, the attendant said, and people came to see him all the time.

When I arrived I was directed to a dining room where I found a man in a white shirt and black tie sitting alert at the table, making notes with a short pencil on a palm-sized notepad. He shook my hand with a deal-making firmness, as if I'd come to offer him a large sum of money.

"Did you have a nice drive?" he asked. "I think the countryside is beautiful this time of year—late winter, everything bare. You can keep your autumn colors, your hot summer days, yessir, you can keep them. Leave me with the winter, that's what I always say."*

His smile had a way of making me feel like there were already secrets between us, and in a way there were, only neither of us knew them. The dining room was empty except for the young women setting the tables around us—little flower vases, salt shakers, coffee cups turned over on saucers.

"A real professional, you are. Not a lot of professionals anymore," he said as I placed the microphone before him.

I asked if he was interviewed often, and he began jotting things intermittently on his notepad as we spoke.

"Yes, why—suppose I've gotten used to it," he said. "Talking about the good old days, the days gone by, days of yore, what have you. I had a good run of it, a very good run."

He then launched into a long story about his work in the State Department in the 1950s, how he'd been a part of a group that had de-escalated a conflict in Vietnam. "It nearly became a war," he said, "but you never hear about the wars that don't happen, you never do."

He told stories with relish and ease, and I'd never seen such a thing—a man at the end of his life, who knew it was the end of his life, who looked back upon what he'd done with natural pride and peace over what had been completed. I'd never, ever reached the end of anything, even things I was glad to be done with, with any feeling other than grief. Every school and university I'd ever attended, for instance, had provided nothing but miserable, friendless years, yet I cried at every graduation.

Eventually, I found a moment to cut into Fred Holton's soliloquy and asked him if he had ever heard of a woman named X.

"Well, sure," he said. "Only that's not what I called her."

I waited for him to elaborate, but he was busy taking notes again.

"What did you call her?"

"I believe we called her Agent Hip," he said. "There's a story there

* Fred Holton, interview with the author, February 13, 2003, tape 61.1–4, CML audio collection, TXA. All quotes from Fred Holton in the following paragraphs are from this interview.

with the name, only it escapes me now. So much does. Who can blame it. Escaping . . . you know."

"What was she like?"

"A very interesting woman," he said, nodding as he put his notepad away again, "though she hasn't come to visit me. She's the only one who hasn't come to visit."

For some reason it seemed like my fault that X had never come to see him—that is, if she had in fact known him. Mr. Holton checked his notepad again, as if it were a watch, then stowed it in his briefcase. After we sat there quietly for a time, I asked him if he and Agent Hip ever went undercover into the ST.

"That's exactly what she did," he said, nodding. "Yes. Quite an expert. I don't think I would have gone at all if it hadn't been for her. Never knew a woman or man as brave as her."

Again we sat quietly. All his loquacity had drained away, and the slow silence discomfited me.

"Would you mind sharing," I said, "what *year* you went into the ST with Agent Hip?"

"Oh, several times," Mr. Holton said. "Let's see, I retired in 1990, or was it 1995? And by 'retired' I mean they asked me to retire. I hadn't been allowed to do much for the last few years there. But it must have been the eighties and seventies with Hip. I must have been doing the trips to the South back then."

"And Agent Hip . . . she was a good deal younger?"

"Than me? Oh hell, everyone's younger than me! I'm just some kind of old penny nobody wants to pick up anymore, ain't it so? Come to think of it, I couldn't tell you exactly how old Agent Hip was, seeing as most of my memories of her have to do with being in disguise . . . That was one of her specialties, as far as I remember. She taught me how to do a fake beard you couldn't tell any different from a real one. Why, I even fooled my own wife with that! She thought I was the plumber for a whole afternoon. Oh, if you could've seen that woman's face! It shocked her half to death when she figured out it was me."

He went on for a while about his late wife, relishing an audience for his memories, and I tolerated him for a little while before I changed the subject back to the disguises.

"See, that's how we did it in the South. You had to. If you gave the guards any inkling that you were someone else, they'd get you. Happened to plenty of other agents before we started getting all the details straight . . . It was probably the most dangerous thing I ever did, those missions, not that I knew it at the time. You can't know it at the time, can you? No, you just can't know anything at the time. That's true for the worst and best things, isn't it? Why, I figure I would have forgotten all about all of it if it hadn't been for these files I got sent."

"Files?" My voice squeaks on the recording.

"Declassified, they said, some of the stuff I did. And I was looking it over and, you know, almost glad that Helga isn't around now to find out what I was doing back then. It would have worried her in reverse, that woman. Even once something was done she kept worrying about it! We got married in 1937, and not a day passed she didn't worry herself over who she'd forgotten to invite or how she stumbled over a word of her vows. Such a worrying woman you've never known. It is a good thing indeed she never knew about the things we did in the South—the mission to that prison, for instance. Before the Hoyne administration came in and ended it, of course, we were planning to liberate that prison since they had so many Northern hostages. But Hoyne thought the number of estimated casualties was too high. A damn shame, you see. And this is the thing—people do get killed, they always get killed, it's just a matter of *which* people. That's what nobody wants to think about, pacifists or whatever. They don't understand it happens either way, you see? It's not how we want it to be; it's just how it is."

He nodded for a while, his eyes grave and elsewhere.

"Was Agent Hip with you on that mission?"

"What I do remember about Agent Hip is that she was very strict about her privacy. I do remember that, but she was a wonderful woman. A very interesting woman. Why, I don't think I've ever met anyone quite as *interesting* as Agent Hip."

He called out to one of the nurses setting tables and asked if we could have two coffees.

"In what way was she interesting?" I asked.

Mr. Holton smiled and took out his notepad again, flipped it open, and began to write as he said, "Well, now, I'm not going to go around violating Agent Hip's privacy, am I? Everything gets back to her, not a single thing escapes her."

Again I considered telling him that she was—if indeed we were talking about the same woman—dead, that I was here because she was dead, that she had no privacy anymore, that death had taken that, too.

"My grandson has lately taken an interest in history, so I had a few copies of these papers sent over. Maybe you'd like to have a look at them, too?"

Mr. Holton took a stack of folders from his briefcase and laid out several papers before us—xeroxed copies of memos, maps, reports with lines blacked out, and a few photographs—

"Here she is," he said, setting a small portrait of a woman in front of me. "Agent Hip."

Though I knew X was accomplished with facial prosthetics and makeup and wigs, I knew her face well enough to find it even when it

Image: Agent Hip

had been purposefully hidden. The fact that there was none of her here seemed to end it—unless, perhaps, she used advanced techniques for such serious and dangerous work. When I later learned that the letter "X" was used on internal FBI documents as a stand-in for agents' real names, I again considered that there had been some kind of misunderstanding, and perhaps she'd never worked for the bureau. Then again, that, too, might have been a coincidence. "X" was often used in such a way, a place-holder for people or things discarded, hidden, or unknown. Malcolm X, Madame X, solving for x.

"Here we are," Mr. Holton said, holding up a page as he read from it. "I was the one to interview Agent Hip, back in . . . The year isn't here, but the seventies or sixties maybe—and I remember this—or I didn't remember it until I read it again, then I remembered—Ah! The things Agent Hip said in that interview! She was apparently quite the prod-igy—'I learnt to write in two weeks,' she said, 'after which I surged for-ward, nothing stopping me . . . I paid no attention to the astonishment of the teachers, the admiration or envy of my schoolmates. The teachers regarded me with suspicion and the pupils began seeking my friendship, but I was busy with this wonderful machine with which I had been en-dowed. I was cold as a field of ice, nothing in the world could shake me.' How about that? She really knew her worth—didn't she?"

It did, I thought, sound like the kind of thing X might say about herself.

"And look at this!" Mr. Holton said, holding up another page from a report that had been redacted to the point of being a solid rectangle of black ink. "Nothing to see here," he said in jest.

Then he unfolded a large sheet of newsprint, a rubbing of what seemed to be a gravestone.

"Well, that jogs a memory, don't it?" he said, looking down at the arti-fact. "Yes. It was that graveyard we sometimes walked around in, the only place you could be sure to be alone."

"And what was this?"

"Well, isn't it obvious?" he asked.

I said nothing.

"It was *her* grave," he said, just as two black coffees were set before us.

She was a Christian.
Humble without meanness;
Pious without bigotry;
Charitable without ostentation;
And while
Most tender and gentle,
She was
Firm and unwavering
in
The performance of every duty

———

This monument is erected to her memory
by
An affectionate Husband.

I kept staring down at the newsprint, the faded crayon.

"I don't need to explain why she might have made a rubbing of her own gravestone, do I?"

Holton finished his coffee as if it were a glass of water, though it was still steaming, then resumed taking notes, glancing up at me every few moments. It was disturbing how quickly he had inverted our meeting, how I now felt like I was the one being scrutinized.

"Did it upset you that the Hoyne administration put an end to your work?" I asked in an attempt to regain control.

"No work is done for nothing," he said, "but if you're asking if I was *disappointed* that nearly all my efforts in the Southern Territory were trashed by the Hoyne administration, well—do you really need an answer?"

It had been a while since I'd thought much about that time, the demoralizing upset of the 1980 presidential election, when Ann Hoyne of the neofascist Growth Party narrowly beat Ronald Reagan of the Green Party. The election of the first female president should have been a victory, but Hoyne believed most women—"With some exceptions!" she always added—were innately inferior to men. She popularized a bogus theory about estrogen being antagonistic to mental acuity, and often bragged that her estrogen levels had been quite low all her life, despite her arrestingly feminine appearance, which she exaggerated with red lipstick and spike heels. It was a particularly menacing time. The Growth Party's propaganda motto, "Let People Live; Make People Work," was blanketed across most public spaces, and Hoyne occasionally suggested the North should bomb the Southern Territory, raze it, and reclaim the land, while she pretended to be acting with "human costs" in mind when she stripped much of the FBI's funding for missions into the South.

"Isn't it funny," Holton asked, "what people think?"

I didn't know exactly what he was talking about, but I agreed to be agreeable. We fell into a silence for a few moments, and I had assumed we were both dwelling—from different angles—on the Hoyne era. I'd been just entering adulthood in the early 1980s, while Holton had been approaching the shrug of years between adulthood and death. I began to ask him what he meant, what was funny about the things people thought, but when I looked at him there were tears rolling down his face, though he appeared oblivious to them.

"She never came to visit me," he said. "Agent Hip."

"She died," I said. "In 1996."

"No," he said, and I left it at that.

For a moment I thought of explaining who I was, but the word "widow" escaped me. I often forgot this word—the word for what a woman became after her wife died. As a sound, it seemed to recall a kitchen with all the cabinets left open, which they often were, I found, now that I lived alone.

"Agent Hip . . . she'll come. I'm sure she'll visit soon," Mr. Holton concluded.

I realized then the error of this trip, how foolish I'd been to believe this theory, based on nothing but hearsay, a single phone call. How utterly stupid and sad I was being.

"I think the world is beautiful this time of year," Holton said, repeating himself as before, "early winter, everything bare. You can keep your autumn colors, your hot summer days, yessir, you can keep them. Leave me with the winter, that's what I always say."

I took this as the right moment to leave, and as I stood I glanced at his notepad and was startled to see that he'd simply been making *X*s across each line. *XXXXXXX*.

Of course, I told myself, it didn't mean anything. An *X* is just an *X*, a shape. Two lines. A sound, a letter, the idle marking of a nervous old man. I put aside my paranoia, thanked him for his time, and shook his hand in that funeral way, soft and lacking meaning.

As I was leaving, the woman at the front desk asked, *How did it go?*

I told her he didn't seem to be all there.

Ah, well, she said, *he has one sort of days, and he has another sort of days. Suppose we all do.*

THE HUMAN SUBJECT

M uch of X's art confused me, or perhaps I should just say it sometimes bored me; I did not think it was uniformly good. Some of it was wonderful—the Cindy O novellas for instance, though it seems I'm alone on that one, as they've all fallen out of print again, and the Clyde Hill novel, *The Reason I'm Lost*, though X regarded that work as juvenile and misguided. However, many of her performances, paintings, and sculptures seem a little heartless to me now, designed not to evoke real feeling, but to get a reaction or a check. She was too smart. She knew what would sell, or stir controversy, and she gave into the ease of receiving that attention—which she pretended to despise but of course was obsessed with—rather than accept the pain of making something sincerely, then being misunderstood or ignored.

Another exception was *The Complete Connie Converse*—the four-record album that X (as "Bee Converse") released with Pulse-Kinsella Records in 1980. It collected almost every song that the two of them had made together. Although it was mostly ignored upon its release, the album was suddenly popular and impossible to keep stocked after Kurt Cobain began covering Connie's songs during his 1992 tour. It was around this time I made the mistake of asking X what had happened to Connie and she gave me the silent treatment for several days. It was only after X's death that I learned the truth.

The afternoon that Oleg told her that X had left for Europe, Connie quit her laundress job in Manhattan, packed up her modest apartment, and moved the short distance to Queens, where she found a nearly identical apartment and job.* New York is a large enough city that a move to another borough is nearly a move to another country. Moving across the river decreased but not entirely erased the possibility of seeing X when she returned from Europe, and I'm led to assume that was part of the point.

Connie lived the last years of her life mere miles from X, but their paths never again crossed, and not even Phil Converse knew where his sister was until her death. She continued to write songs, but she never performed them publicly or recorded them. Yet it also seems that the last years of her life were happy ones. When Connie's boss, the elderly bachelor who owned Buckley's Cleaners, died in 1978, he left the business to Connie, his sole employee. She renamed it Connie's Cleaners and ran it until she died of a heart attack late in 1981. It seems she never found out that X had released an album of her music; it may have been better that way. According to the obituary that her brother wrote after he was called to Queens to identify her body, Connie was beloved by her neighbors. She had a dog named Chipper and washed the clothes of the people living in the streets while they bathed in a metal tub in the back. She then served them tea and cake as she did the ironing.

Phil sent notices of Connie's death to everyone in his sister's address book, including one to "Bee Converse," in care of Oleg Hall. It was New Year's Day 1982 when X found out that Connie had been living nearby all that time but was now gone. Theodore Smith's biography does not mention the event and simply glosses over late 1981 and early 1982 as if X were too busy preparing to debut *The Human Subject* to think of anything else.

It is likely that X used the distraction of her work as a buffer from grief, but her painful, chaotic diaries, which hardly make any grammatical

---

* Connie Converse, memoir, undated pages, folder 5, CML Papers, TXA.

sense (she seems to have been using drugs again), reveal a woman both sharpened and dulled with grief. Several factors contributed to her retiring all her personas and taking the name X in early 1982, but Connie's death was easily the most significant.

A loss tinged with shame, regret, or a sense of something unfinished is the most dangerous sort, a black-hole grief that pulls a person relentlessly toward its center, and when our lives come to one of these we are forced to either bow before it or detach completely. X chose the latter, to proceed as if there had been no Connie at all rather than reckon with a love that was impossible to resolve or fold away neatly. *It is better to cut than to tear*, she sometimes advised. It was years later that I realized this was a translation of a line from X's favorite Camille Bordas film, *Le mauvais paradis*, when the heroine, María del Mar Sánchez Vivancos, calls her husband to break it off abruptly: "Il vaut mieux couper que déchirer."

In December 1981, an article in the *New York Post* had claimed that Cassandra Edwards was a grifter who'd run up tabs all over town in her fictitious father's name;* the next week, *Artforum* published a long essay proving that Yarrow Hall and Věra must have been the same person, and thus that *The Blue Tape* had been a sham.† This crush of press was either well timed or may have sped up X's plans to retire all those names and debut her most influential and lasting work: *The Human Subject.*

Quite frankly, I never quite understood why *The Human Subject* was seen by so many as a pivotal moment in twentieth-century American art. Despite having married two very different artists, I've never comprehended the hidden laws that seem to govern the art world; after I met X, I took some time to study the work that X respected to better understand her references and context. With this in mind, I've briefly outlined the cultural moment into which *The Human Subject* arrived. I do not suggest that this synopsis is comprehensive, simply that it may be helpful for certain readers.

Though it is difficult to imagine now, the occupation of "artist" in America was seen, prior to World War II, almost exclusively as a male calling; it was only through the intersection of a variety of economic and cultural events that this stereotype was inverted and women were seen as the sex to whom "art" belonged. (Why it had to belong to one sex or another is a different matter entirely.) Many have identified the Painters' Massacre of 1943 as a crucial turning point in this reversal.‡ In December of that year, a mob of Southern separatists stormed an opening at the Museum of Non-Objective Painting in New York, killing fourteen male artists—Marcel Duchamp, Alexander Calder, Wassily Kandinsky, and Jackson Pollock among them—while sparing all the women. This act of terrorism might have been more well-known if it hadn't been one of the less-deadly incidents perpetrated by similar groups; as it stands, it appears more often in art history books than in books on the Great Disunion.

---

* Forsyth Harmon, "New Grifters in Town," *New York Post*, December 3, 1981.

† Mary Kate Wilk, "Recent Conspiracies," *Artforum*, December 7, 1981.

‡ Kit Schluter, *The Painting That Never Was* (New York: Pantheon, 1980).

The aftermath of this event reverberated through the work of the female survivors. Dorothea Tanning's series, *Death of the Patriarchs*, in which she used her lover, Max, as a human paintbrush, is seen as an epitomic work of this period.

Shortly after X and I married, she bought a pair from that series—*Death of the Patriarchs No. 13* and *Death of the Patriarchs No. 64*—and kept them in one corner of her studio, leaned against the wall. Ginny Green was driven repeatedly mad over X's lack of reverence for the paintings and begged X to hang them and light them properly or put them in storage if she hated them so much.

A man got smeared in paint—that's all that happened, X often said to Ginny's complaints. *Reverence kaleidoscopes the ordinary into the magnificent.*

When I later asked her why she bought the paintings if she didn't think they were so great, X told me they were her reminder that meaningful work isn't always "*good work*" and a challenge to make things that

Image: *Death of the Patriarchs No. 13* and *Death of the Patriarchs No. 64* as seen in X's studio were both good and meaningful. The paintings were also, though my wife was loath to utter such words, an *investment*.

In the decade before the Painters' Massacre of 1943, radical feminist and anarchist ideas were spreading rapidly across the country, a trend generally attributed to the popularity of Emma Goldman's speeches and policies. Nowhere were these beliefs more apparent or more extremely held than among young artists. Young men who might have otherwise pursued careers as painters and sculptors were pushed toward arts administration, and if they still wanted to work with their hands, then working as an assistant to a female artist was understood to be the most logical option. The belief that the feminine perspective was the only necessary perspective was becoming commonplace at the time; male artists pursued careers with the burden of explaining or accounting for the global history of male violence and destruction; that is—men could only make work about being men. Few took on the task, and those who did were often ridiculed.

A second factor that contributed to the reversal of gender norms in the art world was economic. The potential financial rewards of making art dramatically changed in the early 1940s—all the money that had been poured into the art market from Europe during the 1930s dried up by the Disunion; nearly two-thirds of all art galleries in New York City closed between 1940 and 1960. Though cultural conventions were in flux, most American men, even in the Northern Territory, still felt the need to provide financially for their families. Money itself was seen as a dirty necessity in the Goldman and post-Goldman era, and the task of generating a family's income was understood to be inherently masculine, something unpleasant but still needed, a kind of penance for being a member of the violent sex.

Throughout the twentieth century, similar inversions occurred in the architecture, film, and music worlds—though at different rates and for different reasons. By the 1970s, however, European investment in the American art market had again surged. New galleries and museums opened all over the Northern Territory, and many visual artists—practically all of them women—became enormously wealthy. Whether this financial shift merely *coincided with* or *caused* the increasing unrest of ignored male artists is a topic of robust debate.

Larry Rivers, a struggling middle-aged American painter and truck driver, and his friend Yves Klein staged a guerrilla show of their work outside the Guggenheim Museum in 1972 to protest the fact that it had been over a decade since the museum had exhibited any work of art by a man. Klein was quite successful in his native France, but he was ridiculed in America for copying Dorothea Tanning's *Death of the Patriarch* with a female model instead of male. Attitudes about gender were again shifting in the Northern Territory and the Rivers-Klein protest upended and divided the art world.

In 1980, the critic and scholar Richard Cusk published an essay about this conflict that encapsulated the issue. "Can a male artist—however virtuosic and talented, however disciplined—ever attain a fundamental freedom from the fact of his own malehood?" Cusk asked. "Must the politics of masculinity invariably be accounted for, whether by determinedly ignoring them or by deliberately confronting them? The latter is a fateful choice that can shape an artist's life and work; but does the former—the avoidance of oneself as a male subject—inevitably compromise the expressive act?"* Cusk went on to describe "female art" as having reached a kind of creative plateau, and argued that the dominance of women in the art world since the 1950s had had its intended effect—it had fundamentally changed the way that men made art.

When *The Human Subject* debuted in spring of 1982, it was frequently described as a rebuke of Cusk's thesis. Men had created almost every work of art prior to the twentieth century. They had depicted the female form again and again and thus narrowly and tenaciously defined "the feminine." A few decades of female dominance of the art market was not a sufficient corrective of that imbalance. "*The Human Subject*," one critic explained, "introduces us to a dozen women who lived within one artist, but it will take thousands more to fill the crater left behind by the reckless history of Male Art."†

The Human Subject exhibition charted X's inhabitation of each per-

* Richard Cusk, "Male Artists: Can They Really Be Artists?," *Art in Review*, June 16, 1980.

† Chiara Barzini, "A Thousand Faces Launch One Ship," *The Giancarlo Review*, May 6, 1982.

sona through a series of artifacts. Under a section titled "*Dorothy Eagle, 1968–1978,*" there was a vitrine holding that Montana ID, two handkerchiefs, her white patent leather purse, several letters, two diaries, and a collection of photographs—some taken by "Dorothy" and some portraits of the character. The display for "*Bee Converse, 1972–1977*" held several of her bulky costumes, a wig, a ukulele with her name carved into it, and many handwritten drafts of the songs she later produced with Waits, Bowie, and others. "*Clyde Hill, 1973*" contained one object: the typed manuscript of *The Reason I'm Lost.* To avoid legal trouble, X did not include "Martina Riggio" in the exhibit, but among the many artifacts for "Cindy O" and "Cassandra Edwards" are letters to and from that elusive, tax-evading editor. "Yarrow Hall's" and "Věra's" sections were pushed up against each other, and the series of letters between the two were so intricate that they aroused theories that X may have been schizophrenic, a theory that X often encouraged.

"I'm not at all acting parts in these portraits," X told one journalist. "I think because I'm an artist, my image will always come before me. I am an artist, I am a representation, I think that's the reason why people think that I am directing myself in a little story and acting a part, but this is not a character."* The controversy and scope of the exhibition meant it became one of those rare occurrences that lured in visitors beyond the urbane, self-sacrosanct few who usually fill galleries. Unsurprisingly, the more popular the show became, the more frequent was the complaint that the work was unserious, pedestrian. Initial reviews, however, were effusive.

"The sheer range of self-transformation is astonishing," Calvin Tomkins wrote in *The New Yorker.* "Using only makeup, wigs, clothing, and a few props, she makes herself look vulnerable, sexy, gauche, put-together, a total mess, plump, slender, tough, childlike, worn—every kind of woman except herself. You could study the pictures for an hour and then fail to recognize her on the street."† Tomkins was one of the only critics who

---

* Barzini, "A Thousand Faces Launch One Ship."

† Calvin Tomkins, "The Human Subject Astounds," *The New Yorker*, April 19, 1982.

accepted *The Human Subject* as a work of art without arguing with himself over how to categorize it or whether he should feel betrayed by the fact that he'd also reviewed Yarrow Hall's film and had attended Věra's show at the Philadelphia Institute of Contemporary Art. Tomkins simply called it "a ten-year performance to which the whole world had been the audience."

Richard Cusk, in his *Village Voice* review, called the show "a sublime experience . . . not quite a dream, not wholly a nightmare."* Like others, Cusk seems to have been personally unsettled far beyond the gallery walls: "For days after my first viewing I felt uneasy in eye contact, unsure of my own face in the mirror. I contacted the gallerist and returned to Quarry for a second viewing; I arrived half an hour before my appointment and stood in the unusually cold April morning, smoking in a hurry. Then this terrible realization arrived: this indignant pain I felt was the same feeling I'd had the morning I met my estranged son . . . Our meeting had seemed to be more like theater than like life, which had bothered me . . . Once inside the gallery I could not decide—is this a good work of art? Is it even a work of art at all? Upon this matter, I could never settle myself, but I could not forget how it had pushed me to see something horribly honest about how performance bleeds into life."

Other outlets covered the show more bluntly. The *New York Post* ran a brief summary under the headline "Serial Scammer Says She Did It for Art!"† *Art in America* ran a dry, somewhat confused piece, the writer irritated by X's refusal to be interviewed and her lack of cooperation in fact-checking.‡

Hito Steyerl, in her monograph on *The Human Subject*, used X's effect on David Bowie's music as a framing device. She suggested that the "hero" X had invented for Bowie was "no longer a subject, but an object: a thing, an image, a splendid fetish." She used the 1977 music video for the song as further evidence: "[The video] shows Bowie singing to him-

---

* Richard Cusk, "The Human Subject: Enigma Variations," *The Village Voice*, April 7, 1982.

† Terry Yuval, "Serial Scammer Says She Did It for Art!," *New York Post*, April 14, 1982.

‡ Phyllis Yang, "Human Subject: Subjective Human," *Art in America*, September 2, 1982.

self from three simultaneous angles, with layering techniques tripling his image; not only has Bowie's hero been cloned, he has above all become an image that can be reproduced, multiplied, and copied, . . . a fetish that packages Bowie's glamorous and unfazed postgender look as product . . . endowed with posthuman beauty: an image and nothing but an image."*

Steyerl went on to write that X had begun "the erasure of the self into an image" as the primary new subject for the modern era, though she warned it came with a risk: "Images are violated, ripped apart, subjected to interrogation and probing. They are stolen, cropped, edited, and re-appropriated. They are bought, sold, leased. Manipulated and adulterated. Reviled and revered. To participate in the image means to take part in all of this."

"There is another world," X often said. "I'm not satisfied with this world. And that's why I'm onstage. To be nearer to the other world."†

When an interviewer once asked her what she meant by "onstage," she only said, "That's right. Onstage."‡

"Do you despise these questions?" another reporter asked.

"You want to know what I most despise? Literature? The tragic mis-understanding that goes under the name of love? People in general? That's a hard question. I don't despise anyone or anything. I have no right to . . . But I will not have people lying to me anymore, neither books nor women, and I will have no patience at all with lies I tell myself."§

She ended the interview then by standing abruptly and walking out.

On live radio, a host asked X if she ever missed them, if she ever missed any of those women she used to be.

"Well, do *you* miss them?" X asked in reply. "Now that we know they're all gone and never coming back—do you miss them?"

---

* Hito Steyerl, *The Human Subject in Review* (London: Rizzoli, 1985).

† Pasha Clarion, "10 Questions with X," *Lyonne Magazine*, October 3, 1982.

‡ "X interview with Sara Q. Rich," 92nd Street Y Arts & Letters Festival, 1984. Transcript, item 501.3, TXA.

§ S. N. Prickett, "Various Lies of the Late 20th C.," *Lake Magazine*, March 28, 1982.

"Oh, but I didn't know any of them."

"And neither did I."*

Early in 1983, X was awarded The Essay Prize for *The Human Subject*. At the ceremony she appeared in a black suit and sunglasses, pale hair slicked back, as she was interviewed onstage by Jenna Sauers, president of The Essay Foundation:

SAUERS: Do you agree that *The Human Subject* is an essay?

X: It seems that by your choice you've answered the question and by accepting the prize I have given you my answer.

SAUERS:: How do you define the word "essay"?

X: It's up to you to tell me.

SAUERS: You have said that you both do and don't regret making *The Human Subject*. Several of the "real" people who were involved, in various respects, have objected strongly to the project; do you feel that the work was ultimately worth it? How do you balance the moral concerns of a work like this with the concerns of an artist? Is it a question of the ends justifying the means?

X: Indeed the question is: Was it worth the effort from an artistic or literary point of view? You seem to think so, by giving me this prize. As for me, even if I had regrets when a few people declared that my project had made them suffer (which truly surprised me, since I involved them precisely because they seemed to be the sort of people who would be in favor of the idea of escaping a self). But in spite of these regrets, I cannot deny that my excitement was stronger than my guilt . . . If I had to do it all over I again, I would. During the years I was making *The Human Subject* I abandoned many possible personas because I thought they did not measure up to their potential intrigue or danger or potential cruelty. I do not believe it is always morally wrong to act in a cruel manner, so long as you accept the burden of accurately calculating whether the

---

* Barbara Hosh, *Live at 10 with Barbara Hosh*, WNYC, November 9, 1982.

object of one's cruelty could stand to benefit from pain more than from pleasure. Each person I involved during the course of *The Human Subject* revealed to me whether they should be exploited in this way. Many factors were calculated as I came up with responses to this problem of "ends" and "means." There isn't a general answer. The question is asked every time.*

* Jenna Sauers, "Interview with X," The Essay Foundation Prize, December 8, 1982.

MARION

X once explained to me that her first wife, Marion Parker, had been powerfully charming at first, but soon became cruel and jealous and childish. Once certain lines were crossed, there was no way to go back. I took this as a warning that every relationship contains one-way gates, boundaries you can cross only once, limits I nervously tried to locate and avoid.

After their divorce, Marion had lived abroad for a while, I was told, remarried a few times, tried several self-reinventions. She'd attempted a career as an actress, then as a singer, but even her father's many connections were no help, and his waning reputation likely hung over her. She wrote a memoir, but no one would publish it, and after she paid a gallery to exhibit some of her abstract paintings, the opening received so much laughing press that she moved to the Philippines for a year. Floundering, it seems, became the primary activity of her life, a fate that often plagues those born into a cocoon of wealth or an excess of self-regard; she was certainly the former, if not the latter.

All the while, Marion continued to send long, intense letters to X, which my wife read with a sad smirk before throwing them out and never writing back. The lack of reply was no deterrent, however, and the letters from Marion continued to arrive, sometimes several within the same month. When I noticed one in the mail I sometimes thought of ripping it open and reading it myself, but I never did. Instead, I presented each one to X on a silver platter, trying to transform my disdain into a joke, trying to hide my greed, my immature wish for anyone who had ever come before me to vanish forever and leave no shadow. Occasionally, X read them aloud to me; other times, I simply forced myself not to lift them from the garbage and hold them together at the rip.

By the time I contacted Marion for an interview in 2003, I'd been a widow for long enough that I no longer feared meeting this first wife, though I cannot say I was looking forward to it. I will admit I was intimidated by Marion's effortless grace—who wouldn't be? She is a good deal younger than I am, not so much in years but in the way she carries them, and not only in the way she carries them physically but also in her bright and undiminished gaze, that of someone who seems to know no disappointment. You could argue, of course, that physical beauty indicates nothing of any depth about a person, yet few can avoid falling under its spell.

We met at a restaurant in the West Village that she chose, one with a heated patio and "a marvelous steak frites," which she ordered without looking at the menu. Though I'd studied many photographs of Marion, I found her even more charming in person than I'd expected. She seemed powerfully relaxed, at ease, magnetic.

"I've been rereading the poetry of W. H. Auden," she announced, then recited a few lines.*

To my dismay, I immediately understood how X would have been drawn to her, even all those years ago, and I paid attention to her in a way that went beyond simple research and recalled how I'd look at women when I was a girl, in hopes that I might become one.

"You know—she was such a wonderful woman, a truly remarkable woman," Marion said of X. "And I'm sure you know quite well how utterly magical she was, but the real truth of it was that she and I would have been better suited to be friends . . . I was just *so* young—and I suppose I didn't know to recognize that yet, how powerfully you can love

---

* Marion Parker, interview with the author, December 16, 2003, tape 69.1–9, CML audio collection, TXA. All quotes from Marion Parker in the following paragraphs are from this interview.

someone and still not need to *marry* them. Maybe I never learned!" She laughed, showing all her perfect teeth.

I was embarrassed to hear her say this, as it was the same justification I'd often given for my divorce from Henry—one meant to tidy a wreckage, to absolve all parties. *I was so young.* I knew that excuse as well as I knew my own hands.

I tried to look past Marion's charm, to stick to the task at hand, yet I couldn't help but wonder if she looked at me with pity. My insecurities and plainness had only grown in these years of isolation, and it must have baffled her—how X could have ended up with someone like me. "How many American women of her generation had lovers, male and female, as numerous, beautiful, and prominent," one source in Theodore Smith's book had quipped, "only to run off and marry a mousy little nobody?" *

* Theodore Smith, *A Woman Without a History* (New York: Brace & Sons, 1997), 301.

Image: Marion Parker

Marion could have easily looked at me and declared herself the victor of that marriage—the one who went on to better, more beautiful things.

As she stirred sugar into her tea, Marion confirmed what I already knew of their first meeting in October 1983. Marion's father—Winthrop Parker, the now-disgraced film producer—had sent her to a public interview that X was giving for an arts festival at New York University. Mr. Parker was considering producing X's film, *The Coma Game*, and wanted his daughter's opinion of the writer. The staged interview was going along just fine until the interlocutor crossed her in some way, leading X to toss her microphone across the stage and storm off, a detail Marion happily recalled.

"She wasn't afraid to be hostile . . . and that was something I was very interested in at the time. Unfortunately, I've always been one of those people who wants to be liked, one of the most terrible weaknesses a person can have, but what can you do? Of course, everyone's virtues come with equal and opposite vices, so I was rebelling, I suppose, trying to go against my own nature. And X didn't care what anyone thought of her! No one at all. She didn't wait around on anyone's approval."

"And was it true," I asked, "that you stalked her, that you followed X that night?"

At this Marion twisted a coy shoulder forward and tilted toward me—"Oh, I was nothing if not confident, my dear."

She'd been apprenticing with a private investigator at the time (a lark, it seems), so she was well prepared to track X down—lurking near the building's unmarked stage exit, then following her to a nondescript lounge where she'd become a regular. It was there that Marion approached her—according to X's diaries—or X approached Marion—according to this interview. The two women then spent the rest of that night and the next day together, staying up to walk all over the city, to cross every bridge, to drink a cup of coffee in every diner they came across. At some point it seems they went back to X's loft, and one can assume that they made love, though X—despite all the other sexual dalliances she described in exacting detail—never wrote a word of it. Perhaps this omission indicates the sacred nature of their meeting, too ideal to defile with description, or perhaps she later destroyed those pages in anger or disgust. I fear it was the former, but given the brief and disastrous course of that marriage, I know it is an irrational jealousy, though jealousy is one of the least rational emotions.

Despite her father's disapproval, Marion and X married only two months after first meeting. Marion was twenty-three but looked like a child. X claimed to be twenty-nine, occasionally admitted to being thirty-three, but in fact she was thirty-eight. Their December wedding took place in a massive heated greenhouse. A society-page article detailed the lavish ceremony and reception—Tom Waits, Susan Sontag, and David Bowie were in attendance, huge vases of hydrangeas were everywhere, and a string quartet played Erik Satie arrangements as the two walked down the aisle, a detail that explained why all my Satie records vanished after I moved in with X.*

"Who can stand all that compulsory nostalgia?" she'd asked, and though Satie had long been a favorite, I adopted her opinion immediately, believed all those songs to now be facile and fake.

X later burned the photographs from the wedding, but one remained: X in a white suit and Marion in a bright blue dress, rushing up the aisle, gleeful. Marion is in the foreground, holding her wife's hand to her mouth. Only the couple is in focus, the crowd and foliage blurred around them, an illustration of one marriage myth—that it transforms a couple into a stable thing, around which the rest of the world spins. I found this photograph in the back of a closet just after I had married X. *An impulsive mistake*, X explained, *not like us, nothing like us*, though we, too, had married in the risk-ridden clarity of impulse. I tried to forget this image, but I thought of it often, especially Marion's face, the elation in it. It didn't matter that I knew how quickly their relationship fell apart—the image was a powerful fiction, made only more powerful by how little reality it contained. When I asked Marion about the wedding, she had nothing to say, though I noticed her eyes glassing over for a moment, as if the emotional blackmail of the ceremony still held some sway. Her steak arrived; she cut into it quickly.

X and Marion moved to a "small estate" in Connecticut in January

---

* Annie Getman, "Marion Parker Marries the Artist Known as X," *New York Society Pages*, December 17, 1983.

MARION   [283]

1984. *W* magazine published a profile of them accompanied by Annie Leibovitz portraits of the two, draped across each other on a chaise
longue, several dogs clamoring at their feet.* X is wearing what appears
to be a horse-riding outfit, though she never rode horses, not there, not
anywhere. Marion wears a corseted Victorian dress, blisteringly elegant.
Susan Sontag, X's occasional friend and occasional enemy, wrote the profile and described their marriage to be "unusual in both its swiftness and
in its happiness . . . When you're around them, you believe it—they are
for no one but each other." When Sontag asked X about the move from
the city to the countryside, she gushed: "I love it. I love it. I love being a
juvenile's bride and living in a bungalow and pinching dead leaves off the
rose bushes. I will be God damned."

In a letter to Oleg, I find X's glee to be unrecognizable:

> I love having a house, I love its being pretty wherever you
> look, I love a big yard full of dogs. There are two additions—
> a four-months-old dachshund, pure enchantment, named
> Fräulein, and a mixed party called Scrambles who is, by
> happy coincidence, the one dog in the world you couldn't
> love. This gap in her character causes us to lean over
> backward to ply her with attentions, and so she's worse
> than ever. You don't know anybody who wants a half-Welsh-
> terrier, half-Zambi, do you?†

The dogs accompanied Marion and X everywhere, especially on their
frequent trips into the city. Most of them were badly trained, and neither X nor Marion made any attempt to curb their behavior. In February
1984, an incident was reported in the gossip pages of the *Post*.‡ While
Marion and X were at the Waldorf, meeting Oleg Hall for caviar service, his morbid yearly celebration of his mother's birthday, one of their
three dogs "*misbehaved* in the lobby," according to the *Post*. "The manager

---

* Susan Sontag, "Wives in the Country," *W,* January 1984, 118-28.

† X to Oleg Hall, January 30, 1984, box 1984, folder 2, item 10, TXA.

‡ M. P. Cusick, "The Dog Days of February," Page Six, *New York Post,* February 20, 1984.

promptly appeared. 'Miss Parker! Miss Parker!' he shouted. 'Look what your dog did.' Marion drew herself up and gave the man a withering look. 'I did it,' X said. Then the two women walked away with as much dignity as they could summon under the circumstances."

After this, they left the dogs at home. Though Marion claimed not to remember the incident, she said, "I've always hated the Waldorf."

Later in the interview, I eased toward the more difficult topics. "Did you mind her secrecy?"

"Which one?" Marion replied.

I stammered for a moment, then clarified—the secret of where she was from or where she disappeared to all the time.

"X was a true eccentric . . . and I've always been accustomed to eccentrics. What did it matter where she was from or where she went? Anyway, I suppose I admired her for not having a past. For not having a father, for instance."

(Though Winthrop Parker had been dead for a few years by then, the scandals that engulfed the end of his life had eclipsed his accomplishments as a director and film producer. One can only imagine having such a man as a father was difficult, if not dangerous, but since Marion's father was of no concern to me, I left this issue aside.)

"And what about the difficulties toward the end?"

"To which difficulties are you referring?" she asked.

I read her a few excerpts I'd copied from X's diaries and letters, pertaining to the ugly period that preceded their divorce—Marion's jealous outbursts, her accusations that X was cheating on her, her attempts to disrupt X's work, the fit she threw in the waiting room at Electric Lady when she wasn't allowed into the studio, and the incident on New Year's Eve 1984 when she threw herself down some marble stairs at a party in protest of X's flirtation with someone else.

"Well, to start with, I *fell* down those stairs at the party—some people said X pushed me, but I *fell*. Two twisted ankles, and I'm lucky that's all it came to . . . Listen, I was very young, and I hadn't learned how to really take care of myself yet. You know—I raised myself. I didn't have parents, not really, and I was in the process of growing up . . . Still—I'm not surprised that X rewrote a few stories . . . Of course, it wasn't exactly the most sane or flattering period of her life, either, was it? And she thought *I* was cheating on *her*. She even hired a PI to follow me, which of course I picked up on immediately. Do you need me to go into specifics?"

"What about the incident with the story 'Yvette's Daughter'?" I asked. Marion clasped her hands as if to pray, then exhaled.

"I haven't thought of that in years," she said, her voice softer and weaker than it had been. "It was the saddest thing I'd ever seen. I—well, I could hardly believe what was happening . . . But you have to understand the whole context of this time. She was completely paranoid about everything—wouldn't even accept a cup of tea if I'd made it . . . She was worried I was going to poison her. She refused to see a doctor about it, refused to even *acknowledge* the problem."

"And was it true that you would listen in on her phone calls?"

"Well, I had to—especially after she'd hired the investigator. She seemed capable of doing something, I don't know what exactly, but something dangerous. So, yes—she had her own line at the cottage, but I had it tapped . . . She had stopped talking to me, and she wouldn't even *write* in the house and instead would haul her typewriter into the woods, even in the snow! When I asked her about it she said she wasn't 'alone enough' inside the house . . . Well, of course she wasn't alone! Wasn't that the point of being married? Then she accused me of trying to plagiarize her work—saying that I could somehow tell, from the sound of the keys, the words she was typing. And what do you even say to something like that? Obviously, she wasn't well, but I never thought she'd distrust me so much. I really thought what we had at first was different . . . perfect, even. I never thought she'd give up as quickly as she did."

That winter, X wrote the majority of *The Missing*, the first book she'd written since the Cindy O tetralogy, but among her papers from that time there was also a story titled "Yvette's Daughter," dated February 24, 1985. With it there was a note that indicated the story was never to be published, that it was unfinished, and that Marion Parker had made it impossible to complete. The story begins:

Yvette's daughter told me yesterday that she has many times imagined her death, that when you're born to a certain kind of mother you learn very quickly that it is your job to think about death. Someone has to. In every family. Someone has to be the one thinking about death. Yvette was there, smoking so beautifully, and she said her daughter was probably right, whatever she was saying.

"I don't know what she is talking about," Yvette said, "but she is a smart girl. That's what they tell me."

Yvette may have been drunk. I noticed her daughter was holding the car keys and a large purse while Yvette held nothing but a cigarette.

"I believe," Yvette's daughter said, "that our lives are defined by the generation that came before. In fact, my mother has personally ensured that my life will be defined by death, not just in a generational sense but in a very real, very domestic way."

I nodded at Yvette's daughter—it was a perceptive and not incorrect thing to say—then I looked to Yvette. She only had one shoe on, I noticed, a slip-on half-off. I always liked Yvette. She was smiling, petting her daughter's hair. Her daughter flinched, slightly, each time her mother's hand came down, like a cat who resents her lowly status but is resigned to a life without recourse. I never had any daughters, but I knew that Yvette and I were just the same. We'd fucked it all up. For a moment I wondered about my son, but what business did I have wondering about someone I don't know at all? There wasn't any reason. There was simply no reason at all to even consider that child, a stranger.*

"I *never* read the story," Marion insisted, dabbing at her mouth with a napkin before retouching her lipstick with a tiny mirror. "She kept all her work locked in a safe then—that's how little she trusted me, how bad everything was. And of course there's the problem—it's impossible to prove a negative! And there was never any convincing X of anything! *Nothing* I could say would have made her feel any better. In fact, I really think it was a trap. The whole thing was a trap, to make me feel like *I* was the crazy one, like it was all my fault."

---

* X, "Yvette's Daughter," unfinished manuscript, February 24, 1985, box 103, item 19, TXA.

This "whole thing" Marion was referring to was a sequence of events that X describes in several letters—an afternoon that the character of Yvette's daughter seems to have come to life, a story that Marion confirmed.

In early March of 1985, a teenage girl carrying a large white purse appeared at the front door of Marion and X's Connecticut home. As X stood on the foyer, the girl explained that she and her mother had just moved into the house down the road, but now her mother was quite ill and needed her help. A doctor was on the way, but she needed some help getting her mother into "a presentable state" before he arrived.

My mother will kill me if I let a man see her like this, the daughter explained.

X loved glimpsing the intimate lives of people she didn't know, so of course she went with the girl, and just as they were leaving, Marion appeared with a peacoat thrown over her dressing gown and followed them.

At the house they found the mother in a heap in the hallway, a cigarette between her fingers, wearing only one house shoe. X helped carry the woman to the living room, propping her up on a sofa while the daughter splashed cold water in her face.

Yvette, we have company, the daughter shouted.

That's her name? Yvette? X asked.

That's what she's called, the daughter said with bitterness.

Oh, do we have company? Yvette asked her daughter. *Smart girl, aren't you? Everyone says you're such a smart girl.*

At this X turned to leave without explanation and Marion ran after her, insisting they stay and help, but X didn't respond, didn't say anything until they were home. It was so obvious to her that Marion had broken into her safe, read her story, then hired those women to act it out, and it wasn't amusing, it wasn't clever, it wasn't even particularly sane. It was pathetic. It was cruel. It was an attempt—not a very good attempt, but an attempt all the same—to drive X to madness, and she wouldn't accept it.

"I had absolutely no idea what she was talking about," Marion recalled, "but she told me that the longer I kept lying, the worse it would all become, that I would leave her with no choice. I had no idea what she was talking about and no way to get out of it . . . But she kept saying, 'The story, Marion, my goddamned story—you tried to make it real because you're sick, you're a sick woman!' And it was all so worrying, you know. She wasn't *well*. She was genuinely losing her mind, but what could I do? I was hardly twenty-five years old, and I'd never seen anyone have a psychotic break—I'm not sure I even knew what they were. I tried to reason with her, you know—Yvette's a common name and nearly everyone's a drunk up here—but it was no use. Then, well, I started laughing and couldn't stop."

Marion's recollection matched X's diaries exactly—the denials, the laughing. Each wife saw insanity and cruelty in the other. That night X packed her things, drove back to the city, and, according to her diary, filed for divorce the next day.

"We never spoke again but through our lawyers," Marion said. "It's the saddest thing that ever happened to me, that total, sudden death of us. I'm not so proud I can't admit that I never really got over it." A waiter appeared, and Marion, with tears glittering her eyes, ordered an ice cream sundae.

"She wanted me to have a child, did you know that?"

I didn't.

"She wanted me to have a child using Oleg Hall's sperm . . . We had talked a little about having a family when we first met, but it had all been so vague and I said I didn't think I wanted children, but maybe we could adopt—but, no. She was certain that I'd change my mind. She wanted to see me pregnant—I remember that much. She was fixated on it—even bought a trunk full of maternity clothes right after we got married. But just the thought of pregnancy frightened me. It always has. Of course, we were both a little foolish to think the question of whether to have children would simply resolve itself and leave us intact . . . You know, I think what it was—well, this may sound silly, but I always wanted to be a father—not a father like *my* father had been, of course, but a real father. That's what I wanted. I didn't want to be pregnant. I didn't want to be a mother."

Just as Marion's divorce justification had felt uncomfortably familiar, I recognized my own old hopes in that unattainable plan—to both carry a child and immediately cease to be a body that had carried the child, to be completely entrenched then completely excused from the process. To be, in short, a father.

"It simply wasn't going to work out," Marion continued. "And I think she knew also, as clearly as I did, which is why she became so paranoid, so angry. X was a good woman in her heart—I know she was. But once she saw doom in something, you could never change her mind . . . And isn't it natural for people to behave badly when they feel hopeless? So, I don't blame her, not anymore . . . That's why I never pressed charges. I never even told anyone about anything until long afterward. I felt—well, I felt sure that the violence was an aberration in her character, an illness."

Marion spoke as if I should know what she meant by "violence." The waiter set down the sundae for her and a shot of whiskey for me that I didn't remember ordering.

"She was convinced I had hired those women, and the more I insisted I hadn't, the angrier she became . . . I'm sure she didn't mean to push me as hard as she did, but when she heard the bone crack, well, I think we both knew that was the end. I told her to leave, and she did. The maid was the one to drive me to the hospital—and I told Rhonda that we had been fighting but that I had tripped and fallen, it was an accident. Well. Anyway. I'm sure she was probably never violent with you, was she?"

On the tape I'm clearly startled. "What?" I asked, then immediately answered my own question. "No—no, nothing like that. She was, she was never—no." None of this, however, made it into Theodore Smith's book. I asked her why.

"I didn't tell him—I had planned to, actually, but somehow when it came down to it, I didn't want anyone to remember her that way."

Then why did she tell me?

Marion met my eyes and held the stare for a moment, then sort of shrugged and looked away.

"She had an unhealthy obsession with being alone," Marion said as she slowly ate the perfect spheres of ice cream, one flavor at a time. "And sometimes she'd spend so much time by herself that she'd forget how to be with others. That's why she had to be so intense about love. Don't you think that's right? Don't you think so?"

There was nothing I could say.

"I didn't want to divorce her, but she left me no choice. She wouldn't get help. She wasn't well, and I was simply too young to take care of someone like that. It's all quite sad."

It had never before occurred to me to locate the actual paperwork of their divorce, but later that week I did just that. Though I had always believed that X had been the one to divorce Marion (as she had written in her diary), the opposite was apparently true.

For a while I watched Marion push the maraschino cherry around in the empty dish.

"I hate cherries," she said, letting the spoon fall onto the crystal.

On the sidewalk outside the restaurant, Marion hugged me goodbye. I knew it was a sincere gesture, something people at ease in their lives often do to each other, but it startled me. Just before we parted, Marion asked, *Do you still feel like she's controlling your life?*

The recorder wasn't on anymore. She was looking straight into my eyes. I had no answer.

You're still letting her control you, Marion said, answering herself, *but she was just a woman.*

No, I said, *that's not it.*

No she wasn't just a woman or no she's not controlling you?

I shook my head as she backed away, no longer looking at me but at the sky.

Twenty years, she said.

Still I said nothing. Months later, as I was transcribing the tape, I realized we'd met on the exact anniversary of their wedding.

I watched Marion get into the town car that had been waiting at the curb, and as I walked away I could feel the place on my back where her arms had been.

SCHUSTER

After the divorce, it seems X had to be half-dead to stay alive. Everything she did was lackluster, empty—the paintings, the drawings, the sculptures, the ideas for later work. *A sculpture of a locket, nothing inside. A silent play, no music, no characters; audience is blindfolded, told it is there. Room made of mirrors—no one allowed to see it.*[*] In photographs, her glare is severe. In diaries, she swims in pessimism and mundanity.

In April of 1985, X sent the manuscript for *The Missing* to Tim Holt. He'd been waiting to hear from her for years by then, but found the new book overly difficult, the narrator unsympathetic, the tone a bit maudlin. "Perhaps I expected a sequel, of sorts," he explained in a rejection letter, "that one being *Lost* and this one being *Missing*. I think Clyde Hill's readers will find themselves a bit off-put. I'm very sorry I can't make an offer on this particular work, but I wish you well with it and look forward to whatever is next for you."[†]

X ripped this letter up, put the pieces back in the envelope, and kept it for posterity. It seems she never spoke to Holt again. In an interview, X

---

[*] X, six pages of undated notes stapled to a receipt from a pharmacy, box 223, folder 19, item 1, TXA.

[†] Tim Holt to "Clyde Hill" (X), May 9, 1985, box 1985a, TXA.

claimed to be done with books: "What bothers me about writing is that I'm here and the page is there."*

Her screenplay, *The Coma Game*, had been scheduled to go into production in late 1985, but Marion's divorce from X meant Winthrop Parker dropped the project, sending it into a state of financial limbo that X had no interest in resolving. She turned her attention, instead, to making her least successful (quite frankly, her worst) series of artwork—*Stabbing the Leg*—several encaustic paintings, technical drawings, and sculptures of wax and concrete. Based on the success and impact of *The Human Subject*, X had been selected as one of the subjects of the PBS documentary series *Art20*, one-hour portraits of contemporary artists who were said to be "defining the twentieth century." During one part of the interview, the host of *Art20* walks with X around her studio as they look at her work in progress.

"Whose thigh is being stabbed here?" the host asks.

"This one," X said, pointing to one of the drawings.

"What I mean is—metaphorically. What is the metaphor of the thigh?"

"It's not a metaphor," X says, almost whispering, staring at the floor. "It's a part of a leg."†

"Her draftsmanship was just never that good," Ginny Green had said when we looked at the slides from *Stabbing* during our interview, "so the drawings were imprecise, even anatomically incorrect. Granted, we disagreed about this. X insisted it was her sense of style, that the errors were intentional, that she'd learned how to draw from studying *Gray's Anatomy*. But, really, it was just lazy . . . The paintings were a little better and the sculptures were probably the best of the series, though I can't say I particularly liked any of it."‡

* Linda Masi, "An Interview with 'Cindy O,'" *The Fiction Review*, August 1985.

† Sasha DeRuiter, "X," *Art20*, PBS documentary series, September 1985.

‡ X, *Stabbing the Leg*, 1986. Resin, latex, plaster, graphite. Dimensions variable. Quarry Archive, New York.

It is true that X never had any formal training in visual art and her drawing ability was quite juvenile, and not intentionally so. The works all sold—X's art was a good investment then, even if no one wanted to look at it—but the reviews were uniformly atrocious.

"I don't care if anyone understands," X repeated in almost every interview she gave during this time. "I don't waste my time waiting around on anyone's *understanding*. I'd sooner die."*

In late 1985, she spent a month alone in a cabin in rural Vermont, then two weeks in Japan, though she took no photographs, and only a few notes, and brought nothing home with her. The only postcard she seems to have sent from Tokyo was back to herself: "I can't understand why I made this trip, except in the hope that there is something good in being so unhappy—as if I might use up my large portion of unhappiness + have only joy left."†

The only vivid things from this part of her life are the dozens of letters from a scientist named Alfred Schuster, and copies of some of her replies. It's unclear how X and Schuster first met, though it seems to have occurred in early 1986; he moved to New York in the fall of 1985 to teach in the Neurology Department at Columbia. Details of their daily lives are never mentioned in the letters, which are mostly philosophical and abstract, and though there is a palpable fondness in the tone, the letters are never directly romantic. Often they seem to be straining and struggling to tell each other something—"This isn't the letter I wanted to write," X wrote on the ninth page of a fourteen-page letter. "It's too obscure, too beside the point, and yet I can't seem to step into anything, can't seem to say anything but the things next to what should be said."‡

In one of his letters, Schuster seems to refer to the two of them in the third person—"Of their own volition or owing to an accident which has been chosen for them, they plunge lucidly and without complaint into a reproachful, ignominious element, like that into which love, if it is profound, hurls human beings. Erotic play discloses a nameless world which

* See, for example, Masi, "An Interview with 'Cindy O.'"

† X, postcard sent to herself, box 1985c, folder 6, item 3, TXA.

‡ X to Alfred Schuster, undated, box 223, folders 1–5, TXA.

is revealed by the nocturnal language of lovers. It is whispered into the ear at night in a hoarse voice. At dawn it is forgotten."*

It took me several months to locate Alfred Schuster. He had been living in Finland for many years by then, and though I spoke to him briefly on the phone in late 2002, he insisted that I write to him instead, and though I sent him several letters that detailed every question I wished him to address, he wrote me only one short letter in reply.

"I don't know quite what to make of that time," that letter began. "She and I were not equipped for each other's lives. Over the years I have sometimes wondered if it was all a mistake—only I can never decide whether the mistake came in meeting her or leaving her. Most personal matters will reach an emotional conclusion once enough time has elapsed,

* Alfred Schuster to X, undated, box 223, folders 1–5, TXA.

Image: Alfred Schuster

and yet in this case, time has revealed nothing to me. I still have the bruise."*

Again I tried calling, and again he deflected my calls, having his secretary take message after message over the course of a year, until she became so irritated by the situation that she barged into Schuster's office one afternoon in January 2004, insisting he put an end to my calls.

Angrily, Schuster told me that this was it, that this was all I would get, that he was very busy, that he had more important things to do—very important things to do—and he had no patience for those who wanted to dwell in the past, because there was no such thing as the past, and it was only fools who tried to return to it.

I asked him, quite directly, to tell me what had happened with him and X.

Schuster explained that he had met her on West Twenty-Third Street in February of 1986, that he had been walking to his apartment when she appeared at his side and began talking to him as if they two were already mid-conversation.

"For some reason I did not question her. I cannot explain it. I felt I already knew her. It is not rational, but that is what I felt for whatever reason. It was as if we already knew each other."†

The two of them spoke for many hours that day—first in person and later on the phone—and began writing each other daily letters. For the rest of that year and into the next, they met all over the city without trying. Several times, or so Schuster claimed, he would go out for a walk in a random direction, enter a subway station he had never before used, board a subway car, and find X already on it. He was well aware this sounded impossible, but he insisted he was not exaggerating, that he was not the sort of man who told such stories.

"It was as if there were a force between us that defied explanation, that defied chaos," he said. "I am not one to believe in such things, but it did seem as if we could not be parted. We kept coming across one another in

---

* Alfred Schuster to CML, December 30, 2002, folder 14, item 2, CML Photo and Research Collection, TXA.

† Alfred Schuster, telephone interview with the author, January 12, 2004, tape 71.1–2, CML audio collection, TXA.

the city, and each time we met we began exactly where we left off. Time seemed to move differently . . . as if there were a kind of second present tense between us. I have never again felt so natural with a person." He paused for a long time here, then began again. "You see, most people— really, all people—they do not make sense to me. I have a wife now, and a child, and I love them, but I cannot say I feel natural with them, least of all with my son. He and my wife both know this about me, my unnaturalness, but with her I was someone else . . . I was briefly, well, natural. At ease. And all I am certain of now is that I was given an opportunity to meld my life completely with hers and I did not take it."

The last time Schuster saw X was in a hospital in Manhattan, in March of 1987. Her appendix had burst, and just before she'd been put under for surgery, she'd given a nurse Schuster's name and number as her emergency contact. Even though he had a flight to Belgium in only a few hours, he went to the hospital, suitcase in hand. He was there when she emerged from the anesthesia, and she immediately asked him to move in with her.

Our lives are not so long, she said. *They only seem so.*

"When she'd asked if I wanted to live together, I'd been hesitant, never actually answered. Then I left for Antwerp. We never formally parted," Schuster told me over the phone. "I hardly understood at the time that we were ending, that I had to make a choice. After that, we kept crisscrossing each other's paths. There was a feeling that something existed between us, but it was never said: a potential that was never realized. I never stopped feeling close to her."

I don't know what Schuster meant by "crisscrossing each other's paths," or whether their paths crossed while I was with her. She never mentioned Schuster to me, and I was unable to ask him for greater detail.

"I believe the world—all parts of the world—I believe it is all logical, only there is not enough time in one life to locate every explanation, do you understand?" he asked. "We must live with the explanations we have, and respect the absences of those who are absent."

A few weeks after X saw Schuster for the last time, she sent a postcard to Marion and took a Polaroid of it before putting it in the mail:

Belief is nothing until it is strained. A person may hold a
belief and become emotionally attached to it long before
it's ever put to the test. The same is true of promises and
aspirations. Promises are made when they seem easy to
accomplish. Aspirations, too. Few wed themselves to
anything that seems impossible. And yet so many beliefs or
goals are proven to be impossible. We are, I know not how,
double within ourselves, and as a result we do not believe
what we believe, and we cannot rid ourselves of what we
condemn.

The last sentence is from Montaigne, though she gives him no credit.

THE COMA GAME

I returned to the cabin one evening to an unexpected voice on the answering machine: *My dear, I think it's time we resolve the matter of her clothing. There are several pieces from the early seventies that held a particular meaning between the two of us . . . Let's convene at the loft tomorrow to go through everything. Three in the afternoon is best.*

Oleg Hall. I almost pitied him, yet no amount of pity could make me take his orders. He'd brought up the same issue of the clothes at our last interview, but I'd avoided it, and he ceased all contact with me for more than a year.

When X rewrote her will in 1994, she'd taken Oleg out entirely; he didn't need any money and couldn't be trusted on issues of legacy, and she was sure he "wouldn't be sentimental" about the rest. Upon learning of his exclusion, Oleg had the dignity not to mention it, but now, years later, it seemed his patience had waned. I was still staring at the answering machine in the cabin when the phone rang again.

I let the machine pick up.

Actually, we need not do this in person. I already have a list of what needs to be sent over. There's a pair of Dior trousers, beige linen. A teal paisley shirt-dress with a matching belt. A coral necklace, a very long strand, and matching earrings. A royal-blue silk dress by Chanel. A beaded white purse. All the rubies, if you don't mind . . . He went on until the tape cut him off; then he called back, and again I let the machine answer, at which point he continued his list and concluded, *So—just have your assistant bring them over. You have an assistant, don't you? I can't seem to—*

Something compelled me to pick up—How lovely it was to hear his voice after his vow to never speak to me again!

"Ah, well, bygones and whatever."

In fact, I said, I still had a few questions for him about X about Alfred Schuster.

"Oh, Alfred! Ah! They were so in love. And he was just so marvelous, intelligent, handsome—smoldering, really. Of all of X's suitors, he was by far the most appealing. Everyone agreed—positively *every*one."

And why didn't they work out?

"A logistical matter. He had to be one place or—I don't know, really. It wasn't for lack of love, I can tell you that."

Eventually, Oleg was mesmerized by the sound of his own voice. He went on without pause for half an hour, first describing the intensity of X's heartbreak over Alfred, then how that heartbreak bled into the filming of *The Coma Game*, which had been picked up by a director whom Oleg somehow knew—

"Wim Wenders, perhaps you've heard of him? Ah, well, once it was with Wim, of course, I knew I could donate the use of the penthouse for the set. That was where X had always imagined it happening, and of course *everyone* wanted to work with Wim, so casting was easy. As an executive producer, they all became my friends—Jane [Fonda], Christopher [Walken], Anjelica [Huston]. It was just a shame that X was in such a state about Alfred at the time. She couldn't even bear to watch the filming, just locked herself in one of the bedrooms and wouldn't come out. One day Jane even knocked on the door—you know, Jane is such a wonderful woman, always looking out for everyone—and I remember Jane said, 'Darling, come on out, doesn't misery love company?' And X shouted back—'Misery doesn't love anything.' And that was the joke on set for a while—that misery doesn't love anything, but *some* people sure love their misery. We were filming *The Coma Game*, but she was the one in the coma."

X's diaries and calendars from late 1987 into the next year demonstrate that she did little more than spend her time alone, working, isolated. When asked, Oleg Hall often said he spent several hours each day with her, and claimed to be the first reader and viewer of everything she made.*

"Oleg was here yesterday," X wrote in one journal, "and he encouraged me to write books again because I was complaining about not liking who I am. He said—'To write you have to allow yourself to be the person you don't want to be (of all the people you are).' I think I'd rather paint."†

X did begin painting again at that time, mostly on a series titled *The Amnesia Triptychs*, a series of mixed-media paintings that were not her strongest, but became some of her best known after Ginny Green sold the reproduction license to a poster company. Throughout the 1990s, *Amnesia Triptych* posters lined the walls of dorm rooms and head shops, a fact that enraged X to the point that she nearly fired Green.

Though X had once written several letters daily, the main thing she wrote in the late 1980s were RSVPs of decline. Most repeated her stock excuse—*An unmovable prior obligation prohibits me from attending*—or had no excuse at all. A rare few go into detail, for instance the letter she wrote to decline an invitation to the wedding of a woman she'd once slept with:

> My dearest Lisette,
>
> As we both know, a wedding is a way for the living to attend their own funeral, and since it is likely I won't be around to attend your second funeral, it is such a shame that I must miss this, the funeral rites of your first marriage. Alas, my dear Lisette! There is so much festivity in punishment! I should have liked to see you, before you became improbable! Please remember that no one will ever love you passionately for being *nice*.‡

* Joshua Rivkin, "The Erasing Woman," *Vanity Fair*, February 1988, 45–47.

† X, journal entry, January 8, 1988, box 1988a, item 9, TXA.

‡ X, carbon copy of typed letter to Lisette Musante, March 2, 1988, box 1988b, item 3, TXA.

When *The Coma Game* debuted at Cannes in 1988, audiences were divided. The acting was generally regarded as strong, but critics felt the writing style was either genius or overdone. Many were split about whether the film's bleak and unresolved ending was a weakness or a strength, but all agreed that Christopher Walken, at forty-four, was an odd casting choice to play a man in his late twenties. Wenders had tried to talk X into using a younger actor, but she objected.

He has a young spirit, she said, *and I like his face. It's the face you see when you close your eyes and think of a face.*

Even the actors—Huston, Fonda, and Walken—had trouble speaking about the film without betraying their misgivings about the odd editing choices. "Asked recently at a dinner party what she thought of the film," wrote a gossip columnist who'd been seated next to Anjelica Huston, "she simply draped a napkin over her head."*

Though she never made any mention of it in her papers and was careful never to speak of the film in public, X told me several times that *The Coma Game* had been a failure, that she should have never done it. But her belief in Christopher Walken's skill as an actor persisted; she convinced him to take the role of Blanche DuBois in the production of *A Streetcar Named Desire* she directed at St. Ann's Warehouse in Brooklyn in February of 1989. The production, a collaboration with the Wooster Group, reversed the genders of Tennessee Williams's script—not that the actors played their parts in drag, but that each character's sex was rewritten.

The production was cursed from the start. The theater caught fire twice during rehearsals. Zia Anger, who played Stanley, got in two separate accidents while she was working her day job as a taxi driver—one with a drunk driver who fled the scene, and the second occurring when a manhole cover exploded beneath her car. Nearly everyone involved in the production experienced a death in their immediate family. A group of conspiracy theorists who believed Walken to be responsible for Natalie Wood's death began an aggressive campaign of harassment. During a rare tornado in Brooklyn, a tree fell through a window of the stage manager's apartment. Though there was strong interest from other theaters to

---

* Finny Shukart, "Anjelica Has No Comment," *Inque Magazine*, May 8, 1989.

extend the run, no one in the cast or crew was interested. They'd initially joked that Tennessee Williams's ghost disapproved of the gender swap, but this theory became less amusing as the traumas accumulated.

The Amnesia Triptychs were shown at Quarry in the spring of 1989, X's first show since the widely panned *Stabbing the Leg*. "A sense of gloom seems to have overtaken X both personally and artistically," one review read. "Indeed, we can assume X would like to forget the past few years, and now we have her newest body of work—*The Amnesia Triptychs*. They're fine, I suppose—evocative and eerie—but one would trade in the entire show for simply one frame of *The Blue Tape*, for instance, or even a single page from her least compelling novel."*

"Did you ever find it odd," Oleg asked, "how quickly you two got together?"†

The sun had gone down and I was standing in my dark kitchen. I'd been listening to him monologue for over an hour on the phone. I said I didn't know what he meant.

"It was a low point for her, creatively and emotionally—you know that, don't you? Or were you one of those fools who thought *The Amnesia Triptychs* were actually good?"

I didn't answer this, and Oleg kept on talking for a while before it seems he remembered why he'd called me in the first place.

"I'll be expecting the items to arrive tomorrow," he said. "If I'm not in when they arrive, you can leave them with the doorman and he'll take them up."

It was easy to imagine Oleg draping X's things around his home in order to feel as if she might still be around, that perhaps she'd just gone out to buy a pineapple or a pack of cigarettes and that she'd soon return and put on this necklace, these trousers. But of course I wasn't going to hand anything over to him, and for the time being I had an ideal excuse:

* Hamish Henklin, "To Add Insult to Insult," *The Village Voice*, October 19, 1989.

† Oleg Hall, audio of a phone conversation, January 13, 2004, tape 9.45, CML audio collection, TXA.

the curator Julie Ault was organizing an exhibition of X's costumes and clothing—everything was in her hands. My only error was in naming Julie, who then became Oleg's target for several phone calls a day, first to volunteer himself as an expert on X's wardrobe (services she denied) and then to insist he be named co-curator of the exhibit since he'd been the one to dress her for so long. He was given no such distinction. Apologies to Julie.

A BAD YEAR, A GOOD YEAR

When I moved into X's loft in June 1989 it had seemed empty in a robbed way—bare nails on the wall, hardly any furniture—though I didn't ask why. We spent nearly all our time at home, especially that first summer when heat waves made the city hellish. When we ventured out at night, everything seemed to be under her spell—private admission to empty museums, restaurants entered through hidden doors, taxis appearing when needed as if by her will. At home again she would read to me as I took a bath. She played the piano and sang. Many nights a week she rolled out a projector and screened films for us—classics I'd never seen, French New Wave, Italian romances, Hitchcock, and sometimes new ones—reels that arrived in big crates from studios or directors. She once mentioned that she'd worked as a projectionist long ago, but when I asked where or when, she didn't say. She often left such questions answered; I never repeated myself.

October 1989—the first of her disappearances, the time she vanished while we were making spaghetti—was the first time we'd been apart for more than a few hours. When she'd first told me how I would need to tolerate these sudden departures, she'd advised I find a project or work to absorb or deflect my worry, and remembering this suggestion, I called my former editor at the paper. I told him I'd cover whatever story no one else wanted, which was how I ended up in suburban New Jersey, reporting on an odd set of murders. Two men and one woman had been found dead in their cars the same night. By the afternoon I was in the field, reporting with the verve of an idealistic new graduate, someone who could comprehend neither her present nor her future.

Over the next two days, through a web of details too complex to detail here, I was able to connect these murders with seven other unsolved murders from the past three years.* Every victim had belonged to an organization called the Refinement Group, which ran a series of "career enhancement seminars" called EOT, as well as a "women's group" called HXWZM (pronounced *Hex-whim*). Though I'd only been asked to produce a short article, I decided to join the Refinement Group under a false identity—Brielle Leroy, a young advertising executive frustrated with her stalled career. By now the horror stories from HXWZM are well-known—the sexual blackmail, the rapes, the exploitation of children— and Reif Kanette and his henchwomen have long been in jail.

Before this piece, I'd been a crime reporter only in the most modest sense—I wrote about things that had already happened, held brief conversations with cops, and typed up what they'd said. Though I'd previously wanted my name to vanish into the paper's name, this story temporarily filled me with a fevered ambition. X returned the day I'd gotten the first proofs of the article.

You could have been killed, she said as she read them.

I may still be killed, I said, and we smiled.

Before the article was published, the paper turned over my findings to the FBI, who soon took Reif Kanette and several others into custody. Unsurprisingly, they already had a file on Kanette, who was charged with sex trafficking, rape, manslaughter, identity theft, five counts of conspiracy to murder, and tax fraud.

After publication, hundreds of complaints and warnings came in from members of the Refinement Group who were still devoted to Kanette. X and I lived in a hotel for nearly a month as the threats were investigated.

* C. M. Lucca, "Inside HXWZM," *The City Paper*, December 20, 1989.

Those weeks were some of the happiest I can remember, despite the fact that my life was being endangered or perhaps because of it. X and I ordered banana splits from room service and floated away whole afternoons beside the rooftop pool.

It was during that time that I first met Oleg Hall. X had bragged to him about the article and the subsequent arrests. When Oleg referred to the work as a "short story," I corrected him, explaining it was a heavily investigated work of nonfiction, not something I'd made up. It was simply all *true*.

Oh dear, he said, *we believe in an abstract concept of truth, do we?*

The few times I went into the newspaper's office I felt uneasy with my former colleagues' congratulations. In their eyes I could see it: *I didn't think you had that in you*. And neither did I. Some time later, when the article earned a Pulitzer for investigative reporting, my coworkers' respect deepened, complicated, warped. I mainly felt ashamed, then shame about feeling shame, and more shame, exponentially more shame. It was all a big misunderstanding, I thought. I was not a real reporter; it was simply an accident of luck and timing. When I confessed this anxiety to X she surprised me with a quick slap to the face.

You will not think this way. I will not allow you to think this way.

In retrospect it's obvious this moment must have changed us, pushed us through a one-way gate—now she had hit her wife and now I was married to a woman who had hit me—but I interpreted this moment as an initiation into some hidden chamber of her regard and attention. Had I been less enthralled, I could have seen the slap as no different from the abuse my father brought against my mother. But nothing could be more human than falling prey to the desires that have slipped beyond our control. I desired her beyond reason, beyond self-protection, beyond common sense, and it is just as difficult to call that love from afar as it is not to call it love when within it.

Regardless—it worked. I never thought that way again.

A few weeks after we left the hotel and returned to the loft, X and I began accepting the social invites we'd been declining for months. It was 1990 and thrilling, though at times tiring, to be at her side everywhere. I'd never been much of a night person, but X would transform, it sometimes seemed, in a crowd in the middle of the night.

One night in March of that year, after an opening at Quarry and a dinner party that Ginny had thrown in the artist's honor, I went home early without my wife. The crowd had seemed impenetrable and boring to me, though X had been extra animated. At some point I realized that she'd probably been using cocaine, in which she knew I had no interest. X had done all sorts of drugs in the past and she'd never become dependent, so, not wanting to spoil anything with nagging or suspicion, I thought— Fine, let her have her cocaine. Let her stay out.

My memory is hazy about the precise events of the next few days, but I remember she didn't come home until nearly eight the next morning. She told me she'd taken some MDMA and some kind of amphetamine along with the coke, and though the combination sounded dangerous, her demeanor was remarkably sober. She spoke slightly faster than normal, but beyond that I could not detect any difference. I'd never been interested in taking drugs—as I didn't like staying up late or feeling any loss of control—but I felt mostly sure that X could handle herself. This particular bender went on for another day or two; then she came home, slept one solid night, and seemed to have recovered fully. I didn't know what to make of it, so I didn't make anything of it.

A few weeks later, a young man named Khash stopped by for an afternoon tea. X had never before mentioned Khash, but he'd apparently been an acolyte of X's. In reverence, he told me that X's mentorship had profoundly changed him. He'd come to give her an advance copy of his first book—a collection of poems—which he had dedicated to her.

The book was titled *Never*. X regarded it, held it out at arm's length, then frowned as she dropped it into a trash bin. Khash stood by, abject, looking hurt but not surprised.

Khash, why do you think I had to throw your book away? she asked.

He said he didn't know.

She'd thrown his book away, she explained, because the title—*Never*— was a word Khash was not qualified to use; he couldn't possibly understand its meaning. As Khash apologized, he accidentally knocked over his cup of tea and by the time I'd come back to the room with a rag, he was gathering his things while X shouted at him. He moved quickly toward the door, shut it softly, and was gone. I had no idea what to do but clear away the broken teacup, soak up the mess, and leave everything unsaid.

It was around the same time that X gave the now-notorious radio interview during which she made several incendiary statements.

"I believe very strongly in fascism," she told Brian Lehrer on WNYC. "We need a dictatorial right-wing tyranny. And right away, quite frankly."*

Though the quote was taken out of context, the context wouldn't have helped much; as I listened to the broadcast, I recalled how the previous night X had told me she'd grown tired of her life, that she wanted to go somewhere, start over, maybe learn a trade like plumbing or carpentry, and quit all this art shit. I'd assumed she'd been speaking facetiously, but now it seemed we might be left with no choice, that soon she'd be run out of Manhattan on a rail.

Those who lived through the early nineties in North America will likely not need an explanation for why advocating for fascism in 1990 was so contentious—this was early in the first term for President Bernie Sanders, during which he'd been trying to undo the damage of Ann Hoyne's economic policies, which had widened income disparity. The country was still wounded from a bitter election season, as Sanders's main opponent had been Jesse Jackson, the first Black presidential candidate pick by the Growth Party, which had been banking on Jackson's charisma to revive their unpopular standing in the wake of the semi-dictatorial Hoyne administration. It was widely suspected and later proved that part of Sanders's victory was due to flipping a white supremacist contingent of the Growth Party; nearly a million Growthers cast protest votes. (Sanders appointed Jackson as secretary of state to condemn the racism that had worked in his favor, despite Jackson's conservatism being in direct conflict with the policies of the Goldman Party.) For X to advocate for fascism was to throw gasoline on a fire.

"You don't really mean that," Lehrer replied, aghast, in wait of a punchline.

---

* Brian Lehrer, "Interview with X," *Brian Lehrer Show*, WNYC, April 26, 1990.

"I do mean it. I really do. The Northern Territory is going to fall apart under Sanders—you'll see. And you'll wish we had a dictator. Once everything goes to shit and the white supremacists take over, you'll wish we lived under tyranny. Democracy is only as good as the people can make it, and we're a country of idiots, don't you think so?"

"I don't think so," Lehrer said.

"That's because you're an idiot, too."

Bookstores and libraries removed X's work from their shelves. *The Coma Game*, newly out on video, was removed from circulation. Ginny released a statement saying that Quarry didn't condone X's statements, though they believed in freedom of expression and would continue to represent her. (Their building was extensively vandalized.) David Bowie called X's remarks a disgrace and said he was ashamed of her. Social invites ceased coming in; we stopped going out.

For a few days I left the phone off-cradle, and neither of us left the loft. I tried to broach the subject, but she wouldn't speak about it except to complain that it was all quite ridiculous. "At some point offendability moved its offices to the hip side of town," she wrote in her diaries.* X began locking herself in her studio, doing speed, and leaving a pile of emptied paint tubes and full pails outside the door every few days. For weeks I rarely saw her; then one night she ran from her studio, out our door, down the stairs, and into the street. I followed her for a few blocks, but she was so much faster than I was. At home I waited for a few hours, then fell asleep by the door.

It was dawn when she came in, covered in dirt, her clothes torn, a gash on her forehead. She'd been riding on the roof of the M train as it went across the Williamsburg Bridge, she explained, as if such a thing were a weekly errand. She drew a bath, got in, and asked me to read to her, which I did. The water was dark and cold by the time I coaxed her to bed.

—————

* X, diary entry, April 30, 1990, box 1990b, items 3, 7, 12, TXA.

In late May I woke up from a nap to find X looking at me.

Let's go, she said as she pulled me up.

I didn't ask where we were going. By then I'd learned not to ask. Half an hour later we were at the courthouse, lined up for a marriage license, and I did not wonder if she could have been high—though she most likely was. I had crossed a line, I suppose, and everything that was once strange no longer seemed so.

The marriage application required us to name our prior spouses, and I printed out Henry's name beside our wedding and divorce dates. The bureaucratic compression of that life seemed so odd, as if it were written in a language I no longer spoke.

X wrote out Marion Parker's name as I expected, but then added another—the marriage and divorce dates only months apart. Again, I did not question the existence of this second wife, nor did I permit myself to read her name, feeling that if X had left it out there must have been good reason, and though I always knew I was her third wife, I imagined myself as the second.

By the end of July 1990, she'd produced *The Drugged Martyrs*—frenetic portraits of various martyrs through the millennia. (She later grew to hate the series and referred to them as the *amateur Klimt rip-offs.*) By the time of their exhibition in December, X's reputation had seemed to survive after she apologized in another interview. "I think that was probably a bit coke-driven," she explained. "It was also . . . I fell into the trap of black magic capitalism . . . I really got completely disoriented by all that. It was an awful, dreadful period for me . . . I'm absolutely amazed that I survived that period."*

Marrying me, I assured myself, must have been the sole bright spot of that era, and not one of a string of mistakes. This was the first of many instances when X would make a public statement about something before she'd made a private one to me. She'd never apologized or explained the "coke-driven" behavior of that year. When I came across this interview

* *Portrait of an X,* dir. Ross McElwee, A22, 1994.

during my research, I watched it several times over. I could have hated her if I didn't love her so much.

"I felt done for, an empty burned-out wreck," she said in an interview with Ross McElwee. "Too much static in my head and I couldn't dump the stuff. Wherever I am, I'm a seventies art hack, a pop relic, a wordsmith from bygone days, a fictitious head of state from a place nobody knows. I'm in the bottomless pit of cultural oblivion. You name it. I can't shake it. Stepping out of the woods, people see me coming. I know what they're thinking. I have to take things for what they're worth."

Though she kept diaries all through 1990, many pages in them were smeared over with oil paint and ink. In a notebook some time later she wrote, "Looking back at the pages from [that] period, it is mostly accounts of my drug and alcohol consumption: cocaine, amyl nitrate, Ecstasy, alcohol, grass, as though I were trying to kill something, or bring something in myself to life."* In the safe I had to have cracked after she died, all the way under other pages, folders, clippings, and loose manuscripts, at the bottom of a cigar box full of old theater tickets and receipts and business cards, I found a small piece of card stock bearing the date of our marriage and a few lines: "One realizes everything later. Sorrow always comes late. Sometimes sooner because it gives advance notice. Coming to find you at night, digging holes in your brain and stomach and veins with pain, wounds, something dark comes to you. But you still don't know what it is."†

---

* X, diary entry, December 22, 1991, box 1991c, item 19, TXA.

† X, notecard, May 29, 1990, box 1990b, item 16, TXA.

STRANGERS

I n April 1992, X vanished for three weeks. This was normal by then, and I knew it was best that I occupy myself with something, but nothing interested me at that time and when I went calling around for assignments, everything sounded dull. I forced myself to spend as much time as I could away from home, not to wallow in wait of her return.

I sometimes felt as if my mind were slipping from me—a sudden paranoid feeling that there were slightly too many people idling on a certain street corner, that some kind of conspiracy was under way, that I was being followed, watched. One morning outside my building I noticed a young man leaning against a mailbox, three women huddled together sharing a cigarette, and an older woman in a wheelchair—and I could have sworn that all of them turned to quickly look at me when I came outside, but this must have been impossible. Did they all look familiar to me? Or was I looking for familiarity?

I had good reason to disbelieve these feelings. When I was fifteen my mother had told me that if she'd known how much schizophrenia ran in my father's family, she never would have run off with the bastard. She'd meant this as a warning about men—*The wild ones seem like a good idea*, she often said, *but they never are.* Instead, I worried over the land mines of madness that were surely buried within me. I kept a careful notebook as a teenager, in which I'd scrutinize my every thought, examining it for its possible lunacy, a scrutiny that became its own problem. Though I outgrew the habit, my ability to sit and write for hours led me easily into journalism; most of my colleagues believed the crime desk to be purgatory, a place to pay one's dues, but I had been relieved to no longer be my own subject.

All of this is to say—when I walked past the three women sharing that cigarette outside my building that day, I could not help but notice that their whispers stilled, and the fact that I had noticed this (or believed that I had noticed this) felt like a harbinger of encroaching psychosis. As I turned the corner, I assured myself I was sane—just a little lonely, a little idle, that's all—but I also recalled a somewhat distant memory, the afternoon that Henry and I finalized our divorce papers, during which he said I was giving up too much of myself to be with X, not just my marriage, but my independence, my privacy, my ability to be rational and make decisions on my own.

She has so much power over you, he'd said, his voice neither kind nor cruel. *Maybe no one else can see it, but I can. There's something missing in you—there's something about you that's gone.*

At the time I felt it was his control I was escaping, that the thing that was gone was *his* power over me; I told him he didn't know what he was talking about. Our marriage had always been fragile, I explained, and we'd treated it as if it were much sturdier than it was, perhaps as a way to passively end it.

That's just what she wants you to believe, he said. *She wants you to believe that you're leaving me on your own accord, but you must know what is happening—you've put yourself in her control.* (How ridiculously we use language in such moments—so blunt our accusations, so loud our fears.)

Please don't worry about me, I said, knowing he wouldn't. I'd always loved and hated his ability to focus on what was necessary and immediate—how he lacked the sloppiness of experiencing real passion, and how calmly he lived his dispassionate life.

But as I walked through the city that morning in 1992, trying to pass the time, it occurred to me that everything I had done since meeting X in 1989 had been her idea. She had encouraged me to quit my job—we didn't need the money, she told me, as she made more than she knew what to do with, and I shouldn't spend my life in a cubicle leasing my mind to a corporate media power when I could be at home, with her, living a real life. Though I'd enjoyed everything about my job—even the act of depositing my modest paycheck at the bank—none of it mattered after X diagnosed that work as void of meaning. I quit that very day.

And though the accolades I earned with the HXWZM story had impressed her, she insisted that I'd only been able to write that story because I hadn't been beholden to anyone, that real work occurred only outside the prison of employment. Even after the HXWZM article led to a lucrative job offer as a contributing editor at a weekly magazine, X had been appalled that I'd even considered it.

You'll have to go to an office, waste all your time in meetings, an annual word count hanging over your head, she told me. *Your life won't be your own. Nothing could be worse than that.*

The idea of having a job had been appealing, something to bend the days around other than her, but I took X's advice and turned it down. The editor then asked if I'd at least take a freelance assignment—he was looking for someone to report on a sex-trafficking ring in Bolivia. When I told X about the story she told me it sounded like I was out of my depth. This may have been the only time she ever said such a thing to me, and I immediately wanted to prove her wrong, to impress her again. Weeks later, in a state of emotional paralysis in a hotel room in La Paz, I was too afraid to do the reporting. I had to return to the editor with nothing, repaying the expenses I incurred. After this failure, the phone no longer rang for me, and I lacked the confidence to find work of my own. I became, completely, X's wife, her wife in the most archaic sense of the word—I managed all her appointments, cooked, did the shopping, cleaned the house, went to places she said I should go to and did whatever she thought I should do. Whenever she vanished, I found myself to be useless and confused about what to do with all the time I had on my hands without her.

As I considered all this, walking around the city alone that day in 1992, I walked into a diner, dazed, trying to fight off the sense of a conspiracy. I had nothing to worry about, I knew. My life was fine, was easy, and I was lucky. Absolutely nothing was wrong. As I was eating, three women sat next to me at the counter, and I soon realized they were the same trio who had shared the cigarette outside my building. I asked for the check immediately, put down some loose cash, and—fearing they were following me—quickly headed for the door. A woman wearing one of those bulbous brimmed hats, fashionable for a moment, put her hand on my elbow as I passed.

I'm sorry to bother you, she said, *but I was wondering if you ever knew someone named Yarrow Hall.*

The other women kept their backs to me.

I told her I could not help her, feeling much less afraid now that she had simply revealed herself to be one of those superfans who believed all of X's personas in the seventies were real people, and I felt sorry for her, sorry for this woman, her obsession, and her silly hat.

I know you, the woman shouted as I walked away. *I know who you are.*

This, too, was unsurprising, as my face was often known by such obsessives. I hurried outside and went quickly down Eleventh Street, checking over my shoulder several times.

There was an oddly shaped and shoddily maintained park in the West Village that I often visited on my walks, and in it, beside an elm tree, was an imposing statue of a sea goddess called Nehalennia. It had been made by an Icelandic American artist, Herdis Hoernsdottir, and dedicated in memory of Hoernsdottir's sister, who had died in an apartment fire in 1928. Nehalennia was at least fifteen feet tall and sturdily built, with outlandishly large hands. I'd often seen children burst into tears at the sight of her, but she always calmed me for some reason. When X and I had first gotten together we'd been thrilled to discover we held the same feelings for this statue, though I'd never known anyone else who'd noticed her.

I was standing there—I never sat in the presence of Nehalennia— when I heard a voice several feet behind me.

I believed her, you know, you must know, I believed her, what else was I going to do?

Then the voice fell quiet for a while. I did not turn around. The statue kept looking down at me. I felt so protected when I stood beneath her. The voice returned—

Of course her name was so unusual—

It was then I realized this was the voice of that woman with the hat, and if I'd been in a stronger state of mind I might have left right then— run away or hailed a cab—but for some reason I felt captive. The woman took a few steps to stand beside me, shoulder to shoulder. I did not look at her.

She told me that on the last day of February 1979, she met Yarrow Hall by chance. She'd been sleeping on the floor of a friend's dorm room that week but was beginning to overstay her welcome and was spending most her time walking around, wondering if she should return to Rochester, move back in with her parents. She was walking down Bleecker Street

Image: Nehalennia

when she noticed a group of people going into an apartment building carrying bottles of wine. Lonely and lacking plans, she followed them in. The
party turned out to be a living room concert—a woman playing a guitar
and singing with a strange thorny voice, and another accompanying her
on cello. The small apartment was packed completely, everyone enraptured. Unable to get farther inside, the woman stood near the door by the
kitchen, and in between songs, as applause shook the room, Yarrow Hall
emerged from the crowd, dashed into the galley kitchen, and began to rifle through the cabinets and drawers. The woman watched Yarrow, drawn
in by her confidence and strange clothing—a baggy jumpsuit buttoned to
the neck. In a whisper Yarrow said her blood sugar was crashing, that she
was going to faint. All they could find was an old jar of crystallized honey;
Yarrow scooped out a lump with two fingers, and the two of them left the
concert arm in arm. This was weeks before Yarrow's name became known,
before *The Blue Tapes* had debuted at the AFA, before the scandal with
Vito Acconci and the accusations from Věra had turned her into a villain.
Yarrow, the young woman told me, said she'd been born in Lithuania and
had run away from home and now ran a few laundromats and produced
music on the side. All lies, this woman told me, but Yarrow had her ways
of seeming honest. They had hamburgers and coffee at a dingy restaurant
near the meatpacking district, then took a room at the Jane Hotel, where
they fucked and smoked cigarettes and laughed at their good fortune, and
by dawn it seemed that Yarrow had solved every problem this woman
had. She'd gotten her a few shifts at the restaurant where they'd eaten,
and by chance the manager had a friend who was subletting an efficiency
apartment nearby. The woman felt that her life was finally being given to
her—cramped and unglamorous, but all hers—and Yarrow, having been
the vessel of this new life, was impossible not to love. Yarrow told this
young woman she had *the carriage of a French New Wave actress*, that she
should start going for auditions, that she'd help her get into film, and for
years, long after Yarrow had ceased showing up at her apartment with
flowers, apologies, declarations of her devotion—long after this woman
had given up all hope of becoming the actress she'd once believed herself
to be—even then she'd sometimes catch herself admiring her reflec-
tion in a mirror and repeating Yarrow's line, *the carriage of a French New*

Wave actress. A person can so easily poison you in this way when you're young, the woman told me as we continued to stand side by side under the shadow of Nehalennia.

You must know what I'm talking about, she insisted.

She believed everything that Yarrow told her, and all of it had been lies. She'd fallen in love with a fiction, a figment—even worse than that—a fiction spawned from another fiction, not even a character included in *The Human Subject,* but a rejected prototype, the secret Yarrow Hall beneath the other Yarrow Hall, all of it false. The woman's voice was so pained that it was difficult to listen to her, and though I knew there was nothing I could do for her, I wished there was. She stopped speaking for a while before telling me it was *rape by deception.* Her voice was concretized and clear. *Rape by deception,* she said again. *I want you to know that I intend to press charges against your wife. I don't believe she's changed. I don't believe it's possible—that kind of cruelty. It's a stain.*

The woman left my side, and when I turned to watch her go she was moving with a smooth confidence that I'd often envied on so many other New York women. The carriage of a French New Wave actress.

I took a cab home. A cab has a way of rinsing something off.

It was possible that woman's story was true, but I knew X would have been angry that I'd stood there listening to her instead of escaping, and I knew as well that X would find this accusation ludicrous—*rape by deception*—that she'd insist it was another example of the harmful expansion of the word "rape" by these so-called activists who valorize victimhood and belittle women by insisting we're all martyrs, ever plundered, always fools.

When X came back I had nothing to show her that I had done with our time apart, but she didn't seem to notice. She was more affectionate than

usual, though I feared it was a guilty affection—that she'd done something while away that had put her in my debt, or perhaps I was project-
ing my own guilt onto her. I did not tell her about the woman who'd
followed me or what she'd said. I returned X's affection and we resumed
our routine, our walks, the debates she always led and won, the books we
read aloud to each other. She was working late hours on an installation
called *The Long and Tragic Degradation of Reality As We Know It*, a series
of paintings and sculptures both admired for their originality and decried
as nonsense. As the months passed, I combed the mail daily and always
answered the phone, waiting for the "rape by deception" charges to arrive,
but they never did.

Instead, other stalkers accumulated—covertly at first, then audaciously, like mice in daylight. The first one was a young woman I'd noticed
in the neighborhood for weeks—just another jittery club girl pacing the
sidewalk in a fur stole and jagged lipstick—but eventually she seemed to
be outside our building at all hours, pretending not to notice our coming
and going. One evening she approached us as X and I were getting into
a cab and pushed an envelope into my hands. Opening it as the cab sped
away, I found several photographs of X and myself walking around the
city and three grainy shots of our loft windows taken from a neighboring
building.

I was horrified, but X was amused, and when we came home late
that night the woman in the fur stole was still there. She tried to follow
us into the building, but X pushed her away. She fell to the ground,
crying, shouting at us about the messages that X had been sending to
her, coded in her artwork. Once we'd gotten upstairs to the loft, I drew
all the blinds and insisted that we call the police, but X didn't think it
was necessary. She claimed she'd dealt with things like this for years,
that she knew the difference between the actually dangerous and the
simply weird. I tried to disagree with her because I *felt* unsafe and
shouldn't she at least recognize my feelings? X just laughed, ended the
conversation as she sometimes could, and slept soundly that night,
but I couldn't stop listening at our door, afraid that that woman might
have found a way into the building, that she'd break into the loft and—

what exactly? Try to love my wife? Try to convince my wife to love her? To speak to her directly? What, I wondered, did all these people want from her so much?

The next morning X suggested we pack our bags and go to the airport, that we leave town, leave the country even, and not worry about any of this for a while. We did just that—flew to Lisbon that evening, then to Amsterdam two months later, then to Tokyo a month after that, then back to New York. In each hotel, at least once a week but sometimes more often, I'd catch X staring into a mirror, transfixed. There were no mirrors in our loft, not even in the bathroom—X had claimed to detest them—but in hotels, she would sit there for ten or twenty minutes, staring at herself as I waited for her to finish so we could go to dinner, or for a walk, or whatever it was we did in those places. There was nothing to gain in asking her what she was doing. She did all sorts of things all the time for all sorts of reasons, reasons that were never for anyone else to know.

I remember very little about what we did during that extended vacation. We walked around those cities for hours at a time—got sunburns or ice cream or sat in silence in parks, trading off books as we read them. It seems that neither of us took any photographs, and even my journals from that time were barely used. However, I do remember how X would sometimes announce that she needed to go somewhere for the day, that she'd be back later, and this was already such a common occurrence that I thought nothing of it. I wallowed in the luxurious dislocation of a hotel room alone, dumping the whole tiny bottle of shampoo over my head.

On our last flight, from Tokyo to New York, X told me she had a plan for a new series—that she was going to stalk our stalker and document the process. I thought this was a horrible idea—that it would simply legitimize this woman's belief that she was secretly significant, but X was sure it was the only way out, that the only way to end this woman's suffering was to transform it. There was never any point in arguing with X. Whether through rhetoric or stamina she always won, and by the time we landed in New York I had not only approved her plan but also agreed to work with her on it.

This idea, I can now see, was inspired by her correspondence with an Iranian filmmaker named Abbas Kiarostami, who in the late 1980s had made a film that was part documentary and part fiction about a man who had been trying to impersonate him.* At the time, I knew nothing of the extensive letters she exchanged with Kiarostami, a man she praised with uncommon abandon.

We returned to the loft in October 1992, and I was relieved that the woman in the fur stole wasn't there to greet us. Oleg had been checking in on the place in our absence and had left a tall stack of mail in the kitchen. Among the usual letters were several manila envelopes that contained photographs of us in Lisbon and Tokyo (though not in Amsterdam, for some reason). I insisted, again, that we call the police, but X told me not to worry, that to be afraid was to let them win, and though I was afraid—deathly afraid—I tried to borrow X's attitude, her implacability. It didn't work. It never did. I was nothing like her.

Restless and jet-lagged, I funneled my anxiety into rote errands. As I entered a bank I noticed a man coming in after me, and as I was leaving, he left, too. I took a circuitous route to the drugstore and seemed to have lost him in the process, but then he reappeared at the grocery store with an empty basket, rummaging through the garlic while watching me. I abandoned my cart and fled; blocks away, I realized he was two steps behind me.

Excuse me, I said, turning to him. *Do we know each other?*

He blinked at me, like I was the insane one.

You were at the bank just now, and the grocery store, I said.

I was what?

Do you know me? Do we know each other?

No, lady. I don't know you, he said, quickening his pace to pass me. He

* Kiarostami letters, 1986–1993, box 227, items 1–52, TXA.

looked over his shoulder as he turned a corner, as if to ensure I wasn't following him.

When I returned home I insisted to X that I was being followed, that there was simply no other explanation for it.

No other explanation? she asked. *The only explanation is the one that you've come up with?*

I went to bed and cried.

She petted my hair. *You're just a little tired,* she said, *tired and afraid and you need to sleep it off, that's all.*

When I woke up X rushed me into her darkroom to show me the first of the photographs she'd made of the stalker—that woman with the fur stole from before our travels—as well as a new one, a man whom X had noticed outside the building. She was wired and possibly high as she spoke about this new series. She told me she'd hired three private detectives to follow us and to monitor our building at all hours. And, frantic with happiness, like a child poring over Christmas gifts, she showed me all the cameras and surveillance equipment she'd bought at B&H while I'd been asleep.

As a matter of coincidence, Ross McElwee, a documentarian who'd been working on a film about X, was already scheduled to begin shooting that week. She'd told him he could shadow her for a month, and though I thought she was being overly generous, when X approved of someone, and especially when she approved of their art, she gave them all the space in the world.

In a 1987 interview, X had mentioned that after she'd seen his film *A Meditation on the Possibility of Romantic Love near the South During an Era of Nuclear Weapons Proliferation*, she believed McElwee to be the only true genius working in American documentary.* McElwee had been a toddler when his family left South Carolina for Virginia only months before the Great Division. As a young man he intended to make a documentary about Charlestontown, Virginia, as it held the highest population of pre-division ST defectors and was also the site of the Northern Territory's largest collection of nuclear warheads, all of them aimed at the

* Sinead O'Loren, "Interview with X," *The Film Gazette*, December 1987.

ST. The conflict and division between North and South, a loaded topic that most avoided speaking about, was McElwee's starting point for the film, in which he attempted to interview many women of Charlestontown about whether it is possible to destroy the past. But the women he spoke to never wanted to talk about war and instead repeatedly tried to set him up with their daughters and nieces and other young women they knew. The tension in the film exists between these subjects—McElwee's interest in the looming possibility of war, and the women's preoccupation with the future, marriage, and babies.

When X had praised McElwee in that interview, she didn't know that the director, back in 1982, had stood in line at Quarry several times to see *The Human Subject*. Upon learning of their mutual admiration, he proposed making a film about her, but she declined—"It would make my work look weak by comparison," she told him in a letter.* But in 1990, just after she had made the statements about fascism that had enraged the public, X called him to tell him that if he still wanted to do the film, he had her blessing. Two years later, the work was under way.

I liked Ross—we both did—and while X was happy to talk to him all day, I felt too surveilled at the time to give interviews. It seemed there were cameras everywhere, and the private investigators were trailing us, and the stalkers were still stalking, and X, in turn, was stalking the stalkers. Eventually, X hired another three investigators to follow the stalkers at all hours; we had hundreds of photos of them tacked up around the loft— the stalkers walking the streets, or idly riding the subway, or seen through their apartment windows, eating TV dinners, masturbating, clipping their fingernails. At one point I asked X how she could believe that stalking the stalkers was going to dissuade them, because it seemed to have done the opposite—the more they were photographed and followed, the more they seemed to follow us. Manila envelopes of photographs kept appearing in our mail. At times they accosted us in public. X gave no answers, just repeated herself: *It will all be fine.*

From that autumn and into winter I was frustrated and frayed. I could hardly sleep. I usually felt too nervous to talk to Ross, though I sometimes

---

* X, carbon copy of typed letter to Ross McElwee, November 9, 1987, box 1987c, item 1. TXA.

drifted through the background of a shot, or gave brief off-camera answers to single questions. As agreed, I'd been cooperating with X's project by helping develop photographs, hiring a series of lookalikes for both X and myself to throw the stalkers off, but after more than a month of work my hand tremor—a neurological condition that I've had all my life but am usually able to keep under control—had gotten so bad I was useless in the darkroom and could barely even hold a book still to read.

By mid-November, Ross had gone back to Boston to begin editing the footage and even X seemed a little exhausted by her work on *The Spying Series*. Anytime either of us left home at least one of the stalkers would trail us, and another PI or two would follow. Eventually, I developed weary fondness for them, as if they were my pets, or maybe that I was their pet, and we went around silently together, tethered. It began to seem normal, having so many shadows, but in January 1993, when one of the stalkers was taking photographs too audaciously, a group of tourists mistook me for a celebrity and asked for an autograph. For some reason this burst my usual calm; I shouted at the tourists, then pushed the apparent paparazzi hard enough that her glasses flung off, her camera was crushed, and her arms badly scraped on the sidewalk. There are—I am ashamed to say—several photographs documenting this incident. That evening I told X I'd had enough, and she, as if she'd been expecting my ultimatum, said we were leaving the next day, though she didn't say where to or for how long.

By the next afternoon—after hours of ensuring we weren't being followed—X and I were driving along rural dirt roads somewhere in upstate New York. It was nearly sunset when we arrived at an imposing wrought-iron gate that swung open after X punched in a code, and as we went down a winding, unpaved driveway, X explained she'd bought us a cabin, one that had been designed and once inhabited by Natasha Cyrus. At first I didn't believe her—I couldn't believe her, as it didn't seem possible to *own* a Natasha Cyrus cabin—but after we passed through the thicket of pines I was shocked by the sight of it. A Cyrus.

I had idolized Cyrus since childhood, had gone on pilgrimages to every one of her works that were public, and read her biography several times—*The Mother of Modern Architecture.** Though X also admired Cyrus, she didn't care where she lived so long as there was enough space to work. She'd often told me she'd like to live in an empty Quonset hut, sleep on the floor, and bathe in a steel bucket, so I knew the cabin was her gift to me—the one who sometimes cried at the sight of certain architectural features, like circular windows or poured concrete stairways without railings.

The cabin was on 150 acres of private land, had its own woods, a pond, and a hill large enough to seem like a mountain. The sun was setting as we arrived, and everything was bathed in that uncompromising light of late winter, that which seems to promise so much and so seriously.

That first night in this new home X told me she had to reveal a secret she'd been keeping from me for several months. I braced to learn she'd finally fallen in love with someone else, but instead she told me that the Museum of Modern Art was going to do her retrospective in the fall. She'd known about it for months by then, and though I was elated, I was also irritated she'd kept this news from me for so long. As usual, she had her reasons, and also as usual, she didn't tell me what they were. Instead, she distracted me with odd features about the cabin—the false tile in the bathroom that opened a small door, the hidden fireman's pole at the back of a closet that plunged into the basement, the myriad secret rooms and the puzzling ways to reach them.

I never found out why she kept the news of the retrospective from me for so long, but I could never manage to be angry with her for more than a moment. People sometimes say their spouses know them better than they know themselves, but most of them are lying. Yet I fear that it was true of X and that, without her, no one knows me, not even me.

That first year I hardly left the cabin, though X and I often hosted friends from the city on the weekends. It was then I discovered that X's life had fully engulfed mine, that I no longer had my own people. It had been only

* Summer S. Shapiro, *The Mother of Modern Architecture* (New York: Knopf, 1977).

a little over four years since I'd lived in a small apartment with Henry, working long hours to help cover our modest bills, and while X's mostly bare loft in the city didn't reveal the privileges of my life with her, a Cyrus cabin on a gated property exposed it completely.

How to explain that year? I found I didn't like going into the city anymore, that I didn't miss it, that I no longer understood why I had ever wanted to live there. I tended the house, gardened, learned to sew. I bought eggs, honey, and buckwheat from a roadside stand open a few hours each week. The farmer who ran it always brought his elderly mother with him; her dementia had turned her into a child again, and she often sat in a folding chair nearby with a toy cash register in her lap, shouting out totals, saying thank you and come back. The way the farmer looked at his mother with such loving hopelessness felt sometimes familiar—the way I worried that X looked at me.

What I am saying is, I think there was something wrong with me that year, or else there was something wrong with us, with X and me, and it was showing up in me, and though I sensed something was amiss, I couldn't say what it was, and though most of the time I did not question the illusion I lived within, there were moments when I could see our life clearly and knew that everything was beautiful and nothing was right.

I began writing again, small things, book reviews mostly, the badly paid assignments I could afford (as a kept woman) to waste weeks on. X worked almost without ceasing through 1993 and 1994, though her work took her into the city much more often than I ever went, and sometimes she had to fly somewhere to install an exhibition or take a meeting. When she returned she seemed happier than ever to see me, always bringing gifts—some fabric to add to the quilt I was sewing or heirloom seeds for the garden. Once she brought home a Japanese vegetable cleaver that we both found so beautiful we couldn't bring ourselves to use it. It sat under a glass dome on the kitchen counter; I looked at it with an amorphous sense of identification.

In September of 1993, *The Spying Series* opened at Quarry, but even though I shared a co-credit on the work, I didn't want to go to the opening, nor did I want to see the completed prints hanging up, nor did I want to discuss why I didn't want to discuss it, but the night before the opening, X pressed me to explain.* *Are you frightened?* she asked me, and I scoffed—*No, I'm not frightened, of course I'm not frightened*—but upon hearing myself speak, I could tell it wasn't true.

Where is the woman who went undercover in a cult? X asked. *The woman who risked her life for no reason more than she had a life to risk?*

What was there to say? I had no life to risk anymore. She had my life. I didn't know how she had it or what she was doing with it, but that's what it felt like—she had my life and I had a home.

---

* X&C, *The Spying Series*, 1993, Quarry Archive, New York.

SALIF AND MIDORI

S hortly after someone bought the derelict storefront building across the road from our gate and began to renovate it, we found a pale blue envelope in the mailbox. Our new neighbors—our only neighbors, it seemed—were inviting us over for dinner. It was early summer of 1994, and though I felt sure X wouldn't want to go, she insisted we accept, saying that it would be good for me to meet someone new.

Salif and Midori had just moved to the Northern Territory from Paris, where they'd been raised and lived all their lives. They must have spoken a dozen languages between the two of them, and though I'd estimated they must have been somewhere in their midthirties, they had the exquisite taste of a well-traveled elders. Their home was a perfect mixture of stark and comforting—the ceramics, textiles, and paint colors all understated and elegant. They'd laid the designs for the renovation together, as it seemed they did everything together, and I first assumed from the buoyant way they moved around each other that they must have been together for a short time, but when I asked Midori one night how she and Salif had met, she told me they'd attended the same international school in Paris. Not college, not even high school—they'd been together since she was ten and he was eleven. It was sometimes hard to believe the enormous amount of uncomplicated goodwill that existed in their home.

Salif and Midori ran a design firm together in the city but spent most of their time upstate. I gravitated toward Midori, as she was modest and funny and never made me feel like a fool the way Salif, perhaps unintentionally, sometimes did. While Midori seemed to always be reading or playing her flute, Salif moved around the house with manic domestic energy—cooking, cleaning, bragging about what his garden had produced. While Midori was serene, Salif was unpredictable—as quick to weep as he was ready to challenge X to a drinking game, throwing back several shots of rare whiskey in minutes. He liked to arm-wrestle and hold push-up contests; in fact, he enjoyed competition of all sorts— Ping-Pong, backgammon, dice, cards. After dinner, he and X ran around the house like schoolkids, and when we came home from those nights, intoxicated by wine and their glamorous amity, X intensely recounted her victories and defeats with Salif, stomping around the cabin as if to burn off the excess energy she seemed to gain from him. We had a lot more sex than usual around this time, but as we fell asleep those nights X would often continue to talk about Salif and Midori, recounting each conversation, each joke.

I can do more push-ups than him, she said one night, and without thinking I snapped at her—*You're being the worst kind of man,* I said, immediately regretting the insult, assuming she was going to get out of bed and angrily turn on all the lights and rail at me, but instead she dreamily repeated the phrase—*The worst kind of man*—and fell asleep smiling.

From mid-1994 onward, we spent a few nights each week with Salif and Midori, always all four of us—I never went over there when X was out of town.

In July of 1995, we were at Salif and Midori's house playing croquet when Salif went inside for a moment to answer the phone. He was gone for long enough that we paused the game, settling back at the table to finish the opened bottle of champagne. By the time he'd returned we were all a bit drunk and riotously laughing, which ceased when we looked up to see him looking sober and somber.

There had been several bombings in Manhattan that afternoon, and hundreds, possibly thousands, had been killed. The phone call had been

from one of Salif's employees who wanted to tell him their office building had been partially damaged. It seemed likely that an extremist group
from the Southern Territory was responsible for the attack, but nothing
was yet clear. The golden hour around us took on a surreal, sinister feeling as conversation drifted toward the politics of the division, a topic we
tended to avoid.

Midori offered, and we all agreed, that we shouldn't dwell on what we
didn't know, that when the newspaper came the next day we could talk
about what happened, but for the time being we should just be here in
this yard, not off in some imagined rubble where we did not yet belong.
Salif opened another bottle of wine, which we drank quickly as we tried
to finish the croquet game. For a while we at least seemed to put it out of
mind, but soon X and Salif had descended into a debate about the wall,
about the possibility of it ever falling, about the nature of the theocracy
on the other side. X's tone was much more aggressive than I had ever
heard from her in public, and though she and Salif often had a friendly
combative dynamic, their accusations became darker as the sun set. Eventually, they were shouting at and over each other, and in the midst of this,
X raised her mallet at him. Midori and I both screamed—for different
reasons and in different registers, then X froze, as did Salif, looking painfully into her face and breathing hard. I went to X, took the mallet from
her hand, put it on the ground, and took my wife home.

We never spoke to them again. I was so sorry and I missed them
terribly—I'd never had friends like that, so easy, so near at hand—and
though I often thought of calling Midori, apologizing for my wife, for
that night, there was no undoing the gesture of violence she had made
toward Salif. I knew I would never be able to return to their house. I'm
not sure if they live there anymore.

DOCUMENTARY

———

Ross McElwee's documentary opens with a long static shot of X standing in a greenhouse full of cacti at the Brooklyn Botanic Gardens. Wearing a costume, complete with a latex mask, that convincingly transforms her into a man of about sixty, X stares silently into the lens for a few minutes before walking oddly around the space as McElwee's voiceover narrates, explaining his initial interest in her work:

I came across *The Human Subject* by accident while I was walking around New York City. I'd just ended a long-term relationship with a woman in Boston and I was feeling depressed. The thought came to me about how difficult it was to be the same person all your life, and at that moment I saw people standing in a line and I joined it. The line was leading up to a gallery and when I got inside I was surprised that the artwork was, in a sense, all about escaping the very thing I'd just been thinking about. I found this very moving, but disturbing, too. A few years later I asked this artist—her name is X—if I could make a documentary about her life and work, but she didn't want to do that. After some more years passed, at a time when X wasn't feeling very well, she said I could come film her. A little while after that, I arrived at her loft in New

York, ready to begin our interviews. She only wanted to discuss the present—not the past. This made my task a difficult one.*

Just as McElwee's voiceover concludes, X exits the greenhouse, running. The camera follows X through the gardens, down Eastern Parkway, and into the zoo. His voiceover continues intermittently, describing X's career and his interest in it: "The thing that makes X an artist could easily be, in another person's life, something that would create obsessive, self-destructive behavior." He pauses, then says, "I'd like to know more about that."

Later in the film, when McElwee is pressing her to explain why she won't say where she was born, X picks up Marguerite Yourcenar's *Dear Departed*—

* *Portrait of an X*, dir. Ross McElwee, A22, 1994.

Marguerite is looking at a photograph of herself as a child, but then what does that mean? A photograph of yourself as a child? Because it isn't you at all, not anymore—and here she writes, "In order to overcome the feeling of unreality that this identification gives me, I am forced—just as if I were trying to recreate some historic personage—to seize on stray recollections gleaned secondhand or even tenth-hand." What's the self, huh? What's the me here, really? Is it in, as she puts it, the "registries and archives for original documents whose legal and bureaucratic jargon is devoid of all human content"? Of course not. And yet what are you asking me to do? Marguerite already told us trying to nail down an image of the self will just come up with something that's "flat, like items written on the dotted line of a passport application" or "inane, like oft-told family anecdotes" or "corroded by gradual accretions within us, as a stone is eaten away by lichen or metal by rust!"

"But what about the future?" Ross asks from behind the camera. "The past has to be able to reach the future, but if we can't recollect, if we can't—"

X interrupts him again. "Every word I've ever written or said has been the same word—Goodbye!—every one of them—Goodbye! Goodbye!"

Later, during a very slow, quiet scene on the roof of our building, Ross asks X how she is feeling and she replies, without pause, "Undervalued." The shot lingers on her for a while, then cuts to one of X aimlessly pacing her studio, looking at some unfinished painting. Ross narrates: "X had been feeling undervalued for a while. Even when she was honored, she often felt that the venerators weren't venerating her appropriately."

I did not watch McElwee's documentary until years after X had died. I knew that as she sat there saying she felt undervalued she was aware that the MoMA retrospective was approaching, perhaps the highest indication of veneration in the art world, something she'd wanted since the moment she knew it was something to want. Her disappointment in her life, it seems, was intractable.

1995

It was Oleg Hall's tradition to spend New Year's Eve with X, and even though she and I had been mournfully hibernating through the end of 1994—sleeping late and walking around the woods hand in hand in silence—I had no choice but to make the bed in the guest room for Oleg's arrival. He drove in on December 31 with a whole case of champagne, full caviar service from Brenda's, and a toy poodle—Dominic—that he'd purchased that fall. Though X always had an uncharacteristic superstition about being kissed through the year's threshold, that night she didn't protest when I retired early, leaving Oleg and X to their warm fireplace and full coupes.

The next morning I discovered that Dominic had shat on the center of the dining table; the dog sat in a chair at the other end of the room, looking at me. The entire kitchen stank of shit, but I refused to clean it up and began preparing a vindictively elaborate breakfast. Hours passed before Oleg and X appeared in the kitchen, each icily regarding the other; I assumed they must have had one of their spats after I'd gone to bed.

What's this? Oleg said when he saw his dog's shit on the table.

He made no move to clean up the mess; he simply sat some distance from it, apparently awaiting his breakfast, at which point I shouted that I wasn't his maid, that he had to clean up after his own dog, to which Oleg got up, taking Dominic but leaving the mess, and began to pack up his car. X ran after him, trying to cajole him back inside for omelets, telling him that *she* would clean up the table, that it was really no problem, but he couldn't be stopped. From the kitchen window I watched him lecture her briefly before he sped away.

He can be such a child sometimes, I said to X as she came back inside.

He is a child, she replied. *That's why I love him.*

A week later X went to the city for a few days to show Ginny a new photograph series, but I stayed behind, ostensibly to receive an electrician who needed to fix something in the guest room—a wiring problem Oleg had found. I'd already made an appointment with the electrician he'd referred me to, someone named Olivia who was trusted to be discreet in the homes of public figures.

When Olivia arrived, I immediately liked her. She was quite tall and wore those striped train-conductor overalls and had her abundant, wild hair tied up in a knot—a look of masculine femininity that never fails to stir my deference. I showed her to the guest room, pointed out the outlets that weren't working, and told her how to get to the electrical box through the crawlspace in the back. A few minutes later she told me she couldn't fix the problem—*It's simply beyond me*, she said while giving me the name and number for someone she said was *a real electrician.*

I didn't understand what she meant, though I was still under her charm when she confessed that Oleg Hall had arranged for her to pose as an electrician because she needed to tell me something. Olivia explained that she had been X's second wife, that they had met and married in November of 1988 and had been divorced a few months later. She had been the one to leave, Olivia explained, as there had been some kind of abuse. *It was quite complicated*, she explained, *the reason we got together in the first place, but that's not what I need to tell you.*

I could barely breathe or move as she spoke for the next few minutes. She said she'd recently met another woman at a bar in Manhattan, an aspiring actress who—when Olivia asked her what the most challenging character she'd ever had to play was—told her the story of very unusual job she'd once had for neither theater nor film, but for life itself. The actress had been hired to follow a certain woman around the city until she found an opportunity to approach her and recite a monologue she'd been hired to deliver, a sort of customized real-life theater. The actress told Olivia she couldn't tell her who had hired her for this part, as she'd had to sign a strict nondisclosure agreement, but Olivia thought it sounded like X and asked her if that was so—to this, the actress simply looked away, blushing, said she couldn't say.

I knew exactly what it was, Olivia said. *I'd been aware that X had married again soon after me . . . I've always kept up with her career and with her life so far as I could see it in the papers. You probably think I envy you or something, but I don't envy you. It's just that—I wondered if you were all right, and I assumed X must have done the sorts of things to you that she did to me, even though you two did seem, from afar, to be suited for each other, maybe even happy—*

We were happy, I interrupted, the tense surprising me. *We are* happy, I corrected.

Of course, it isn't my business, Olivia continued, *and it was never my business, and anyway it doesn't matter what she did to me—it's so far in the past now, and I always believed she, of all people, she always had the capability to change. It was what attracted me in the first place, you know, how mutable she was, how she might become someone else right in front of you.*

We stood there quietly for a moment, then Olivia said she had to go, apologized for the deception, but she was still in touch with Oleg Hall sometimes—*He speaks very highly of you,* she said, though I was unsure if this was a taunt, a lie, or some odd truth—but maybe this hadn't been the right thing to do, Olivia admitted, coming here and saying this, but she'd had to do it. She apologized for the fifth or sixth time, said she'd never bother me again, went out to her truck, and was gone.

The afternoon hadn't even passed yet before X called to tell me she would be gone a couple of extra days. I didn't pick up, and instead sat listening to her voice filtered through the machine. She explained through the tinny speaker that Ginny had lined up a meeting for her in L.A. and she had to fly out that night, and I knew it wasn't true, but it didn't matter what was true anymore. I tried to forget about what Olivia had said.

I tried to forget who I was now and tried to continue being who I had once been.

When X returned the next week she asked who had visited the cabin while she was gone.

No one, I said. *You know I hate having visitors.*

She shook her head at me and squinted. *Don't lie.*

I'm not lying.

There's a swerve of tire tracks off the side of the driveway, she said, and she knew that they were too wide to be from my car.

The electrician. They must have been from her.

X's expression was skeptical for a moment, then almost unbothered as she asked what the electrician had come to fix.

I don't remember.

But it's fixed now?

Oh, no. It's not. She didn't know how, I said.

Apparently, she doesn't know how to drive either, X said.

We left it at that.

A month later, as I was trying to fight off a growing sense of suspicion about X, I found myself asking her, quite suddenly, about those months when we'd been sieged by the stalkers. We'd just eaten lunch and were lingering over our empty soup bowls. Where had they all come from and why?

She told me that there was no sense trying to rationalize the actions of irrational people. *We made the best of a difficult situation.*

An idle silence returned, and something in my face must have discomfited her—there was never any feeling or thought, it sometimes seemed, that I was capable of hiding in her presence.

She leaned toward me. *Is there something you need to know?*

I tried to insist there was not, but my insisting was too insistent and I could tell she didn't believe me as she began a familiar lecture about how there are people who hated her, people who would do anything to make her unhappy, to sabotage her, to sabotage us. I backed away from her and approached the sink; then, as I washed our dishes, I told her about that day nearly three years prior when that stranger had followed me through the city and told me of her affair with Yarrow Hall, but I had not yet reached the heart of her allegation when I turned to X and saw her take a paring knife from the counter and slash her own cheek, a shallow slit that began to cry blood.

I grabbed my own face, as it flashed with mirrored pain. Then the memory blurs. I remember her leaving the room. All was silent. I stood at the sink for a long time, afraid to move.

X came home hours later, when the sun was nearly gone. A wide streak of blood had caked and dried on her face, down her neck, into her sweater. You cannot safely look at a person like this, a person who will bring a knife to her own face and cut it in order to make a point, whatever point it was. This put an end, for a time, to any of my idle wondering, to my asking questions, to my hope for clear explanations from her.

I realize none of this may seem to be a scene from a happy or even reasonable marriage, and who would believe me if I tried to say that the rest of this year was the most peaceful we'd ever had together? Who could accept that one of the strongest and most intimate physical memories I have of X is from that night in our bed? It's the sense memory of her arm bent around my chest and her fingers holding on to my clavicle as she whispered *Stay here, stay here* into my ear. Does time clarify or distort these memories? So many claim that distance from an event or a year or a person helps us see meanings and truths more precisely, without the muddle or myopia of the immediate moment—but is that so?

Relief is often a stronger and more layered pleasure than happiness, and it was relief that washed over me when she returned that evening, and relief when she held me, relief even as I felt the part of her sweater hardened with blood, and all this relief was enough to carry me, to carry us deeper into love.

Now, nearly a decade later, the corporeal jolt and fizz I felt in moments such as these is gone, wholly gone, and cannot be reconstructed or felt again. Time takes those sensations away and without them the story seems simpler and we hold that simplicity up and call it clarity.

There is almost nothing else to report from 1995. The gash healed. There were many dinners and baths. We went about our lives together.

SANTA FE

She had been dead for nearly eight years before I entered her office, the room where she had died. I was, surprising even myself, selling our cabin and moving away, as what had once been unthinkable had now become the only way forward, the only way toward anything. The chair she'd collapsed from was still tipped on its side, and on the desk there was a just-begun letter, one fountain-penned fragment:

Forgive me for

Silently and without hesitation, I began moving everything out. A small bookshelf and a few books. An electric tea kettle full of moldy water. I removed the chair, the desk, a floor lamp, the vitrine filled with pinecones and animal skulls and antlers she'd collected on her walks. By sunset I had cleaned the windows, dusted, swept, and mopped, but it was only then I noticed a simple canvas bag hanging on a hook on the back of the door. It looked empty at first but contained a small, hand-bound notebook. Inside the front cover was a quarter-sized stamp of a cicada— the exact same image she'd come home with tattooed on the left side of her ribs just a few months before she died. (I didn't ask what it meant or where it had come from, and she did not speak of it.)

The notebook had three addresses written in it—all in New Mexico—

and some driving directions that began at the Santa Fe airport. There were several receipts stapled together—rental car, gas station, diner—and a note in green ink:

> A perfect week—I looked forward to it, and now I will look backward to it.
> —Always, Shelley

It was 2005 before I was able to visit Santa Fe. After a series of bombings carried out by the American Freedom Kampaign in the Western Territory, flights had been restricted for a few months.

It did not take me long to find Shelley. The driving directions went right to her house, a pale blue adobe in that vulval style that Natasha Cyrus first popularized and lesser architects tried to replicate. Shelley answered the door and invited me in without introducing herself or asking who I was or why I was there. She was beautiful in that impish way that X tended to gravitate toward. There was no need to explain my presence, no need for introductions.

She offered me a glass of water. I accepted. With ice? Yes with ice. *Make it nothing but ice*, I did not say, *a sea of ice, a whole river of ice to pour down my throat.* Her living room was furnished with battered old furniture—not the expensive sort that wealthy bohemians use to instill a false disorder in their overly comfortable lives, but the truly disgusting things students drag home from street corners. I turned on my tape recorder without asking.

"I almost feel I should apologize," Shelley said, nervously smoothing her skirt against her thighs as she smiled and squinted at me.* I did not ask for what she might almost apologize, and instead—unable to control myself—asked how old she was.

"Thirty-three," she said. "Next month."

We sat in silence and I did the math—she would have been about

---

* Shelley Carlos, interview with the author January 14, 2005, tape 102.1–5, CML audio collection, TXA. All quotes from Shelley Carlos in the following paragraphs are from this interview.

twenty-five to X's fifty at the time—and if I hadn't been so horribly tired of all this perhaps I would have felt something about that. I'd long ago accepted that X likely had had an affair or several, but I'd never imagined she might fall for someone quite so mundane, so *Shelley*. Her ceramics were all over the room—hideous teal and bright pink glazes—and I wanted to ask her what the deal was with all these repulsive, overwrought colors, but I didn't. I picked up one of the vases nearby and turned it over. On the base, stamped into the naked clay, was the same cicada from the notebook and tattoo. I put the vase down. I did not throw it across the room. Shelley was watching me like a guilty child and I thought, *I could kill you, but what would be the point?* I remained silent and motionless as this notion paced in me—*I'd kill you, but why? Why go through the trouble? What for?*

Shelley, in her flowery, uncertain voice, began to explain herself. I looked at her wavy blond hair, linen skirt, and pink tank top. It must be a kind of suicide to love a person like this, a person so edgeless. It must be like drowning. Shelley explained to me how they met, how close they were, how immediate that closeness was. She told me the places they went and the things they did, but her affair—like all such affairs—was simply boring; she was stupid enough to believe she is the only person who has ever known such a thing, as if she alone had discovered the intensity of deceptive love. I considered telling her.

For some reason I asked her if there was anyone in her life now.

"Yes," she said. "I'm in love again."

"How wonderful."

"I'm happy," she said.

"Of course you are."

For a moment we were quiet.

"She didn't love me," she said. "She said she did, but I knew she didn't."

"I don't need you to reassure me of anything," I said, though I know now that reassurance had always been my goal in this—to be reassured that our life had actually happened, that I had been there with her, and that I hadn't imagined all those years, her company, our life, the home we had in each other—though I was forgetting her every day, forgetting whatever was between us and whom she'd been to me and who I'd been beside her.

"All she ever talked about was you. She thought you were the only real person in the world—you must have known that. And from the very beginning she made it clear that she'd never leave you."

"Well, she did," I said. "She did leave me."

"She died," Shelley said.

"She left. She was leaving when—"

"She's dead."

"She left me," I said, and certainly she would let this stand, let me pretend that X had simply wandered off somewhere, that she'd simply gone away.

Shelley tilted her head downward, pietà-like, and for a moment she reminded me of someone, only I wasn't sure who.

"I want you to know I'm sorry. I'm sorry for what you're going through," she whispered.

But no one has any use for consolation from a young woman in love, a pretty young woman who is probably always in love, both with herself and with others who always return that love, always reflect it brightly back in her direction. Without thinking, I pushed a teal vase from the side table to let it shatter on the floor. A moment passed. I did not apologize.

"That's exactly the sort of thing I'd expect you to do," she said, smiling. "X always said how honest you were, and real."

Her repetition of this idea—and what did being *real* have to do with anything?—was badly scripted, badly acted, and quite obviously far from the truth. Reality hadn't had anything to do with me in quite some time.

"That's why she was here, you know, doing this work. It was for you, all of it. She wanted to understand you more than she wanted anything."

"Oh, I'm sure," I said.

I wanted to break everything in the room, but instead I did nothing at all.

"I suppose you'd like to see the materials now."

And if I had known what she was talking about, maybe I would have declined to see the *materials* and abandoned this hideous diversion, but I wanted Shelley to believe I was prepared for whatever it was, that I knew what I was getting into, so I said, "Of course I do. Don't you understand that's why I'm here?"

———

As she drove us to a storage facility, she glimpsed in my direction several times in silence before she said, "It's strange to see you in person," and this statement loitered between us for a moment, then drifted away.

Strange to see me? What did I care what felt strange for her? As we parked beside a large garage door I looked at her briefly, and again I felt a troubling familiarity in her face, something in the nervous twitch in her mouth or the length of the neck, an echo of someone I didn't particularly enjoy.

She unlocked and lifted the metal garage door to reveal another door centered on a wall painted black, and as she struggled with the keys, I recognized this door as the former entrance to our loft in Manhattan, a door that X had replaced without warning during our first winter together. The lion's-head knocker was still there, too, still glossy at the handle where it had been touched so many times, and recalling the moodiness of this door—how it would swell with the weather and refuse entry unless the locks were handled with just the right amount of force and knowledge—I took the keys from Shelley's little hand and opened it myself. She said nothing, then reached toward me as if to delay my entering the room; I recoiled.

"I wanted to tell you something," she said, but she told me nothing, just stared.

"What?"

"It's just that—it's all set up the way she wanted the work exhibited in the end, but she wasn't quite done. And some of it was going to be taken out—some of it, some of the pieces, she never wanted you to see them. Only I don't know which ones . . ."

Too late for that, I thought, and pushed my way past this old door to find a storage unit transformed into a gallery—high white walls glazed with that indifferent light. The words *You Ruin Things* were painted in black directly onto the first visible wall, and below it several photographs hung in a row. The first few of them were—I was quite surprised to see—of my ex-husband and me, black-and-white images taken through restaurant windows or on the streets near our apartment, specific evenings I thought I could remember, but some of them looked strangely unreal, as if Henry and I had been replaced with replicas of ourselves, replicas that lacked some crucial but indecipherable substance. I did not stop, however, to study those images too closely, as the walls beyond this first wall were crowded from the floor to the ceiling with more photographs—some of X and me together and some of me alone—all taken from the early years of our relationship, and just as with the photographs of Henry and me, a few of them had this semi-replica quality, dipping into an uncanny place between memory and nightmare.

Along the floor were hundreds of Shelley's urns, and when I lifted the lid on one of them I found a tangle of ripped fabric—a pair of ochre trousers that I'd bought for X in Amsterdam and that she had worn almost daily for a while before they vanished, unexplained. A second urn held the square-shaped pocket knife I'd had carried since college until it had gone missing during our trip to Lisbon. Other urns hid other objects, each tied to a specific memory or moment—a wooden spoon, a novel ripped apart at the spine, a missing backgammon piece, a broken porcupine figurine that she had once thrown against a wall in anger—but I could not bring myself to keep opening those urns, distracted as I was by several large and intricately detailed graphs titled *Her Progress*, each of which measured some abstract quality over time—Intellectual Capacity, Aesthetic Intelligence, Depth of Love, Rhetorical Strength—wide charts with lines that rose and fell and X's meticulous, tiny handwriting noting the moments that occasioned an increasing or decreasing score. My score. *Her Progress.* My progress.

I turned to Shelley, who was facing away from me as if I were a stranger getting undressed. The line dipped down sharply at the end of the graph for Depth of Love. I wanted to know why, but unlike the other points of ascent and decline there was no explanation, no paragraph detailing an inciting incident with a date and time. *Perhaps it takes something to receive love*, I thought as I felt my jaw lock and stay there. *Perhaps your ability to feel it waned, perhaps you are the one who ruins things, it was you, you*—and there it was again, that useless, human blame two people will toss between each other when they become too tired or weak to carry the weight of love.

Beside the photograph of me staring up at the statue of the goddess Nehalennia were many columns of text running the height of the wall, and I had to stand close to it to see it was a transcript of a conversation between *X* and *C*. There was a sliding ladder beside the text, and I ascended it to begin at the top, descending it, then ascending again to read it column by column, though I could not recall (could I?) having ever said or heard any of this.

x: The image you have of our love will always be incomplete.

c: But my image is no less complete than your image of it.

x: That is not true.

c: Please explain.

x: If you cannot tolerate the image I have of our love, and the image I have of you, then you will never have a full picture.

c: Who is to say I cannot tolerate your image of—

x: It's quite obvious that you cannot.

c: How is it so obvious?

x: If you cannot see how obvious it is that you refuse to tolerate the way I see us and the way I see you, then that is all the more troubling—a double refusal. It's clear you are obstinate.

c: I'm not obstinate.

x: The obstinate are often obstinate about their obstinance.

c: But how can you prove that you accept the image I have of *you*, of us—

x: Because I love you anyway. I love you despite your refusal to see me.

c: I don't refuse to see you—

x: But at a certain point I won't be able to keep going on like this.

"Ginny called it *The Second Human Subject*," Shelley said, interrupting my reading, saving me from it.

I climbed down the ladder, my vision narrowing as if I might faint, but I held still for a moment and my body returned to me and I returned to myself and as I turned to look back over the room, I felt it was absolutely fetid with X, with her aesthetic, her vision, her meticulous rage and need to categorize everything she did not understand or could not control or abandon. Enough, I thought, okay, *fine*, you win or neither of us win, no one wins this, no one wins, but it is over. It is done. We've lost, I've lost, you've lost, and I've lost my self most of all and I hope to never find her again.

Shelley stood there with her hands behind her back and just behind her I noticed a narrow black curtain. I moved toward her, pushed past her, and the moment I stepped into the curtained room a film began.

It was X in her truck, driving, the film shot through the windshield, and there I was sitting next to her, the passenger, always the passenger in the passenger's seat—only I wasn't me. I looked like me and I wore my clothes, but it was clear I was someone else, someone who looked quite a lot like me and wore my sunglasses on not-my-face, and my scarf tied around not-my-neck. X drove down a gray highway before dawn. Light shards flicker across her face—streetlights, headlights—and when the terse silence is broken it all becomes clear: it's Shelley, playing at being me. Her voice pretending to be my voice came out of not-my-body, which was her body. The sunglasses in the dark made sense then—a modesty, a decency, an admission to the fiction of it.

c: Where are you taking me?

x: To the airport.

c: Why are you taking me to the airport?

x: Because you are leaving.

c: Where am I going?

x: I don't know where you're going.

c: When will I be back?

x: You're not coming back.

c: Ever?

x: Ever.

c: Am I leaving or are you sending me away?

x: Why are you doing this?

c: Doing what?

x: Asking these questions.

c: Because love requires knowledge.

x: This doesn't seem like love.

c: What does it seem like?

x: An interrogation.

c: You think love isn't an interrogation?

And I couldn't remember, couldn't recall, couldn't touch any memories or thoughts or archives that could confirm or deny whether any of this had any truth in it—it had not happened in fact, but had it happened in spirit?—but it did seem then, as I watched, that perhaps X hadn't died and perhaps she hadn't left, but it was possible, instead, that I had been sent away, that I had been sent away from her some time ago and blacked it out in order to continue. I felt all our years together mounting up in me, full of things, full of words, positively saturated with sentences spoken that were meant to vanish immediately, or sentences spoken that were meant to stand forever, words we gave each other to explain ourselves, words that were misunderstood, words we stole, images we held in private, moments made significant to one and not the other or to the other and not the one, two realities pressed against each other, stupid impossible human points of view, views of nothing, conflicting views, incomplete views, impossible to reconcile, impossible to forget.

At some point I realized I was running from the room. Shelley was following me saying whatever, saying nothing I needed to hear, nothing I could believe, nothing of which I could make any sense anymore. I had tipped over inside myself and I had put myself in the position of having to interpret this, X's final work, yet who could be less capable of understanding it than I? What did that work mean? And what was it for, whom was it for? And what had my work, this work, meant and whom was it for beyond my rage at Theodore Smith and beyond my juvenile need to assert myself as some kind of authority on this woman, just a woman, just a dead woman I thought I knew? I did not know her, and I do not know who she was, and I do not know anything of that woman, though I did love her—on that point I refuse to concede—and it was a maddening love and it was a ruthless love and it refuses to be contained, and it is not true that it was in decline toward the end—in love, I made her soup as she was dying, and I was picking rosemary for her in the garden as her heart was going useless in her chest, and I was simmering potatoes and onions together with the herbs, as I knew how much she liked her lunch to be simple, as simple as possible, almost nothing at all, and I made this for her while I did not know she was dying, served it in bowls while I did not know she was dead—and I cannot explain my wife or myself for even a moment longer and I confess all this now, full of well-earned shame that I should have known better than to have even tried to explain even a minute of her life.

I stalked down the road as if I had been physically beaten, stepping unevenly. A dreadful, deadly feeling. I have no choice but to put it here, to put it somewhere, to translate it into language so it won't hang around my neck like a locket filled with poison.

I walked the few miles back to Shelley's neighborhood. For a mile or so, Shelley trailed behind me in her truck, calling out every few minutes that I should get in, that it was hot out, that I'd get a sunburn, but I didn't listen and eventually she gave up and drove away. The long walk in the heat scorched my skin and blistered my feet, but I made it back to the rental car alive, mostly alive, fathomless.

On the plane back to New York I was seated next to a man reading *The Journal of Neurological Disorders*. It was Alfred Schuster (or was it?), a man I'd known only in photographs, somehow sitting there, breathing beside me.

I tried to ignore him, to remain within myself, but by midflight he must have picked up on my agitated interest. He put his journal away and began—hesitantly, then without reserve—one of those sterile yet intimate plane conversations in which names are never exchanged, as if sitting this close to someone made a name unnecessary. When he asked what I did for a living I said I was a journalist, part lie, part truth, to which he raised his eyebrows. Had I ever, he asked, tried to force someone into an interview? I told him I had not, that I was not that kind of writer, that I didn't write about anything that really mattered. (I recalled all those phone calls and letters, the messages left with Schuster's secretary, the pleading voicemails, my desperation to speak with him, an aggression I could no longer understand.)

He explained to me that he'd been hounded by a writer some years earlier, and it made him glad he worked in science, where measurements could be discerned and conclusions reached.

There are never any conclusions with people, he said, *are there?*

He winked at me as he sipped his drink. I froze, and in the moment's silence between us I wondered if he knew who I was, if this was some kind of trap. Or maybe it was worse than that—maybe some force or pattern beyond human comprehension had drawn us to each other, the same way he and X had been drawn together, again and again, in the city, all those years ago.

A flight attendant appeared and handed us new drinks, and she, too, winked at me. Alfred Schuster (was it really him?) went on a long diatribe about how he had to admit that even in science there was so much we didn't know, so much that kept changing, and that was frustrating enough, wasn't it? For instance, about once every two years he found himself afflicted by an acute episode that seemed to be an irregularity in adrenaline production, yet he was unable to adequately diagnose the issue. *It begins as a kind of shaking fit*, he explained, and then it became an issue of temperature regulation and involuntary lacrimation. Standing under a cold shower usually helped it pass a little more quickly, he said, but it tended to last at least an hour, sometimes two hours of trembling, nausea, teeth chattering, sweating, freezing. It had first occurred in a waiting room in Shanghai, he said, and had once happened after he'd had a fight with his wife, but another time it had come on during a very pleasant picnic at a park, and yet another time—perhaps the longest and most painful instance—this problem had come after he'd learned of a woman's death, a woman he used to know quite well but to whom he hadn't spoken to in some time.

He stirred his drink, and his expression was one of deadly seriousness and regret before he brightened and smiled and turned to me. *Ah, listen to me*, he said, *giving my entire medical history to a perfect stranger.* All he meant to suggest, he went on, was that there really was mystery everywhere, at all times, and as a scientist with every known resource at his hands, a person who was often awestruck about how much there was to know and learn about the material world, he found it humbling that he could still not always discern what was happening in the most intimate of intimate spaces, within his own body or mind or the spirit—*for lack of a better word*, he said—if there was such a thing as the "spirit," of which he was not sure.

Later he fell asleep with his head lolling to the side and I looked at his eyelids. Everything vanishes, I thought. Everything vanishes and nothing returns, but what, what on earth, whatever are we supposed to do about it?

RETROSPECTIVE

---

x: There was nothing that didn't interest me, I still do have a burning curiosity about just about everything—except the pursuit of political office, of course—but other than that, I'd really like to understand the society that I'm living in and how it works, how it functions, and what people are thinking. You can't be a writer in any other way, I think—you have to sort of know where you are to write.

WALTERS: Is that how you see yourself—mostly, or primarily, as a writer?

x: I think up until the last couple of years I would have said yes, absolutely, but I think most people are surprised to know I never really enjoyed performance very much. I never really felt like the natural performer. I wasn't an outrageous person at heart . . . so it seemed to me that I could use characterization as a way to perform.

WALTERS: So you're saying the characters came about in order to do the performing?

x: It's odd, isn't it?

WALTERS: What is?

X stares at Walters for a long interval, until she looks away, shuffles her notes, repeats herself.

WALTERS: What's odd?

x: The way . . . the way that people try to escape their pasts. And it's a way through characters, it's always through inhabiting characters that a person moves forward . . . or tries. And for some reason, I'm working out all of those characters in public and having to answer questions about them. But don't you see that the choices I've made are no different from the choices you've made?

WALTERS: Me?

x: Yes. Only you get to keep them private, in a way, move through your characters in your head. What I mean is that the move from the street into museums was not the most comfortable one. Anonymity was taken away . . . In the best of worlds, the work would be seen, and I would remain a shadowy figure.

WALTERS: Well, a lot of people would like to know . . . Who are you? Who are you really? Under all the costumes.

x: I never ask myself "who am I?" . . . I ask myself "who are I?" . . . Who can say who I are, how many I are, which I is the most I of my I's? What is a human subject, Barbara, what is it that makes us live so well and so badly, so that after millions of years we still do not know how to die or what death is? A subject is at least a thousand people . . . Don't you think so?

WALTERS: Oh, I, well, I suppose that's one way of looking at it.*

I didn't believe her when I heard her say this back then, and I still don't believe her now. She never wanted to remain anonymous or to remain in the shadows. She was so childish, so naked in her desperation to be known. And that was the year—1994—that she received all the acclaim and burn of the spotlight she had wanted all along.

In moments that year I thought I saw X relax a little, as if this achievement had really changed her, but I found several pages of handwritten notes picking apart a single essay that the writer Elvia Wilk published in *Future Looks Magazine* just weeks before the retrospective opened. One line in particular seemed to have driven X mad: "The problem with her oeuvre, which is also a problem with her personas—her oeuvre and per-

* Barbara Walters, "Interview with X," *Barbara Does Culture*, NBC, 1994.

sonas cannot be dissociated—is that it fights a merciless battle against complicity with the existing culture, against the incomprehension that accompanies each social and professional recognition, beginning with X's own."* All her notes amounted to a single question that Wilk raised and X was unable to resolve—could she both disdain the state of this country's culture as a whole and still reasonably desire or accept its approval?

"The happiest years are the shortest. We only notice them after they're gone," X wrote in *The Reason I'm Lost*. "Therefore, the attempt to avoid suffering is the most suicidal impulse of all. It is to ask your life to go by so quickly that you never see a moment of it."†

I thought of those lines often that year, as I saw how displeased X seemed to be with her success. McElwee's documentary had been released to great acclaim. Ginny had sold every piece of *The Spying Series*. The reviews and attendance for her retrospective, *The Place to Be*, had exceeded all reasonable expectations. No matter how strange or rude she was to a journalist, the many profiles throughout that year always portrayed her as a genius who lived beyond the confines of normalcy—never a narcissistic maniac who didn't care what she destroyed in her making.

In public and in interviews, she exuded the confidence of a woman who'd sated her most ferocious ambitions, but the moment we were alone again in the back of a car or at the apartment in the city or alone in the cabin, she was listless. I made many excuses for her moods, but none of them make any sense now. There was simply no limit to the pain she could wrench from even the most pleasurable experiences. As I write these words now I gawk at them. Is this sort of love always tinged with such contempt or was that contempt something special to ours? Is "contempt" even the right word for it?

A few times that year, though I knew how much she hated this question, I stooped so low as to ask, "What's the matter?" and each time she scowled at it, never answered. A page in her diary confirms the fissure:

---

* Elvia Wilk, "The Desire to Fail," *Future Looks Magazine*, issue 22, March 1994.

† Clyde Hill. *The Reason I'm Lost* (New York: New Directions, 1973), 111.

*Often enough she has asked, "What is the matter?"—that continual re-proach which was meant as a continual reminder of her love.**

Again, my worrying returned. The few times I came into the city to go with her to some event, I couldn't help but later complain about how some woman had doted upon X a little too dutifully, laughed at her jokes with just a little too much throat. I was well aware that Ginny and Oleg and presumably others thought me to be plain and glamourless. I was not a star and I was not even someone aspiring to stardom.

Sometimes another guest at one of those endless parties and dinners would ask me what I did for a living. My answer always seemed like it was more about the past than the present. If X was nearby, she'd some-times brag, explain that one of my stories had gotten an evil man arrested and earned me a Pulitzer, but inevitably the guest would ask what I'd been working on lately—*A book review*, I often said, which equated to slightly less than nothing among people who did not read books. Though I was thirty-five or thirty-six, I became accustomed to looks of belittling patience, those given to children who have not yet found their way.

Journalism—now there's a tough business, someone once said. *Anytime I ever think the entertainment business is tough, I'm just glad I didn't go into newspapers! At least people still want to be entertained.*

One night during the holidays in 1994, after we'd been at a dinner party celebrating the engagement of two beautiful young actors we didn't know that well, X and I were back at the loft getting ready for bed when I turned around and found her pointing a gun at me. She wasn't smiling. It did not seem to be a joke. I must have looked afraid.

Oh, you can't possibly think I'd hurt you, she said, but she still was not smiling and I could not imagine what point she was trying to make.

Eventually, she put the gun down and tried to touch me, but I would not allow it. Wearing only my robe and house shoes, I left the loft, walked

* X, journal entry, November 11, 1994, box 49, item 4, TXA.

down the street to the parking garage, and drove that night to the cabin. At the time it seemed impossible that we would ever recover from this. We didn't speak for a week, and I, with no place to put my anger, sprained both my wrists thrashing the punching bag in the garage. X gave up waiting for me to call her and showed up at the cabin, and though she didn't apologize, there was a sense of apology in her gestures, which was as much of an apology as she could ever manage. I do remember— though this memory is suspiciously clear—that the first thing she said to me the day she arrived at the cabin was, *I've figured out what your problem is.*

Oh, have you? I was still angry but unable to do anything about that anger other than sit there and listen to her as bags of frozen peas softened on my wrists.

You rely on me too much. You don't have your own life, your own work.

I objected, but she insisted.

It's not true, I said a second time. We sat quietly for a moment, and now that she is dead I can admit she was right. She was my life. I knew it then and I know it now.

I'm happy to support you, she continued after a moment, *but you don't seem content to be supported. It seems there is something else you need, something only you can give yourself.*

I don't know how this discussion ended; all I remember is an over-whelming nausea and the feeling of cold, wet plastic on my wrists, and anyway how do any such discussions ever end? Conclusions are never reached. Resolutions are never adopted. A marriage continues because it continues.

X and I didn't speak for the rest of that day, but we held each other in that way that people will hold each other when they're trying to resist their lives. If X had lived much longer, perhaps we would have later concluded this was the beginning of the end, as they say, or maybe we would have gotten through it, transformed ourselves. I never asked her why she pointed that gun at me, and she never explained what she was trying to prove or do. Her diaries never mention it. Nor do her letters, her various unfinished drafts, and sometimes I wonder if I hallucinated the whole event. Either that or I was feeling, as X wrote in *The Missing*, the "sheer good fortune to miss somebody long before they leave you."*

In X's papers, I found a single note from that time, dated Christmas 1994, though we did not celebrate such things:

> *I'm sick of thought. I want something palpable and beautiful . . . But nothing a human can do is palpable. The history of art is women consoling each other in the face of this fact . . . The idea of getting somewhere with love is even more frustrating and futile than the idea of getting somewhere with art.*

* X, *The Missing*, unpublished, undated manuscript, box 56a, item 1, TXA.

NOVEMBER 11, 1996

I t is sometimes the case that you call your wife to come down for lunch and she doesn't come and you go upstairs to knock on a door and she doesn't answer and you knock again and hear nothing and you go away, go halfway down the hall, then turn back in anger for being ignored, and you open the door slowly, fearing this is a mistake and she'll shout at you to leave her alone, that she's working, can't you see that she's working, but she doesn't shout at you because she is lying on the floor like so much laundry or a blanket kicked off the bed.

When I found her—when I found her body and she wasn't there— what I want to say is, when I went to look for her and did not find her—when she died, that is, or after—after she died and I looked at the body left behind I knew immediately what had happened—there is the smell of death, but also its light, its sound—and yet I also knew she was still there, that she was watching me from the corner, that this was one of her games and soon she would appear again and I could be angry with her for fooling me again. She had done this many times. I would go looking for her in the house and she would hide behind a dresser or fold herself onto a high shelf in a closet or beneath the sofa, the bed—and she would let me go around screaming for her until I eventually found her—or else she'd play dead and I'd come into some room or another to find her slumped on the floor, one arm splayed to the side, and I hated this then and still hate the memory of it now. How often she pretended to be dead when she was still living, as if she were training me for it, as if she wanted it to happen soon.

What will I do when you're really gone? I sometimes asked her, half in jest and half in earnest. *Why would you want me to think of that now while you're still alive?* I pleaded with her not to play dead, never to play dead, that it was simply too much for me, but she always laughed, laughed so much, she found it all so funny.

Not knowing any better—or knowing better but not wanting to know better—I spoke to her dead body. I said, *Get up.* I said, *Stop this, it isn't funny, get up, get up now.* I said, *Lunch is ready.* I said, *It's getting cold. It's soup and you hate it when it's not hot enough. I won't heat it up again if you're late to come down, you know, not this time.*

I went to the kitchen and ladled two bowls of soup and set them on the table, as if I only needed to wait for her to give up this game. I waited for what—half a minute or five minutes or thirty—then phoned for an ambulance.

The police came, the coroner, other people. I don't remember what happened. I sat in the front yard staring at a pine tree—how impossible it seemed that this tree was still standing—and I know if she were here to read this scene, she'd cross it all out. *No—you've got it all wrong, too self-aggrandizing, you know that death comes for everyone and there's nothing at all special about it, nothing particular, nothing particular at all.*

At some point I was taken away to fill out paperwork. That is how it goes. Someone has to put the dead in writing.

The soup stayed out for some time in the kitchen. It dried and congealed in the pot and bowls, then hardened and cracked. Eventually, someone did something about it, though I can't remember who. There were people in the house, people trying to do something, people busying themselves. I can't remember who those people were anymore. Can't remember, that is, or simply will not.

Several times I called the coroner's office, and after I had spoken with the coroner a few times I never made it past the secretary who tried in vain to volley me away. Eventually, she suggested I contact a social worker, but I had no use for such a person. I wanted to speak to the coroner again. It was all very simple. He had not adequately answered my questions—

I wanted to know if there was any chance that X had killed herself. I also needed him to explain to me again whether it was possible that I had killed her—for some reason it did not frighten me to consider this. Had I killed her by not responding quickly enough? By not hearing her body fall to the floor? By not dragging her down the stairs and into my car and driving her to the hospital? Had I killed her years or days before she died? Was I responsible, or if I was not responsible, then how was I not responsible?

No, he said. No, she had not killed herself, and no, I had not killed her. Instead, he explained, it was all very simple. *Her heart gave out, it just gave out, just like that, happens all the time.*

I may have been briefly assuaged by his explanation, but each time the phone call ended, I was enraged. Stupid man—how could her heart give out? How dare he try to tell me what was in her heart?

And furthermore, how did he know that the dead body he examined was truly *her* body? Was he completely sure that the autopsy was done to X's body and not to some other body, some other woman, some corpse that happened to be in her office, somehow?

But the coroner stopped me there. *You want me to tell you that your wife was your wife?*

And when he put it like that I wasn't so sure anymore.

At last the coroner agreed to meet me in person, at Finney's sandwich shop on Highway 232, a place that always looked like it was closed, though it wasn't. It was a dim diner, heavily fragrant with old oil, and I felt horribly sad that X and I had never come here together. It was exactly the sort of place that she would have loved, and it wasn't so far from the cabin. How had we always missed it? What else had we missed?

I waited in a vinyl booth in the back corner for the coroner to arrive. He recognized me immediately, walked straight over, laid a medical

textbook on the table, and opened it to some pages about the human heart.

She wasn't any different from you or me, he said, *not as far as her organs were concerned. When we love people, they seem different from all the people that we don't love, but everyone is the same. Everyone is made of the same stuff, and everyone reaches the same conclusion.*

He told me what he'd learned about her heart in the autopsy, how one of the valves was deformed, which had made her heart beat irregularly, how it labored more than other hearts, how amazing it was that she had weathered the years as long as she had, as her heart could have given out long ago, years before I'd met her.

We all have a heart, he said, *and they can only take so much.*

Before he left, the coroner ripped the page from the textbook and gave it to me.

Please don't call me again, he said.

And I didn't.

For days I left the gate wide open and all the doors unlocked, living in disarray. The phone rang. Letters piled up. Reporters appeared at the door, rang the bell, peeked in windows, asking *Hello, hello,* asking again—

TWO LATERAL VIEWS OF THE HUMAN HEART.

Drawn by G. Kirtland, from a preparation in the collection of S.t Thomas's Hospital, London.

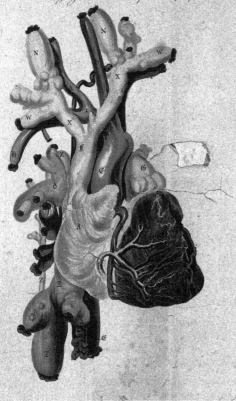

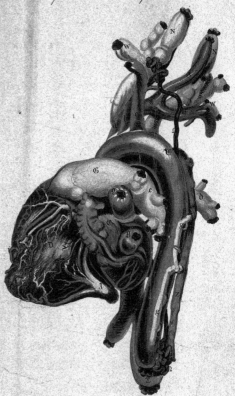

Hello? Later, I installed a larger gate, security cameras. I bought a gun. I stayed inside. I hated them, every one of them, the whole world. Some nights I practiced shooting glass bottles in the yard.

There was a magazine story about an anonymous source at the coroner's office who'd told them they'd found poison in her bloodstream but had left that out of their report. It was theorized that the coroner had been paid off—though the source admitted he didn't know for sure. Still, I was a suspect, of course. Oleg, too, and a few of X's former lovers, Ginny Green, and X herself. (When the source from the coroner's office was found to be schizophrenic, the story went away.)

A supposedly reputable journalist wrote a long article for a supposedly reputable newspaper in which he interviewed every resident in a small seaside town who swore that a secretive woman who'd just bought a villa at the edge of the cape must have been her—there was no other explanation, they said.

Who else would be so strange?

On the radio a man's voice tallied up the rumors, the conspiracies—an overdose, a cancer left untreated, a ploy, a "pseudocide"—or no, it must have all been a part of a plan—no, it was just a heart attack—no, it was something worse than that, something more gruesome. And wasn't it strange that the widow wouldn't go on the record and wasn't it strange that Oleg Hall had held a press conference and cried all the way through. *Something's strange,* Oleg said, *something's not right,* and the simplest explanation—that she had died—he refused to accept.

Who knows what they said on television. The only way in which my life had improved after X was that I carried her stupid television out of the cabin, put it in my car, drove seven miles to a bridge, pulled over, took the television out, and threw it into a lake.

I speak to her all the time. I tell her we're out of milk, of bread. I ask her where the Band-Aids are—that I've got a paper cut—that I can't remember the last time I had a paper cut and how is it that they hurt so much? I tell her I'm running an errand, will be home soon, then I talk to her the whole way into town, all around it, and home again, then I tell her I'm back, tell her how it went, how the hardware store didn't have the right kind of bolt—what is the world coming to when even the hardware store can't carry the right kind of bolt—and sometimes I imagine her response—a laugh, a complaint—and though it has been years since I've heard her voice I still refuse to believe I won't hear it again. Dead all these years and I've never been without her, not for a moment, not for even one moment, and no matter how much I want to be through with this life, no matter how much I want her memory gone, gone completely, she will not leave me. Alone all these years, and yet I want nothing more than to be even more alone.

At the morgue they weighed her body, measured it, measured each limb, weighed each organ, determined the cause of death. They gave me a document that described her body in the most discrete terms, as if we could ever say for certain where she ended and where the world began.

IMAGE SOURCES

32 1989, box 10, item 144, TXA.

43 Courtesy Missoula Public Library.

46 Box 32, item 3, TXA.

49 Box 32, item 8, TXA.

53 1993, NASA Public Archive.

56 EG 009–4, Charleston Archive.

62 PP 102–7, Charleston Archive.

69 Folder 6, item 3, CML supplement, TXA.

75 Courtesy FST Travel Mentors Information Commission.

84 Courtesy FST Travel Mentors Information Commission.

94 Box 1, item 19, TXA.

94 Box 1, item 19, TXA.

97 Greenwood Men's Facility.

104 CML, photo from 1999, TXA.

123 Courtesy Ted Gold / FBI.

124 Ted Gold file 2, item 18, TXA.

133 Courtesy Susan Lorde Shaw.

134 Folder 9, item 17, TXA.

141 Creative Commons.

147 Courtesy Oleg Hall.

148 Sentimental #129, TXA.

150 Courtesy Oleg Hall.

154   Courtesy Frank O'Hara.

169   Courtesy New Directions.

171   Courtesy New Directions.

173   Folder 12, item 19, CML photo and research collection, TXA; Courtesy Denis Johnson.

178   CML photo collection 2, item 4, TXA.

202   CML photo collection 3, item 15, TXA.

204   Carla Lonzi by Lonzi Bassa.

212   Courtesy Gioia Realto.

223   CML photo collection 3, item 19, TXA.

226   Knife Fight collection, folder 2, item 9, TXA.

228   Knife Fight collection, folder 3, item 1, TXA.

229   Knife Fight collection, folder 3, item 13, TXA.

235   Courtesy FST Travel Mentors Information Commission.

242   In cooperation with Quarry Gallery.

248   In cooperation with Quarry Gallery.

249   In cooperation with Quarry Gallery.

257   Courtesy Fred Holton / FBI Archive.

261   Courtesy FBI Archive.

263   CML supplement, folder 5, item 4, TXA.

268   Creative Commons.

270   CML photo collection 2, item 25, TXA.

280   Courtesy Marion Parker.

294   Portrait of Alfred Schuster, CML photo collection 3, item 32, TXA.

316   CML supplement, folder 22, item 3, TXA.

332   Still from *Portrait of an X*, dir. Ross McElwee, A22, 1994.

361   Creative Commons.

362   Public domain.

A NOTE ABOUT THE AUTHOR

C. M. Lucca (born 1957) was a staff writer for *The City Paper* from 1982 to 1989. Her reporting on the HXWZM cult won a Pulitzer Prize for Investigative Journalism in 1990. This is her first and last book. She is the widow of X.

NOTES

REGARDING MR. SMITH

10   *"If you truly want to write"*: Patty O'Toole, late 2016.

16   *"line by line"*: Renata Adler, "The Perils of Pauline," review of *When the Lights Go Down*, by Pauline Kael, *The New York Review of Books*, August 14, 1980. I've changed "piece by piece" from the original to "page by page" to fit with the narrative.

21   *"they know what they're doing"*: Clarice Lispector, *The Hour of the Star*, trans. Giovanni Pontiero (1977; repr. New York: New Directions Publishing, 1992), 85.

LETTERS

26   *The Reason I'm Lost*: The fictional novel in the Denis Johnson story "Triumph Over the Grave," in *The Largesse of the Sea Maiden: Stories* (New York: Random House, 2019), 101–50.

1989

29   *"voracious for people"*: Jean Stein, *Edie: American Girl*, ed. with George Plimpton (New York: Grove Press, 1994). Quote by Chuck Wein as told to Jean Stein.

30   *"beaten up"*: Kathy Acker, letter to Ron Silliman, September 1975, MSS 75, Ron Silliman Papers, Special Collections and Archives, University of California San Diego Library. The full sentence in Acker's letter reads:

"Maybe I should go fuck Richard Serra (there are hints of it in the air) and, as a friend of mine says, get beaten up."

35   *"To be rebellious"*: Susan Howe, *My Emily Dickinson* (New York: New Directions Publishing, 2007), 114–15.

35   *"This cowardice, unknowingness"*: Susan Sontag, *Reborn: Journals and Notebooks, 1947–1963*, ed. David Rieff (New York: Farrar, Straus and Giroux, 2009), 274, 140.

MONTANA

39   *"You're born naked"*: RuPaul, quoted in *Queer Quotes: On Coming Out and Culture, Love and Lust, Politics and Pride, and Much More*, ed. Teresa Theophano (Boston: Beacon Press, 2004), 109. According to Wikiquote, RuPaul was paraphrasing Tede Matthews in *Word Is Out*, a 1977 documentary film directed by Nancy Adair, Andrew Brown, and Rob Epstein; see https://en.wikiquote.org/wiki/RuPaul.

40   *"Maybe the closest friends"*: Quoted in Benjamin Moser, *Why This World: A Biography of Clarice Lispector* (Oxford, UK: 2009), 2–3. Moser cites the source for this quote as "Meus livros têm 'recadinhos': Quais? Os críticos é que dizem . . . ," *O Globo*, May 15, 1961.

40   Moby-Dick: Maya Jaggi, "George and His Dragons," review of *Grammars of Creation*, by George Steiner, *The Guardian*, March 17, 2001. Jaggi writes of Steiner: "Once asked if he had ever read anything frivolous as a child, he replied: 'Moby-Dick.'"

40   *"Who knows if it was"*: Nathalie Léger, *The White Dress*, trans. Natasha Lehrer (St. Louis, MO: Dorothy Project, 2020), 17.

40   *"You have to get through"*: Amanda DeMarco, "Nathalie Léger," *BOMB* 153 (September 11, 2020): 105. I have augmented Léger's words in this paragraph.

50   *"This is the poetically licensed story"*: Robert Storr, "Narcissism and Pleasure: An Interview with Yvonne Ranier," *The Paris Review*, November 17, 2017, https://www.theparisreview.org/blog/2017/11/17/narcissism-pleasure -interview-yvonne-rainer. I have altered and added to Storr's and Ranier's words to fit the narrative.

THE SOUTHERN TERRITORY

57   "WE WANT QUIET AND ORDER": Marc Fisher, *After the Wall: Germany, the Germans and the Burdens of History* (New York: Simon & Schuster, 1995). This slogan (in German, *Ruhe und Ordnung wollen wir!*) appeared

on recruiting postcards for the anti-Communist, extrajudicial Bavarian Einwohnerwehr (Citizen Protective Force) in 1920.

57 *"the original American conflict"*: Susan Howe, *My Emily Dickinson* (New York: New Directions, 2007), 74.

59 *"Jobs, housing, childcare"*: Fisher, *After the Wall*, 115. Quote extensively altered.

CAROLINE

63 *"The more cultivated elements"*: Renata Adler, "The Talk of the Town: Notes and Comment," *The New Yorker*, July 16, 1966. I have substituted the term "theocratic fascism" for Adler's "the segregationist community."

66 *"So I said to her"*: Jean Rhys, *Smile Please: An Unfinished Autobiography* (London: Penguin UK, 2016). I have altered the quote.

67 *"What I am asking for"*: Flannery O'Connor, *A Prayer Journal* (New York: Farrar, Straus and Giroux, 2013), 38.

77 *Around 1:45 a.m.*: I have based this story, including names and ages of the people involved, on the description of the March 6, 1970, Greenwich Village townhouse explosion given in Kirkpatrick Sale, *SDS* (New York: Random House, 1973), 1–2. I heavily manipulated the excerpt to suit the needs of the story.

80 *"Revolutions do not follow precedents"*: Oliver Wendell Holmes to Cornelius Conway Felton, July 24, 1861, Harvard University Archives, UAI.15 .890.3, 170–71.

80 *"I do not want pity"*: Susan Howe, *My Emily Dickinson* (New York: New Directions, 2007), 115.

85 *"Today Momma took me"*: Candy Darling, *Candy Darling: Memoirs of an Andy Warhol Superstar* (New York: Open Road Media, 2015), 82.

99 *"But the dark has advantages"*: Barbara Demick, *Nothing to Envy: Ordinary Lives in North Korea* (New York: Spiegel & Grau, 2010), 4–7. I have borrowed details from the anecdote Demick presents but altered much of the wording.

100 *"Tied me to the bed"*: I have drawn the story of tying a man to a bed from the life of my ancestor General Edward Lacey, who, according to lore, tied his father to a bed to keep him from sending a warning to the British during the Revolutionary War.

101 *"I marry"*: Susan Sontag, *Reborn: Journals and Notebooks, 1947–1963*, ed. David Rieff (New York: Farrar, Straus and Giroux, 2009), 62. I have changed the name "Philip" to "Paul" to fit the narrative.

101   *"I smiling wife"*: Howe, *My Emily Dickinson*, 103–104.

101   *"In marriage, every desire"*: Sontag, *Reborn*, 18.

101   *"Whoever invented marriage"*: Sontag, *Reborn*, 81.

104   *"I do not know which of the two courses"*: Tayeb Salih, *Season of Migration to the North*, trans. Denys Johnson-Davies (1966; repr. New York: New York Review Books), 66–67.

106   *Equality of the sexes*: Kristen R. Ghodsee, "Why Women Had Better Sex Under Socialism," *The New York Times*, August 12, 2017. I've drawn on details from this article throughout this paragraph.

114   *"Hitler and Gandhi"*: Ewald Althans, quoted in Marc Fisher, *After the Wall: Germany, the Germans and the Burdens of History* (New York: Simon & Schuster, 1995), 235–36.

118   *"the myth that the critic"*: Adrian Piper, *Out of Order, Out of Sight: Selected Writings in Meta Art 1968–1992*, vol. 1 (Cambridge, MA: MIT Press), xxix.

118   Love Is The Message: Arthur Jafa, *Love Is The Message, The Message Is Death*, 2017 (video, 7 minutes).

119   *Black Futures*: Jenna Wortham and Kimberly Drew, eds., *Black Futures* (New York: One World, 2020).

TED GOLD

125   *"Men don't protect you anymore"*: See, for example, Jenny Holzer, *The Survival Series: Men Don't Protect You Anymore*, 1983–1985, aluminum plaque with varnish, 6.5 × 25.5 cm.

128   *"I entered the art field"*: Francis Alÿs, quoted in Hans W. Holzwarth, *100 Contemporary Artists A–Z* (Köln: Taschen, 2009), 36.

129   *"Beware of anything"*: Susan Sontag, *Reborn: Journals and Notebooks, 1947–1963*, ed. David Rieff (New York: Farrar, Straus and Giroux, 2009), 287.

129   *a young woman*: Ted Gold's assassination is modeled on the 2017 assassination of Kim Jong Nam, half brother of North Korean leader Kim Jong Un. See, for example, "Murder at the Airport: The Brazen Attack on Kim Jong Nam," Reuters, April 1, 2019.

131   *"I want it more than both ways"*: Collier Schorr, "Seeing and Being Seen on St. Mark's Place," *Frieze*, June 16, 2020, https://www.frieze.com/article/seeing-and-being-seen-st-marks-place. I changed this quote from past tense to present tense.

132   *"You must seem totally harmless"*: Catherine Lacey, *Nobody Is Ever Missing:*

A Novel (New York: Farrar, Straus and Giroux, 2014), 5. I have changed some of the wording in this quote from my own book.

134 "*If They Don't Come Tomorrow*": This song is from the album *Like a Dream*, by Francis and the Lights, 2013, lyrics by Francis Farewell Starlite (used with permission of the artist).

136 "*The price of having an identity*": Louis Menand, *The Metaphysical Club: A Story of Ideas in America* (New York: Macmillan, 2002), 365.

136 "*You have had an abnormal childhood*": Chris Kraus, *After Kathy Acker: A Literary Biography* (Cambridge, MA: MIT Press, 2018), 268.

CONNIE

142 "*I only know*": Sheila Heti, *Motherhood: A Novel* (New York: Holt, 2018), 1–2. I changed this quote from past tense to present tense.

144 "*We are a pair*": Vivian Gornick, *The Odd Woman and the City* (New York: Farrar, Straus and Giroux, 2015), 45.

145 "*People do cling*": Elizabeth Hardwick, quoted in Darryl Pinckney, "Elizabeth Hardwick, The Art of Fiction No. 87," *The Paris Review* 96 (Summer 1985).

OLEG HALL

151 "*Like all famous people*": Edmund White, *City Boy: My Life in New York During the 1960s and '70s* (New York: Bloomsbury, 2009), 278. I have altered pronouns and verb tense in this quote (which in reality is *about* Susan Sontag, not *by* her).

157 "*complex arrangement of love*": Joshua Rivkin, *Chalk: The Art and Erasure of Cy Twombly* (Brooklyn, NY: Melville House, 2018), xiv. I have changed the plural "arrangements" to the singular "arrangement" to fit in my sentence.

159 "*an astonishing number*": Rene Ricard, speaking about Ed Hennessy, quoted in Jean Stein, *Edie: American Girl*, ed. with George Plimpton (New York: Grove Press, 1994), 125. I have substituted "Ed Hennessy" with "Oleg Hall" in this quote.

160 *I sleep without a home*: These are fictional lyrics inspired by "Trouble" by Connie Converse, except for the last lines, which are hers.

160 *Big Bar*: The real Big Bar, on East Seventh Street, did not exist until 1990.

161 "*possessed the touching temerity*": Parul Sehgal, "A Rebellious Victorian Woman Rescued from History's Shadows," review of *The True History of*

the First Mrs. Meredith and Other Lesser Lives, by Diane Johnson, *The New York Times,* June 24, 2020.

DOWNTOWN

164 *"And now there is the nightmare"*: Fleur Jaeggy, *I Am the Brother of XX: Stories,* trans. Gini Alhadeff (New York: New Directions, 2017), 17.

170 *"I opened a musty copy"*: Denis Johnson, *The Largesse of the Sea Maiden: Stories* (New York: Random House, 2019), 131–32.

171 *"Whatever happens to you"*: Johnson, *The Largesse of the Sea Maiden,* 106.

171 *"I once entertained some children"*: Johnson, *The Largesse of the Sea Maiden,* 106.

172 *"an unwinnable battle"*: Merve Emre, "Misunderstanding Susan Sontag," review of *Sontag: Her Life and Work,* by Benjamin Moser, *The Atlantic,* October 15, 2019. I have changed the names in this quote; also, the second sentence I attribute to Emre is my own addition.

173 *"Thank you for your letter"*: *Jean Rhys: Letters 1931–1966,* ed. Francis Wyndham and Diana Melly (London: Andre Deutsch, 1984), 301. I have changed the names, left out the name of the crematorium, and omitted a sentence from the original.

174 *"I have earned the right"*: Adrian Piper, "Dear Editor," January 1, 2003, Adrian Piper Research Archive Foundation Berlin, http://www.adrian piper.com/dear_editor.shtml. The second sentence is my own addition.

177 *"incapable of returning friendship"*: Tina Weymouth, quoted in Guy Blackman, "Byrning Down the House," *The Age,* February 6, 2005, https://www.theage.com.au/entertainment/music/byrning-down-the-house-20050206-gdzi09.html. Weymouth was speaking about David Byrne; I have changed the gender in this quote.

178 *"At readings when people ask"*: Chris Kraus, *After Kathy Acker: A Literary Biography* (Cambridge, MA: MIT Press, 2018), 29. I have altered this quote.

179 *"In one of their routines"*: Kraus, *After Kathy Acker,* 28.

179 *"I'm sick of fucking"*: Kraus, *After Kathy Acker,* 65.

CONNIE, AGAIN

183 *"All pain enrages"*: Susan Sontag, *As Consciousness Is Harnessed to Flesh: Journals and Notebooks, 1964–1980,* ed. David Rieff (London: Penguin UK, 2012), 292. I have added "And there's no conclusion. I conclude nothing" and "(rebellion)" to this quote, along with mentions of Bee.

183 *"I can't think of anything more warping"*: Kaitlin Phillips, "Lower Middle Class & Loving It," *Spike*, August 19, 2020, https://www.spikeartmaga zine.com/articles/immediate-release-lower-middle-class-loving-it.

183 *"I talk about depression"*: Sontag, *As Consciousness Is Harnessed to Flesh*, 292.

183 *"Could I write to C"*: Sontag, *As Consciousness Is Harnessed to Flesh*, 295.

183 *"This is the loveliest place"*: *Jean Rhys: Letters 1931–1966*, ed. Francis Wynd-ham and Diana Melly (London: Andre Deutsch, 1984), 26. I changed "Hampstead" to "Morningside Heights, who are they kidding."

184 *nearby clinic*: The clinic Connie goes to is a total New America fantasy—a well-staffed free clinic with a psychiatrist in-house at all hours. Imagine not going broke because you get pink eye while you can't afford health in-surance. Imagine being in distress and getting free mental-health attention at a walk-in clinic. What is it that stops us from building such things?

185 *"the importance of succeeding"*: Fleur Jaeggy, *I Am the Brother of XX: Stories*, trans. Gini Alhadeff (New York: New Directions, 2017), 13.

185 *"like a broken toy"*: Tom Waits, quoted in Jon Pareles, "Ralph Carney, Saxo-phonist for Tom Waits and Many Others, Dies at 61," *The New York Times*, December 27, 2017. I have changed "He" to "She" in this quote.

186 *"likes something"*: Benny Blanco (speaking about Francis Farewell Starlite), quoted in Reggie Ugwu, "Francis and the Lights, Pop Star Interrupted," *The New York Times Magazine*, March 12, 2020. I have changed the gender of the pronouns in this quote.

186 *"She's a remarkable collaborator"*: Tom Waits (speaking about his wife, Kath-leen Brennan), quoted in Laura Barton, "Hail, Hail, Rock'n'Roll," *The Guardian*, December 2, 2010, https://www.theguardian.com/music/2010/dec/02/hail-hail-rock-n-roll-tom-waits.

186 *"Rumor and hearsay"*: Chris Kraus, *After Kathy Acker: A Literary Biography* (Cambridge, MA: MIT Press, 2018), 83.

187 *"I'm writing now because I just shot a little cocaine"*: Richard Hell, diaries, October 29, 1976, box 1, folder 6, MSS. 140, series I, Fales Archive, New York University.

EUROPE

191 *"You're such a weird person"*: David Bowie, "Breaking Glass," from the album *Low* (1977). I have altered the lyrics.

192 *"It just seemed so perfect"*: David Bowie, speaking to Kerry O'Brien, in "Da-

vid Bowie Reflects on His Career," *The 7:30 Report*, February 16, 2004, posted on YouTube, https://www.youtube.com/watch?v=ahT4xFY49w4, 4:22.

192   *"They say that I have no hits"*: Tom Waits, in *Tom Waits: Tales from a Cracked Jukebox*, BBC documentary, dir. James Maycock, 2017, https://www.daily motion.com/video/x6c0vx9, 1:36.

193   *"It's a lie"*: Lou Reed, press conference in Sydney, Australia, August 19, 1974, posted on YouTube, https://www.youtube.com/watch?v=2UrhX1il wwc.

193   *David Bowie's performance of "Heroes"*: The anecdote about Bowie singing "Heroes" in Berlin in 1987 is true.

GIOIA

209   *"Men must just be 'abandoned to themselves'"*: Claire Fontaine, "We Are All Clitoridian Women: Notes on Carla Lonzi's Legacy." *e-flux journal* 47 (2013). All of the Lonzi-related quotes in this chapter are from Fontaine's article.

213   *"She never spoke"*: Chris Kraus, *After Kathy Acker: A Literary Biography*. (Cambridge, MA: MIT Press, 2018), 267.

KNIFE FIGHT

222   *"More depressing than The Bell Jar"*: This is my favorite negative reader review for my novel *Nobody Is Ever Missing*.

223   *"It gave you a thrill to look at him"*: Nancy Hale, "That Woman," in *Where the Light Falls: Selected Stories of Nancy Hale*, ed. Lauren Groff (New York: Library of America, 2019), 86.

224   *at the Ritz-Carlton*: The anecdote of the lunch at the Ritz is based on a story told by Ed Hennessy in Jean Stein, *Edie: American Girl*, ed. with George Plimpton (New York: Grove Press, 1994), 131–33.

225   *"Warren is not my problem"*: David Yaffe, *Reckless Daughter: A Portrait of Joni Mitchell* (New York: Sarah Crichton Books, 2017), 169.

GINNY GREEN

236   *Tall and sturdy*: Ginny Green's style was inspired by the late Richard Howard's style, as observed in his D. H. Lawrence lectures at Columbia University in 2009.

239   *"I haven't answered my phone in years"*: Cy Twombly, quoted in Alan Cow-

ell, "The Granddaddy of Disorder," *The New York Times*, September 18, 1994.

240 *void artists*: See Audrey Wollen's "Girls Own the Void" post on Instagram, October 2015.

243 *"Continuation d'un chemin"*: This is the title of a 1970 work by the French artist Gina Pane, 1970. See https://kamelmennour.com/artists/gina-pane/continuation-d-un-chemin-de-bois.

244 The Blue Tape: This is the title of a 1974 film by Kathy Acker and Alan Sondheim.

245 *"The thing that still interests me"*: Vito Acconci, quoted in Richard Prince, "Vito Acconci," *BOMB* 36 (Summer 1991): 52–61.

245 "The Blue Tape *played later*": Alan Sondheim, quoted in Chris Kraus, *After Kathy Acker: A Literary Biography* (Cambridge, MA: MIT Press, 2018), 108.

247 24 Hour Psycho: This is the title of a 1993 art installation by the Scottish artist Douglas Gordon.

248 *"I don't think so"*: "Sophie Calle, in Conversation with Catherine Shaw, Hong Kong, 10 December 2014," *Ocula*, https://ocula.com/magazine/conversations/sophie-calle/.

DISAPPEARING

253 *"The early work applied stress"*: Vito Acconci, quoted in Richard Prince, "Vito Acconci," *BOMB* 36 (Summer 1991): 52–61.

253 *"For me, insanity would be like a vacation"*: Vito Acconci, quoted in Prince, "Vito Acconci."

262 *"I learnt to write in two weeks"*: Tayeb Salih, *Season of Migration to the North*, trans. Denys Johnson-Davies (1966; repr. New York: New York Review Books), 66–67.

THE HUMAN SUBJECT

272 *"Can a male artist"*: Rachel Cusk, "Can a Woman Who Is an Artist Ever Just Be an Artist?," *The New York Times Magazine*, November 7, 2019. I have switched the genders in this quote.

273 *"I'm not at all acting parts"*: Audrey Tautou, quoted in Hettie Judah, "Audrey Tautou: Superfacial," slide 3, slide show accompanying Judah's article "Audrey Tautou's Very Private Self-Portraiture," *New York Times Style Magazine*, June 20, 2017. I've changed some words in this quote to fit the narrative.

273   *"The sheer range of self-transformation"*: Calvin Tomkins, "Her Secret Iden-
       tities," *The New Yorker*, May 8, 2000. I have changed "Cindy Sherman" (the
       subject of Tomkins's piece) to "herself" to fit the narrative.

274   *"no longer a subject"*: All quotes attributed to "Hito Steyerl" in this passage
       are from Hito Steyerl, "A Thing Like You and Me," *e-flux Journal* 15 (April
       2010): 1–7.

275   *"There is another world"*: Richard Foreman, quoted in Richard Schechner,
       "'We Still Have to Dance and Sing': An Interview with Richard Fore-
       man," *TDR/The Drama Review* 46, no. 2 (Summer 2002): 110–21.

275   *"You want to know what I most despise?"*: Sándor Márai, *Portraits of a Mar-
       riage* (New York: Vintage, 2011), 108–109.

276   *"Do you agree"*: Sophie Calle, quoted in Jenna Sauers, "An Interview with
       Sophie Calle," trans. Elizabeth Carroll and Stephanie Kupfer, The Krause
       Essay Prize, https://krauseessayprize.org/winners-2/sophie-calle/sophie
       -calle-interview/. I have heavily altered this interview to fit the narrative.

                              MARION

280   *"How many American women"*: Benjamin Moser, *Sontag: Her Life and Work*
       (New York: Ecco, 2019), 10. I've added "only to run off and marry a mousy
       little nobody" to Moser's question about Susan Sontag.

283   *"I love it. I love it"*: Dorothy Parker, quoted in Marion Meade, *Dorothy
       Parker: What Fresh Hell Is This?* (New York: Penguin, 1987), 240.

283   *"I love having a house"*: Dorothy Parker, quoted in Meade, *Dorothy Parker*, 245.

283   "misbehaved *in the lobby"*: Meade, *Dorothy Parker*, 245. I have altered the
       quote to fit the narrative.

                             SCHUSTER

292   *"What bothers me about writing"*: Vito Acconci, "I Never Liked Art," video,
       Out of Sync, September 2015, http://outofsync-artinfocus.com/video/art/
       vito-acconci/i-never-liked-art/, 2:43.

292   Gray's Anatomy: Jean-Michel Basquiat was the one who was rumored to
       have taught himself to draw using Gray's Anatomy.

293   *"I can't understand why I made this trip"*: Susan Sontag, *Reborn: Journals
       and Notebooks, 1947–1963*, ed. David Rieff (New York: Farrar, Straus and
       Giroux, 2009), 314.

293   *"Of their own volition"*: Jean Genet, *The Thief's Journal*, trans. Bernard
       Frechtman (1949; repr. New York: Grove Press, 1994), 9.

296   *"When she'd asked if I wanted to live together"*: Sylvère Lotringer (speaking about Kathy Acker), quoted in Chris Kraus, "Cancer Became My Whole Brain: Kathy Acker's Final Year," *The New Yorker*, August 11, 2017.

THE COMA GAME

300   *"To write you have to allow yourself"* Susan Sontag, *Reborn: Journals and Notebooks, 1947–1963*, ed. David Rieff (New York: Farrar, Straus and Giroux, 2009), 280.

300   *"I should have liked to see you"*: Emily Dickinson to T. W. Higginson, February 1863, quoted in Susan Howe, *My Emily Dickinson* (New York: New Directions, 1985), 127.

300   *"no one will ever love you passionately for being nice"*: Charles Baxter, *Burning Down the House*, 2nd edition. (New York: Graywolf, 2013), 104. From the essay "Counterpointed Characterization."

301   *"Asked recently"*: Joseph Giovannini, "Demolition of LACMA: Art Sacrificed to Architecture," *New York Review of Books*, October 2, 2020, https://www.nybooks.com/daily/2020/10/02/the-demolition-of-lacma-art-sacrificed-to-architecture/. I have altered this quote to fit the narrative.

301   *reversed the genders*: I conceived of a staging of *A Streetcar Named Desire* with reversed genders years ago, as the play seems to naturally suggest it as a possibility. It turns out I was not alone in noticing this; I've since discovered a British company that had the idea before I did. See Deborah R. Geis, "Deconstructing (A Streetcar Named) Desire: Gender Re-citation in *Belle Reprieve*," in *Feminist Theatrical Revisions of Classic Works*, ed. Sharon Friedman (Jefferson, NC: McFarland, 2009), 237–46.

A BAD YEAR, A GOOD YEAR

307   *trash bin*: Louise Bourgeois threw away a student/friend's book without reading it because she didn't like the title, according to Jean Fréman *Now, Now, Louison*, trans. Cole Swensen (New York: New Directions, 2016), 102.

308   *"I believe very strongly in fascism"*: David Bowie, quoted in Jessica Lee, "Did David Bowie Say He Supports Fascism and Call Hitler a 'Rock Star'?," Snopes, December 23, 2020, https://www.snopes.com/fact-check/rock-star-david-bowie/.

309   *"At some point offendability"*: Laura Kipnis, "Transgression, An Elegy," *Liberties* 1, no. 1 (Autumn 2020): 28.

310 *"I think that was probably a bit coke-driven"*: David Bowie, speaking to Kerry O'Brien, in "David Bowie Reflects on His Career," *The 7:30 Report*, February 16, 2004, https://www.youtube.com/watch?v=ahT4xFY49w4, 11:17.

311 *"I felt done for, an empty burned-out wreck"*: Bob Dylan, *Chronicles* (New York: Simon & Schuster, 2004), 147–48. I've changed "'60s troubadour, a folk-rock relic" to "seventies art hack, a pop relic."

311 *"Looking back at the pages from [that] period*: Hanif Kureishi, *My Ear at His Heart: Reading My Father* (New York: Simon & Schuster, 2010), 165.

311 *"One realizes everything later"*: Fleur Jaeggy, *I Am the Brother of XX*, trans. Gini Alhadeff (New York: New Directions, 2017), 17.

STRANGERS

321 *a film that was part documentary*: The film by Abbas Kiarostami, titled *Close-Up*, was released in 1990, not the late 1980s, and the director who was impersonated was Mohsen Makhmalbaf, not Kiarostami.

322 A Meditation on the Possibility of Romantic Love Near the South During an Era of Nuclear Weapons Proliferation: I have used the actual subtitle of Ross McElwee's documentary *Sherman's March* (1985), changing only the word *in* to *near*.

DOCUMENTARY

332 *"The thing that makes"*: David Yaffe, *Reckless Daughter: A Portrait of Joni Mitchell* (New York: Sarah Crichton Books, 2017), 340. I have changed "Joni" to "X" in this quote.

333 *"In order to overcome"*: Marguerite Yourcenar, *Dear Departed*, trans. Maria Louise Ascher (New York: Farrar, Straus and Giroux, 1991), 4.

333 *"Undervalued"*: Yaffe, *Reckless Daughter*, 337. I have changed "Joni" to "X" in this quote.

RETROSPECTIVE

352 *"There was nothing that didn't interest me"*: David Bowie, speaking to Kerry O'Brien, in "David Bowie Reflects on His Career," *The 7:30 Report*, February 16, 2004, posted on YouTube, https://www.youtube.com/watch?v=ahT4xFY49w4, 5:23. I have changed "country and western" to "the pursuit of political office."

353 *"In the best of worlds"*: Jenny Holzer, quoted in William Oliver, "Jenny Hol-

zer: Texty Lady," *Dazed*, February 8, 2015, https://www.dazeddigital.com/artsandculture/article/23205/1/jenny-holzer-texty-lady.

353 *"I never ask myself"*: Hélène Cixous, in the preface to *The Hélène Cixous Reader*, ed. Susan Sellers (New York: Routledge, 1994), xvii. I have reversed the order of the two sentences in this quote to fit the interview format.

353 *"The problem with her oeuvre"*: Claire Fontaine, "We Are All Clitoridian Women: Notes on Carla Lonzi's Legacy." *e-flux journal* 47 (2013). I have changed the original to make "persona" plural and to use "X" instead of "Lonzi."

355 *"Often enough she has asked"*: Djuna Barnes, *Nightwood* (1937; repr. New York: New Directions, 2006), 6.

357 *"sheer good fortune to miss somebody"*: Toni Morrison, dedication, *Sula* (1973; repr. New York: Vintage, 2004), vii.

357 *"I'm sick of thought"*: Richard Hell, journal from Patti Smith, box 1, folder 3, MSS. 140, series I, Fales Archive, New York University.

Thank you, Jin, Eric, Jackson, Alexandra, Elizabeth, Alba, Ekin, Maggie, Jessica, Martina, Teresa, Anne, Jason, and DW.

Thank you, Tims, Booths, CB, Goose, 1364 Wolcott, Sara, Sean, Kendra, Haroula, and both Brendas.

Thank you, Guggenheim Foundation, Illinois Arts Council Agency, Omi International Arts Center, the librarians at the Fales Archive, and the many people who helped credited elsewhere.

ILLUSTRATION CREDITS

150   Found by author.
154   Found by author.
169   Commissioned. Art by Alex Merto.
171   Found by author.
173   Commissioned. Art by Maryse Meijer.
178   Found by author.
202   Found by author.
204   Carla Lonzi by Bassa Lonzi.
212   Photograph by author.
223   Found by author.
226   Commissioned. Art by Alex Merto.
228   Found by author.
229   Photograph by author.
235   Found by author.
242   Found by author.
248   Photograph by author.
249   Photograph by author.
257   Found by author.
261   Found by author.
263   Commissioned. Art by Rebecca Novack.
268   Photograph by author.
270   Photograph by author.
280   Portrait by Isabella Watling.
294   Courtesy of the Tejchman Brothers.
316   Photograph by author.
332   Manipulated video still of a performance by Yanira Castro, "Paradis" (2011), shot by Peter Richards at the Brooklyn Botanic Garden. Performer: Peter B. Schmitz.
361   Creative Commons.
362   Public domain.

A NOTE ABOUT THE AUTHOR

Catherine Lacey is the author of the novels *Nobody Is Ever Missing*, *The Answers*, and *Pew*, and the short-story collection *Certain American States*. Her honors include a Whiting Award, a Guggenheim Fellowship, and the New York Public Library's Young Lions Fiction Award. Her work has been translated into a dozen languages.

This book is for my mother, Susan